Drowthers might have no magery, but they built this. *What mage had ever* built *anything? All right, yes, mages worked with the natural world, so great artificial things like this building were not even interesting to a mage. But still—without any particular powers except the skill of their hands and the thoughts in their minds, the drowthers had built great and beautiful things. Ugly things, too—but the Aunts always spoke of drowthers as if all they ever made were wars and stinks and stupidity. But it was not true. Drowthers also sometimes made things that were beautiful or mighty or clever or useful, or all of these at once.*

Maybe Loki noticed this, too. Maybe Loki came to care about the drowthers and realized that if he closed all the gates, tying the gods to the place they were in and taking away the vast increase in power that came from gating between the worlds, then the drowthers could come into their own. The world would belong to them, and not to the mages anymore.

But he still had to learn how to be a gatemage. Because he was going to open a gate to the other world. To Westil, the ancient homeland of the mages. Loki might have been moved by compassion for the drowthers, but it had been nearly fourteen centuries, and the drowthers had come into their might and power. Surely now a Great Gate could be opened. What else was Danny born for, if not for that?

I'm not another Loki, he thought. *I'm the anti-Loki, the opposite. What he closed, I'll open. What he broke, I'll fix. What he hid, I'll find.*

He opened a gate into the Library of Congress.

BY ORSON SCOTT CARD
FROM TOM DOHERTY ASSOCIATES

Empire
The Folk of the Fringe
Future on Fire (editor)
Future on Ice (editor)
Hidden Empire
Invasive Procedures
  (with Aaron Johnston)
Keeper of Dreams
Lovelock (with Kathryn Kidd)
*Maps in a Mirror: The Short
  Fiction of Orson Scott Card*
*Pastwatch: The Redemption
  of Christopher Columbus*
Saints
Songmaster
Treason
The Worthing Saga
Wyrms

ENDER
Ender's Game
Ender's Shadow
*Shadow of the
  Hegemon*
Shadow Puppets
Shadow of the Giant
Speaker for the Dead
Xenocide
Children of the Mind
First Meetings
Ender in Exile

HOMECOMING
The Memory of Earth
The Call of Earth
The Ships of Earth
Earthfall
Earthborn

THE TALES OF ALVIN MAKER
Seventh Son
Red Prophet
Prentice Alvin
Alvin Journeyman
Heartfire
The Crystal City

WOMEN OF GENESIS
Sarah
Rebekah
Rachel & Leah

FROM OTHER PUBLISHERS

Enchantment
Homebody
Lost Boys
Magic Street
Stonefather

Stone Tables
Treasure Box
*How to Write Science
  Fiction and Fantasy*
Characters and Viewpoint

THE LOST GATE

A Novel of the Mither Mages

ORSON SCOTT CARD

TOR®

A TOM DOHERTY ASSOCIATES BOOK
NEW YORK

This is a work of fiction. All of the characters, organizations, and events portrayed in this novel are either products of the author's imagination or are used fictitiously.

THE LOST GATE

Copyright © 2010 by Orson Scott Card

A Tor Book
Published by Tom Doherty Associates, LLC
175 Fifth Avenue
New York, NY 10010

www.tor-forge.com

Tor® is a registered trademark of Tom Doherty Associates, LLC.

ISBN 978-0-7653-6538-5

First Edition: January 2011
First Mass Market Edition: December 2011

Printed in the United States of America

0 9 8 7 6 5 4 3 2 1

To Phillip and Erin Absher
After all we've shared over the years,
From California to Kansas,
From Provence to Myrtle Beach,
With all the magics along the way:
This book is for you.

CONTENTS

1. Drekka   1
2. The Greek Girl   33
3. The Man in the Tree   58
4. Shoplifter   70
5. The Gate Thief   89
6. Fistalk   107
7. Stone's House   137
8. Safe Room   171
9. Orphans   188
10. Inside Man   202
11. Servant of Spacetime   238
12. The Queen's Hero   263
13. Veevee   282
14. Public Gate   301
15. The Queen's Squirrel   317
16. Warden   331
17. Birthday Present   339
18. The Father of Trick   360
19. Rope Climb   365
20. Locks   387
21. Great Gate   405
22. Justice   418
23. Gatefather   435

THE
LOST
GATE

1

Drekka

ℒ

Danny North grew up surrounded by fairies, ghosts, talking animals, living stones, walking trees, and gods who called up wind and brought down rain, made fire from air and drew iron out of the depths of the earth as easily as ordinary people might draw up water from a well.

The North family lived on a compound in a sheltered valley in western Virginia, and most of them never went to town, for it was a matter of some shame that gods should now be forced to buy supplies and sell crops just like common people. The Family had spliced and intertwined so often over the centuries that almost all adults except one's own parents were called Aunt and Uncle, and all the children were lumped together as "the cousins."

To the dozens and dozens of North cousins, "town" was a distant thing, like "ocean" and "space" and "government." What did they care about such things, except that during school hours, Auntie Tweng or Auntie Uck would rap them on the head with a thimbled finger if they didn't come up with the right answers?

School was something the children endured in the mornings, so they could spend the afternoons learning how to create the things that commoners called fairies, ghosts, golems, trolls, werewolves, and other such miracles that were the heritage of the North family.

It was their heritage, but not every child inherited. Great-uncle Zog was notorious for muttering, "The blood's too thin, the blood's too thin," because it was his considered opinion that the Norths had grown weak in the thirteen and a half centuries since the Evil One closed the gates. "Why else do we have so many weaklings who can't send their outself more than a hundred yards?" he said once. "Why else do we have so few children who can raise a clant out of anything sturdier than pollen and dust, or heartbind with one of their clan? Why do we have these miserable drekkas like Danny in every generation? Putting them in Hammernip Hill hasn't made us stronger. Nothing makes us stronger."

Danny heard this when he was eleven, when it wasn't a sure thing yet that he *was* a drekka. Plenty of children didn't show any talent till they were in their teens. Or so Mama said, reassuring him; but from Great-uncle Zog's words Danny began to doubt her. How could it be "plenty" of children who showed no talent when Danny was now the only child in the Family over the age of nine who couldn't even figure out whether he *had* an outself, let alone send it out to explore. When the other kids used their outselves to spy on Danny's school papers and copy them, he couldn't even detect that they were there, let alone stop them.

"Drive them away, can't you?" demanded Aunt Lummy. "You're the only decent student in this school, but they're all getting the same marks as you because you let them cheat!"

"I know *how* they're doing it," said Danny, "but how can I drive them away when I can't *see* them or *feel* them?"

"Just make yourself big," said Aunt Lummy. "Hold on to your own space. Don't let them crowd you!"

But these words meant nothing to Danny, no matter how he tried to act them out, and the cheating went on until Lummy and the other Aunts who taught the school were forced to make separate tests, one for Danny and one for all the others at his grade level. The instant result was that by age twelve, Danny was soon the *only* student in his grade level, the others having been put back where they belonged. In the outside world, Danny would have been doing ninth grade work, two years ahead of his age.

The other kids resented him more than ever, and therefore taunted him or froze him out as a drekka. "You're not one of us," they said—often in those exact words. During free time they refused to let him come along on any of their escapades; he was never chosen for a team; he was never told when one of the Aunts was sharing out cookies or some other treat; and he always had to check his drawer for spiders, snakes, or dog poo. He got used to it quickly, and he knew better than to tell any of the adults. What good would it do him? How much fun would he have if some adult forced the others to take him along? What kinds of pranks would they do if they had been whipped for pooing his clean clothes?

So in this idyllic world of fairies and ghosts, gods

and talking animals, Danny was a profoundly solitary child.

He knew everybody; everybody was kin to him. But he had been made ashamed of everything he did well, and even more ashamed of everything he could not do, and he regarded even those of the cousins who treated him kindly as if their kindness were pity. For who could genuinely like a boy so unworthy, whose existence meant no more than this: that the bloodlines of the North family were weak and getting weaker, with Danny the weakest of them all.

The irony was that Danny had been kept as a child apart since he was born—but for the opposite reason. His father, Alf, a Rockbrother with an affinity for pure metals, had found a way to get inside the steel of machines and make them run almost without friction, and without lubrication. It was such a useful and unprecedented skill that he had been made ruler of the Family, and was therefore renamed as Odin; but Danny called him Baba.

Danny's mother, Gerd, was only slightly less remarkable, a lightmage who had learned to change the color of reflected light so that she could make things nearly invisible, or hide them in shadows, or make them glow as bright as the sun. For years Alf and Gerd had been forbidden to marry by old Gyish, who was then the Odin, for fear that the joining of two such potent bloodlines might create something awful—a gatemage, which the Norths were forbidden ever to have again, or a manmage, which all the Families were sworn to destroy.

But when Gyish retired after losing the last war, and machinemage Alf was made Odin in his place, the Family voted almost unanimously to allow the marriage. Danny's birth was the result, as close to a royal child as the Norths had had in many generations.

In his early childhood, Danny was pampered by all the adults. He was the golden boy, and great things were expected of him. He had been bright as a child—quick to read, clever with all the family languages, dextrous with his fingers, an athletic runner and leaper, curious to a fault, and clever of tongue so he could make almost anyone laugh. But as he got older, these traits could not make up for his utter lack of harmony with any of the magics of the Family.

Danny tried everything. He gardened alongside the cousins who had a way with herbs and trees and grasses—the ones who, as adult mages, would continue to make the North farms so astonishingly productive. But the seeds he planted grew weakly, and he could not feel the throbbing pulse of a tree.

He roamed the woods with those who had a way with animals—the ones who, if they could only form a deep bond with wolf or bear or (failing everything grand) squirrel or snake, would become Eyefriend or Clawbrother and roam the world in animal shape whenever they wished. But the creatures ran from him, or snarled or snapped at him, and he made no friends among the beasts.

He tried to understand what it meant to "serve" stone or water, wind or the electricity of lightning in the air. But the stones bruised his fingers and moved for him only if he threw them; the wind only blew his hair into a tangled mop; and storms and ponds left him wet, cold, and powerless. Far from being precocious, with magic he was slow. Worse than slow. He was inert, making no visible progress at all.

Yet, except for the loneliness, he didn't hate his life.

His long rovings in the woods were a pleasure to him. Since neither tree nor animal was drawn to him, he simply ran, becoming swift and tireless, mile after mile. At first he ran only within the limits of the family compound, because the trees that guarded the perimeter would snatch at him and then give the alarm, bringing the adult Seedguards and even Uncle Poot, the only Sapkin in the Family right now, to warn him not to leave.

But during this past winter—perhaps because the trees were dormant and less alert—he had found three different routes that allowed him to avoid the sentinel trees entirely. He knew that as a probable drekka he was being watched—Danny never knew when the outself of some adult might be following him. So he took different routes to these secret passageways each time. As far as he knew, he had never been seen leaving. No one had challenged him about it, at least.

Liberated now, he would run and run, miles in whatever direction he chose. And he was fast! He could cover miles and still be home by suppertime. He would only stop when he came to a highway, a fence, a house, a factory, a town, and from the shelter of the woods or hedges or weeds he would watch the drowthers go about their lives and think: I am by nature one of *them*. Without affinities or powers. Living by the labor of their hands or the words of their mouth.

With one slight difference: Drowthers didn't know they were bereft of all that was noble in the world. They had no sense of lost heritage. The North family ignored them, cared nothing about them. But if Danny tried to leave, all the Family secrets would be at risk. The stories told on dark nights, of traitors, of wars between the Westilian families, all ended the same way:

Anyone who defied the Family and fled the compound without permission would be hunted down and killed.

In these twilight times Norths may not have all the power they used to have before Loki closed the gates, before the centuries of war with the other families. But they were superb hunters. Nobody evaded them. Danny knew he took his life in his hands every time he left. He was insane to do it. Yet he felt so free outside the compound. The world was so large, so full of people who did not despise him yet.

They have no talents like ours, and yet they build these roads, these factories, these houses. We have to import *their* machines to air-condition our homes. We tie in to *their* internet to get our news and send emails to the trusted rovers the Family sends out into the world. We drive in cars and trucks we buy from *them*. How dare we feel superior? None of these things are in our power, and when the Westilian families ruled the world as gods of the Phrygians, the Hittites, the Greeks, the Celts, the Persians, the Hindi, the Slavs, and of course the Norse, the lives of common people were nasty, brutish, and short—nastier, shorter, and more brutal because of our demands on them.

The world would be better if there had never been such gods as these. Taking whatever we wanted because we could, killing anyone who got in our way, deposing kings and setting up new ones, sending our disciples out a-conquering—who did we think we were? In the long-lost world of Westil, where everyone was talented, it might have been fair, for everyone might have had a chance. But here in Mittlegard—on Earth—where only the few Westilian families had such powers, it was unjust.

These were the thoughts that Danny was free to think as he watched the teenagers come out of the high schools of Buena Vista and Lexington and ride off in buses or drive off in their cars. At home he never let himself think such things, because if he did his face might reveal his repugnance or dismay at something that a relative did or some old story of an ancestor's adventures. His only hope of having any kind of useful life was to convince them that he could be trusted to be allowed out into the world, that his loyalty to the Family was unshakeable.

Meanwhile, he pored over the books that children were allowed to read, especially the mythologies, trying to understand the real history of the Westilians from the tantalizing tales the drowthers had collected. He once asked Auntie Uck which of the tales from *Bulfinch's Mythology* were true, and she just glared at him and said, "All of them," which was just stupid.

Somewhere there were books that told the true stories. He knew that family histories were kept—histories that went back thousands of years. How else could the adults make their cryptic references to this or that person or event in the distant past? All the adults knew these histories, and someday the other cousins would be given these secrets—but not Danny, the one best suited to read, understand, and remember. If he ever learned the truth about anything, he would have to find it out himself.

Meanwhile, he had to stay alive. Which meant that as much as he loved to run outside the compound, he only did it now and then, when he couldn't stand to be confined in his loneliness another day; when it began to seem that it might be better just to go up to

Hammernip Hill, dig his own grave, lie down in it, and wait for someone to come up and finish the job.

When he was analytical about it, he realized that running outside the compound *was* a kind of suicide. A game of Russian roulette, without any idea of how many chambers there were in the revolver, nor how many bullets there might be. Just run to a secret passageway and keep on running—that was how he pulled the trigger.

His life was not unrelenting solitude and hostility, of course. There were aunts and uncles who had loved him from childhood on, and they seemed to love him still, though some were certainly more distant now. And since Baba and Mama themselves had never particularly doted on him, certainly he could detect no difference in their indifference now. In many ways his life at home was normal. Normal*ish,* anyway.

And maybe he would find a way to make himself useful to the Family so they would let him live.

He had tried to get them to let him become the family computer expert. "Let me set up a local area network," he said. "I've been reading about it online. We could have computers in every house, in every *room,* and they could share the same internet connection so we wouldn't have to pay the cable company a dollar more."

But all they could think to say was, "How did you learn about these things?"

"I googled them," he said.

The result was that the family made a new rule that kids could access computers only with an adult in the room, and you had to be able to demonstrate at any moment just how the stuff you had on the screen was related to the classroom assignment you were supposed to be doing.

"Thanks a lot, drekka," Lem and Stem said as they beat him up a little behind the haybarn the next day. They were particularly annoyed because Danny's inquiry had led to Auntie Tweng finding their files of pornography, which got them a screaming tongue-lashing from their drekka mother, Miz Jane, and a whipping from one of Uncle Poot's most savage hickories.

So now Danny was trying to make himself useful by helping train the kids who were just learning to create clants with their outselves. Not that Danny knew anything about clanting, but since the kids couldn't see their own clants, Danny watched how the clants took shape and then reported to them on their results. Pure observation, but because Danny was doing it, an adult was free to do something else.

The trouble was that the three children whose clants he was supervising were Tina, Mona, and Crista, and instead of working on their assignment—to make their clant as close to lifesize as possible—they were remaining under a foot in height and trying to make themselves as voluptuous as they could. All three girls were just starting to develop as women in their real bodies, but the miniature female bodies they were forming out of fallen twigs, leaves, and nutshells were shaping up with huge breasts and exaggerated hips. Forest fairies, a drowther would have called them. Or sluts.

"I'll report this, you know," said Danny. But it was wasted breath—none of them was good enough at clanting to be able to hear anything through their clants. They could see, however—the outself could see whether it was formed into a clant or not—and one of them noticed Danny's lips moving.

Almost at once, all three of the forest fairies turned to face him. Two of them flaunted their chests; the other turned around, thrust her buttocks toward him, and waggled it back and forth. They could not have made their contempt more clear.

Danny didn't care. It was better than getting beaten up by Lem and Stem. But it was his responsibility to make sure they worked on what they were supposed to work on. He had no authority himself, and even if he had, he couldn't have done anything if they chose to defy him. Adults could use their own outselves to give the girls' clants a shove, which they would feel in their own bodies as well. But Danny had no outself, or hadn't found one, anyway. The only thing he could do was find an adult and report them—but by the time an adult arrived, they'd be working on what they were supposed to work on, and the adult would be annoyed at Danny.

Not that the adult would doubt Danny's word—he was known not to lie, and besides, they knew exactly what Tina, Mona, and Crista were like. But the very fact that Danny had to fetch an adult to enforce the rules meant that he really wasn't worth very much as a clant-minder. Sometimes Danny was conscientious enough to report such antics as these, but most of the time he put his own survival ahead of the goal of pushing the children to develop their skills, and let them get away with whatever they wanted.

The danger was that when these children grew up, they would remember how worthless Danny had been as a child-minder, and far from being grateful that he hadn't reported them when they were young, they'd realize he couldn't be trusted to take care of their own children. Then he'd just be Poor Uncle Danny the drekka. Or Poor Old Danny, the body under the nameless headstone on Hammernip Hill.

All he could do was kick out at them, dispersing the stuff out of which their clants were formed, so they'd have to take a few moments to gather them up and shape themselves again. It took only a second or two—they'd been making forest fairies of *this* size since they were nine or ten, and Danny was the darling little eight-year-old that they liked to pamper when adults were around or torture when they weren't.

Well, even though Danny couldn't make a clant the size of a thimble, he had listened well during the early lessons and remembered things that those with talent often forgot. For instance, he knew the warning about letting drowthers capture a small and fragile clant. "You hold the clant," Uncle Poot had told them, "and the clant holds *you*. If you let them capture you when you're little, they can keep your outself from returning to your body, which leaves you completely helpless."

"Why can't we just toss away the clant?" Danny had asked—for in those days, he still expected to be able to use these lessons.

"You have to be able to spin and leap to cast away the bits from which you made the clant," said Uncle Poot. "If they trap you so you can't move far enough, the bits of clant stay bound to you. It's just the way it works."

"I'll just make *my* clant with scissors," Friggy, Danny's best friend in those days, had boasted. "Then I'll cut my way out."

"Make your clant with scissors?" Uncle Poot had

laughed. "Why not make it with a gun and shoot your captors through the sack they caught you in?"

"The clants that children make are faint and small," said Danny. "They have no strength in them."

"That's right," said Uncle Poot. "The son of Odin never forgets. It's only truly a clant when it's full-size and every bit as solid as you are in your own body. Until then it's a small or a faint or a face, and it could no more lift a pair of scissors than a boulder."

Remembering such lessons, Danny pulled his tee-shirt off over his head and then idly scratched his side, as if that had been his purpose. The girls made their clants point at him and pantomime rolling on the ground with laughter—they really were quite good at giving lifelike movements to their smalls— but all that mattered to Danny was that they weren't paying attention to the danger they were in. It took only a moment for Danny to have his shirt down on top of the two nearest fairies and another moment for him to gather it into a sack containing them.

The third was free, and it leapt and scampered up the sack, up his arms, into his face. But it was a mere annoyance—he swept it away with a brush of his hand and the pieces of it fell to the ground. He expected that girl—he had no way of knowing which it was, since they weren't good enough yet to put their face on the clants they made—to drop her outself back to the ground and form the clant again, so he didn't wait around to see. Instead he gripped the tee-shirt in his teeth and began to climb the nearest branchy tree.

No one climbed trees better than Danny, and this time he moved so fast it seemed to him that he was flying, just tapping the branches with his hands and feet. Meanwhile the fairies in the bag kept trying to jump and spin so they could shed their clants and return to their bodies, but they didn't have the strength to do much more than jostle the bag a little.

At a high branch, Danny stopped climbing, took the tee-shirt out of his mouth, and tied it so tightly to a slender branch that there was hardly room for the clants to move at all. Then he let himself back down the tree, taking much longer jumps downward than he had managed on the way up. When he reached the bottom, the third girl's clant was nowhere to be seen.

So Danny walked back to the house, to tell Uncle Poot what he had done.

But it was Great-uncle Zog and Grandpa Gyish who intercepted him on the path, and they gave him no chance at all to explain that he was only teaching the girls a lesson.

"Where are they!" screamed Grandpa Gyish.

"What kind of drekka bags a child!" Great-uncle Zog bellowed at him. "I'll have you up the hill for this, you fairy-thief, you child-abuser!" And then he was shaking Danny so hard that he was afraid his head would come clear off. Years of flying with the eagles had caused old Zog's arms and shoulders to bulk up and he had so much strength that he could break a big man's neck with a swipe of his hand—he'd done it more than once in the wars. So it was a relief when Auntie Uck and Auntie Tweng showed up and clung to both Zog's arms, dragging him away from Danny.

As it was, Zog didn't let go—the Aunts dragged him, but he dragged Danny, his grip like a talon on Danny's shoulder. He staggered to keep his feet under him so that he didn't have his full weight dangling from Zog's massive grip. Who would have thought an old man could be so strong?

A few minutes later, the adults who were in the compound had gathered, and Danny found himself in the midst of something like a trial—but without the legal forms they saw in the TV shows. There was Danny and there was his accuser, Crista, the oldest of the girls, and there was Gyish, presiding like a judge in Baba's absence, with Zog as the prosecutor.

But that's where the resemblance to a fair trial left off, for there was no one to speak in Danny's defense. Not even Danny—whenever he tried to speak, Zog slapped him or Gyish shouted him into silence. So the only story anyone could hear was Crista's.

"We were trying so hard to make our clants big," she said, "that we didn't even see that Danny was sneaking up on us with a giant sack. He caught all three of us but I just barely managed to get out before he sealed the neck of it with Tina and Mona inside. And then he broke my clant in pieces and before I could put myself together he was gone, up in the sky."

"He flew?" demanded Gyish.

"Yes!" cried Crista. "He flew away and dropped the bag outside the compound and now we'll never get them back!"

It took a moment before she realized that she had pushed too hard. For the adults were all shaking their heads and some were laughing derisively.

"Danny? Fly?" said Uncle Poot. "If only he could."

"You can see that Crista's lying," said Uncle Mook. "Maybe everything she said's a lie."

"It's not a lie!" shouted Gyish—he had made no pretense of impartiality. "I saw the poor girls' bodies lying helpless in the house! Children so young don't have the strength to bring their outselves back when their clant is captured! Nor the skill to wake up their own bodies when their outselves are clanting! They might never wake up!"

"Let's hear from Danny," said Aunt Lummy mildly.

Zog turned on her savagely. "A drekka has no voice here!"

"But the son of Odin and Gerd has the right to speak in his own defense," said Lummy. And Mook, her husband, moved closer to her, standing beside her, to give more force to what she said.

"What will we hear from *him* but lies?" said Gyish. "I know what drekkas and drowthers are—they'll say anything to save their worthless lives!"

"If he is so determined to save his life," said Aunt Lummy, "why would he harm these children, whom we trusted to his care?"

"Because they hate us! Drekkas hate us worse than drowthers do!" Gyish was almost frothing at the mouth. Danny realized that he was seeing now what lay behind the muttering and grumbling that were Gyish's usual form of speech. The old man's wrath and shame at having lost the war and the seat of Odin had made him into this poisonous old gnome—or so he seemed, because he stooped to point a quavering finger at Aunt Lummy as if he meant to jab it through her heart if she took one more step toward him.

"Piffle," said Auntie Uck. "You're behaving like a child, Grandpa Gyish, and Zog, you're just a bully. Let go of the boy at once—you've probably broken his shoulder and you know we don't have a first-rate healer anymore." She turned to Gyish again. "Which *you'll* rue if you let your anger give you a stroke!"

It took Uck's no-nonsense tone and unintimidated look to get Gyish back to his normal level of grumbling, while Zog tossed Danny on the ground and stood there, fists clenched, waiting for Danny to be such a fool as to try to rise again.

He needn't have worried. Danny's shoulder hurt so badly that he could only lie there, holding it with his other hand, trying not to cry.

"Danny," said Uncle Mook, "tell us what happened."

"I already told you what happened!" shouted Crista.

Uncle Poot silenced her with a glare. "We already heard your lies, girl. Now we'll see if Danny can come up with better ones."

"Well, boy?" asked Zog. "You heard them! Answer!"

"They were staying small," said Danny, "and giving themselves huge boobs."

"So what!" shouted Gyish. "So what if they were! It's what they do! They're stupid little girls, it's what they do!"

"I knew that if I went to fetch you, Uncle Poot, they'd lie and say they were trying to be big."

"I wouldn't have believed them," answered Poot.

"But you wouldn't have punished them, either," said Danny. "So they'd just have kept on doing it." He heard the other adults murmur their agreement.

"So now you're a critic, is that it?" Uncle Poot replied. "Telling me that I'm not good at training youngsters?"

"It doesn't excuse you putting them in a sack!" said Zog. And the adults murmured their agreement at that, too.

"I didn't have a sack," said Danny. "I stood there right in front of them and took off my shirt and walked right over to them. It was plain enough what I was doing—if they'd been paying any attention. I didn't expect to actually *catch* them with my shirt! I just wanted to give them a scare, remind them to take their study seriously. But when I found that two of them were in the shirt, I didn't know what to do. If I just let them go, they'd mock me and I'd never be able to get them to do what's right without bothering some adult. The whole point of having me watch them is so none of you has to be bothered, isn't it?"

Even as he said it, though, Danny realized that he had just declared that it was impossible for him to tend the clants if the other children didn't want him to; he wouldn't save the adults any time at all, and so they might as well have one of them do the minding and leave Danny out of it. But what choice had he had? The accusation Crista made was so terrible, and with Gyish and Zog calling him a drekka, one who could be killed whenever it was convenient, there was a great danger that the trial would end suddenly with Zog tearing his head off and tossing it into the trees.

"So you trapped them in your tee-shirt," said Aunt Lummy. "And you didn't let them go. Where are they now?"

"Crista's clant was going for my eyes and so I did brush her aside. And then to get away from her, I climbed a tree."

"And yet you are not in a tree," said Uncle Mook. "And you seem to have neither your shirt nor the clants of two disobedient and stupid girls."

"I tied the shirt to a branch and climbed down and I was just going to fetch Uncle Poot and turn their clants over to him when Great-uncle Zog and Grandpa Gyish attacked me."

"No grandpa of yours!" shouted Gyish, though this was only partly true, since Danny's mother, Gerd, was Gyish's firstborn granddaughter.

"I believe you," said Mook. "But what you don't know—what you could not possibly understand—is how terrified those girls are now. There's nothing worse for an inexperienced child than to have your outself trapped and be unable to bring it back. It's like you're suffocating and can't draw breath."

The others present murmured their agreement.

"I'm sorry," said Danny. "I really am. It's not as if I planned it. I only did what came to mind, to try to get them to work on what they were assigned. I didn't know that it would hurt them."

"Look at his shoulder," said Auntie Tweng. "Look at that bruise. It's like a truck ran over him."

"He was trying to get away!" said Zog defensively.

"He was in agony," said Tweng. "How dare *you* punish the boy before the rest of us were called?"

"I didn't punish him!" Zog roared. "I *brought* him!"

"You know your strength, and you're responsible for what you do with it," said Tweng. "You and Grandpa Gyish did *this* to him? It's at least as bad as anything he did to those two girls—why, I wouldn't be surprised if his clavicle was broken along with a few thousand capillaries."

Since neither Zog nor Gyish was even slightly educated in the drowther sciences, they had no idea what they were being accused of having done, but they were clearly angry and abashed at having the tables turn like this.

"And while you're torturing this child," said Tweng, "and refusing to let him speak, has anyone thought that only *he* knows where he hung that tee-shirt with a brace of stupid disobedient fairies inside?"

Danny could have kissed her then and there, if he'd thought that Auntie Tweng would stand for it. Within a few moments, uncles Poot and Mook had Danny on his feet and helped him keep his balance—he was faint with pain—as he led them back to the tree.

It was farther than Danny had remembered, or perhaps pain magnified the distance, since every step jostled him and made it hurt worse. But finally they were there, with all the Aunts and Uncles—and now a fair entourage of cousins, too—staring up into the tree.

"I don't see it," said Zog. "He's lying."

"He said he put it high in the tree," said Auntie Tweng. "Of course you can't see it. The leaves are in the way."

"I can't climb that thing," said Uncle Mook.

"Can you get the tree itself to bring them down?" Aunt Lummy asked Uncle Poot.

"Is it on a living branch?" Poot asked Danny. "Green with leaves?"

"Yes," said Danny.

"Then we should try another way," said Poot, his voice now gentle, "before we ask this scarlet oak for such a sacrifice."

"Then Zog," said Auntie Tweng. "Send up a bird to untie the shirt and bring them down."

Zog whirled on her, but then seemed to swallow the first terrible thing he had meant to say. Instead he spoke softly. "You know my heartbound died in the war. Such birds as I can speak to now have no such skill as the untying of a knotted shirt. I can make them attack and kill, but not untie a knot."

"Then someone has to climb the tree," said Uncle Poot.

"Make a clant first," said Auntie Tweng, "and see how high it is, and how dangerous the climb might be."

Uncle Poot was one of the foremost clanters of the Family, and he must have been showing off a little, for he sat down at the base of the tree and formed his outself into a clant using the leaves and twigs of the living oak. The smaller branches merely bent toward each other to form the leaves into the vague shape of a man. It progressed up the tree by joining higher leaves into the shape and letting lower ones fall away behind it. Soon it came back down, little more than a rapid quivering of the leaves and branches, yet always shaped like a man, and Uncle Poot opened his eyes again.

"How could you climb so high?" he asked Danny. "How could such slender branches bear your weight?"

"I don't know," said Danny. "I climbed up them and they didn't break and I didn't fall."

"I can't send another child up there," said Uncle Poot. "As we were so recently reminded, we have no healer capable of dealing with grave injuries."

"Then let me go," said Danny.

"With that shoulder?" asked Aunt Lummy. "I don't think so!"

"I can do it," said Danny. "It's only pain. I can still move my arm."

So he climbed the tree for the second time today, slowly this time, testing the strength in his left arm and shoulder every time before relying on them to hold him.

When he was far enough up the tree that he could see none of the people below him, he came to a place where he couldn't find any kind of handhold at all. The next higher branch was simply out of reach. Yet he had come this way. This high in the tree there were no alternate routes.

I was moving faster, Danny thought. I was almost *running* up the tree. I must have leapt upward and reached it without realizing it.

Yet he knew this was not true. Such a leap as this he would have noticed and remembered—if for no other reason than to brag that he had done it.

He had climbed the tree in the same kind of single-minded trance that came over him when he ran. He didn't remember picking his way or watching his footsteps when he ran his fastest, and likewise he had no memory of gripping this branch or that one when he had made his first climb, though he remembered every handhold and every reach on this second time up the tree.

He closed his eyes. How could he possibly go back down and tell them that what he had climbed before, he could not climb a second time? What could they possibly think, except that he refused to go? What if someone else got to this same place, and saw the tee-shirt hanging far out of reach? What would they think? Only that Danny didn't want to free the girls from their imprisonment. Then Uncle Poot would ask the tree to sacrifice and break the living branch, and Danny's punishment would be severe indeed. Who would think him anything but a drekka then?

Yet he knew there was a way up, and not just because of the logic that the tee-shirt was knotted around a branch, so Danny must have been there; he knew there was a way because he could sense it, where it began and where it led, even though there were no handholds that his eyes could see.

So he closed his eyes and reached upward, sliding his hand along the rough trunk. Ah, if only you could speak to me, Scarlet Oak, if only we were friends. If only you could bend your branch to me.

And as that yearning mixed with his despair, he twisted and flung his body upward. What did it matter if he missed the branch and fell? His days were numbered anyway, if he did not bring those girls back down.

His hand gripped a branch. He opened his eyes.

It was not the next branch up, the one that he had reached for in vain a moment before. It was the very branch the tee-shirt hung on.

How did I get from there to here?

But even as he asked himself the question, he answered it. I could not have done it with hands and feet. Nor is there any magic that lets a twelve-year-old boy leap upward three times his own height.

No, there *was* such a magic, only Danny had never seen it. The whole world had not seen it since 632 A.D. He had to close his eyes and breathe deeply as he took it in.

I must have made a gate. A little one, a gate that takes me only there to here. I must have made it when I climbed the first time, and when I leapt again just now I passed through it.

He had read about gates like this in books. They were the gates that were within the reach of Path-brothers, or even Lockfriends sometimes, back in the days when gatemagery was still practiced in the world. And now that he was thinking of it this way, Danny could see just where the gate began and ended. It was nothing visible, not even a quivering in the air or a rearrangement of the leaves, like Uncle Poot's temporary clant had been. He simply knew that it was there, knew where it began and ended, *felt* it almost as if it were a part of him.

Danny had *made* a gate. How many others had he made, not knowing it? It must be gates like this that had allowed him to get past the watching trees at the perimeter. How long had he been making them? How many were there?

As soon as the question formed in his mind, the answer came. He could sense the placement of every gate that he had ever made. There were scarcely two dozen of them, but from his reading he knew that this was really quite a lot. Even a Pathbrother could only make a dozen gates of any size, because each gate required that a portion of the gatemage's outself remain behind with it. A trained, experienced gatemage could close the gates that he had made himself, erase them and gather his outself fragments back into the whole. But Danny had no idea how such a thing was done. And there was no one to teach him.

I've made two dozen gates without knowing that I was doing it, without feeling it at all. Yet I've been finding the ones that lead outside the compound, because I could sense without realizing it exactly where they were and where they led and how to use them.

Now every one of them is lying about inside the compound, waiting for someone to stumble into it and find himself abruptly in another place. It only had to happen once, and the discoverer would know there was a gatemage in the world again, and one with strength enough to make a gate rather than merely find and open up a gate that someone else had made.

Danny exulted at the knowledge that he was not a drekka at all, but instead a rather powerful mage of the rarest kind. But eating away at the thrill of triumph was the fact that to be a gatemage in the North family was worse than being drekka.

For the last gatemage in the world had been Loki the trickster, the monster Loki who had sealed up every Great Gate in the world so thoroughly that all traffic between Westil and Mittlegard was cut off at once. It had shattered the power of every Family in the world, for the mightiest of powers could only be sustained by frequent passages back and forth. Magic gathered in one world was magnified a hundred times by passage through a Great Gate into the other. Little gates like the ones that Danny made had no such power— they led from Earth to another spot on Earth, and meant nothing except that his body moved from there to here. But the Great Gates had been what turned the mages of Westil into gods when they came here to Mittlegard.

And when they closed, when Loki made it impossible for anyone to even find them—even the gates that had stood for three thousand years or more before his time—the gods became mere mages, and easy to find and kill if someone was determined to; they could die from the blows of drowther swords or the darts from drowther bows. They had to learn caution, to isolate themselves, to pretend that they were ordinary people. To hide, as the North family was hidden here in the Virginia hills, where people who kept to themselves were not exceptional and others mostly left them alone.

The wars had been fought at first to force the Norths to reopen the gates, for no one believed that Loki's actions were not part of some nefarious plan. Only after the Families had decimated each other and the Norths had fled with Leiv Eiriksson to Vinland—only then, seeing how helpless the Norths had been against five centuries of onslaughts, did the other Families finally believe that Loki had acted alone, that the Norths were not holding on to some secret Westil Gate that would enable them to build up power that no other Family could withstand.

Even so, once America was conquered the Families made war on the Norths again from time to time, whenever the pain of being cut off from Westil became too much to bear, if only to punish the Norths or perhaps destroy them utterly—what else did they deserve?

But as truces and treaties were formed and broken, made anew and once again broken, they always included this clause: that if any gatemage was born into the world, into any Family but most especially the Norths, he would be killed. And not just killed, but his or her body cut up and one piece sent to each of the other Families as proof that it was done.

Otherwise, whichever Family got a gatemaker first would have a devastating advantage and could destroy the others if they were not stopped in time. All the Families feared the others would cheat, because that's what they themselves would do.

If any of the adults had sent a clant to watch Danny and saw what he just did to reach this spot, then when he came back down they'd hack him to death on the spot, and care nothing. For if the Norths were caught with a gatemage of any degree of power left alive and making gates, the other Families would unite again and this time they would not stop till every North was dead.

I am a mage with power to do what no other living mage can do; and yet I am a dead man. If Loki had not played his monstrous, inexplicable prank and closed the gates, the discovery of my power would be a cause for celebration. I would at once become one of the leading members of the Family, and mere beast-mages like Zog would defer to me, and Lem and Stem would never dare to raise their hand against me. But Loki closed the gates, and now it's a crime for me to breathe. If I were a good boy, I'd fling myself from this tree and die, saving them the trouble of killing me.

But Danny was not that good a boy.

He owed them nothing. He was not one of them. He did not accept their power over him. He would not let them kill him if he could avoid it.

The only trouble was, he didn't actually know how to use his power. He had made a gate, but unconsciously; he could map with his mind all the gates that he had ever made, because they were a part of him. But he had no idea what to do in order to create another. Useful as it might be right now to make a gate that would take him from this treetop to a place somewhere in Canada or Brazil, he had never made a gate that took him more than fifty yards, and never made a single one on purpose.

So he inched his way out to where he had tied the shirt, unfastened it, opened it, and released the two feeble fairy clants. At once the girls' outselves let go of the pieces of their clants and let the twigs and leaves and nutshells tumble or flutter to the ground.

Upstairs in the schoolhouse, their eyes were opening; no doubt they were wailing and clinging to each other and making noise about how terrified they'd been.

And it's a near certainty that they'll never wave their clanty boobs and butts at me again, thought Danny, if I were ever set to watch over them again. So my plan *was* a good one, except for the part where it nearly got me killed.

Danny made his way slowly down the tree, pausing here and there to try to hear what was going on below him. Then he noticed that his shoulder did not hurt at all anymore. That it had not hurt since he made the leap through the gate and hung from the branch where his shirt was tied. He looked at his shoulder and saw no trace of injury—not a bruise, not a scratch.

Gates heal. He had vaguely known that, but since it was a positive aspect of gatemagery, no one spoke of it much. When Auntie Uck referred to not having a first-rate healer, she was talking about the lack of a Meadowfriend who specialized in herbs and could enhance their healing powers. But before 632 A.D., any injury could be healed by pulling or pushing someone through a gate.

If they saw his shoulder, they would know. The injury had been severe enough it could not have healed without a mark. Only a gatemage could be unscathed.

Pulling on his shirt would not be enough. One of the aunts would insist on seeing the wound, dressing it. He had to have a suitable injury to show them. Yet how could he inflict it on himself, here in the tree?

He gripped his shoulder with all his might, jabbing his longish, dirty thumbnail into several spots. It hurt, and there were red marks, but had it been enough to bruise himself? He could only hope as he pulled his shirt on again.

When he got to the bottom of the tree, only Uncle Mook and Aunt Lummy were waiting for him. Lummy was Mama's youngest sister and looked like her, only plumper and not as irritable as Mama always seemed to be. But then, Aunt Lummy was not a great lightmage; she was good with rabbits, a skill not much called for once she had persuaded them to leave the vegetable garden alone. So she spent her days trying to teach all the useful languages, written and spoken, to children who mostly could not understand what they might ever be used for.

And she was kind to Danny. So was Uncle Mook. And these were the two who had been left behind to wait for him.

Danny dropped from the lowest branch to the ground and faced them. "How much trouble am I in?" he asked them.

"With me," said Aunt Lummy, "none at all."

"Those girls should have been wrapped in a sack long ago, to teach them sense and manners," said Uncle Mook.

"But Zog and Gyish are now your enemies," said Aunt Lummy, "and they want you dead, to put it plainly. And many there are who think they have a point, and that the only reason you're still alive is because your parents are who they are."

"As if Mama would miss me if I died," said Danny, "or Baba would even notice I was gone."

"Don't be unjust," said Uncle Mook. "Your parents are complicated people, but I assure you that they care a great deal about you and think about you all the time."

"But if the Family decided I was drekka and dangerous and had to be killed, Baba would put me up in Hammernip himself, and Mama would shovel on the dirt."

"Nonsense," said Aunt Lummy.

"Of course they would," said Uncle Mook. "It's their duty."

"Now, Mooky," said Aunt Lummy.

"The boy is old enough to know the truth," Mook said to her. And then to Danny, "They know their duty to the Family and they will do it. But right now the madness is over and it's time for you to come back home to eat. With *us,* I think, in case somebody takes it in their head to make a preemptive strike before your folks come home."

"Oh, Mooky," said Aunt Lummy impatiently. "Don't scare the boy!"

"He should be scared," said Mook. "He should have cut off a hand before he put those children's clants in a sack. Now he knows it, but the deed's been done. Everything he does from now on will be viewed with suspicion. If we mean to keep him safe, we have to help him learn to be as innocuous as possible. No more strutting around about how smart he is in school—"

"He never struts," said Aunt Lummy. Danny was grateful that she defended him, but he realized that there *had* been times when he flaunted his superiority in classwork.

"It looks like strutting to the other children," said Mook, "and you know it."

Aunt Lummy sighed. "If only he could leave here and grow up in safety somewhere else."

"Don't put a thought like that into his head!" cried Mook.

"Do you think I haven't thought of it a thousand times?" said Danny truthfully. "But I know they'd track me down and find me, and I won't do anything like that. The only life I'll ever have is here, and all I can hope to affect is how long it lasts."

"That's the attitude," said Mook. "Humility, acceptance, willingness to sacrifice."

They led him back to the house, and Danny ate well that night, since Lummy's best talent was neither with rabbits nor students, but with cooking. After dinner, she insisted on applying her favorite and smelliest salves to his injuries, and when she pulled his shirt off, he was relieved to see that his self-inflicted replacement injuries had left bruises, though small ones.

"Well," said Lummy, "either Zog is getting weaker in his old age or he was being gentler than it seemed, because you're only bruised a little."

"Danny has the resilience of youth," said Uncle Mook. "They're tougher than they look, these children."

Well-salved and stinking to high heaven, Danny went to bed. Only then, alone in the darkness, did he allow himself to know what he must know: that he intended to survive, no matter what.

Now the entire business of his life was to figure out a way to escape from the North Family compound in such a way that they could never find him. Fortunately, unlike so many others who had ended their lives on Hammernip Hill, Danny had the power to move himself from anyplace to anywhere—if only he could figure out just how his power worked, and how to make it do things that he consciously desired.

2

The Greek Girl

᎐

It was Christmastime when the Greeks came.

Not that any of the Families would be so weak-willed as to celebrate Christmas. It was merely the time when most of the Indo-European world took at least a few days off work. It was the Indo-European tribes that had once worshiped the mages of Westil as gods, so most of the Families got a holiday right along with the descendants of their worshipers.

The Persian Family had been wiped out quite accidentally by Tamurlane a thousand years before, while the Sanskrit Family lived in shabby isolation on a compound in the lower reaches of the Himalayas. But the Greeks had prospered, primarily because they had had an unbroken string of Poseidons—seamages who could make sure that their ships prospered and those of their rivals did not. They had been weakened severely since Loki closed the gates, but such powers as remained were enough to provide a competitive edge.

So when a trio of long black cars made their way

unerringly through the magics designed to make the North Family compound hard to find, everyone knew at once that it was the Greeks arriving for one of their periodic "surprise inspections."

Not that the adults were really surprised. Thor had come home a few days before the Greeks arrived. It was his job to maintain a network of drowthers who watched the other Families for him—nowadays consisting mostly of computer wizards—a metaphorical term—who tapped into the electronic communications of the Families. They had picked up chatter that an inspection was in the works, and since the Greeks had more money than anybody, they were the ones most likely to carry it out.

The Norths always had to make a great show of cooperation and humility in order to avoid provoking another war. The last one had left the North family even smaller and weaker than the Sanskrits—but none of the other Families relaxed their vigilance, least of all the Greeks.

So Danny, thirteen since September, lined up with all the cousins. He was tall enough to be in the second row now, and to avoid the jostling (or worse) of the bigger boys, or the obvious snubbing of the girls, he took his place at the farthest end, keeping his head down. But not too obviously, either—the last thing he wanted was to attract attention by having a posture too abject.

The Greeks got out of their cars in the dooryard of the old house. No one lived there anymore, but once it had been a beehive of family life. In the early days of the compound, they had kept adding wings and stories onto the house, so it crept up the hill like the labyrinth of Crete. The oldest sections had thick beam-and-girder construction, so that the facing of the outer walls was nearly a foot from the inner lath-and-plaster walls. Between them was nothing but air, and Danny had long since found a way into that space, where he could roam through the edges of the house unseen and unheard.

That was how he had first learned the true use of Hammernip Hill, and how he had heard old Gyish's grumblings about the weakening of the Family's blood. Ever since the business with bagging the clants, however, Danny hadn't chanced any such spying. He made it a point to be visible to someone almost all the time, so that nobody could accuse him of anything or even wonder where he was. And he was glad he had made that his policy, because Gyish and Zog had enlisted several of the boys and girls to spy on Danny. As the children got better with their clants, Danny became less and less certain of whether he was being watched at any given moment. For the last little while, he had even given up leaving the compound through the gates he had made.

But today he knew there would be serious meetings between the Greeks and the Family council, and he wanted to hear them. He had never been old enough to understand anything when other Families had sent observers before. And since the Greeks would be most alert to any sign that a gatemage had emerged among the North Family—a "new Loki," they would call any such—Danny wanted to be there to hear if there were any accusations. Because if there were, he would have no choice but to run, even though he still had no real plan for how he would get away and keep from being caught.

Right now, though, they were still outdoors in the

cold December air, being inspected by some of the people who had killed a lot of the Family in years not long past.

The Greeks walked up and down the line of children, looking at everyone closely. Some of them—especially the middle-aged women—gave them all a look of disdain. And why not? The North cousins were mostly barefoot, even in the cold weather, with hair that only vaguely remembered having been touched with brush or comb. They were all suntanned and dirt-smudged, and their clothes were patched-up hand-me-downs or offerings from Wal-Mart or Goodwill, chosen by thrifty grownups guessing at the child's size.

By contrast, the Greeks were all dressed as if they were going to a rich man's funeral—dark suits and dresses, all looking like they cost serious money, with hair perfectly coiffed and fingernails manicured. Above all, they were clean. Yet they wore their perfect costumes with ease, as if they dressed this way every day, and didn't care if they got dirty as they walked through the mud of melted snow from the storm a week ago. They could always replace whatever clothes got mussed. They could buy a small planet, Thor had once said. Not that any amount of money could buy passage to the one planet where they all had wanted to go for nearly fourteen centuries.

From time to time as they walked along the line, the Greeks would pause in front of a child and ask something in the ancient tongue of Westil—the original from which Indo-European sprang five thousand years before—and one of the Norths would answer. If they had spoken louder, Danny could have understood them; he was the only one of the lined-up cousins who had achieved real fluency in the language. But they spoke softly, so it was not until they came quite close that Danny realized that these murmured words were questions about what branch of magery a particular child was showing affinity for.

It should have been Baba who answered them, but he was away buying new equipment. Danny suspected that the Greeks had waited until Baba was gone, so they could speak to others less accustomed to answering questions without revealing anything interesting. The result was that Auntie Tweng usually answered—she being the most taciturn of the adults—though sometimes Uncle Poot would answer, since he worked most closely with the children. One thing was definite: Every question was answered, and promptly, too.

The little children directly in front of Danny were not interesting to anyone—they hadn't shown any particular affinities yet, though of course they could already raise a bit of a clant. But the girl just to Danny's right was Megan, Mook and Lummy's daughter, just turned fifteen, and a very promising windmage. So there was some discussion of her, and Danny noticed that while Poot praised her highly, the particular feats he mentioned were actually things Megan had done when she was ten. So every word was true, but the impression Poot made was that the Norths were such a pathetically weak Family that they boasted when a fifteen-year-old did things that a talented ten-year-old should do.

Danny wondered about this. Years before he had overheard an argument about whether the Family should appear strong, to deter attacks and insults, or appear weak, so that no one would feel envy or resentment. "They don't attack us because they fear us,"

Baba had said, "they attack us because they think they can get away with it."

But Gyish, perhaps because he had led the family during the last war, took the opposite side. "All the Families are getting weaker and they all blame us. The flames of hatred burn deep and long, Odin—they need to see that we are weak so that their hate for us is satisfied."

Apparently Baba had given in to Gyish's view—or, in Baba's absence, Gyish had bullied the others into following the strategy of humility.

"And this one?" asked the short, slightly heavy woman who seemed to be the Greeks' chief inquisitor.

Danny raised his head to look Poot in the eye. Poot said nothing.

It was Auntie Tweng who spoke. A single word. "Drekka."

A little smile flickered on the Greek woman's face. "And still here?"

"We still have hope for him," said Poot, and then turned and walked away. The others followed him, though Tweng took a moment to glare at Danny before she strode behind them.

That's all I needed, thought Danny. One more reason for the Family to wish me dead.

Danny noticed now that there was a girl of about eleven or twelve among the Greek adults. She was the only child that they had brought along; Danny wondered why they had brought any. The girl stayed well back and looked bored. Maybe she was the spoilt child of the woman who always took the lead—certainly the Greek leader took the girl's arm and hustled her along, which suggested that the girl was her daughter. A bratty child, perhaps, who threw a tantrum when they thought to leave her behind. It pleased Danny to imagine her that way, because as the son of Odin he was always accused of being that way, though he was pretty sure he never had been.

The children had been told to stay out of sight as soon as they were dismissed, and most of them took this to mean it was a play day, as long as they took their games to remote locations within the compound. The whooping and hollering began the moment they were out of the dooryard.

Naturally, no one invited Danny along. He made his way toward the schoolhouse as if he intended to study something in the one place where none of the other children would willingly go during a play day, but after entering the school he waited only a little while before he slipped out the back and made his way around behind Hammernip Hill to approach the old house from the most isolated side.

A steep slope on Danny's left side led to a runoff ditch on his right. The ditch ran right under the crawl space of the newest wing of the house—it had obviously been dug long before the wing was built, and Danny knew that was more than a hundred years ago. Danny made a point of *not* checking to see if anyone was watching him. He knew that a glance around would make him seem furtive, whereas if he just ducked under the house without the slightest concern about who might see him, he would seem innocent. If anyone asked, he would say that he liked to nap in the near darkness there. That story was a bit more plausible in summer, because it was so much cooler under the house. In winter, though, it provided shelter from the wind, so he could still make a case for its being his private hideaway.

And it was, wasn't it? The only thing he concealed was that instead of lying down on the cold earth of the crawl space, he made his way to the cranny through which he entered the wall spaces.

He had discovered it first when he was only five, small enough to fit through the passage more easily. But long habit had taught him how to bend his body to fit around tight corners. He had grown quite a bit in the months since he had last crept inside, and he worried that he'd have to turn back at some point, or—even worse—get stuck and have to call for help. But no, he moved smoothly through the familiar passages.

The leaders of the two Families would meet in the library, at the opposite end of the house, because that's where the important meetings were always held. There was a big table in the middle of the room, and several extra side chairs around the walls.

The books that filled the shelves, written in every Indo-European language and sometimes in Westil itself, contained all the lore of the North family clear back to the ancient time when the tribes began splitting off, each taking a Family of gods with them to lead them to victory and guarantee them the support of heaven and earth, beast and tree. In those days the power of the Families had been unstoppable, and the Indo-Europeans—Hittite and Persian, Aryan and Celt, Illyrian and Latin, Dorian and Ionian, German and Nord and Slav—prevailed over the locals wherever they went. Their conquests only ended when their gods got bored or distracted, and refused to help them invade the next land and subdue or slaughter its inhabitants.

The Families that prospered most were the ones

that worked hardest at supporting their worshipers in battle and in agriculture. But the more a particular tribe succeeded in spreading across a large area, ruling over subject nations, the more likely it was to fragment into smaller clans or city-states. When they divided, the clans vied for the attention of their favorite gods. Sometimes a Family divided, some following one clan, some another. Sometimes the divided Families fought each other for decades, using their worshipers as surrogates.

More often, though, to keep up their strength a Family would simply pick one of the tribal clans and stay with it, letting the others fend for themselves without the help of gods. But if the Family felt itself to be ill-served by their worshipers, they would choose another clan or city, and leave the first bereft of Westilian help. That was the secret history behind the histories, behind the waves of invasion, the ups and downs of a city's fortunes. And drowther scholars actually thought that Homer had made up the doings of the gods! That the Eddas and Vedas and Sagas were a kind of religious fantasy! Drowthers convinced themselves so easily that gods they hadn't seen with their own eyes must not exist. But then, compared to earlier days, the Westilian Families were not gods at all, but mere shadows of the old glory.

Danny slid along through the west wall of the library, the one with no windows in it. There *had* been windows, back when it was a dormitory, but it had been turned into a library back in the 1920s and the windows were sealed up. Where they had been, the casements remained, and Danny had to crawl under them if he wanted to go all the way to the end of the room. But he didn't need to go that far. Years ago he had pushed pins through the plaster, right through the wallpaper on the other side, so he could see into the room. As he got older and taller, he had created new pinholes higher up.

Now he didn't poke any more, but just bent himself enough to see with one eye through the highest of the old holes. He could hardly make out faces, but he could get a good count of how many were present. He had long since learned that seeing wasn't as important as hearing. Once he knew who was in the library, he would recognize the voices and know who was speaking.

He knew none of the Greeks, however, so he bent to take a census of who was in the room. They hadn't brought the girl in with them, so there were seven Greek adults, three women and four men. Danny didn't bother trying to learn their names, beyond the fact that their last name was Argyros. He would google them later if he was curious. This conversation was about Greeks against Norths, and what mattered to Danny was what might be said about *him*.

The pleasantries lasted a long time. He was astonished that they actually reminisced about the last war. The Greeks talked about a time when one of their number found himself trapped inside the North compound, holding only an axe to defend himself against the North treemages.

"Oh yes," said Gyish. "Alf was just a lad, we didn't know yet all he could do. He loosened the head on that axe, so when your boy went to take a swing at one of the trees, the axe flew apart and there he was, ready to do battle against trees with a stick of wood!"

"Beat him to a pulp," said Zog. "Pounded him into the ground like yams."

Danny could hardly believe they would brag about such a thing right in front of the dead boy's family—but to his surprise, the Greek men laughed just as hard as the Norths.

The women of both families kept stolid faces and said nothing.

There were more stories, snide remarks about the "magery of money," and other nonsense, before Auntie Tweng cleared her throat and said, "Well, you inspected our lot. What did you think?"

"That perhaps you should acquire more soap," said a Greek woman.

One of the men started to chuckle. "No, no, Valbona. Agon was saying, They obviously have a dirtmage and he's been practicing on the other children!"

At that, all the men again burst into laughter. Again, the women made no sound.

How could these enemies laugh together?

Maybe there was a camaraderie among warriors, now that the war was over. Or maybe laughter was how they pushed painful memories out of their minds. Perhaps laughter was the only way they could keep from killing each other.

"It's the country life," said Aunt Lummy with a smile in her voice. "You wash them, but five minutes later they're dirty again. We could raise them in air-conditioned boxes, I suppose, but the fresh air is so healthy, and the exercise makes them strong."

"Shoeless even in winter?" asked the Greek woman called Valbona.

"You'd be amazed how tough one's feet can become," said Aunt Lummy.

"Oh, I'm sure they become like hooves," said Valbona. "Shoes, though, you can change with the styles."

Again the men laughed as if this were the most hilarious jest.

"I think it's time to bring in a bit of refreshment," said Auntie Tweng. "It's winter, so the tea is hot, but we just got a refrigerator this year, so if you want lemonade or cold iced tea, that can be arranged as well."

Danny almost laughed at that, partly because he enjoyed the irony—the Norths had owned refrigerators Danny's whole life—and partly because he had never known that Auntie Tweng had a sense of humor, still less one with a nasty bite to it.

"And cakes," said Aunt Lummy. "Tea and cakes."

"How British," said a Greek woman.

"Actually, the tea comes from Indonesia," said Aunt Lummy. "Odd that we call coffee 'Java,' when the island of Java produces nothing but tea."

"It produces many things," said one of the men, "and we transport a great portion of the island's exports. But it's true that the mountains are one big tea plantation."

So he had been to Indonesia. Big deal, thought Danny. He couldn't get to Westil, and that's the only thing that any of the Westil Families cared about now.

He heard the door open as Auntie Tweng and Auntie Uck went out for the refreshments that were waiting on carts at the head of the stairs.

Someone came in when they went out. It took a moment before the Greek girl came into view, walking slowly and taking everything in, looking up and down the bookshelves. The Greek adults couldn't take their eyes off her—but they didn't rebuke her for coming in, either. They just watched her explore the room, and because their attention was so focused on her, all the Norths began to watch her closely, too.

From across the room, the girl turned and faced directly toward the spot where Danny was watching through a pinhole in the wall. "What is it, Yllka?" murmured one of the Greek men; one of the women shushed him.

The girl walked around the table and out of Danny's range of vision, but in a moment she reappeared, much closer now, and immediately walked right to where Danny was watching and put her eye up to the pinhole.

Danny was so startled that he tried instinctively to back away. Of course there was nowhere to back *to*, so he ended up banging his head against the clapboard of the outer wall, making a thump; and the pain of it made him utter a sound. Halfway between a groan and a cry, instantly stifled—but it had been heard, and Danny knew that he was dead.

"Someone's spying on us," said Uncle Mook.

"Out of the way," said Gyish. And then there was a crash as the shovel from the fireplace shattered the plaster and broke through some of the laths, right where the pinhole had been.

Danny went from sick fear to absolute panic. He threw himself toward the passage that led outside, only to discover that it didn't exist. He had never had trouble finding it before, but now all he could feel with his hands was the solid wood of the tall eight-by-eight timber that ran all the way up that corner of the room, from deep in the earth to hold up a roof beam.

There was no secret passage. Without ever thinking

about it, in the darkness Danny had created a magical gate, just as he had done in the tree when he tied up the girls' clants in his shirt. And now he couldn't find the gate. He'd be trapped here like a bug under a glass.

Crash! The shovel came through the wall again, lower down. And then someone started pulling away the laths, letting even more light into the gap between walls. In a moment one of them would stick his head in and recognize Danny.

The girl had done something, he realized that now. She had hidden the gate from him so he couldn't get away.

Well, she couldn't hide a gate that didn't exist. Danny didn't know how to consciously *make* a gate, but he knew what it felt like to be rushing somewhere and have a gate simply *happen*. In this moment of extreme danger, it was time to run.

So he threw himself toward the great timber, while thinking of his goal—to get out of the house, out of the compound, so that he could absolutely prove that he had been nowhere near the house.

He threw himself . . . and of course banged into the heavy timber.

I need more of a head start, he thought. So he forced himself to move back toward the place where the wall was getting smashed in, and threw himself toward the place where he had always thought his secret passage was.

He struck solid timber again, and fell.

Only this time it was different. He was outside, and though the spot was shady, there was winter sunlight filtering through pine needles. His hands were full of fallen leaves and needles. The timber he had bumped into wasn't part of the structure of the house. He had passed through a new gate and struck the trunk of a living pine, and his forehead was bleeding.

He knew the spot. One of his secret gates that bypassed the watching trees was only a few paces away. He was outside the compound. He had made a gate that went all the way from the library wall to a place beyond the Family's protective barrier.

I made a gate when I needed it most, thought Danny. I can go anywhere.

But this was no time to feel boastful, even in the privacy of his own mind. If he were found outside the compound, when none of the sentinel trees remembered his passing, it would be almost as bad as being found inside a wall space that had no nonmagical entrance. He had to get back inside the compound if he was going to bring off the claim that he could *not* have been the spy in the walls.

Unless the girl already knew, and told them. How could Danny guess how much the girl understood about gates and gatemages? Obviously she must be nothing more than a Doormouse—if she were so much as a Keyfriend, all the Families would insist that she be killed. Sniffers and Doormouses were allowed to live, as the weakest kind of gatemage, for the sole reason that if there was a living gate somewhere, the Sniffer would find it. Ostensibly the purpose of keeping Sniffers alive was because finding a gate was proof that one of the Families had broken the law and had a Pathbrother or Gatefather who could create gates where none had been before. Then war would begin again.

But the real hope of all Families, whenever they had a Sniffer or Doormouse, was that they would find a longforgotten gate to Westil that Loki had somehow overlooked when he was closing all the gates in the world. Then the Family could pass through to the other world, return with their power vastly increased, and rule all the Westilian Families in Mittlegard.

No passage to Westil here. Only the criminal existence of Danny North, child gatemage, who should be put in Hammernip Hill to keep the war from breaking out again. The Greek Doormouse had found him. But she could not possibly know that he was the one she found. He could bluff this out.

"You're not thinking of going back, are you?"

And just like that, his hope of escape was over.

It was some adult's clant, of course, so the voice did not sound like himself. More like a whisper in the woods. The rustling of leaves. But the voice was clear enough.

"Thor," said Danny. "Of course I'm going back."

"I understand. Life is burdensome for you. You think of Hammernip Hill as a fine resting place."

"No one knows it was me inside that wall."

"Well, now *I* do," said Thor.

Danny refused to take the bait. If Thor's clant was waiting for Danny here, then he already knew. "You knew about this place."

Thor formed a little whirlwind, picking up leaves and pine needles to give him a tiny tornado shape. "We've taken turns watching you come and go. We argued a little, sometimes—does he understand that he's making gates, or does he think he's simply a fast runner?"

"I realized it last summer. When I took Tina's and Mona's pathetic little clants to the top of a tree. A place so high I couldn't get back there by climbing."

"Don't call 'pathetic' a thing you cannot do," said the whirlwind that was Thor.

"Oh, I'm quite aware that I'm the most pathetic of all. But then, I've had no training."

"And who would train you? I hope you're not resentful."

"Your sons beat me up. A lot."

"Nasty little brutes, aren't they?"

"They're your sons."

"I was assigned to get a drowther wife. I did. The results were disappointing."

"But they can make clants."

"Apart from that, and copious amounts of urine, manure, and trouble, they produce little else. But one does what the Family needs."

"And yet you've apparently known about me for a long time, and you said nothing."

"Gyish and Zog would never let you live, Danny. You know that. And there are plenty in the Family who would back them to the hilt."

"But not you. And not . . . who *are* the others? And what exactly do you expect me to do?"

"I can't tell you until I'm sure you're not coming back," said Thor. "Because it's possible you're such a donkey pizzle that you'll turn yourself in and name the people who protected you, and then die beside them to prove your loyalty."

"And how do *you* prove *your* loyalty?"

"The way we've always done it in the North Family. Look for a gatemage to be born among us, and then shield him and protect him until he's old enough to escape this prison compound and reach adulthood."

Danny sat down and thought about this. "So our compliance with the treaty is all pretense?"

"Oh, Zog and Gyish mean it with all their hearts. Gyish was never in on the secret, even when he was Odin. He was always just mad enough to take treaties seriously. Honor, you know. I don't have any. Not where our enemies are concerned. No, the only honor is doing what will allow the Family to rise again from the ashes of Loki's madness. You're the first gatemage since Loki to be clever enough to stay alive this long."

"I wasn't clever, I just didn't know I had the knack of it."

"Yes, but when you found out you didn't brag or ask questions or suddenly start looking up Loki in the library. And before you knew, you didn't boast about how fast you could run and then get yourself observed making instantaneous jumps through space. That's how most of the others got themselves up in Hammernip Hill."

"And yet you knew about me."

"Knew about you? Hoped for you is more the truth. Your mother and father—so powerful, so unusual. Why do you think they wanted to make babies together? They'd had children in their first marriages. Pipo and Leonora were very promising. Quirky in their own way. Alf and Gerd, your parents, the two mightiest mages in generations. They won the war for us, you know."

"I thought we lost."

"Lost? That's what we called it, for the other Families' sake. 'We surrender! Do with us what you will!' " The mini-tornado sank down and seemed to grovel. "But they would never have made a treaty and kept it this long if they weren't deathly afraid of us. Even now, they are making no accusations. Because they're afraid of your mother and father."

"Why not? So am I."

"They have to keep moving, so they won't fall into a trap. The other Families want them dead. And they shivered with fear when they heard that your mother was pregnant with Alf's child. And then Alf is made Odin, and the word gets out that their only child together is . . . a drekka? Oh, I'm sure they absolutely believed us on that one."

"*I* did," said Danny.

"How would you know that gatemages don't make clants? It's a closely guarded bit of information. Why do you need to make remote copies of yourself, when you can go, just *go,* as with the winged heels of Mercury, to whatever place you wish to see? But we knew. Your seeming drekkitude was just another hopeful sign to us."

"Who is 'us'?"

"Just the five of us. Your parents and Mook and Lumtur."

Aunt Lummy and Uncle Mook. And Thor, of course. And Mama and Baba.

Danny found himself crying. He didn't know he was going to, didn't feel it coming. He was just . . . crying. And then sobbing into his hands. Loud sobs. And he wasn't even sure why. Except that it had to do with Mama and Baba.

"Don't you see they had to keep their distance from you?" said Thor. "What if one of them was caught looking at you with love? Or pride? What would they say that they were proud of, without rousing suspicion? But you have to know that they *are* proud of you. Of how well you've done in your studies. Languages—what a marker for a gatemage! Amazing that no one guessed just from that alone! And how resourceful you've been. You realize that you were leaving the compound for months before we finally saw you do it and months more before we saw you use all three escape gates. That was very impressive. Your gates still go only a short way, like the gates of a Pathbrother, but you're what, thirteen? Oh, yes, they're proud of you."

Danny got control of himself. He was ashamed that Thor had seen him cry, but he couldn't do anything about it now.

"So Mama and Baba don't want me dead?"

"Oh, don't get this wrong, Danny. If you come back into the compound now, you'll be killed. Maybe not at first—maybe they'll wait for your mother and father to come home. But only so they could lead the attack on you. Do you understand?"

"No." Danny wasn't sure if he was furious at Thor for saying Danny's own parents would have him killed, or furious at his parents because it was true.

"Stop being angry, it just makes you dumb. They'll *have* to show that they were absolutely heartless— the law that applies to other people's children applies to their own. It's not as if they could save you at that point. The moment they seemed to be wavering, Zog would peck your eyes out and Gyish would boil your blood."

"So now they'll track me down and find me."

"Think, Danny. Why do you think I was put in charge of our network of informants? The only person tracking you will be me."

"What am I going to do? In case you didn't know it, thirteen-year-olds aren't safe out in the drowther world, even if they don't have mages from another world hunting them."

"Danny, Danny, we're not from another world. We're from *this* world. For thirteen hundred years we've been from this world."

"You're still not answering my question."

"You'll get along, Danny."

"How?"

"You're one of *us,* Danny. You might be one of the most powerful mages in the family—we're certainly hoping so, because all this will be wasted if you can't learn how to open a gate to a world you've never seen."

Danny thought about that for a while. "I opened a gate to *this* place when I had never seen it."

"Very impressive. Let's see . . . two miles, to a place you can see from Hammernip. Why, you'll be ready to go to a planet in another star system tomorrow!"

"I don't even know what's hard or what's easy!"

"Well, I can tell you this. The gates you're making aren't yet *open* gates. You have to learn how to make them and then leave them open for *other* people to follow. Then you'll be a Gatefather."

"You've tried to go through my gates?"

"You should have seen me. Running starts, great leaps, I always just stayed in the same part of the compound. Your gates are real, but they only work for *you.* So far."

"How do I open them?"

"Am I a gatemage?"

"Then I need books."

"Gatemages never told, never wrote things down. Liars, tricksters, deceivers, that's what gatemages are. Along with being healers, guides, interpreters, ambassadors."

"Healers?"

"Think about it, Danny. Have you ever passed through a gate and come through in any condition but perfectly healthy and uninjured?"

Danny shrugged.

"Something happens during the passage through a gate. It heals you. The body that emerges on the other side is perfect, exactly what it should be at the age you are. There are no blind or one-legged gatemages."

Danny remembered now. Loki wasn't known as a healer, but Hermes and Mercury were.

"Go far from here," said Thor. "Talk to people in their own language, but also say as little as possible. Let them teach you, by what *they* say, what you need to know to stay alive. Drowthers can be cruel, but they're not all alike, and many more of them are kind than otherwise. Stay alive until you can make a gate that stays open. Then come back here. Don't just walk in—gate yourself in to Lumtur's and Mook's bedroom. They'll be hoping for you. Waiting."

"What will happen then?"

"Then we'll talk about whether and how you're going to get us all to Westil. The five of us first. We'll come back powerful enough to subdue anyone who tries to hurt you. When they see the result of the passage to Westil, they'll be clamoring to do the same. You'll be the hero of the Family."

Danny thought again. "So that's the plan. I leave in order to keep the Family from killing me, and I live in hiding while you pretend to search for me, and when I learn the forbidden gatemagery without a speck of help from you, I'm going to come back and just *give* you all this power?"

Thor laughed. "Ah, Danny, it's good to hear you talk like one of the Family. Of course you won't give us anything. You'll demand power. You'll insist on being made Odin in place of your father. Do you think you'll be the first? Your father will usher you in and bow to you. Whatever you make us pay, it's worth the price."

Thor hadn't understood at all. It hadn't crossed Danny's mind to become head of the Family, least of all while Baba still held the office. But let Thor think he knew what Danny would do. It would make it all the easier to deceive him.

"North, south, east, west. Make plenty of jumps. The longer, the better. Though don't try making gates that end over water, not until you figure out how to make a gate while drowning."

"I made a gate while people were crumbling down a lath-and-plaster wall with a shovel and poker."

"A promising step. Just don't tell me where you're going. Make it hard to spot you, so I can really look for you without accidentally finding you. And take care that this absurd little girl of the Greeks *not* find you first. You can be sure they'll have her looking for you."

Danny nodded as he rose to his feet. "Do you have anything else useful to tell me?"

"You sound so bored. 'And the voice of God was in the whirlwind after all,'" said Thor. "We gods just aren't as impressive as we once . . ."

Danny wasn't there to hear him finish the sentence. He had learned all that Thor intended to tell him. Danny had reached several clear conclusions.

First, his parents and Lummy and Mook and Thor might have watched over him, but if he screwed up and got caught, they would have killed him and still *would* kill him just as quickly as anybody else. So they were no friends of his, especially because Danny had no idea what "screwing up" might consist of.

Second, if Thor's clant could watch him pass through gates for years, long before Danny even understood that they *were* gates, then who else might have a clant here, listening to the whole conversation? Thor's boys, Lem and Stem, were stupid, all right, but Danny didn't think they got their stupidity from their drowther mother.

Third, Danny really was getting the idea of what he did inside himself to make a gate. The one he made to get from the house to here was his first act of deliberate gate creation, and to make it with only one false start wasn't a bad thing. He believed he could make a gate whenever he wanted. He didn't even have to be walking, let alone running or leaping. And now was as good a time as any to see whether he could do it.

He could. He thought of where he wanted to go, and there he was, standing just outside the fence that marked the edge of the I-64 freeway right-of-way, watching the cars and semitrucks approach, then whiz by, then cruise on out of sight.

And then, without another thought, he was on the other side of the freeway, up on the hill. Another gate now existed behind him—and if Thor was telling the truth, no one could follow him through it. Why would he ever, ever want to make a gate that other people could pass through? They could follow him then! And the last thing he wanted was to be followed.

Another jump, and he was in the Wal-Mart parking lot. If there was one thing he knew, it was that he'd need better clothes than what he was wearing in order to pass for normal in the drowther world. And shoes—he had to have shoes. Running shoes. The kind he'd seen on television and internet ads. The kind that drowther kids his age all wore. The kind that the Aunts had absolutely refused to buy for him. "Bare feet are better, Danny. It toughens you up." Well, screw you, all you cheap murdering bastards. If you think I'm ever coming back, think again.

3

The Man in the Tree

The kingdom of Iceway has no eastern border. It runs up against Icekame, the ridge of mountains that form the northern spine of the great continent of Westil. The peaks of Icekame are always deep in snow, and their glaciers creep downward year after year, plowing the poor soil and stony earth of the high valleys before them.

Many miles below these valleys, in his castle of Nassassa by the city of Kamesham on the Graybourn, the King cared nothing for that edge of his kingdom. Beyond Icekame there were no marauding hordes eager to pour over the high passes. There was only the Forest Deep, where no one dwelt but thornmages, who sought no visitors and never left.

From a king's point of view, Icekame was better than a border. On that edge of his kingdom, there was no one who coveted his crown or his lands, and he need not spare thought or money to guard that border. And the higher one journeyed up the valleys, the poorer the people were, so there was no purpose in trying to tax them. A king could only do it once, and then, deprived of the slight margin of survival, the people would either die or become expensive refugees farther down the valley.

So the people in the high valleys were left alone. Poor and powerless, scrabbling in their poor soil for food enough to last out the winter, eking out a bit of meat by killing a bird or a squirrel now and then, they buried many a child, and a man was old at forty.

Between hunger and loss, however, they found time to live. The children had games and rhymes and contests and grand adventures between the labors that helped their families survive. They got older and felt the stirring of the hot sap of love rising through them like trees in spring. The women built their mud-daubed hovels and symbolically sang their lovers into husbands at the hearth, and then babies came and they delighted in them and taught them and raged at them and clung to them for however long they might survive.

The people in the King's city of Kamesham thought that these highvalley folk lived like animals. But in truth these villagers lived pure human life. They needed each other to survive, and knew it. They had no conspiracies and no secrets, no ambitions and no feuds. They couldn't afford the luxury of treating any man or woman or child as expendable.

The highvalley villagers knew one thing that the King in Kamesham did not even think about: They knew every passage over Icekame into the Forest Deep. In high summer, when the crops were doing well and could take care of themselves, families would pack up a bit of food and hike over a pass and then down the other side.

As they walked, the parents taught the children what

they could and could not take in this place: Food enough for meals while they were there, but nothing to carry away. Water enough to drink, but nothing for the return journey.

"Will we see a thornmage?" a child would ask. Always they hoped to see one, and feared to see one.

"We will tread in their homes and their hearts," the parents would always answer, "and you will never see one because they are the whole forest. Nothing here goes unseen or unfelt by them. They tend it all."

"And they share with us?"

"They see that we take nothing from their land, but only live here for a day or two as honest as the animals. We live here like squirrels or birds, and they let us be."

Since most children had licked the last scrap of meat and fat and marrow from the bones of squirrels and small birds in order to survive a hard winter, this gave them a bit of a shiver. No wonder they came only in summertime. Who knew how hungry the thorn-mages would be in wintertime?

Such was the family of Roop and Levet, a man and woman married long enough to have had seven children, and astonished that six of them were still alive. Their oldest was Eko, a girl of eleven, who had a bit of a knack with root vegetables; not enough that anyone would call her a mage, but she could find edible tubers even under the deepest snow, and that was part of the reason they survived. The other children looked up to her and endured her endless bossing, because they knew she loved them and looked out for them.

The family always went to the same place, the meadow of the Man in the Tree. Other families had come with them in years past, but the Man in the Tree unnerved them and they never came back. That was all right with Roop and Levet. It was a lovely meadow for children to romp in, and fruit trees and berries provided sweetness and tartness that could never be found in their high valley.

Why didn't the Man in the Tree frighten them?

The great oak stood alone in the middle of the meadow, as if all other trees had shied away from daring to grow too close. The massive trunk proved the tree to be of great age—the whole family could not join hands around it, or even get halfway around the trunk.

Ten feet above the ground, the bark was distended in the shape of a man, as if someone were imprisoned between the bark and the heartwood. This was not a vague impression of a man, a trick of the eyes. The man was in perfect proportion, with knees slightly bent, one more than the other, and hands splayed so that in a certain cast of light you could count all five fingers. But he had no nose or eyes, no mouth or belly, no toes sticking out, because his face was inward, toward the heartwood, his back turned to the meadow.

"I think," Eko told the younger children, "that he is a treemage who defied the thornmages and came to the Forest Deep and tried to turn this great tree into his clant. And the thornmages punished him by trapping him inside the tree, not just his outself, but his inself too."

"You don't know anything about magery," said her next sister, Immo. "How could a man live inside a tree?"

"Then what do you think it is?"

"I think it's a fungus growing under the bark," said Immo.

"That's silly. You don't really think that."

Father heard them and came over. "I think the tree eats children who play too long around its roots, but it takes so long to digest the children that they have time to grow up into fullsized men."

The children laughed, for it was always fun when Father told them a story. Mother even turned to face them, as she sat in the grass, in the sunlight, nursing the youngest.

"How long, Baba?" asked Eko. "How long has this child been inside the tree?"

"My parents brought us here," said Father, "and the Man in the Tree was already there. But not as high as he is now. My father was as tall as me, and he could still touch the man's heel without standing on tiptoe." Father stood up against the tree but could not touch the man at all, even when he jumped a little. "He's been there for hundreds of years. Our family always comes here to watch him. My father said that our family was the first to notice him, back when his head first rose up here."

"There?" said Immo skeptically. "But that's not even on the same side of the tree."

"He hasn't just been rising through the bark," said Father, "he's been circling the tree. All the way around, the long way. They say that when he completes the circuit, he'll be set free."

"Who says that?" asked Eko.

"My father's father. Or someone in the family. Or some stranger who visited this place with our family. Or me."

"Is there really a man in there?" asked Bokky, the oldest boy, who was only six.

"Yes," said Father. "I believe there is. Because why else would a great oak like this bother to make the shape of a man in its bark? Trees have no reason to lie to us. Does a sycamore pretend to be a hickory? Does a walnut pretend to be a willow?"

"But how could he live?" asked Immo.

"Who says he's alive?" challenged Bokky.

"Well what's the point of having a dead man in there, then?"

"I've heard two stories about that," said Father. "One is that this man is the one who invented fire and burned the first tree. The treemages couldn't stop others from learning the secret and burning wood, but the trees took their vengeance by holding the man inside the heart of the wood."

"What's the other story?" demanded the children.

"That he was a hunted man, and a great king sought him to kill him because he had dared to love his daughter. He was slain against this great tree, and his blood soaked into the roots, and in pity the oak opened its heart to him and brought him back to life. The king's daughter came here every year in those days, in a great procession up the valley, and here she wept beside the tree, and inside the bark he heard her, until at last she grew old and died. It broke the heart of the man in the tree, and that's when he turned his back on the world. He still lives, but he sees and hears nothing, because his love is dead and gone, and he still lives on inside the tree that saved him."

Eko brushed a tear from her eye, and Immo jeered at her, but Father held up a hand. "Never mock a tender heart," he said.

Abashed, Immo rolled her eyes but said no more against Eko and her tear.

"Isn't the bark getting thinner over him now?" asked Bokky.

"It might be," said Father. "But it might just seem that way because he's so far above us."

"What if he comes out of the tree while we're here?" asked Bokky.

"Then we'll greet him," said Eko, "and ask him which of the stories is true."

"You wouldn't dare talk to him," said Bokky.

"I think she might," said Father, "because your sister is a brave one."

"She wouldn't jump across the runnel in the north glen," said Bokky.

"It doesn't take bravery to do every foolish dare that someone puts to you," said Father. "Only stupidity."

They all laughed at Bokky for that, because *he* had taken the dare and Father had to climb down and get him where he dangled from a branch over the runnel far below. Half the village men were in on that rescue, holding the rope that held Father, and then dragging them up together.

That night they slept without blankets, the night was so warm. The moon was high and in the middle of the night, Eko awoke and looked at the oak and for a moment did not realize what she was seeing. She thought it was a snake in the tree, and she glanced around quickly to make sure that none of the children was too near. Only when she was sure that the snake couldn't drop onto anybody did she look again and realize, through her sleepy eyes, that it was not a snake at all. It was an arm, an elbow and arm, and the palm of the hand was pressing against the bark, pushing inward as if the man were trying to pull himself out of the tree.

Which is what he was doing. Only the arm looked smaller than it should have, and as the shoulder emerged, as the body turned sideways, Eko could see that it was a slender boy, not a man's body at all. Taller than Bokky, but no thicker, no more manly.

I should wake someone else to see this thing, she thought.

But she couldn't bring herself to make a sound or even move to poke somebody. What if she frightened the man? What if he did this every night when no one was looking, and then scampered back inside the bark before dawn? If she made a noise he might stop coming out, and no one would believe her when she told what she had seen.

So she watched him in silence. His body rotated so his shoulder and arm were straight out. And when he got his right leg out, too, he rotated even more, so now he faced outward. Both legs came free, and then both arms, and . . . and he was dangling, painfully it seemed to Eko, by his neck, for no part of his head had come forth from the bark. And without the tree holding up any part of his lower body, the boy struggled and wriggled but had no leverage. He slapped and pushed against the bark, but he couldn't get his head free.

Eko worried that he might be suffocating. Or strangling. Or simply helpless, and what would he do if he could never get his head out of the oak? Hang there till he starved? Or until some bear decided to eat him? If there were bears in the land of the thorn-mages. She had never heard of a bear in the Forest Deep, but you never knew.

By the time she thought of bears she was already halfway to the tree. Still none of the family awoke, so she was alone when she stood under the boy in the tree and tried to reach up to help him. She couldn't, of course, so she went back and woke Father, pressing her finger against his lips to keep him from speaking.

She led Father to the tree, and then showed him what she wanted, without saying a word. He lifted her and sat her on his shoulders. Now she could reach the boy's feet and help hold up his weight.

Now he could reach up his hands and push against the bark much nearer to his head. Eko could hear Father beginning to pant with the exertion of bearing both her weight and half the boy's. "Come out come out," she whispered. "The moon's about." The rhyme was supposed to be about the sun, but Eko was adaptable.

The bark didn't tear, it merely opened, or not even that, it simply receded so that his face emerged as if from water. He was not a beautiful boy. His face was stretched. His nose scooped downward and out as if it were some sort of bird's perch. And when he got free, he was pushing so hard against the bark that he toppled all three of them down into the meadow.

Still no one woke.

Eko got up and went to the boy. He was naked, curled up in the grass. She touched his shin. He gasped and quickly withdrew his leg as if her touch had stung him.

She sat down before him, looking at him, marveling. None of the stories said that the Man in the Tree was just a boy.

"Is that a dingle or a dong?" whispered Father. "Is he a man yet or not?"

Eko shook her head. It's not as if she knew anything about how a boy became a man. She was having trouble enough making sense of the nasty things involved in becoming a woman.

At the sound of Father's voice, the boy slowly moved his hands to his ears and covered them. Then he tucked his body into a ball, ears tightly covered, eyes squinted shut.

"He wants to be alone," Father whispered.

Eko nodded her understanding, but not her agreement. As if Father understood both messages, he crept back to the spot where he had been sleeping near Mother, while Eko continued to sit and watch.

Eko woke at the first light of dawn. The boy was gone. Instinctively she looked at the tree to see if it had been real or a dream.

Real. There was no manshape now. Nor was there even a scar in the tree where the boy had broken free.

The boy had not stayed to speak to her. Had not stayed for daylight. Somehow she had fallen asleep and he had crept away while her eyes were closed. It hurt deep inside her, to have been present at his— what, birth? emergence, anyway—only to have him sneak away while she slept. She never heard his voice. More to the point, he had never shown a sign of hearing her, or remembering that she had helped him get free of the oak.

I didn't do it for thanks, she told herself. So it doesn't matter that he never said thanks.

Maybe he couldn't. Maybe he speaks only tree language now.

Or maybe he was born inside the tree . . . somehow. Maybe he was never human. Maybe *he* is the *tree's* clant. Why shouldn't there be trees that had the talent of manmagery? Then the outself of the tree would ride inside the boy, struggling to understand the world around him.

Eko lay there, weeping quietly, until the others awoke and saw that the Man in the Tree was no longer there. They were all so frantic with questions and disappointment that Eko could barely get them to listen to her as she told what she and Father had done that night.

"But you let him go!" said Immo.

"If he was done with being the tree's prisoner," said Father, "why should Eko have tried to make him *her* prisoner?"

All morning Father and Mother tried to restore the sense of frolic, but it was wasted effort. Everyone could see how Father grieved. The Man in the Tree really had been part of their family's life from his youngest memories. And now he was gone.

By noon everyone knew that it was time to go. It was no longer the meadow of the Man in the Tree. It was just an oak meadow now, and no place special. Now other families could come here with no mysterious trapped man to frighten them. But *their* family, who had not feared the Man in the Tree, *they* would not be back to this place again in their lives.

As they walked home along the barely detectable track, which was nevertheless engraved in memory, Eko thought she caught glimpses of movement in the woods to either side. Was the boy dogging them, keeping them in view? Was he hungry? Thirsty? What if he broke the rules of the thornmages?

Ridiculous. The thornmages surely knew where he had come from and would not begrudge him a sip or two from whatever stream they passed.

They emerged from the woods and began the long climb toward the pass. They had left too late in the day to make it all the way home, so they camped in a cold clearing high up the slope, where the ground slanted so much that Mother and Father tied the little children to sapling trunks so they wouldn't roll away in their sleep.

"Maybe this is how the man got caught in the tree," Bokky joked. "He was a baby that his mother tied to the tree and then forgot."

"I can't believe he's gone," said Immo.

Gone, but not far, thought Eko, for she had caught another glimpse of a shadow moving just at the edge of her vision.

The next day, if he followed them through the pass and down to the village, Eko never saw. And yet she knew that he had done it somehow, naked as he was, cold as it was. That's why, when they got home, she took a ragged old outworn tunic of Father's that Mother was saving to cut up into rags or maybe make into something for the baby to wear—she hadn't decided yet—and, along with a bit of her own dinner, left them at the edge of their potato field, in the shade of a slender oak sapling—in case the boy had some particular affinity for oaks.

The next morning, food and raiment were both gone, and Eko could only guess where he had gone. Perhaps downriver. Perhaps back over Icekame. Or maybe he had flown away like a bird, or burrowed down into the earth to find the roots of yet another tree. Who could guess, with such a magical being?

4

Shoplifter

In all his previous ventures outside the compound, Danny had taken great pains to be seen by no one. His pleasures came from watching the drowthers and from knowing he was temporarily outside of a place he was constantly reminded that he did not belong.

Now, though, it wasn't enough to watch the drowthers. He had to pass for one of them. Inside Wal-Mart was every item he needed to pass for normal. But it would cost money, and Danny didn't have any. He had never even held money in his hands. From the internet and from books he knew about money; he had even learned the denominations and knew what they looked like. But knowledge didn't put money into his pocket.

Soon enough he'd need money even to eat and drink. But there was no chance anyone would hire him to do anything while he was wearing homemade clothes that, to tell the truth, didn't fit all that well and were tattered and grubby-looking. Nor was he qualified to do any kind of work, even if it were legal for people to hire a thirteen-year-old.

Clothes first. He ran into the first problem as he was coming into the store. An old man was greeting people at the north entrance. He took one look at Danny, pointed at his feet, and said, "Shoes."

"I'm not wearing any," said Danny.

"No shirt, no shoes, no service."

"But I have a shirt on," said Danny.

"No shirt *or* no shoes, no service."

Danny stood there flummoxed, and nearly turned around to go back out. Then he saw a mother carrying a two-year-old who was wearing flip-flops on her feet.

"What about flip-flops?"

"Flip-flops count as shoes," said the old man. "Except that you're not wearing flip-flops."

"Because my little brother stole them. You saw him come in, didn't you? He was running and *carrying* my flip-flops. Do I have to wait out in the cold because my brother stole my flip-flops?"

"I didn't see anybody like that," said the old man.

"Come on," said Danny. "You aren't *that* old."

The man bristled, but then Danny grinned. "Come on, let me find my brother, then I'll have my flip-flops, he'll have an Indian burn on his arm, and everybody's happy."

"Except your brother," said the man, a little bit amused now.

"Oh, he'll tell you, stealing my flip-flops and *almost* getting me kicked out of the store was worth it."

"You're completely full of b.s.," said the old man. "Just don't tell anybody you came in through this door."

Danny knew what he needed to get, and without anything on his feet, he knew he had to get it fast and get out. But he couldn't help wandering around Wal-Mart for a while just looking at things. The whole place was a fantasy of Christmas. Everything had holly or Santa faces or elves on it; everything was red and green. Christmas lights, phony-looking plastic trees, pre-stuffed stockings. Christmas was apparently an even bigger deal to the drowthers than it looked like on TV or the internet.

Even ignoring the Christmas stuff, Danny was in awe. So many things that the Family had never provided for the cousins. Foods that didn't look edible, but plenty that did. Drinks whose flavor he had no idea of. Labels that meant nothing to him. Implements whose purpose he couldn't guess.

But flip-flops he knew. Even in the winter, they had some. He walked up to them, pulled them off a rod without even pausing, dodged around a corner and again into the next aisle, and by then they were apart and he was wearing them.

By now, though, there was a man following him around. Wherever Danny stopped to look at something, there was the man nearby, pretending to look at something else.

Danny knew everybody in the Family, but not the drowther spies that Thor worked with. Still, Danny imagined that Thor's informants would be a little more subtle. A pedophile? Danny had read about them, but he didn't think he was young enough, and even if he was, the guy would be chatting him up, making friends.

Store detective, that's what he was. And now that

Danny thought about it, he was probably acting like a shoplifter—looking around at stuff, seeming to have no purpose.

Well, my purpose is to get clothes that fit me and then get out of the store with them, without spending money. That means you've tagged the right kid to watch.

Danny stopped looking at the array of things for sale and started paying more attention to the people. How did regular shoppers act?

First, they weren't thirteen. Danny realized that kids by themselves had to look suspicious to the store employees. Serious purchasers were older than thirteen—anybody who wasn't old enough to have a driver's license would have to have come with a parent or adult or older sibling. Since there was no such person in Danny's vicinity—and hadn't been from the moment he walked into the store—they had to assume he had no money. Especially the way he was dressed. He might as well have hung a sign around his neck that said "Thief."

Second, most regular shoppers had shopping carts and put stuff into them. If you put stuff into your basket, you weren't going to steal it, right? You were going to push it around and get more and more stuff, and then take it to the front of the store and pay. As long as you had a basket, you weren't sneaking stuff into your pockets.

So Danny walked to the front of the store to get a cart. *Not* near the entrance where he'd lied to the old man about having a little brother. He didn't want to have to produce the little brother.

The trouble was that the detective was right behind

him, and as Danny went into the recessed area where the carts were waiting, the detective stopped him. "Come with me," he said.

"Why?" asked Danny.

"Just come with me."

Danny spoke loudly. "I don't go anywhere with a strange man."

The old woman who greeted people at the door stepped into the space. The detective flashed some kind of i.d. and the old woman relaxed, but Danny said, "I don't care what he shows you, I don't want to go anywhere with this man."

The detective sighed elaborately and turned to face Danny. "Turn out your pockets."

Danny turned them out. There was nothing in them.

"Lift up your shirt."

"You like to look at the naked bodies of little boys?" asked Danny.

"You're not that little, and I want to see what you've been stuffing up under your shirt."

Danny pulled his whole shirt over his head, then stepped out of the flip-flops and dropped his pants. One of the Family's concessions to modernity was that they bought their underwear at drowther stores, so Danny was wearing tighty-whities.

"Good heavens," said the old woman. "How far do you need to go with this? He hasn't stolen anything."

"He's going to, even if he hasn't yet," said the detective.

Why don't you check out the flip-flops? thought Danny. Out loud he said, "I'm *going* to pick out clothes and put them in a basket and when my mom gets here, she'll pay for them. And I can't wait to tell her about

the Wal-Mart guy who had to look at me in my underwear."

"I didn't ask you to drop your pants."

"Yes you did," said Danny.

"I did not," said the detective.

Danny looked at the old woman. "You heard him."

She looked confused. "I don't remember . . ."

"Oh, come on, what kind of witness *are* you?"
asked Danny.

"He's playing you," the detective said to the old
woman.

"May I get a cart now?" asked Danny.

"You can get out of the store," said the detective.
"When your mother gets here, *if* she gets here, then
you can come back in with her."

"Whatever you say," said Danny. Carrying his
pants and shirt, Danny headed out of the recess into
the main store.

"Put your damn pants back on!" said the detective
sharply.

Danny was out in the open now, and people were
already staring at him, there in his underwear. "You
made me take my clothes off, and now you're throwing me out of the store," he said loudly. "Wal-Mart
must hate poor people. My mom's coming and she's
got a little money, and we thought she could buy me
my Christmas clothes at Wal-Mart because you sell
things cheap, but no, I'm too poor, you accuse me of
stealing and make me strip and then you throw me
out into the cold! My mom's going to buy me a coat,
but you're going to make me wait outside with no
coat at all!"

It was quite a speech, Danny knew, but the detective was completely helpless and they both knew it.

Even the old woman knew it—she was giving him a twisted half-smile and she even winked at him. And the people entering the store had stopped near the carts and were looking at him and listening to him and then looking at the detective, and they looked a little hostile now.

For a moment Danny thought of talking directly to the onlookers and talking about how lucky *they* were that they weren't getting thrown out of Wal-Mart into the cold, but he decided that would be pushing too hard. Instead he started for the doors, awkwardly stepping into his pants as he went. "I'm getting out, I'm getting out." Then he deliberately tripped over his own pants and fell to the floor.

That did it. Immediately there were people helping him up, holding the shirt he had dropped, and standing between him and the detective.

"What are you doing to this boy?" a woman demanded.

"He's a shoplifter," said the detective.

"He didn't steal anything," said the greeter, with a shrug. "You proved *that*."

"I was just trying to get a cart," said Danny.

"You can shop with us," said a man. "We'll vouch for you."

"If you throw him out," said the demanding woman, "you're throwing us all out."

The detective made a dismissive gesture and walked away. But Danny knew he hadn't given up. It was a tactical retreat—Danny had done the same thing himself, when he was little and the cousins played war. You pretend to run away, but then you lay an ambush for the guys chasing you.

"Thanks," Danny said to the people who had helped

him—but he kept his eyes down, as if he was ashamed to have needed help. Hadn't he used the same technique to deflect attention a thousand times before? And it worked even better with these strangers than it did with the Aunts and Uncles. "Just want a cart."

"Stick with us," said the man. He had three children with him.

Danny took note of his face, in case he needed to run to him for help later. But for now, he didn't need someone watching him closely. "Thanks," he said, "but my mom's going to get here soon and I'm supposed to pick out the clothes I like the best. She got her Christmas check from Dad today and she just went to cash it."

That was a good story, Danny knew. Single mom, raising a kid alone—and not doing too well, from the fact that he was barefoot in winter and had no coat. And Dad was such a cheapskate he didn't even send the Christmas check until the day before Christmas. But it also meant that this man really didn't want to be near Danny when the purported mom arrived—needy single women were not part of this man's plans for friend-making, not even at Christmastime.

I'm pretty good at this, thought Danny. Fooling people by telling them stories that make sense in their view of the world—they had no reason to doubt you, and so they didn't. And it helped that Danny never looked like he was lying. He had perfected that during years of playing pranks on the cousins and getting away with it most of the time.

And now that he thought of it, of *course* he was good at tricks and pranks and lies—he was a gatemage, wasn't he? The first loki since *the* Loki who wrecked everything by pulling off the biggest prank in history and closing all the gates. Deception was part of the talent with gates—that's why Hermes and Mercury and Loki and the gatemages from all the other Families were the ones most likely to have dealings with drowthers. That's why they went by so many names— Eros and Cupid could always get into any bedroom. God of Love indeed! As if there were any such thing!

But even as he gloated a little, Danny made sure that his face showed no sign of anything but a poor boy who had just been through an ordeal. He walked to the carts and someone pulled one free from the stack and offered it to him. "Thanks," he said again, with downcast eyes.

As he passed the old woman greeter, her hand clamped down on his shoulder. He looked at her—she wasn't much taller than he was—and saw that she was smiling. "You're the smoothest I've ever seen," she said softly, right in his face. "Just try not to take too much—nobody should lose their job over you, not at Christmastime." Then she winked.

Danny showed nothing on his face, and said nothing. He just pushed the cart onward. But he felt a great deal less pleased with himself. The old woman had seen through his lies. He wasn't as clever and talented at deception as he had thought.

And yet she had also backed him up with the detective, making sure everybody else heard her bear witness that Danny hadn't been caught stealing anything. And she let him go with a warning not to take too much—not a warning that he shouldn't steal anything at all. Apparently Wal-Mart could hire her to be a figurehead representing their compassion for the elderly, but they couldn't buy her loyalty.

Drowthers were more complicated than anybody

in the Family thought. They always lumped them together as if drowthers all thought alike. But she was smart enough to see through him, yet lenient enough to help him get away with at least a small amount of theft. And her grip on his shoulder had been almost as strong as Great-uncle Zog's, and *he* was beastfriend with the eagles!

Peril is everywhere, but there are also allies in places least expected. Sometimes even the people who know you're lying will help you and trust you a little. The things he had learned in his first hour of freedom.

Pushing his cart, he went back to the boys' clothing section. Danny soon learned that he was exactly the wrong size for everything. Too tall for most of the boys' clothing, and too short and skinny for most of the men's. He stripped off his shirt and pants again, not caring who stared, so he could try things on right out in the open—he figured it would be pushing his luck to try to get permission to use a dressing room. There was the detective again, watching him from afar—let him see how Danny carefully hung things back up when they didn't fit, or put them neatly in the cart, so his mom could decide which ones to buy.

It was getting so Danny was almost disappointed to remember that she didn't exist, and no one would ever come to pay for anything he took.

Getting shoes that fit was the hardest, because he couldn't tell anything about the fit unless he had socks on, and he couldn't buy any socks. He ended up taking two pairs of socks, each clipped together at the top, and then put on one from each pair, slipped the shoes on and tied them, and then walked around with the extra socks flopping around his ankles. Then he took off the shoes and socks, tossed them in the cart, and put the flip-flops back on his feet. Then he set out to get the rest of his drowther wardrobe.

Don't be greedy, he told himself. The detective won't believe the story if I overload the cart—or put in any toys. A package of three tee-shirts, a package of three more tighty-whities, four pairs of socks, one pair of shoes, a pair of jeans and a pair of nicer pants maybe for church, two long-sleeve button-up shirts, a small backpack, and a nice winter jacket. Exactly what Danny imagined a mother might buy for her son, if the Christmas check had to go entirely for clothes and other useful things.

Then, just to gild the lily, he went to the Christmas card section and stood there reading cards in the "to Mother" section. Every now and then he'd look toward the entrance as if looking for his mom.

Time to go.

As he looked toward the door, he suddenly brightened, stood taller, waved. Then he began to push the cart at a run, weaving among people heading for the checkout counters. But—as if his mother had gone up one of the aisles—he suddenly cut to the left and started racing up an aisle. Let's give Mr. Detective some exercise, Danny thought. At the end of that aisle, Danny dodged down one of the central corridors, with narrow aisles going off to either side. As soon as he reached one that contained no shoppers—an office-supply aisle—he called out, "Mom!" and whirled and raced into the space . . .

And then he was in the woods behind the store, shopping cart and all.

It was such a relief to know that he could bring the cart with him. He had almost stopped in the aisle to load up his purchases in his arms, but then he thought, why not hold tight to the cart and see if I can bring the whole thing with me through the gate? And it worked.

Danny stripped off his old clothes and discarded them, including the now-useless flip-flops. He put on the jeans, a tee-shirt, and one of the button-up shirts over it. Then he pulled the jacket on over everything, and stuffed the other stolen clothes into the back-pack.

He was warmer right from the start. And the Nike shoes were comfortable enough that they didn't bother him much—and it felt good not to have the stones and sticks on the ground be more than bumps under the soles of the shoes. These were a lot better than the "best dress" shoes that got passed from child to child. Danny had never been the first to wear a pair of shoes in his life.

He looked at the now-empty cart and it bothered him to leave it there in the woods. So he hitched the backpack up over one shoulder and then wrestled the cart through the woods and bushes until he reached the asphalt that ran along the back of the Wal-Mart property, where several trucks were getting offloaded. He left the cart behind as soon as it was on asphalt, and walked south, toward the small row of stores separated from Wal-Mart by more parking. He toyed with the idea of sauntering along in front of the stores just like a regular person, but decided to go behind them, after all.

And that decision shaped the next few years of his life.

There were a couple of guys smoking behind one of the stores, sitting on some steps with a handrail.

They were teenagers, eighteen years old or so, Danny guessed. One of them was dressed in an employee uniform of some kind, and the other one was scruffier, with a sad-looking jacket and a beat-up backpack beside him. They looked at Danny as he walked by.

"Kid, you must be the dumbest shoplifter ever," said the scruffy guy.

Danny stopped and turned to look at him. "Shoplifter?"

"Come here," said the guy. "Look at him, Tony. Look! He didn't even take the store tags off."

"Yes I did," said Danny.

"Maybe you took off some of them, but look at that, what's that sticking out of your collar? Is that from the shirt or the jacket?" Scruffy Guy Who Wasn't Tony was standing up now, and Danny let him yank something out of the back of the jacket. He held out a tag as big as a brochure, touting the virtues of some kind of fabric and some designer's name that Danny never heard of.

"Thanks," said Danny.

"Dumb as my thumb," said Tony.

"Naw, he's not dumb," said the guy who had called him the dumbest shoplifter ever. "He's just unobservant. That right kid? You *unobservant*?"

"I guess," said Danny.

"Take off the jacket and let me see if anything else is dangling. And let me guess what's in the backpack—more stuff with the tags on, right? So if somebody stops you they don't even have to *ask* if you stole it?"

Danny took off his jacket and the guy pulled something else off the back of his pants.

"How did he miss *that* one, Eric? You going to tell me he's blind?"

Danny now had his backpack open and was pulling tags and labels off the other clothes. "Where can I put these?" he asked, when he had a fistful of them.

"Just drop them in a trash can somewhere," said Tony. "Or toss them in the woods. But *not* here. Manager would just make me come out and clean it up."

Eric had his hands on his hips now and was looking Danny up and down. "So I wonder what you were wearing before."

"Other clothes," said Danny.

"But not anything you wanted to keep."

"Old, lousy, ugly hand-me-down clothes," said Danny. "Since you seem to want precision."

"Oh, listen to him, Eric," said Tony. "A real intellectual. Pre-*ci*-sion."

Danny kept looking at Eric. "*You* said 'unobservant.'"

"Because I'm a high school graduate," said Eric. "Not college material, mind you—my counselor was very clear about that. But I did attend enough days to graduate. Next day I was out of the house and on the road."

Danny liked hearing that. "That's what I'm doing."

"Yeah, I can see that," said Eric. "In brand-new clothes that say, 'Come rob me and beat me up too.'"

"That what you're going to do?" asked Danny. He wondered if he should disappear right now.

"What are you, twelve?" asked Eric.

"Fourteen," said Danny.

"Thirteen then, right?"

Danny nodded.

"See, here's how it is, kid. The road's a tough place. How you going to live? Me, I'm eighteen. If I felt like it I could get a job. Or join the army. But what are you going to do? Look for some nice man who'll give you a good place to live as long as you let him *do* a few little—?"

"I'm not looking for anybody like that," said Danny. He remembered what he had accused the Wal-Mart detective of, and now he had a sick feeling that all by himself, he might run into somebody who really was like that. Not that he couldn't get away easily enough. But what if somebody drugged him? Or knocked him out? He couldn't make a gate and get away in his sleep.

"Yeah, but, see, *they*'re looking for *you,* and a kid your age—a little bit pretty, too—new clothes, looking like you ain't got a brain in your head and ain't scared of nothing . . . tell him, Tony."

"As long as he stays away from my stepdad, he's got nothing to worry about," said Tony.

"Your stepdad isn't the only asshole on planet Earth," said Eric.

"I know that," said Danny. "Got my share of them back home."

Eric slapped him on the shoulder. "See, Tony? This is a man of the world!"

"I'm not," said Danny. "Never been out of the . . . homeplace. Farm." He had almost said "compound" but he decided that would have conveyed a wrong impression. Like he was from some religious group somewhere. Though come to think of it, the Family *were* gods, or at least descended from them, and that was kind of like being from a religious group, wasn't it?

"Country boy!" cried Eric. "Yee-haw!"

"Nobody in my Family ever said 'yee-haw' in their

lives," said Danny. Though he wouldn't put it past Lem and Stem, if they ever thought of it.

"I'm just thinking something, kid. You got a name?"

"Danny," said Danny, since there was no particular reason to lie.

"I tell you, Danny," said Eric. "This is a hard world and you're just too damn young to do the road by yourself. You need somebody looking out for you."

"What he means," said Tony, "is that he's thought of a use for you."

"Well duh," said Eric. "Pitiful kid, and I can say, 'Got nothing to feed my kid brother, you spare us a couple of bucks, ma'am?' Bet we do okay with that."

"Not with his clothes looking all new like that," said Tony.

"Well, he's going to have to dirty himself up anyway," said Eric. "He's not going to make it far with all his clothes looking new like that."

Danny looked down at himself. "They won't look brand new for very long. And I'm not going to dirty them up. I could have kept the clothes I came here in if I wanted to look dirty."

"Any chance you can still lay hands on those clothes?" asked Eric. "I mean, not for wearing now or anything, but so you can change into them when you need to beg."

"Are you kidding? I don't want to beg."

"Oh, you got a junior executive job in a Fortune 500 company waiting for you in Philadelphia? Atlanta maybe?"

"No," said Danny.

"You don't look big enough to be worth anything

at digging ditches," said Eric. "You box flyweight? What about tag team wrestling? Or maybe you're a mechanic for a NASCAR team. Begging's how you stay alive on the road, Danny. You too good to beg? You better go home to mommy and daddy."

"I've just never done it," said Danny.

"You go get those clothes. They far away?"

"Back in the woods."

"You go get them," said Eric. "I'll be here waiting for you. You can keep all this stuff you stole, that's good, you must be one hell of a lucky thief to get away with all this on your first try."

"How do you know it was my first try?" asked Danny.

Tony hooted. "The tags? The labels?"

"So I was lucky," said Danny. "I'm good at getaways."

"A useful skill," said Eric. "But this is my home town. Don't steal anything more from my home town, get it?"

"Got it," said Danny.

"I still got a lot of friends here, like Tony. You planning to steal anything from his store?"

"No," said Danny.

"Good thing, because then we'd have to beat the crap out of you."

"If this is your home town, what do *you* know about the road?" asked Danny.

"Because I've been on the road since June. Came back for Christmas. Say hi to my mom, tell my dad to eat shit and die."

"You already do that?" asked Tony. "Cause I don't see any bruises."

"I left him a note," said Eric. "And besides, he's not

as big as your stepdad. I don't think he could lay a hand on me now. I'm taller."

So neither one of these guys felt safe living with their families. Danny wondered how they'd feel if their family had a Hammernip Hill.

"Go get your clothes," said Eric. "I'll wait here, and then we'll get us a ride up north. No money for begging around here. But in DC now, there's plenty of people with a few bucks for a guy and his kid brother. You'll see."

"Who's going to give us a ride?"

"Somebody," said Eric. "You getting those clothes, little brother, or do I kick the crap out of you?"

"Think you can?" asked Danny, getting into the spirit of the game.

"Think I can't?" said Eric. "Move your butt, little bro. Don't make me wait any longer than the next cigarette."

So Danny jogged and then ran back around behind Wal-Mart, put back on his discarded shirt and pants, stuffed the new ones into the backpack, and ran barefoot back to where Eric and Tony were still waiting.

"Man, the kid wasn't kidding," said Tony.

"His name's Danny," said Eric.

"I don't have to remember that," said Tony. "I'm not going with you. I'm a working man."

"BFD," said Eric. "Those clothes are great, Danny. You're a natural."

"Come on, he's a complete hick, that's what those clothes mean," said Tony.

"But he doesn't talk like a hick," said Eric. "He talks like he's read a book in his life. He'll be good company. I'll teach him to beg and he'll teach me how to make clean getaways. We'll be such great brothers we'll start thinking we really grew up together."

Eric and Tony said their good-byes and a half hour later, Eric and Danny were in the back of a pickup truck that was going as far as Staunton. Danny figured it was the luckiest thing in his life, that he walked behind those stores and not in front of them.

5

The Gate Thief

෴

King Prayard of Iceway was a Wavebrother—a seamage with the power to make currents flow where he needed them to.

This was no surprise. The inhabitants of Iceway, lacking in good agricultural land, and so far north that the growing season seemed to pass in a few weeks, had long found that trade or pillage were essential to survival; and, rimmed with mountains as their lands were, the ocean provided the only means of accomplishing either.

In such a land as Iceway, seamages were essential to making long voyages even when winds were contrary. A ship with a good stillsea mage aboard would never sink in a storm; a fleet led by a ship with a Wavebrother could always follow currents that led precisely where he wanted them to go. And if they had a Tidefather, the strongest of seamages, he could invest a portion of his outself in a particular current so that it would continue to flow exactly as he shaped it, for decades or centuries, no matter how long he himself remained alive. So long had Iceway depended on detailed maps of all the ancient currents made by the Tidefathers of the past two thousand years, and on the work of present-day Wavebrothers, that they had long since ceased to build their great trading and raiding ships with sails, or with any means of propulsion except the sea itself.

In such a land, it was inevitable that great seamages would rise to political power, and just as inevitable that seamagery was the power most sought after. Thus most children were tested for seamagery, and if they showed even the slightest talent for it, they were trained to the extent of their abilities, however meager they might be.

It was not that other mages were without value, for a Siltbrother could help improve the soil, a Galebreath could turn aside an unseasonable, crop-wrecking storm, a Cobblefriend could lead miners to productive veins of a desired ore, and a Meadowfriend could bring reliable harvests, and sometimes even spectacular ones. The people of Iceway were grateful for any such mages.

But seamagery had become something of a religion with them. To have a child with such abilities was to be raised into a different rank of society; no social barriers stood in the way of a child who could flatten the sea or kindle a current in the desired direction.

Kings of Iceway almost always married the daughters of seamages, or women who were skilled in seamagery themselves, for there was a strong belief in Iceway, and some evidence, that a predisposition toward seamagery could be inherited by children.

There is a subtle distinction here: It was absolutely known and repeatedly proven that if both of a child's parents were powerful mages in any discipline, their children were likely to have great power in whatever magery they found an affinity for. But in most of the world called Westil or Mitherkame it was considered just as certain that the *kind* of magery a child excelled in had only a chance relationship with the particular talents of either parent.

In Iceway, however, the importance of seamages was so great that a seamage king, in order to produce seamage heirs, would mate only with women who were proven seamages.

Here is where King Prayard's life became complicated. For his father, King Oviak, having started a war with the Jarl of Gray and having then promptly lost it, was forced to accept a state marriage between his son, Prayard, and Bexoi, the sister of the victorious young Jarl. Bexoi had no shred of seamagery in her, and only the slightest talent as beastfriend.

It would be generous to say that Bexoi was talented enough with birds to call herself a Feathergirl—they would come when they were within earshot, and then only small and rather useless birds, not even geese or ducks that were large enough to be worth eating, or hawks or other birds of prey that might be trained to hunt.

To everyone in Iceway—and Gray, too, for that matter—it was obvious that the marriage with Bexoi was meant to put an end to the hereditary line of seamages that had culminated in Prayard, who was the most powerful Wavebrother in the recent history of Iceway. Prayard's and Bexoi's children would have sharply reduced talent, and far less likelihood of having affinities for the sea.

Prayard was a gracious man, and accepted Bexoi as

his wife for the sake of the nation, even as he grieved over his own lost progeny. Not for a moment did he expect that any child of his and Bexoi's would be seamage enough to succeed him as king. Rather, he expected that the royal succession would pass into another house—whichever noble family of Iceway *did* produce a notable seamage in the next generation. In other words, it did not cross his mind that Iceway would have a ruler who could not command a fleet of sailless ships; rather, he took Gray's action in forcing this marriage to be an act against this particular royal family.

But the terms of the treaty did not stop with the marriage. For along with Bexoi there came to Iceway a host of Grayish "servants" and "stewards," all of whom were assumed to be, and were in fact, spies and overlords, and sometimes both at once. And it soon became clear that Gray would not accept any change of the royal house. The Jarl's goal was not to end the power of Prayard's family, but to force upon Iceway a king who was half-Gray by birth and magically weak and misdirected into some channel other than seamagery: in other words, the perpetual subjugation of Iceway.

So the fortress of Nassassa, where King Prayard lived, became a constant silent war between the Icewegians and the Grays. Prayard gave every outward respect to his wife, even to the sharing of her bed at least once in every month; her lack of children was blamed entirely on Bexoi's barrenness and not on lack of effort by Prayard. She sat beside him in court, attended all his official meetings, and was given an ample allowance with which to support the large contingent of servants and stewards who constantly meddled with the government and business of Iceway.

At the same time, Prayard was well known to have a mistress—no, a concubine, Anonoei—who had given birth to two sons, Eluik and Enopp, whose resemblance to Prayard was constantly remarked upon by Icewegians who already regarded them as their father's heirs.

If Anonoei had been a seamage, or even a powerful mage of any sort, then those sons would long since have been murdered in some untraceable way by one of the Grayish agents in the queen's employ. Or, failing that, their mere existence would have provoked a war. But as far as anyone could tell, Anonoei had no magical ability at all, not even Bexoi's feeble beast-magic. She formed no clant, practiced no discipline, served no aspect of the natural world. She seemed to live for no other purpose than to please King Prayard and lovingly raise her boys.

Thus King Prayard could be believed, or mostly believed, when he declared to the Grays that his sons by Anonoei, though he openly acknowledged them, would not inherit the throne, but would merely be his support and comfort in his old age. Yet at the same time, the common people of Iceway, as well as the noble houses, constantly hoped that Eluik and Enopp would be trained in the early aspects of seamagery like most other children in Iceway, and would show great talent and be worthy to succeed their father. Then they could lead a fleet to avenge their grandfather Oviak's defeat and their father Prayard's constant humiliation by the Grays.

So the Grays in Nassassa kept constant vigilance to

make sure that Eluik and Enopp never received any training in seamagery—indeed, they insisted that the boys should never so much as ride in a boat or see the waves beating upon the shore. Meanwhile, the Icewegians of the royal house kept equal vigilance to try to find some hopeful sign that despite all the outward evidence, the boys were actually getting that vital training.

It was into this castle of intrigue, distrust, resentment, and barely contained violence that a stranger came, who might have been a slight and slender man or a tall-grown lad, whose face was beardless yet whose eyes were deep with the wisdom of age, and who spoke not a word of any language for long enough that most people in the castle of Nassassa assumed that he was mute.

They had no idea how many centuries he had lived inside a tree, or how such a thing might even have been possible; they could only have known it if they had talked to a certain peasant girl from the high country.

The strange silent boy showed up one summer in the kitchen garden, wearing peasant clothing that did not fit and looking miserable and hungry. It was nearly night and Hull, the night cook, was up to her elbows in flour dust, kneading each of the prentices' wads of dough to see if they had the consistency right. Each prentice stood across the table from her as she worked his or her dough, sweating as much from dread as from the bread ovens heating up across the courtyard.

Young Jib, a promising soup girl, came and stood at the end of the table, waiting. Hull saw her at once and was irritated—how could anyone be fool enough to interrupt her when she was doughing? Yet Jib was doing exactly what she had been taught to do when a matter had come urgency but she did not want to break Hull's concentration. So despite her annoyance, Hull could find no fault with the girl.

Hull finished with the current wad by splashing a double handful of flour onto the table, then plopping the dough onto it with a distinctly wet-sounding splonk. "Have we given you a name yet?" she asked the prentice.

"No, Mistress," said the hapless boy, who had dared to offer her a wad that was still spongy.

"Good," said Hull. "Because if you thought that dough was ready for loaving, you'll never have a name in the King's house."

The prentice blanched and immediately plunged his hands into the wad, kneading in the flour Hull had added. It would take more flour than she had put there, Hull knew—it would be interesting to see if the boy had sense enough to add even more. In fact the prentice was promising—his breads had a good flavor to them—but it did them no good praising them too much or too early in their prenticeship.

"Well?" said Hull, turning to Jib at the head of the table.

"A boy in the garden," said Jib. "Or a man. In the dark it's hard to tell."

"And this boy or man sent you in from the garden, your hands empty of the herbs I sent you for? Coriander? Rosemary? I don't even smell them on you."

"In the shade garden, when I went for the cumin," said Jib. "It was locked from the outside, and nothing broken inside, yet there he was."

"What do you think, then?" asked Hull. "The

peppers are bearing a strange new fruit?" But she was washing the flour and dough off her arms. She would go and see what was going on.

Jib made as if to lead her there. "Do you think I can't find my way to the shade garden without you to lead me, Jib? Go get the rosemary, and try not to find any strange intruders there."

Jib hesitated for a moment, as if she thought to defend herself from the ludicrous idea that finding intruders was a matter within her control. Poor girl—like all the others, she was utterly without humor. Or, rather, she was unable to conceive of Hull having a sense of humor, which meant her jests were all counted as madness in the lore that grew up around her. Well, the mighty authority of night cook carried a heavy burden of loneliness. Again, an ironic joke; but since she didn't voice it, her entire audience—herself—was filled with mirth.

An intruder, with no locks opened. Hull refused to let herself feel any hope, though a person appearing in a locked room was a sign that had been drilled into her as a child. In this case it meant nothing—the shade garden would be easy enough to slip into, since the gossamer covering could be loosened at a corner—or torn with a fingernail.

Jib had relocked the gate when she left—Hull marked that as a sign that the girl had some sense. Hull could easily imagine one of the other kitchen servants leaving it open, so that Hull would find the garden empty and some assassin would then have free rein of the castle.

Hull unlocked the gate, stepped inside, and closed it behind her.

The boy—the man—sat on the ground in the middle

of the garden, between planting beds. The full moon was much dimmed by the gossamer roof, as it should have been, but the intruder was plainly visible. He hugged his knees and looked at her impassively, then looked back down at the planting bed he was more or less facing.

"So is it the coriander that fascinates you?" asked Hull. "Or were you hoping for a midnight assignation with a fat old cook?"

The intruder did not look up at her.

Hull walked around the perimeter inspecting the gossamer where it was joined to the roof. No sags, no gaps. It was as tight as when she last had it tightened two weeks ago. If there was one thing the sailor folk of Iceway knew how to do, it was stretch a cloth tight. She glanced back at him from time to time—he made no movement and showed no interest in what she was doing.

She stifled her excitement. It was not possible. Even though her grandfather had taught her the signs, her father had taught her even more sternly that there were no gatemages in the world.

But the first sign, the very first, was a person appearing in a locked place with no sign of how he got there.

Not possible. Gatemages existed, yes—grandfather had been one, to his sorrow. It was *gates* that could not remain.

So the question now was not whether this intruder was a gatemage, but whether he had been discovered by the Gate Thief. Perhaps that's why he sat here in the middle of her shade garden, unable to leave because the gate he came in through was gone and he could not understand why.

"I know what you are," said Hull. She approached him from the side, so he could see her but would not feel confronted by her. She took care to move at a middling gait—not so slowly that she looked furtive, not so quickly that it would seem to be an assault. "I know you came here by way of a gate no other can see. Did you make it yourself?"

He showed no sign of hearing her.

"Is your passageway still open? Can you leave the way you came in?"

He turned his head to look, not at her face, but at her knees. Then he looked back toward the planting bed. It was the basil starts that he seemed intrigued by.

"I will tell no one what you are," said Hull. "No one. Didn't I keep my father's secret his whole life? But I'll tell *you,* so that we each know a secret about the other. My grandfather was a gatemage, and my father had a talent for it, too. My grandfather lived in the Forest of Mages, sheltered there from all kings, from all enemies, from all eyes. His gates were short passages within the forest, and all seemed well. Other mages, when they noticed or talked to him at all, gave him great respect, for he was the most gifted gatemage known in many a century."

The intruder—a boy, a mere boy, he could not be an adult, his skin was so unlined—nodded slowly, though she could not tell if he nodded at what she was saying or at some unguessed inward thought.

"But then he decided to create a Great Gate. One that you make twice, coming and going. One that leads from this world to the Lost World of Mittlegard."

The boy stopped nodding.

"Yes, he was that ambitious. He wanted to restore

magery to its former greatness, for mages who pass
from one world to another and then return come back
not only healed of all physical ills except age itself,
but also strengthened tenfold in their power. A hundred-
fold. So he gathered a dozen of the mages who had
been most respectful to him and told them that
he knew he probably could not succeed, but what if he
did make the Great Gate, but then died? Or half-made
it, and failed to return? Someone needed to be a witness of where it was. And perhaps if he made gate
enough to pass through it himself, some might want
to follow him. My grandfather was generous; he had
forethought; he was a natural leader of men. My father
said he was a fool, but that was after he had failed, of
course.

"For he did fail, you guessed that already. Grandfather began to turn and turn, and then to spin and
spin. For the gate he was making was not a mere jump
between one place on the surface of the world and
another. He was drilling down—or up, no one is quite
sure—a great hole in the universe, a tunnel leading to
a place on another planet that circles another star. It is
the deepest secret of the gatemages, and why theirs is
the most coveted and resented of all mageries.

"Though never tell an Icewegian that—to them, it's
seamages or nothing, that's how short-sighted they
are. Why, if a seamage could pass through a gate to
Mittlegard and back again, he would be able to put
ships inside great bubbles and float them underneath
the surface of the sea so no enemy could see them! He
could turn the sea into solid glass that you could walk
on, or drain a bay of all water and then send it crashing back! Powers no seamage has had in a thousand
years or more.

"But who believes those tales now? Too much time has passed. My grandfather left the Forest of Mages when his outself was taken from him. Did I tell you? That's what the Gate Thief does, when a gatemage is truly powerful. You know that Gatefathers and Pathbrothers make their gates out of a portion of their outselves—just like a clant. That's why an early sign of such mages is they can make no clant. For they must leave a tiny portion of themselves in every gate they make, and the greater the gate and the longer it is meant to last, the more of themselves they put in it.

"But the Gate Thief, he finds their outself and steals it. That's right. Snatches it away and won't give it back. The more of themselves they put into their gates, the more he takes from them. My grandfather put everything into the Great Gate he was making, and when the Gate Thief took it, my grandfather had nothing left. He could make no gate, not even the smallest one. My father taught me that my grandfather was a fool, to risk all on a single gate. But I knew that my grandfather had done what a great man must do—commit all. For if he had committed less of himself, he would always have had to wonder—if he had done more, might he not have succeeded? Grandfather held nothing back, so he did not have to wonder what else might have happened.

"His gate was working, you see. That's what Grandfather himself told me. 'I could feel the connection,' he said. 'And then it was gone. Like a hand in a crowd slipping the coins out of your purse. Gone before you know they're going.'"

Hull reached out her hand to touch the intruder gingerly on his upper arm. "Is that how it felt for you?

Did the Gate Thief take your outself after you came into the shade garden?"

The intruder looked at her, and now she was close enough that even in the dark she could see into his eyes. They looked deep and old. If he had looked at Jib, then Hull could understand why the girl had been unsure of the intruder's age. Ancient eyes, newborn skin. A very strange person. And so silent. Was that grief? Or was he mute?

"Can you talk at all?" asked Hull.

Just the tiniest hint of a shrug.

"What? You don't *know* whether you can speak? You understood me well enough—you knew what I was asking. Or at least that I was asking something. Do you understand me? Nod your head like this if you can."

The intruder looked at her steadily, then nodded slightly.

"Then here's what I offer you. I will tell a lie—I'll make a slight parting of the cloth of the roof and say you slipped in that way. No one will guess what you are. For we're not in the Forest of Mages, and gatemages are much feared and hated, for you know what they say about that ancient Trickster, Loki of the North of Mitherkame—that he stole all the power between the worlds and then hid it away. Because of what he did, if folks think a man might be a gatemage, the ignorant ones will cast him out or kill him, while kings will seek to trap him and use him as a tool in their plans. So you must hide what you are, and I will help you.

"If you wish to stay here, that is," she went on. "I'm a cook—it's within my gift to make sure all who work for me have food, or anyone else it pleases me to feed. Food and shelter—for you can sleep in a corner of the kitchen, with the prentices and scrubs. I can offer you no better, because then I'd need the approval of Rudder, the steward of the house, and he'll have no patience with a speechless boy. Or man. But I'll call you a boy, because that's the look you have. As long as you don't meet anyone's gaze, eye to eye. Can you do that? Look down and never let anyone gaze into your eyes? No harm to let *me* see your eyes, but they're strange. Do you know you have strange eyes? They'll make some folk wish to have you put out of their sight, and there are those with the power to do it. Don't look them in the eye, do you see what I mean?"

The boy nodded.

"So you can stay here as long as you need. It will look better if you do some work for me. Errands, perhaps. Or washing up. Are you willing to do that? Then I can justify feeding you."

The boy nodded again, and a tiny smile flickered at the corners of his mouth.

"Ah then, you do understand," said Hull, though in truth she had no idea what his tiny smile might have signified. "You must understand that for my grandfather's sake—and my father's, too, for he also had the seeds of great magery in him, but he stifled them his whole life, for fear that the Gate Thief would take his outself, too, and leave him like a cripple among mages, as Grandfather was. Like a one-legged man. No, a man without legs or arms, for what can you do without an outself?" She caught herself. "Oh, forgive me if that's your case as well—you never did answer me. And you need not. For the sake of the magery you had—or have—I will give you shelter here as long as you need it. Do you want that? Will you stay, under the terms I just described?"

The boy looked her in the eye again—and oh, how she felt the depth of those eyes, worse than looking over the north parapet at the great drop down to the river harbor, a thousand cubits of fall, they said—that was how it felt to fall into his eyes.

He opened his mouth.

"Thank you," he said.

His words had an accent—but it was her own accent, a mixture of the way her father and grandfather talked and the way the Icewegians spoke. No one spoke like that, and perhaps in those two words she had heard too much. But it was as if her own voice spoke back to her—though pitched a little lower, in the range of a boy whose voice was in the midst of changing.

He could not have come by that accent naturally. He had learned it only just now, and the first words out of his mouth echoed her voice exactly, without a chance to rehearse. The second sign of a gatemage. He will have a way with languages, and know languages he should not know, just from hearing them, for his outself finds them in other people's mouths.

If he found her language, her exact language, then that meant he still had his outself, or some portion of it. He was still a mage, then.

She rose and walked to the darkest corner, the one nearest the entrance, so Jib could not have seen it if she didn't actually walk into the shade garden. There she unhooked the gossamer of the roof, three hooks' worth in both directions from the corner; then she rehooked the very corner itself. She would show it to

Jib later, to explain how he got in and then rehooked the single spot. She could not bring herself to tear the gossamer itself. It was so perfectly made and she nursed the ambition of detaching it and folding it up at summer's end, to use again another year.

When she turned to fetch the boy, she was startled that he had gotten up and moved silently to a place right by the gate. He was looking at her with those eyes. She smiled at him. "I'm such a liar," she said, indicating the corner of the roof. "But I said no lie to *you*."

He smiled at her. Then he cast his eyes downward, and instantly all warmth had fled from him. He looked small now, though he was just as tall as before—about her height, and she was tallish for a woman.

She led him out of the shade garden. He waited, eyes downcast and beggarly, as she relocked the gate, then padded quietly behind her as she threaded her way among the stone slaughtering and butchery tables to the kitchen door. There she paused when she felt his hand touch her arm.

His voice was quiet, yet she heard each word clearly. "Are you like your father and grandfather?"

There it was—the great question of her childhood. For despite her dread of the Gate Thief, she thought it was to be expected that she would be a gatemage like her father and grandfather. Or, failing that, at least a mage of some considerable ability.

But Father had married a woman without a scrap of magery in her, and Hull had inherited her lack in its entirety. Mother had been a sweet and patient woman, but without any particular talent except one: the ability to love her children with her whole heart, so they grew up full of confidence and trust in the world.

"The only gift I have," said Hull, "is the gift of remembering all kindnesses, and trusting those worthy of trust."

He waited a moment longer, his hand still lightly touching her arm—an exact copy, she realized now, of her own touch on *his* arm back in the shade garden.

Though no word was said, she understood the question, because it was the second half of the joke she told only to herself. "Yes, I also have the curse of remembering all slights and ills, and of giving my trust just as readily to those who *don't* deserve it."

She chuckled at that, and then opened the kitchen door and led him inside.

The prentices were all hard at work, but she knew that it was her pause at the kitchen door that had saved them, for they had certainly been looking out the high kitchen windows—she could see the flour marks where they had clambered up onto the counters. But she was feeling good—or at least mellow, nostalgic at so many memories of her father and grandfather, and rueful at what they had lost—and so she allowed them to get away with their time-wasting disobedience.

"Jib?" asked Hull.

The girl stepped forward from the table where she had been tearing the herbs.

"He came in through the corner of the roof and then refastened a single hook, which is why you didn't notice the gap."

Jib nodded.

"I blame no one for this except the wind," she said.

There was a slight lessening of tension.

"Nor do I blame this boy for being hungry and coming into a place where there might be food. He's a traveler, not from Iceway, or at least not from this part of it. He says little. He may not be full-witted. But I'll tolerate no unkindness. He is under my protection, and he serves in the kitchen as I ask him to, and owes no duty to anyone else. Do you understand?"

Jib spoke up boldly—a good girl, Hull thought again. Bold as brass. "I don't understand—is he below us or above us?"

"He is below no one and above no one," said Hull. "He is mine, as long as he chooses to stay."

"Has he a name?" asked Jib.

Hull looked down at the prentices' wads of dough on the table, now looking better but still not ready for loaving.

"Wad," she said. "We will call him Wad, when we must call him anything at all. He'll have a place to sleep among the boys who bed beyond the stoves. Not the best place, but not the worst." This last was as much for Wad's benefit as anyone else's. "Now get a bit of bread and cheese and chilled lemon water for the new boy." She pointed at Jib. "You do it, since you found him. The rest of you, it's time for me to tell you why your wads of dough are as unworthy to be called 'bread' as any mud ever daubed on a wattle."

As Hull walked around the table, inspecting the wads of dough and finding what faults still existed, she could see that Jib was doing a good job of swiftly getting food and drink for the boy, and that Wad kept his eyes downward so deferentially that he almost disappeared. Good, thought Hull. No one outside the kitchen will even notice that he's here.

6

Fistalk

Cadging enough money, food, and free rides to get to DC wasn't hard—not with Eric in charge. He knew what they needed, when they needed it. He also knew who they should talk to.

"She looks nice," Eric would say, or, "He'll want to show off to his girlfriend." Or, "Look, he's got room and he's on a long haul north, he can drive us."

Then it was Danny's job to walk up to them in his ragged clothes and ask for a few bucks. "Got to get home to my folks in Maryland," he'd say, "but no way my dad's going to send me money."

Or, if Danny and Eric approached them together, like they had to do when they wanted a ride instead of cash, Eric would say, "I left the keys in the car at a rest stop and it wasn't there when we got back to the parking lot. Now I've got to get my little brother home to Maryland anyhow I can. Our folks don't have another car, not that's working right now."

And as often as not, people forked over money or offered them rides.

When they were alone, Eric was almost ecstatic. "Why didn't I get me a kid like you before? She gave us a twenty instead of a one!"

The upshot was that by the end of the second day they were on the Mall in Washington and Danny insisted they had to walk the whole length of it, despite how cold it was.

"Begging's a serious job, man," said Eric. "You got to stick with it or you don't make enough to live."

"Come on, I've never been here," said Danny. "I want to see it."

"Don't pull that big-eyed sad-kid crap on me," said Eric.

"Yeah, I'm pretty good at it," said Danny. "Thing I'm wondering is, why do I need *you*?"

Eric had obviously thought of the same question himself, because he immediately launched into a list. "First, you don't know where anything is and I know this town."

Danny wanted to argue—hadn't he learned the map of the Mall? Lincoln on the left, Capitol on the right, Washington in the middle, White House on the north. Museums here and there along both sides. But there was no point in saying this—the point was that Danny wasn't going to let Eric order him around, and that was that.

"Second," Eric continued, "there's guys who prey on kids your size and you ain't gonna be able to fight them off. Third, there's cops'll notice how you're dressed and take you to the station and turn you over to Social Services and they'll find your family and send you home, which I think you don't want."

Danny listened to the whole thing, not dropping his innocent, needy, wide-eyed expression. This used to get laughs from the Aunts, but not for a long time—they stopped thinking Danny was funny quite some time ago.

"I can see by that pitiful act you're putting on that you're not listening to a word I say," said Eric.

"That sounds word for word like somebody's mom talking," said Danny.

Eric's face went grim with anger. "Say that again and I *will* leave you."

Danny shrugged. What Eric didn't know—and Danny wasn't going to tell him—was that Danny wasn't going to get caught by anybody. Not child molesters and not cops or social workers. It was too easy to make a gate and get away.

Eric didn't know this—couldn't know it—wouldn't believe it if Danny told him. Instead, he glared for a long moment and then walked away.

All right, Danny wanted to say. All right, we'll do it your way.

But after a moment or two, the sense of being abandoned left him. He had done all right in the Wal-Mart before he met Eric. He would do all right here. And Eric's company wasn't worth giving up any choice in what they did. Either Eric would come back or he wouldn't. Meanwhile, Danny wanted to see the Mall.

Their ride had left them off not far from the Vietnam Memorial, so Danny walked the length of the Mall. He could see that other people's eyes filled with tears—and not just the ones in their fifties and sixties, who would have known some of the names on the wall. And there were little artifacts left at the base of the wall—flowers, plastic and real; one little plastic army man; letters and notes and cards. But to Danny, this all meant nothing. The wars and suffering of drowthers rarely had anything to do with the Families, except when they were using the drowthers as puppets to act out the Family battles. Drowthers simply did these things—fought over things that never seemed to be important. The pride of nations? Who would get to rule over this or that obscure people? Freedom? What difference did it make to drowthers whether they were ruled by this set of clowns or that one? None of them were free, because they couldn't do anything.

Danny felt a twinge at this thought, because it hadn't been that long since Danny himself thought he would probably end up one of them—if he lived at all. But now he was full of his power as a gatemage. Of course, Danny had no idea whether he was a weakish Pathbrother or a powerful Gatefather—but whatever he was, even if he had been only a meager Sniffer like the Greek girl, he was far more powerful than any of these people gathered at the Vietnam Wall.

At the same time, he had studied history from American books; he had followed the news, when that was possible, from American websites. It didn't make him feel the ancient anguish of these people for their war dead. But it made him *wish* that he felt it.

What was the Family's equivalent to this wall? Hammernip Hill?

Danny walked west, as if lost in his thoughts, though he didn't actually have anything in his mind coherent enough to be called "thought," until he reached the Lincoln Memorial. He climbed the stairs, walked into the lofty chamber, and looked up at the heroic-scale statue of a man sitting in a chair. Or was it a throne? An ugly man, gaunt as a zombie in a bad movie. Just a statue anyway, not the man himself. A face that was on every penny—the cheapest coin.

This is the god that the drowthers worship, thought Danny—echoing, he realized, the contempt that the Aunts had for drowther heroes.

So, in defiance of *their* dismissal of all that the drowthers valued, Danny stayed and read everything that was inscribed on the walls.

At first, by reflex, he mocked. Government of the people, by the people, for the people? What were these people, and who cared who governed them!

But Danny had now spent two full days among the drowthers. He had asked them for money and food and rides, and half the time they had shared with him what they had. Why? No one in the Family would do that for anyone who was not one of the Norths. Danny doubted anyone but, say, Auntie Uck would even notice that some drowther kid was asking for a few bucks.

Of course, Danny had lied to them every time—but even if what he said was true, what business was it of theirs? Why should they care whether somebody else's kid was hungry or got home?

The god of these Americans wasn't one of the old pantheons of the Norths or the Greeks or the Indians or Persians or Gauls or Hittites or Latins or Goths or any of the other bands that had been thriving until Loki closed the Gates. The god was the people themselves. Imagine—a nation that worshiped each other. Not individually, but as an idea. The highest ideal was to make sure that every other drowther in this place had his freedom and enough to provide for his family. Other people *mattered*.

Danny had been on the receiving end of his family's callousness. And he had just run away from the fiercest sort of thoughtless cruelty—the end of his life because he was the wrong sort of mage. This Abraham, this Lincoln—would he have fought for the rights of such a one as Danny? A gatemage who had the misfortune of being born when gatemages were treated as the enemies of the gods?

What would it have mattered if he had? There was little enough a drowther like Lincoln could do for Danny, even with a whole nation—or half of one, anyway—arrayed behind him and armed for battle. Any drowther's life could be snuffed out whenever a powerful mage noticed he was alive.

Besides, the drowthers themselves snuffed out Lincoln's life without even waiting for the gods-in-residence in the North Family compound.

Too much thinking. Too much time spent standing in one place. The need to run came upon him.

Danny whirled around and ran from the building. He nearly flew down the steps, three at a time; barefoot as he was, with his feet horned and callused, he was surefooted, he could feel everything he stepped on yet feared nothing. No one here could catch him; the ground could not hurt him. Danny ran the length of the reflecting pool, ran around the hill of the Washington Monument, then dodged his way across the few streets that crossed the Mall. He ignored the White House when he passed it on his left. It was the opposite end of the Mall he wanted. Not the Capitol—what was the Capitol to him? What was *behind* the Capitol: the Library of Congress.

He was a little out of breath when he got there, but only because it was uphill most of the way, and he hadn't eaten anything since morning, and Eric had all the money—that had been a bad plan, hadn't it? Besides, he had his backpack on, which changed his gait a little, which wearied him.

It was only as he approached the entrance to the library that he realized that he was still dressed for begging. And barefoot! Drowthers had a thing about shoes.

Where could he change clothes?

He jogged around behind the building—a surprisingly long way—till he came to a long street with row houses lining the other side. Most of them had stairways up to the front door, and several of them had basement entrances under the stoop. Danny looked for a house that looked unoccupied at the moment, then lightly vaulted the iron fence and ducked under the stoop. It didn't take him long to swap clothes. Now he looked newer. Closer to normal. And he had shoes on.

The trouble was, he was still a kid. Would they even let him in?

The answer was simple enough.

No.

"What do you think I'm going to do, steal stuff?" asked Danny.

"Or color on the walls," said the security guy—but with a smile, as if to say, I don't make the rules and I know they shouldn't apply to you, but that's how things are.

And Danny couldn't explain: I'm hoping that somewhere in here—the Library that has everything—I'll be able to find something about gatemages. Even if it's written about as a collection of folklore or ancient legends, I need to find out what I'm supposed to be able to do and maybe find some clue about how to do it. Gatemages are supposed to be really powerful and dangerous, but except for getting out of tight situations, I can't think of anything remotely perilous that I can do with my gatemaking. So I need a *book*. I need a *clue*.

He thought of the library in the old house in the North compound. All the answers he wanted were there, he knew it. And what would any book in the Library of Congress be able to tell him? The best he could hope for would be ancient legends, treated by modern authors as mere folklore or even fantasy, but containing some kernel of truth that might guide him.

Every other kind of mage got training from others with his skill. Treemages were introduced to the trees by a Treefriend, beastmages to their beasts by an Eyefriend or Clawbrother.

The unfairness of it, the frustration, it all struck home at that moment and he felt tears come into his eyes. He brushed them away.

"Crying isn't getting you in here," said the security guy. But he wasn't smiling now.

"I know," said Danny. And, though his emotion had been real, he immediately thought of ways he might exploit it, lies he might tell. In the next moment, he rejected the lies. This drowther was a decent guy. It was his job to keep out unaccompanied children who might damage things. If he let Danny in he would be risking his job. Why should Danny bring so much trouble into *his* life? Especially considering that there was another way. For a gatemage, there was always another way into or out of a place.

Danny stepped back from the security gate and peered through into the room. There were no visible books, but he could see that there was a kind of alcove. Leading to restrooms. He fixed the location in his mind so he could come back to it later, by other means. Then he turned and left.

Outside the building, he stood for a while looking up at the Capitol dome. Drowthers might have no magery, but they built *this*. What mage had ever *built* anything? All right, yes, mages worked with the natural world, so great artificial things like this building were not even interesting to a mage. But still—without any particular powers except the skill of their hands and the thoughts in their minds, the drowthers had built great and beautiful things. Ugly things, too—but the Aunts always spoke of drowthers as if all they ever made were wars and stinks and stupidity. But it was not true. Drowthers also sometimes made things that were beautiful or mighty or clever or useful, or all of these at once.

Maybe Loki noticed this, too. Maybe Loki came to care about the drowthers and realized that if he closed all the gates, tying the gods to the place they were in and taking away the vast increase in power that came from gating between the worlds, then the drowthers could come into their own. The world would belong to them, and not to the mages anymore.

But he still had to learn how to be a gatemage. Because he *was* going to open a gate to the other world. To Westil, the ancient homeland of the mages. Loki might have been moved by compassion for the drowthers, but it had been nearly fourteen centuries, and the drowthers had come into their might and power. Surely now a Great Gate could be opened. What else was Danny born for, if not for that?

I'm not another Loki, he thought. I'm the anti-Loki,

the opposite. What he closed, I'll open. What he broke, I'll fix. What he hid, I'll find.

He opened a gate into the Library of Congress and found himself standing in the restroom alcove. He could see, not all that far away, the guard who had denied him entrance. But the man's attention was directed toward the outside and the other guards near him. He was not scanning for intruders who had somehow slipped in behind him.

As long as he was there, Danny used the restroom. It felt good to wash his hands and face. Days without washing were good for begging, bad for personal comfort.

A man came into the restroom and stopped and looked at Danny. No, not at Danny, at his backpack.

"How did you get that in here?" he asked.

Danny remembered the signs outside, that all bags and backpacks had to be scanned. Nothing about their being prohibited. But apparently the fear of book-stealing meant that it was suspicious for a kid to have a backpack with him in the restroom. And this guy looked like the kind of jerk who would be delighted to drag Danny out by the ear and have him arrested for stealing, simply for the sheer pleasure of adding to the sum of human misery in the world.

So Danny opened his backpack, showing that there was nothing inside but clothes.

The man nodded. "All right, but check that bag at the desk before you go anywhere else." Then the man went into a stall, dropped his pants, and began to stink up the place.

Danny's first impulse was to flee—to make a gate to the outside, or at least to get out of the now-unpleasant room and into a place with cleaner air. Instead, he stood there contemplating the problem of the backpack. He couldn't have it with him, but he didn't want to lose it. He could go back outside and hide it somewhere and then return, but he ran the risk of someone finding it and stealing it while he was gone. Besides, it just felt . . . wrong. Inelegant, perhaps, as Auntie Tweng used to say of kludgy solutions to math or programming problems. "Yes, it works," she would say, "but it's not elegant. Truth is simple and elegant. That's how you know it when you see it."

What Danny needed to do was find a place to put the bag where no one would find it. Couldn't a gatemage open a way into some small compartment—like the paper towel dispenser?—and push something through it?

Danny had never yet made a gate without pushing himself through it in the process. But he certainly couldn't push himself into the towel dispenser, not without blowing it all up when he tried to put himself into the same space as the wall—or breaking every bone in his body to make himself fit.

So he stood there, ignoring the man's groans and stinks as he continued to relieve himself copiously. Danny thought: The guy really *is* full of shit.

He stood in front of the paper towel dispenser and contemplated it. It was embedded in the wall, a tall metal contraption that was mostly wastebasket below and towel dispenser above. The wastebasket was overflowing. Still, it was the obvious place to stash the backpack. Danny thought of just jamming it down into the trash, but by now he was committed to at least trying to create a gate without going through it. A tiny gate that would simply let him push the backpack through a thin sheet of metal into a narrow enclosed space.

What could go wrong? The worst that could happen would be a huge nuclear explosion when the atoms of the backpack tried to occupy the same space as the atoms of the dispenser, the wall, and the trash. And in that case, he wouldn't care anymore. Heck, he wouldn't even be in trouble, because they'd blame it on some terrorist or foreign power and it would trigger a devastating war that would slaughter millions or billions of drowthers. Doing some stupid impulsive thing that caused the death of drowthers was practically a family tradition. The only unusual thing would be that Danny would die as a consequence of his own stupidity.

But the fact that there were no legends about huge explosions from the idiotic actions of untrained gatemages suggested that either it could be done safely or it couldn't be done at all.

So he stood there, trying to make a gate without going through it. The trouble was, he didn't really understand what he was doing when he made a gate of any kind. He just knew how it *felt*—what he was doing inside himself while thinking of a place he wanted to be. How could he feel that way, including visualizing the inside of the trash receptacle, without moving himself into the place?

The man in the stall sighed with relief. How nice for him, thought Danny.

"Oh, damn," whispered the man. "Damn damn damn."

Danny pressed the backpack against the trash receptacle and tried to think of it being inside. Nothing happened.

I might as well cross my fingers and wish, thought Danny.

"Are you still there?" asked the man.

"Yes," said Danny.

"This stall is out of toilet paper. Can you get me some toilet paper from the other stall?"

Danny set down the backpack and went into the other stall. Danny thought of unrolling long sheets of toilet paper and lofting them over the wall between stalls. Then he noticed that there was a spare roll of toilet paper behind the partial one. Only a thin sheet of metal stood between him and that entire roll.

The idea formed in the process of carrying it out. Danny *would* move through a tiny gate in a metal sheet—but it would be just his hand, not his whole body. He reached out his hand while producing that gatish feeling inside himself and his hand pushed through the metal as if it weren't there—though he could still see it. It was his hand that disappeared. He thought: Hi, I'm one-handed Danny, the gatemage who drops off pieces of himself in every metal box he passes.

He felt his fingers close around the spare toilet paper roll. He pulled it out. It came easily. His hand was intact. So was the surface of the toilet paper dispenser.

He pushed his hand back through the surface and there was no resistance. He could feel around the empty space where the spare roll had been. He pushed the roll back through and it went, fitting nicely into the space. Danny pulled his hand back out—the roll was where it belonged.

"What are you doing?" demanded the man.

"Getting toilet paper for you," said Danny.

"Can you hurry it up?"

Danny wanted to say, You're pretty snotty-sounding for a guy trapped on a toilet who needs a favor.

Instead, Danny reached back into the little gate he had made. This time he had no gate-making feeling. The gate was simply . . . there. And he knew it was there, he could sense it, it was part of his mental map. He wondered if the gate would be there now for everyone else to use—if the janitor could now re-load the dispenser without using his little key to open it up.

"Come *on*!" the man insisted. And then, as if on cue, he let go with an enormous prolonged fart and there was another plop.

What flashed into Danny's mind was a perverse version of a line of Lady Macbeth's: "Yet who would have thought the old man to have had so much poo in him?" Auntie Uck would have been proud of him for finding just the right quote.

Danny reached the roll of toilet paper to the top of the stall divider. "Catch," he said.

The man groaned.

Danny let go of the roll. It hit the floor and rolled back under the divider into Danny's stall.

"I missed it," the man said. His voice sounded agonized. More noises.

Danny nudged it back under the divider with his foot. The room stank worse than ever.

"Thanks," said the man. "For getting it dirty with your shoe."

Danny almost laughed at the man's stupidity. "Any time," he said.

He walked back out of the stall and went straight

for the trash receptacle. He made a gate in it by pushing his hand through to grab trash. He pulled out a handful of damp, wadded up paper towels and dropped them on the floor. Now the gate existed. It was a simple matter to push the backpack through it and jam it into the space.

When he had withdrawn his hand, Danny wondered why the backpack didn't just pop right back out through the gate. Then it occurred to him to wonder just how big the gate actually was. He pushed his finger against the metal surface just beside the spot where he could sense the gate was. Nothing. He touched a lot of other spots, and the metal was impermeable. He had to be reaching for the *exact* location of the gate—a place that no one else could possibly distinguish from any other—and then his whole hand went through as if the metal weren't even there.

So that's why it took magery even to *find* a gate. A Sniffer might not be able to make anything or open a closed gate, but he could tell where one existed. A Keyfriend could reach through a gate like this one, even though he couldn't make one. So gates didn't actually have to be hidden. They were unfindable to those without gatemagery.

Or maybe it was only lame, half-assed gates like the kind an untrained gatemage like Danny could make that were automatically hidden. Maybe if he were a really powerful mage, he could make gates that anyone could use.

Anyway, the backpack was hidden inside the dispenser, Danny could get it out any time, and judging from the condition of this restroom, the trash receptacle wasn't going to be emptied anytime soon. Then again, the fact that the toilet paper dispensers were mostly empty might suggest that it was about time for the janitor to show up.

Well, if he finds my backpack, I'll just shoplift another. I can live without my old raggedy begging clothes. Maybe I'll stop begging anyway.

Danny gathered up the paper towel litter he had pulled out of the receptacle when he made the gate, and jammed it down into the trashbin from the top.

He heard the toilet flush. He heard the man stand up, the sound of pants being fastened. The man was sighing with relief when Danny reached the door and was gone. Only later did he realize that his encounter with this dump-taking jerk was precisely the kind of thing that the Family expected of drowthers. Danny remembered how sentimental and admiring he was about drowthers while looking at the Capitol dome, and he felt as if he had learned something. He wasn't sure what. Maybe just that nobility and baseness could coexist in the same species. Maybe even in the same person. And that was just as true of the Westil Families as of drowthers. Great heroes, officious dump-taking morons—maybe they were even the same guys. For all he knew, this clown had won the Congressional Medal of Honor when he was younger.

Danny strode purposefully into a large open room—no, a *vast* room—filled with tables and counters and computer screens, and now there were shelves here and there with books on them, though it was obvious that these could not be a significant part of the vast collection of the Library of Congress. Probably you had to look up the title you wanted and then ask for it to be delivered to you.

Danny sat down at a computer and began to feel his way through the software. On a whim he tried "gate magic" as his search terms. He expected to get either thousands of hits or none at all, depending on whether the search engine scanned through the contents of books or insisted on finding only that exact combination in a title.

There were thousands of hits. Of course—the search engine had a notation: POWERED BY GOOGLE. Drowthers could do magic with data, as surely as treemages did magic with trees. Was it possible that this really was a power? That if he could bring one of the Google programmers through a great gate to Westil and back again, his power would be vastly increased? Then again, why would he need to? Computers were a kind of magery in themselves, or might as well be—to people who didn't understand them, they were every bit as inscrutable. The programmers got to know them and love them and understand them in order to coax the right results out of them—just as beastmages did with their beasts, or stonemages with stone.

Danny smiled at the thought of all the great mages in the history of the Westil Families as if they were stereotypical computer geeks.

"Young man, can I help you with something?" asked a woman. Her i.d. made her an employee of the library.

"My dad's in the bathroom," said Danny.

She smiled. "I just wondered if I could help you find something." She looked at the screen. "'Gate' and 'magic,'" she said. "Is this a research project?"

"I wanted old legends," said Danny. "About . . . magical travel. Getting from one place to another."

"Seven-league boots," said the woman.

"Maybe," said Danny, who had never heard the

term but guessed at its meaning. Boots that could take you miles with every step—maybe that's how gatemagery would seem to drowthers. "Or, like, the winged feet of Hermes."

"Oh, excellent," she said. "You've already done some research before you came—you'd be surprised how many people come here without having done enough research to know how to recognize what they're looking for even if they find it. Here, let me narrow your search a little." She sat down in the next chair and typed in a list of search terms and various pluses, minuses, and parentheses. In moments she got a much smaller, more refined list of book titles, and then entered another command. "The list is printing out at my desk right now," she said. "I'll get you the top six books and you can pick them up over there in about fifteen minutes."

"Wow," said Danny. He really was impressed.

"We're here to serve the public," she said. "And . . . we finally have decent software. You should have seen what a mess it was before. It was a miracle if you could find *anything* if you didn't already know exactly what you were looking for."

And then she was gone.

Ah, drowthers, thought Danny. Sometimes you love them, sometimes you hate them.

Then for the first time it dawned on him that classing all drowthers together made no more sense than having a word for all animals that can't stand upright on two legs for more than a minute, or all animals with dry noses. What possible use could there be for such classifications? The word "drowther" didn't say anything about people except that they were not born in a Westil Family. "Drowther" meant "not us," and anything you said about drowthers beyond that was likely to be completely meaningless. They were not a "class" at all. They were just . . . people.

Danny didn't want to loiter around doing nothing, so while he waited for the books he went into another room, a smaller one where people were sitting at tables reading or studying or taking notes. There was art on the walls and Danny walked around the room looking at it. Nobody did more than glance up at him—apparently being an unaccompanied child in this room was okay, as long as he didn't make noise or touch anything.

I'm just six inches away from being a human being, thought Danny. Just a little taller, maybe a touch of moustache, and I won't have to put up with all the suspicion.

Then again, dump-taking man would probably have treated me with disdain just for being younger than him and not wearing a suit.

I need a suit. Not right now, but eventually. I need to be able to look as if I come from more than one social class. I need clothes that look rich, and not just Wal-Mart clothes. What good does it do for me to gate my way into a place, if I immediately look out of place there, and everyone stares at me? Just getting from place to place is nothing if I can't appear normal in the new place.

I wonder what they wear in Westil? When I make a Great Gate and go there, will they dress like us? Or something as different from shoplifted Wal-Mart clothes as our modern clothes are from ancient Egyptian or Chinese costumes?

It had been fifteen minutes. He didn't have to look at a clock, he just knew. He had always had that knack—waking up when he planned to, staying away from home until an exact time, even though he didn't own a watch. When he returned late, having missed dinner, it was never because he lost track of time. It was because he got better food after his parents made the rule that if he was late, he'd get no food in their house. Then he'd stop by Aunt Lummy's on the way home and get a great sandwich even as she scolded him for his irresponsibility. "But a growing boy can't miss meals, it's just *wrong*," she'd say, and Uncle Mook would roll his eyes.

Danny stood up. The nice library woman must be back by now. That is, if her estimate of fifteen minutes meant anything.

There she was at the counter, and there were six books beside her, just as she had said.

"These are almost the best I could do," she said as soon as he was close enough that she didn't have to raise her voice.

"Almost?" asked Danny.

"Maybe you don't care about oddities in the collection, but I'm afraid they're my favorite thing," she said.

"I guess it depends on what you mean by 'oddities.'"

"Come with me and see," she said. "Of course, you can't touch it."

"Touch what?"

"You'll see."

She led him through an employees-only door and up a flight of stairs. At the top, there was a door with a keypad, and when she entered the code and pulled open the door, there was a whoosh of air. "Climate controlled," she said. "Try not to do any global warming while you're in here." She chuckled.

He followed her inside. It was a large room full of books in acrylic boxes. But she led him to another area, where books were shelved without separate cases. On a low table an oversized book was lying open.

"The book itself is only a couple of hundred years old," she said, "and it isn't in English, so I don't know what use it would be to you."

"It's in Danish, isn't it?" said Danny.

She looked at him a moment. "You recognize Danish?"

Danny shrugged. Of course he did, it was one of the languages descended from Old Norse, but he could hardly explain to her that he had grown up with Old Norse. Along with Fistalk, the ancient language of the Germans before their language was bent by the Phoenician colonies along the North Sea and Baltic coasts. It was one of the languages of the Family, one that some of the old books were written in. It wasn't exactly taught, but the books were there, and some words and phrases of it were spoken when the Family was speaking Old Norse. Danny picked up languages as easily as breathing. He could read Fistalk in the runes that it used to be written in. Runes like the ones reproduced on the open page of the book.

"When this book was catalogued," the woman told him, "it was placed in the American history section because it was supposed to be about the colonization of New Sweden. But then somebody who read Danish said that it was nothing of the kind, it was actually about Eric the Red and Lief Ericson and the colony in Vinland. So it was moved here. Then, when I was doing my graduate work here before I got this job, I found the book and realized that it was something else. It's a book *about* a book *about* an ancient runic record."

"You read Danish?" asked Danny.

"I *am* Danish," said the woman. "I moved here with my parents when I was seven, which is why I don't have a Danish accent. But I had already learned to read in Denmark and I haven't forgotten because there were lots of Danish books in the house. You see, this book is describing an old manuscript that the author discovered in an old accounting house in Copenhagen, where some of the library of a monastery had been deposited when the monastery was closed. The book he described was written in a combination of Latin and Old Norse, and *it* was reproducing a supposedly ancient runic record in an unknown language. The Danish author of *this* book had tried to decode it—there are two chapters on his efforts to do that—and he *did* succeed in translating the Latin and Old Norse sections of the old manuscript, but he had no luck at all with the runes."

Danny wanted to be bored—this had nothing to do with his quest for knowledge about gates—but in fact he was fascinated. Because he could read the runes right off the page, the very ones that the author had failed to decode.

"'Here Tiu dashed the ships of Carthage against the rocks, because they would not pay tribute to the valkyrie,'" said Danny.

"What?" asked the woman.

Danny kept reading. "'Here Loki twisted a new

gate to heaven and the valkyrie passed through it many times, because the Carthaginians had eaten the old gate. Here Odin raged with the sky and crushed the might of Carthage until the survivors wept in the blood of their children.' "

"What are you talking about?" asked the woman.

Danny nodded. "This *is* what I was looking for," he said. "How did you know?"

"I remembered that his translation of the Old Norse sections was full of references to the old gods and the magic of doors and gates. And there you were, googling 'magic' and 'gate,' and I knew that this book would never pop up on your search so I thought you'd want to see it. But what you said before, what were you quoting?"

"I wasn't quoting," said Danny. "I was reading."

The woman scanned the pages that were open. "Where did you read that? There's nothing like that in the Danish."

Danny pointed at the copied-out runes. "That's what it says."

"Talking about Carthaginians and Tiu and Loki and Odin?"

"What I can't figure out is how the Carthaginians could have eaten a gate," said Danny. "Is this the whole runic inscription?"

"There are three others," said the woman. "On the next three pages. But . . . are you saying that you can *read* this?"

"Of course not," said Danny. "I'm just imagining what it might say." He couldn't help lying. He was enjoying this game of telling her a truth he could not possibly know, and then pretending that it wasn't true after all. He shouldn't toy with her like this, it wasn't nice, and she had been very kind and helpful to him, but Danny sometimes couldn't resist doing such things. Showing off. The other kids had resented it, but the Aunts and Uncles had often seemed to enjoy it, back in the days before they began to think of Danny as drekka.

"How could the runes say anything about Carthage?" asked the woman.

Danny pointed to a few characters. "It's written in the way Semites write their words and names—no vowels. K-R-T-G. Back when the Germans were just separating from the Norse, they were under the domination of a Carthaginian colony at the neck of the Jutland peninsula." Danny had this much of the story from the version of Family history they taught the children.

"I've never heard of this. Was it discovered by archaeologists? Because it's in none of the histories."

"From the time when Carthage was at its peak, before they went to war with Rome for the first time. The German gods broke the power of the Carthaginians. This has to date from that time. But I'd never heard of any reference to Loki or a gate to heaven."

"That doesn't even sound Norse—they don't talk about heaven."

"But the Carthaginians did. It's referring to another planet—so far away that the light of its star can't be seen even on a clear night. High in the sky, see? Heaven. And Loki made a gate to take them there."

"So that's the kind of magical gate you were looking for?" asked the woman.

Danny didn't answer her directly. "I never heard it said that Loki would *twist* a gate. See? That's the same word you use for making rope. Wouldn't you think that a gate would be 'cut' or 'opened' or 'built' or 'carved' or something like that? How can you *twist* a gate?" Danny knew she couldn't understand what he was talking about. His questions were real enough, but they weren't for her. What he was doing with her was breaking the Family's taboo against telling Family business or Family history to strangers. And it felt good to do it.

The woman looked baffled. "Who are you? Where are you from? What school do you go to?"

"I was home-schooled," said Danny. "May I see the other runes?"

"What language *is* it, then, if you can read them?"

"Widdensprak," said Danny, using the term for "the way the people we know talk." But it wasn't true— nobody talked quite this way. But it was close to Fistalk.

"I've never heard of it," she said.

"Am I allowed to turn the page, or is that something you need to do?"

She reached down and turned the page, carefully and slowly.

Danny scanned the runes. Just as before, the words were ones he knew or were like words he knew, and the grammar was easy. Where it differed from Fistalk, it was more like Westil, though Westil was normally written with yet another alphabet. Or, rather, syllabet, since there were separate characters for every consonant-vowel combination. There were also separate characters for each of the common noun and verb endings. It took up far less room on the page, but you had to learn 181 separate characters, and some of them were pretty hard to tell apart. On the whole, Danny preferred alphabets. Fistalk was written with the runes used as an alphabet, though some of them sometimes stood for syllables, too. It was confusing, and most of the cousins had simply refused to make any serious effort to learn to read or write Fistalk *or* Westil. Aunt Lummy had often said that she expected the knowledge of Westil to die, "so if a Great Gate were ever opened, we wouldn't even know how to talk to our distant kinfolk from our home world."

The message on the page was a continuation of the previous one. "'Hear us in the land of Mitherkame, hear us among the great ships of Iceway, among the charging dunes of Dapnu Dap, among the silent mages of the Forest and the swift riders of the Wold: We have faced Bel and he has ruled the hearts of many. Bold men ran like deer from his face, but Loki did not run.'"

"You're just making this up," said the woman.

"Next page?" Danny suggested.

"There is zero chance that the Semitic god Bel or Baal was ever spoken of in any Indo-European language, let alone some ancient form of German."

"You lose the bet," said Danny. "Do you think the Hittites never spoke the name?"

To Danny, the Hittites were just another branch of the Family, albeit an extinct one. To this woman, though, it seemed remarkable that he even knew of them. "How old *are* you?" asked the woman. "What are you really doing here?"

"I'd like to read the next page," said Danny.

"You aren't reading, you're just playing. This is just a lark to you, but it's my life's work to me."

Danny shook his head. "Really, ma'am, it's at least as important to me as it is to you."

"I thought you'd like to see something old. I didn't expect you to mock me by pretending to read it."

"I'm not pretending."

The woman closed the book. "Come on, we're done here."

She was right, of course—Danny *was* playing with her, though not in the way that she supposed. But he was through playing with her now. He reached down and picked up the book.

Immediately she grabbed for it. "How dare you touch that!" she said. "I trusted you."

"The book belongs to the one who can read it," said Danny.

She pulled harder. He held tighter. If he made a gate right now and passed through it, would she be dragged along with him, because she was holding on to the book that he was holding on to?

"The book belongs to the Library of Congress, for the use of serious scholars."

Again, Danny resorted to truth, because he knew he would not be believed. "These inscriptions are about Loki, a gatemaker. I'm a gatemaker, and I have to learn whatever it has to teach me."

"This is a nightmare. Let go of the book, you're going to damage it."

"And if I do, who will lose her job? Not me," said Danny. "Just let me read the rest of the runes and you can have it back."

"Security!" she shouted.

Danny made a gate and let it suck him through.

He was in the restroom again, holding the book. She was not with him. She must be back in that employees-only room, clutching at nothing. Let her tell security what happened. See whether they believed it.

He took a paper towel and dried the counter around the sink, then set the book on it and opened it.

The third page of runes said:

Loki found the dark gate of Bel through which their god poured fear into the world and through which he carried off the hearts of brave men to eat at his feasting table.

Loki's heart was stabbed with the fear of Bel and the jaws of Bel seized his heart to carry it away.

Loki held tight to his own heart and followed the jaws of the beast.

Danny read it twice to make sure his reading was accurate and it was locked in his memory. Then he turned to the next page that held a copy of the untranslated runes:

Loki tricked Bel into thinking he was captive, but he was not captive.

His heart held the jaws; the jaws did not hold his heart.

And when he found the gate of Bel, he moved the mouth over the heart of the sun.

Let Bel eat the heart of the sun and drag it back to his dark world!

He has no more home in Mittlegard.

Well, how nice. A commemorative inscription about the achievements of the Loki of that age. No pariah then—there had apparently been some kind of war with the Carthaginian god, or perhaps merely with the Carthaginians, and Loki was given credit for shutting down the enemy. By moving the entrance to a gate, apparently, though Danny had no idea how such a thing might be done, especially if he really moved one end of it to the center of the Sun.

Enough. Danny had read it now. It was memorized. He had it.

Danny reached into the bottom of the trash receptacle and pulled out his backpack. He shouldered it, picked up the book, and made a gate back to the room where the woman had shown him the book. He could hear her in the hall, shouting for Security. Poor foolish drowther. Did she think she had any kind of control here?

He set the book right where it had been and opened it to the first runic inscription. He was tempted to stay long enough to smile at her when she returned, but no, he really did not need to be any more flamboyant than he had already been. In fact, he felt more than a little ashamed of himself now, for having responded to her trust and kindness by flaunting his knowledge and then doing something in front of her that was undeniable magery.

At the same time, he still felt the thrill of having done it—of having proven before a witness that he, too, was one of the mages of the North Family, and not a trivial mage, either. A dangerous one—so dangerous that he should be killed and put into Hammernip Hill.

He used his gate to the restroom again and then immediately outside to where he had been when he first gated into the library.

Eric was standing there, grinning. "You kept me waiting a long time in this cold, boy," he said. "You got some explaining to do."

7

Stone's House

෴

Danny thought of simply making a gate and getting away. Or going back through the gate into the library.

But then he remembered that Eric was useful. And then Danny remembered that he didn't like thinking of drowthers the way the Family did—dividing them into the two categories "useful" and "expendable." No, if Danny was going to get the hang of being a human being and not a sort of pathetic halfway wannabe god, he was going to have to think of Eric as something else. Perhaps "friend."

"What did you see?" Danny asked.

"It's what I didn't see," said Eric.

"And what was that?"

"You." Eric grinned. "Neat trick, turning invisible like that."

"Is that what I did?" asked Danny.

"That's what I saw," said Eric. "Come on, you can tell me. The whole way here to DC from Lexington, you were holding out on me, you owe me now."

This irritated Danny. "I think we're about even. You got more from begging *with* me than you usually do without me. And you kept all the money."

"I shared the food," said Eric.

"I earned my share of the food. Nobody owes anybody anything."

"Yeah, I think you do," said Eric. "For instance, what if I tell the cops about you?"

"Are we five years old?" asked Danny. "'Do what I say or I'll tell Mom'?"

"I think there are some government agencies that would love to study you."

So maybe Eric wasn't a friend after all. Then again, his life had been all about hustling, turning anything he could to his advantage. All Danny had to do was let him see how little hold he had over Danny, and that old cooperative big-brother attitude was bound to come back.

"See, that's not going to happen," said Danny.

"You think it's not?"

"First," said Danny, "who's gonna believe you when you tell them all about this kid you met in Lexington? What are you going to tell them about me?"

"You can turn invisible."

"Yeah, they always listen to teenage beggars who tell them stories about invisible kids. They got a whole department full of agents who investigate claims like that."

"All right," said Eric, dismissing the whole idea with a wave.

"Plus, if you gave it about three seconds' thought, you'd see a huge hole in the idea of turning me over to the government."

"What?"

"Three seconds," said Danny.

"Don't screw with me, kid."

Danny counted to three on his fingers.

"All right," said Eric again. "All you'd do is turn invisible and they'd never be able to get you. But what if they surprised you and got handcuffs on you? What good does it do you to be invisible if you've got handcuffs on?"

"And that's the third thing," said Danny. "I have never, not for one second, been invisible."

"I know what I saw."

"You did not see an invisible kid," said Danny.

Eric was about to say something scornful when Danny held up three fingers and began the count again.

"What were you if you weren't invisible?" demanded Eric.

"Not what, but *where*," said Danny.

"Oh," said Eric. "You weren't there-but-invisible, you were visible-but-not-there."

"And as for telling you," said Danny, "would you have believed me? And what if somebody overheard me as I told you? We were always around people."

"So if you can just go away, why didn't you split when I surprised you here?"

"I thought about it," said Danny. "But I decided that even though you ditched *me* just because I wanted to see all the tourist stuff on the Mall, I wasn't the kind of guy who ditches a friend."

Eric rolled his eyes at first, then closed them, nodded, and stuck out his hand. "Okay, man. Friends."

"Well, I know *I'm* a good friend. But you just got through threatening to turn me over to the cops or the government. How do I know I can count on *you*?"

"I didn't have to bring you with me in the first place,"

said Eric. "And I also didn't have to follow you up and down the Mall, Lincoln to Washington to the Capitol."

"Why didn't you just come walk with me instead of stalking me?" asked Danny.

"Can we just drop it?" said Eric. "I was worried about you."

"Yeah, that's what I thought."

"What did you think?"

"That you *care* about me."

"Okay, now's when I puke," said Eric.

"So you aren't going to try to boss me around?" asked Danny.

"Of course I am," said Eric. "It's just not going to work."

"As long as you know that."

"We decide stuff together," said Eric.

"Works for me," said Danny.

"But first you have to tell me how this thing works, this thing you do."

"And there we are, back to 'have to.' "

"How can I figure out how to turn it to our advantage if I don't know how it works?"

"*Our* advantage?" asked Danny.

"Friends and partners, aren't we?" said Eric. "You didn't mind using the stuff *I* knew how to do. Can you teach me to do that? Disappear and reappear somewhere else?"

"In a word—no."

"Can't or won't?" asked Eric.

"I'm still trying to figure it out myself," said Danny.

"So when you disappeared from here, and then came back, where did you go?"

"Into the library," said Danny.

"What, you were having a library emergency? Jonesing for a book?"

"Needed the restroom," said Danny.

"So that's really where you went?" asked Eric.

"Really."

Eric studied his face. Seemed satisfied. "Well, there you are. You can go through walls."

"Of course I can," said Danny.

"Why 'of course'?" said Eric. "Why would I know you could go through walls?"

"Okay, *not* of course. But yes, I can go inside buildings and leave buildings the same way. Without doors."

"Do you make holes in the walls?"

"No," said Danny. "It's a *gate.*"

"Please stop talking like you think this is stuff any idiot would know," said Eric.

"Sorry," said Danny.

"How far does it work? How far can you go?"

"I don't know," said Danny. "Most I've ever done is a couple of miles, maybe."

"But you can go anywhere?"

"Anywhere I wanted to, so far," said Danny.

"Can it be a place you've never been before?"

Danny thought about it. When he first made gates through the perimeter of the Family compound, he hadn't known where he was going on the outside. And when he gated his way into the space inside the wall of the Family's library in the old house, he certainly didn't know what it was like in *there.*

"Yes, it can," said Danny. "But I'm not sure how I do it. I keep worrying that I'm going to gate myself into a tree or a stone wall or something and blow up half the city."

"But you haven't so far," said Eric.

"I'm still in existence," said Danny, "so no, I haven't so far."

"Can you take me with you?" asked Eric.

Danny shrugged. "I don't know." He held out his hand. "Want to try?"

Eric hesitated. "What happens to me if it turns out you *can't* take me with you?"

"I don't know," said Danny.

"Or what if you can only move me away from *here*, but you can't deposit me *there*? Do little bits of me get scattered all along the way?"

"You really do have a weird imagination," said Danny.

"Got to try to think of the consequences," said Eric. "There's always consequences."

"I don't know how any of this works, Eric."

"I think I'll pass on testing whether you can take me with you or not."

"For what it's worth, I take my *clothes* with me every time," said Danny. "And all the stuff in my pockets. And I've pushed stuff through gates without going all the way through myself."

"That's 'clothes' and 'stuff.' You tried it with anything *alive*? And was it still alive when you got there?"

"Never tried it."

Eric grinned. "See? I don't want to be the first experiment, in case I end up having my body half-swapped with a fly and I'm trapped in a spider web waving my arms and saying, 'Help me! Help me!'" He said this last in a high soft voice.

"What are you talking about?" asked Danny.

"You never saw the old black-and-white *The Fly*? Not the Jeff Goldblum but the good one?"

"Movies? You're talking about movies?"

"Why not?" asked Eric. "This *is* a movie. I mean, I'm just minding my business and along comes a kid and I take him under my wing, and then it turns out he can disappear in one place and appear in another. I'm in a *Twilight Zone* episode. Teleporting. *Stargate*!" Whatever "Stargate" was, Eric apparently thought it was brilliant. "Why didn't I think of that already? Of course, *you* don't need some pyramid or a big machine or anything so it's not the same."

"I don't see a lot of movies," said Danny.

Eric shrugged. "Let's see what we know. You can go through walls. And you can push stuff through gates without actually going through yourself, right? So you're, like, the perfect burglar."

"Burglar?"

"You know, guy breaks into a house, steals stuff without waking up the people."

"I know what a burglar is."

"How would I know you know that? If you don't know *The Fly* or *Stargate*, I figure you might not know how to put your pants on frontward."

He said it with a grin. Danny grinned back. "I'm not a burglar."

"Really?" asked Eric. "Where'd you get those clothes?"

"Wal-Mart," said Danny dryly.

"Credit, debit, or cash?"

"Shopping cart plus gate," said Danny.

"So you're a burglar."

"Shoplifter."

"So you'll steal stuff from Wal-Mart and that's okay, but stealing stuff from rich people's houses . . ."

"You gotta draw the line somewhere," said Danny.

"Stealing from Wal-Mart just causes them to raise prices a tiny bit to amortize the cost."

"'Amortize'?" Eric said it slowly and mockingly, as if there was something wrong with knowing the right word.

"Breaking into somebody's house is different, Eric, it's stuff they own personally."

"So . . . what if I promise that we'll only steal stuff from the houses of people so rich they'll barely notice that it's gone?"

"What kinds of things do we steal?"

"Whatever the fence wants to buy," said Eric.

"In your life of crime in Washington, you know who deals in stolen goods?"

"No, but I know people who know people who probably know people who deal in stolen goods."

"And we trust these friends of friends of friends? *That* experiment worries me a lot more than trying to take you through a gate."

"Why should *you* worry?" asked Eric. "No matter what happens, *you're* okay. I'm the one taking all the risks."

"So does that mean you think you deserve more than fifty percent of what we make?"

"Yes," said Eric. "I deserve twice as much as you."

"Even though I'm the one who goes into the house and risks getting caught."

"But it's not a risk for you. You *can't* get caught."

"I can get recognized. Posters can go up with my face on them."

"So what?"

"That happens, I can't go into stores, I can't walk the streets."

"Nobody pays attention to that kind of thing. Come on, there are neighborhoods in DC where *everybody's* on a poster somewhere."

Danny still hated the idea of burglarizing people's houses. At the same time, it sounded better than begging. Indoor work, more money for the time expended, and as long as they only went into the houses of rich people, who would they be hurting?

Danny heard voices and looked up to see several uniformed men with guns. They were skirting the library and looking down at Danny and Eric.

"Let's get out of here," said Danny.

"Too late, they've seen us," said Eric. "If we split, they'll be sure they've got the guys they're looking for."

"But I *am* the guy they're looking for," said Danny.

"Oh, so you were getting a little burglary practice in the library, were you?"

"I put it back."

"So your backpack's got nothing bad in it?" asked Eric.

"I'm clean," said Danny.

"Then talk your way out of it and you won't be on a wanted poster."

"I've never talked to a cop," said Danny. "I'll screw it up."

"These aren't cops, they're building security guys, and let's get real about this, kid, you can talk a one-armed woman into knitting you a sweater."

Since Eric had just talked Danny into becoming a burglar, it seemed to Danny that it was Eric who could talk anybody into anything. But the security guards were yelling at them to stay *right there*, so there wasn't a chance to argue the point.

"Open that backpack," shouted the guard as he approached. "And both of you turn out your pockets."

"Yes sir, right away sir," said Eric.

Danny unzipped all the openings on his backpack. As he did, it occurred to him that this was just like when the security guy at Wal-Mart accosted him. There weren't any passersby to serve as witnesses, but the same idea should play—go way farther than what they asked for, and throw them completely off balance.

So Danny pulled his shirt off over his head, stepped on the heels of his shoes to get out of them, then started pulling off his pants.

"I said to turn out your pockets!" yelled the guard who was doing the yelling. "What are you doing!"

The other one was smirking.

"I'm letting you examine my clothes for yourself," said Danny, "so I don't have you putting your hands all over me."

"I don't mind," said Eric. "You can put your hands all over *me*."

Danny handed his pants and shirt to the one who yelled, and his shoes and socks to the other one. They both stood there holding them, looking like idiots because they had no plan for what to do with them. Then, on impulse, Danny turned his back to them, bent over, pulled down his tighty-whiteys, and spread his butt cheeks. Man it was cold.

"Stand straight and pull your shorts up!" The yelling guard was practically screaming now.

Danny complied.

"I think he was mooning you, Barry," said the guard holding the shoes.

"I think he was mooning both of you," said Eric helpfully.

Danny was facing them now, his briefs pulled up. "I don't know what you're looking for, but I wanted to make sure you knew I didn't have it."

"I ought to run you in for indecent exposure!" Barry shouted.

"I think he was cooperating with an officer of the law," said Eric. "I think our government-appointed attorney can make a case for your having overstepped your bounds in questioning a child."

Barry looked at Eric with murder in his eyes.

"What are you looking for?" asked Danny.

"A book," said the one who wasn't Barry.

"I can't fit a book up my rectum," said Danny. "I don't think anybody can."

"Nobody said you could!" yelled Barry.

"Then why are you holding all my clothes?" asked Danny.

Barry threw Danny's clothes onto the ground and stalked away.

The other guy handed Danny his shoes and socks. "You're one funny smartmouth kid," he said with a smile. "If you were my son, I'd be laughing the whole time I beat the crap out of you." Then he turned and jogged to catch up with Barry.

"That was extreme," said Eric. "I couldn't believe you mooned them from three feet away."

"It seemed like the right thing to do at the time." Danny didn't explain about what he'd done at Wal-Mart. Pranks weren't as funny if people knew you'd done something too similar before.

"Come on, let's get out of here," said Eric. "That

one guy, Barry, he might be thinking about things he *can* fit up your butt."

"Excuse me while I put my clothes back on," said Danny.

"Hurry up," said Eric. "You're embarrassing me. Skinny little hairless legs covered with goosebumps, you're like a Chihuahua. Or a Mexican hairless or whatever they call it. Ugliest dog I've ever seen, like looking at your grandfather naked."

Danny thought of Gyish or Zog starkers and he had to smile. Of course, if Zog brought down a bunch of hawks on your head, especially if one of them was his clant, there wouldn't be much to grin about.

It took the rest of the day to get a meeting with an Arab-looking guy in the back of a little corner grocery. The guy couldn't take his eyes off Danny. "Come on," the fence said. "He's a kid."

"He just looks like a kid," said Eric. "He's really twenty-five, but he's got, like, a glandular condition."

"I'm fourteen," Danny lied. His real age was just too young, and nobody would believe fifteen until he got taller. "I didn't know you had an age limit on who you'll buy stuff from."

"Tell me what you've got," said the fence.

"We've got whatever you want," said Eric. "Just tell us what you want that isn't too big for us to carry down the street."

"You mean you haven't even done it yet?"

"Done what?" asked Eric. "We find stuff, that's all. We're lucky. People drop things, we find them. So you can imagine it's not going to be any high-def big-screen television, you know? Too heavy for my cousin here to carry."

The fence made a dismissive gesture. "Put it on eBay. Put it on Craig's List."

"Right," said Eric. "Like we've got a website or email or a computer or even a camera to take a picture."

"*Find* one," said the fence. "Now get the hell out of my store."

"Just one question," said Eric. "Jewelry? Nice art pieces? Laptops and iPads? What?"

"And don't come back," said the guy.

"Laptops it is," said Eric.

The man stood up. He wasn't much taller than Eric, but he was wearing a wife-beater and he seemed to be made of rope underneath his skin. "Anything you bring me, I'll smash with a baseball bat. Starting with your head. Why aren't you understanding me?"

"We look forward to doing business with you," said Eric. "Come on, cuz. I think it's time for his next appointment."

Danny gladly followed Eric out of the back room into the grocery store.

"I'm hungry," said Danny, looking over some of the snack foods near the checkout counter.

"Not here," said Eric. "You want to get us killed?"

Out on the street, Danny had to ask. "Is this how you usually do business?"

"Are you kidding?" said Eric. "That went great."

"He threatened to kill you!"

"Us. He was including you in the baseball bat thing."

"Only *I* won't be there for him to hit me. What are we going to do now? Nobody told you about any *other* fence. Your friends aren't really all that tied in with the DC underworld."

"Oh, he's going to buy our stuff," said Eric.

Danny had to laugh. "I get it now. You con *yourself*."

"It's no con," said Eric. "He's afraid we're from the cops, wearing a wire, whatever. So he puts on a big show of throwing us out. But we bring the stuff around tonight, he'll take it."

"No," said Danny. "I'm pretty good at knowing when somebody's sincere, and he really meant the part about us not coming back."

Eric shrugged. "Aw, well, you know. It's easy to turn down stuff you haven't seen. When we have the stuff, he'll change his mind."

"Or he'll change *our* minds. Into puddles on the sidewalk."

"Trust me," said Eric.

"And you're the one who thought it was too risky to go through a gate."

"That's why we're such a great team," said Eric. "We're both completely stupid about different things."

Danny wasn't sure about this "great team" thing. It seemed to him that Eric's team had only one member, and it wasn't Danny. It was the way Eric looked at him with the exact intensity he used when he was talking up a mark. Believe me believe me believe me, his face said. Which by now Danny well knew was a sign that Eric wasn't so much lying as simply in need of something from you. Trust me until I have from you the thing I want.

Well, what Eric wanted from Danny was burglary without the hard bits. Entering without breaking. And Danny could do that.

While Eric was in search of a fence, he wangled two different invitations to crash with friends. One of them had a roommate and they could only stay a night or two.

The other, a guy named Ced who was about two years older than Eric, sounded like he was pimping the place where he lived. "It's this great three-story townhouse in a decent part of town and Stone, the guy who owns it, he just likes the company, as long as you don't back up the toilet or do boinky-boinky on the sofa. You can stay as long as you want, even keep stuff in the fridge. Run the dishwasher now and then. Do an errand if he asks, but he almost never asks. He, like, calls us his 'staff' or his 'entourage' but he's cool."

As far as Danny and Eric were concerned, the operative words were "stay as long as you want." The place was about six blocks east of the Library of Congress and two blocks west of Lincoln Park. Danny had no idea what would make a part of town indecent, but decent was pretty nice, especially for a boy from a Virginia farm. The houses all butted up against each other, with short stairways coming up from the sidewalk. Under the stairs there were usually walkout cellars or a ground floor. Lots of fences and gates, but low ones, mostly, that you could vault over if you felt like it. People walking dogs in the gathering darkness. Or coming home from work. Or heading out for the evening.

"Three blocks from a Metro station," said Eric. "Not bad."

"We're not dressed right for this neighborhood," said Danny.

Eric held up fingers to enumerate why Danny was too dumb to live. "*A*. We're kids. We're dressed like kids. It's a uniform, and we're wearing it. *B*. We don't have to look right in *this* neighborhood. *This* is the neighborhood where we're gonna *live*. We have to be dressed right for the neighborhood where we're going to find expensive stuff just lying around. *That's* the neighborhood where it matters that we don't have any cops stopping us to find out what we're doing there."

"So *are* we dressed right for that neighborhood?" asked Danny.

"Are you already forgetting number *A*?" asked Eric. "We're kids."

Danny muttered, "*A* isn't a number," and Eric gave him a shove toward the street. Danny stumbled on the curb and nearly fell but then Eric was there helping him so he didn't lose his balance after all. And Eric was laughing.

Eric might be completely selfish, but it's not like Danny didn't have cousins just like that. And none of the cousins was ever *playful* with him, not anymore.

"So where is that wonderful neighborhood?" asked Danny.

"I don't know yet," said Eric.

"I thought you knew DC."

"I know the parts where you beg and the parts where you get drugs, to put it plainly. Those parts, there's nothing to steal. Or there's a lot to steal but if you do somebody hunts you down and kills you extra dead."

Danny grinned, thinking it was a joke. "'Extra dead'?"

Eric wasn't laughing when he said, "They cut parts off you before they kill you, so the people who find the body will tell the story and other people will think twice before stealing from them."

So there were people in the world worse than Danny's family. He sort of knew that—he got plenty of news from the internet and history in class. But he didn't think of them as living and working in a place like Washington DC.

They got to the address Ced had given them. It was freshly painted and had a profusion of flowers in pots, window boxes, and in the tiny patch of ground that served for a garden. In the dead of winter, everything was in bloom. The smell of them got into Danny's nose and he stood there reveling in it, wondering for a moment if it was possible their host—Stone?—was a Seedservant or some other kind of plantmage. But that was too improbable—that the first place he found to stay in DC happened to be in the house of a member of some other Family.

Ced had told them to just walk in, but that seemed to bother Eric. He stood outside for a moment and then knocked and rang the bell. They could both hear a bustle of activity inside and then, finally, someone came to the door. It was a woman—no, a girl of about sixteen—wearing a man's oversized white button-up shirt with the sleeves rolled up, and quite possibly nothing else, which Danny found distracting. He couldn't take his eyes off her, yet felt he *had* to look almost anywhere else.

The girl looked them up and down. Then she called over her shoulder, "It's nobody, just somebody crashing with his little brother."

"Can we come in?" asked Eric.

She gave him a look of such compassionate scorn that Danny blushed for him.

"I think that's a yes," said Danny.

"Are girls all born with the ability to rip your balls

off with a look?" murmured Eric. Then he led the way inside.

Ced was walking into the messy living room, looking pissed off. "I told you to just walk in, morons. Anybody rings the bell, we assume it's the law. I was *this* close to flushing my stash."

"I thought we weren't supposed to stop up the toilets," said Eric.

"Oh, you're funny," muttered Ced.

"Are you going to introduce your little friends?" asked the girl.

"They stopped being my friends when they rang the doorbell."

Danny stuck out his hand. "I'm Danny."

"How old are you?" asked the girl. "Twelve?"

"Thirteen," said Danny.

"Ma-CHEWER," she said. "Got any hair on your chest?"

Danny wasn't even sure what she was asking. "I don't think so," he said.

"Or *anywhere*?" she insisted.

"Lighten up," said Eric. "He's a kid."

"Said the old man. Who are you?" she asked.

"I'm Eric. Do you have a name?"

"What's today?" she asked.

"Thursday," answered Ced from the floor, where he was rolling a cigarette. Danny had a pretty good guess what kind of cigarette.

"Then my name is Lana," said the girl.

"And if today had been Wednesday?" asked Eric.

"I would have unzipped your pants instead of talking," she said. "On Wednesdays I'm such a *slut*."

"I'm glad we caught you on Nun Thursday," said Eric.

"That's your best shot?" Lana asked, again with the look of scorn.

"I have snappier comebacks, but I don't just give those away," said Eric.

"Yeah? You have to grind them up and mix them with applesauce before anybody will swallow them?"

"Look," said Eric to Ced. "We don't just need a place to crash, we need some advice. Is Mr. Stone in?"

Lana gave one whoop, which apparently passed for a complete laugh.

"Not *Mister* Stone," said Ced. "Just Stone. It's his first name. Maybe his only name."

"It's a translation," said Lana. "Of the unpronounceable name his parents gave him in their native language."

At the mention of languages, Danny perked up. "What language?" he asked.

"Amazian," she said. "Amazon? No, that's the online bookstore. Umbilical?"

"She doesn't know." Ced handed the joint to her.

"Not now," said Lana.

Ced shrugged and kept the joint, though he didn't light it.

"Why do you want Stone's advice?" asked Lana.

"I figured he's lived in DC for a while, he could steer us to a neighborhood where we're likely to find small expensive things lying around where guys like me and Danny here can find them."

"You don't have to ask Stone," said Lana. "Where are you *from*? Everybody knows you're looking for Georgetown."

"I thought that was a college," said Eric.

"University," said Lana. "It's also a ritzy neighborhood. Or you could go out to Chevy Chase, Maryland.

Basically, go west, and the incomes go up. I assume you expect to find these expensive things lying around *inside* people's houses?"

"I think we'd have better luck there," said Eric.

Danny was appalled that Eric was just telling their business to strangers. How did he know that none of these people would tell the cops?

"Your little friend thinks you shouldn't be talking about your criminal conspiracies," said Lana.

Eric looked at Danny. "He's still not completely into it," he said. "But he can't help it—he's so good at it that he just can't stop. Talent is destiny."

"Good at what, exactly?" asked Lana.

"Getting into locked places," said Eric.

"How does he do it?" she asked.

"I make a wish," said Danny. He knelt on the floor and started looking through magazines on the coffee table. Anything to distract Eric. It didn't work, though.

"It's magic, all right," said Eric. "He doesn't touch the doors or windows. He doesn't leave footprints or fingerprints. He just *appears* inside the house."

Danny hated this. "Eric, come on, stop it."

"Don't get so upset, or she's going to start *believing* you can do magic," said Eric.

"Oh, I believe it," said Lana. "He has the look of magic about him." Suddenly she was off the sofa and kneeling in front of him. She was so close he could feel her breath on his face and he felt like she was a quarter of an inch from pushing her chest against his. He wanted to turn back to the coffee table but if he did, then *he'd* bump into *her*, and that might look like he was making some kind of pass at her.

"Come on, Danny," she said. She put her hands on his shoulders. "Do some magic for me."

"Leave him alone, Lana, he's a kid," warned Ced.

"Jailbait? He's jailbait?" asked Lana. She brought her face very close to Danny's and locked her arms around his waist. Now her breasts were pressed against him and her breath was right in his nose and mouth and her lips were brushing his as she talked. "Jailbait boy, why aren't you kissing me yet?"

Danny pulled away from her, but since he was on his knees it's not like he could have done anything but rock backward. Which was apparently what she was counting on, because she basically rode him down onto the carpet. In a moment she was pinning his shoulders to the floor with her hands, but since his knees were still folded under him, his body was arched, with his pelvis at the apex. The pertinent fact, however, was that she was straddling him, and he was feeling things that he'd never felt before. The only girls he knew were his cousins, whom he'd been raised with. They were like sisters. Less than sisters, since he knew them well and also despised them. Lana was not his sister, and he didn't despise her, he was incredibly fascinated with her and what she was making him feel. Yet with every movement of her body under the white shirt, he was also feeling more frightened. What kind of magic was *this,* that worked on people instead of animals or plants or the elements? Was this the forbidden "man-magic" that was only whispered about?

"Come *on,*" said Eric. "I didn't bring him here to catch whatever disease you're carrying."

She turned the upper half of her body so she could give him some kind of withering glare. Danny couldn't see her face, but with the twisting of her body she let up on his shoulders and he propped himself up on his elbows. Almost at once he wished he hadn't, because seeing how her body pressed on his intensified every-thing he was feeling to the point where he was getting light-headed.

"Like what you see?" asked Lana.

"He doesn't even know what he's seeing," said Eric.

"He doesn't have to *know*," she said. "I'm the only one who has to know." She knelt up higher, reached behind and between her own thighs, snaked her fingers into Danny's waistband on both sides, and started to pull down his pants and underwear.

Danny was so surprised and scared that he cried out and tried to scramble backward on his elbows. But that only helped her pull down on his pants and instead he wriggled the other way, toward her. It kept his pants on.

"Help me get her off him before she rapes him," said Eric to Ced. Eric hooked her under one armpit and had her halfway up before Ced joined in on the other side.

"You boys will just have to wait your turn," she said. But in a moment they had her up and off of Danny.

"Pull your pants up," said Eric with withering scorn.

"I'm trying," said Danny. But in fact she hadn't pulled his pants down very far at all, and it occurred to him that maybe she had never intended to, that maybe what she really wanted was what she was get-ting right now—Ced pushing her roughly out of the room.

"I'm the boy's education," she was saying, with a giggle. "He got a scholarship to my private school!"

Ced had her out of the room. Danny could hear him say, more sadly than angrily, "Sometimes you just got no judgment, Lana."

Danny was relieved when she was gone. And disappointed. But definitely more relieved than disappointed.

"Who *is* she?" asked Eric, as Ced returned to the living room. "A one-woman government welfare program for the horny?"

"She's my wife," Ced replied. He sighed. "But don't feel sorry for me. She was like this before I married her."

"Then why did you bother?" asked Eric.

"Believe it or not, she's a lot calmer now than she used to be."

Then, to Danny's surprise, he heard a woman crying in another room. "Is that . . ."

"Yeah, it's her," said Ced. "Now she's totally ashamed and filled with self-hatred and all, so I get to spend the next hour or two talking her out of jumping into the Potomac or volunteering to be a suicide bomber for Greenpeace or PETA." Ced padded back out of the room.

As soon as he was gone, Eric flopped onto the couch and laughed silently, rolling around as if he were screaming instead of stifling it.

"I don't think it was funny," said Danny.

"That's because you couldn't see your face."

"I don't want to stay here," said Danny. "What if she tries that again while we're sleeping?"

"See?" said Eric. "You're already fantasizing about it."

"No I'm not, I'm—"

"You're about ready to explode," said Eric. "She was just teasing you, don't you get it? Because you're so young and a virgin."

Ced and Lana came back into the room. Lana was

smiling shyly and wearing some kind of athletic shorts now that stuck out below the hem of the shirt. "I'm sorry," she said. Her eyes were red-rimmed from crying, but Danny thought she had stopped awfully quickly, if the tears were all that real.

"Don't worry about it," said Eric. "Danny's from the farm, he just wasn't used to doing it with girls."

Danny had no idea what that meant, but it set Lana and Ced to laughing and Danny was pretty sure they were laughing at him. "What are you talking about?" Danny asked.

"You and the sheep, of course," said Eric. "Come on, you can't tell me you didn't get some quality time with that special ewe."

Danny's face was burning now with shame and rage. "That's not—that's not even *possible*," he said.

"I think that means he's done it a lot," said Eric, still laughing. "But she broke up with him."

Danny was thinking of how the beastmages would react if anybody in the Family did such a thing to one of the animals. "Animals are—they're looked after, they—if one of us did something like that, Grandpa Gyish would have him killed. Great-uncle Zog would do it himself."

They laughed right through what he was saying. But when he was done, they stopped laughing and just stared at him.

"Really?" asked Lana softly. "Your own family would . . . ?"

"And then they'd bury him in the family graveyard on Hammernip Hill," said Danny.

"That's just . . . sick," said Lana.

"It's a crime," said Ced. "It's abuse. Worse than abuse, it's *murder*."

"Calm down," said Eric. "He didn't say they've ever done it, he said they *would* do it if somebody started humping the sheep. Come on, this has all gotten so totally out of hand. I didn't bring him here to be sexually molested. He's so underage that you could find yourself with a sex-crimes rap."

"I wasn't going to *do* it," said Lana.

"You were already *doing* it," Ced corrected her. "You were way past *going-to* or *not-going-to*."

"Can we please just go somewhere else, Eric?" asked Danny. It wasn't because he feared further approaches from Lana. It was because he was now completely ashamed of the way they all regarded him—as a joke instead of a person. And also very worried about how much he had said about the Family. He had even told them Zog's and Gyish's names. Why didn't he just give them a printout of Google Maps directions to the compound while he was at it? All he wanted now was to get away.

"Lighten up," said Eric. "Come on, if you didn't like it on some level, you would have just . . . left, wouldn't you?"

Danny didn't know what was worse—that Eric was once again talking about Danny's gatemagic in front of these two strange people, or that Eric was kind of right. Why *hadn't* he just made a gate and gone through it? Of course, with their bodies in contact, Danny might have taken Lana with him right through the gate. That would have gotten her to stop.

But that was not why he hadn't made a gate and left. It just hadn't crossed his mind. He didn't have it down as a reflex yet. If she'd been stabbing him with a knife or slashing him with a razor, he still would have forgotten about his ability to gate himself away, probably. Was there ever anybody as stupid as Danny?

What had he even *done* since he found out he had this power? Run away from home, which he kind of had no choice about, after the Greek girl as much as caught him red-handed. But everything since then—he'd stolen, he'd begged, and he was going to break into people's houses now and steal their stuff. And he'd also blabbed. And been caught—Eric had seen him going and then seen him come back. It was a miracle the Family hadn't caught up with him already.

"Can I trust you to let him sleep here tonight without having some demon attack him in his bed?" Eric asked Lana.

"I'd worry more about Ced than me," said Lana. "Ced's gay, you know. That's the only reason I married him."

Ced rolled his eyes. "This is how she punishes me for helping you pull her off the kid."

"Come on, Eric," said Danny. "Let's get out of here and find something to eat." Not that Danny was hungry—he just hoped he could get Eric alone somewhere and then refuse to come back to this place, ever.

"Stone keeps the fridge completely stocked," said Lana. "Frozen pies and dinners. Ice cream. Juice—but nothing with preservatives or MSG or high-fructose corn syrup. Also lots of fruits and vegetables. Cucumbers are my favorites."

"Lana," Ced warned her.

"Well, they *are*. I like to eat them whole. Bite down on them and hear the crunch." She turned to Danny. "Did you know that vegetables scream when you eat them raw? It's a little-known fact, because it's so hard to hear, but scientists have picked up the screaming on very sensitive instruments and it's true. But I don't care. I think their sappy little bodies deserve to suffer."

"Is she off her meds?" asked Eric.

"She doesn't take meds," said Ced.

"Obviously," said Eric. "But is she *supposed* to?"

"She's just trying to be colorful and free-spirited. Somewhere between Madonna and Mae West and Britney Spears."

Danny had read the names "Madonna" and "Britney Spears" on the internet and knew they were singers. Mae West was a name that meant nothing to him.

"I'm above and beyond any of those bitches," said Lana as she flipped off her husband—really, her *husband*?—and sashayed out of the room again. As she walked away, the athletic shorts, which were too big for her, slid down her legs. She stepped out of them and kicked them back into the room as she left. This time there was no crying from the kitchen; they heard her storm on up the stairs.

"See what I have to live with?" asked Ced.

"Actually, except for the child-molesting, what I saw looked pretty tolerable," said Eric.

"I'm not gay, you know," Ced assured them.

"Until this moment I didn't think you were," said Eric. "But the fact that you felt a need to say it—"

"Go to the kitchen and get something to eat," Ced told them. "By the time you get back I'll have her calmed down and you'll see that she's actually a sweet and funny girl. She just has trust issues with men. Her mother had a lot of boyfriends and if they paid extra, she threw in Lana as a bonus."

"Oh," said Eric.

Danny, for his part, wasn't quite sure what Ced meant. Or rather, he was, but he couldn't believe such a thing could be true. Then again, if someone had told him about a girl acting the way Lana had just acted, Danny wouldn't have believed it, either. His girl cousins were starting to seem normal now. When they knocked him to the floor it was always to pummel him or rub something in his face. It had never made him feel the way Lana had.

"Why would having 'trust issues' make her . . . like that?" asked Danny.

"Well, it gives her control, see?" said Ced. "She had you completely under her power, didn't she?"

"She pushed me down onto the floor," said Danny. "And she took me by surprise."

"Took you by surprise?" asked Eric. "Or by something else?"

Eric and Ced were both laughing silently, presumably to keep Lana from hearing them.

"Is there somewhere I can go in this house to get away from you both?" asked Danny.

"Why not just disappear?" asked Ced, and then he and Eric laughed all the harder. Danny knew that Ced was laughing because he thought it was a joke, and that Eric was laughing because Ced thought it was a joke, and it wasn't, which was an even better joke. Danny didn't feel like laughing at all. In fact, he felt like disappearing and never seeing Eric again. Only then he would be back to begging and trying to find someplace to sleep in a strange city after dark.

"I'm tired," said Danny. "We're not going to do anything tonight anyway, and I want to sleep. Without jerks like you laughing at me."

Which triggered another burst of barely contained laughter.

Danny walked out of the room and went up the stairs. He tried all the unlocked doors on every floor, hoping to find a bedroom that looked completely tidy and unslept-in, but there was no such room. Finally, in the attic, he ducked into a small storage room or large closet lined with boxes and racks of clothes. He took some of the clothes off the wheeled storage racks and spread them on the floor to make a bed, with a few more to cover him. Then he turned off the light, closed the door, and felt his way to the makeshift bed in the dark.

It took him a while to go to sleep, because he kept thinking of Lana, and then how Eric and Ced laughed at him, and then about Lana again, and then about home, which he now missed so badly that it would almost be worth getting killed just to go back. Finally, half-crying from homesickness and half-wishing Lana had stuck with molesting him just a little longer, he fell asleep.

He woke up in total darkness but it could have been morning for all he knew. There were no windows in the attic closet, so no kind of light from the street made it inside. He needed to pee. He had gone to bed without stopping in any of the bathrooms he had passed on the way up three flights of stairs. Now he was going to have to pay for that by creeping through a dark house.

Well, no, he didn't *have* to do that. He had seen the bathrooms, he could just make a gate to one of them and . . . no, what if somebody was *in* one and suddenly there was this thirteen-year-old boy? Then he remembered that the bathroom at the landing between the

second and third stories had been kind of badly retro-
fitted into the landing and there was an alcove right
near the door.

He had no more than thought of it before he had
made the gate and gone through it. There was light
here, though not much. The bathroom door was open.
There was not a sound nearby, though there was
some laughter and talking two floors down. Danny
padded into the bathroom, closed the door, turned on
the light, and did his business. He thought of using
one of the toothbrushes—he had a nasty taste in his
mouth—but settled for cupping water in his hand and
swishing it around in his mouth. He flushed, washed
his hands, dried them, and then put his hand on the
door to leave. Only now he could hear that people
were coming up the stairs. Maybe they were still far
enough down the stairs that he could get to the gate
and be gone before they got to this floor. And maybe
not.

He unlocked the door and turned off the light, but
left the door closed while he made a new gate and
stepped through it.

He was in the attic room, right by his makeshift
bed, which he could see was just as he had left it.
He lay down and snuggled into it and rearranged the
clothes on top of it.

He was almost asleep when he realized: When he
left the attic closet, he hadn't been able to see anything. Now he could see.

Had his eyes gotten used to the darkness? No, that
was stupid—when he first woke up, his eyes were totally used to the dark, but when he came back he was
coming straight from a bathroom where a bright light
had been on until a moment before he made the gate.

Danny opened his eyes. The door between the closet and the open part of the attic was open. It had been closed when he left. Who could have been up here?

He made a guess. "Mr. Stone?" he said, very softly.

"Don't worry," said an even softer whispery voice. "Your secret is safer with me than it is with that idiot who brought you here."

Danny could see the shape of a man get out of a chair not far from the door.

"Sleep well," said the man when he was silhouetted in the doorway. Then the door closed behind him.

On the one hand, it was cool that Stone could see Danny materialize in the attic closet and not even freak out.

On the other hand, did that mean that he knew what he was seeing? That he was from one of the Families? Or maybe one of Thor's observers? And what did he mean that Danny's secret was *safer* than it was with Eric? Safer didn't necessarily mean *safe*.

I really am the stupidest person alive, thought Danny. So stupid that I probably won't remain alive much longer.

So stupid that when I just realized that I'd probably get killed, my only thought was to wish Lana would come up here and hump my brains out before I die. I'm thirteen and I'm already completely evil and have no judgment. It will be Darwinian justice if I die without ever having a chance to reproduce. An improvement of the gene pool by removing my genes from it.

Wouldn't that be ironic if I ran away from the Family because they were going to put me in Hammernip Hill, only to get myself killed here, saving them the trouble? Because that's what's going to happen.

I'm going to burgle somebody's house and they're going to blast me with a shotgun. I don't think I'm quick enough to make a gate and get through it between the squeezing of the shotgun trigger and the arrival of the buckshot at my body.

His mind was in such a whirl that he was sure he'd never get back to sleep. And then it was morning, and he could smell coffee all the way up to the top of the house, and the door to his closet was open, letting in the light, and he actually felt kind of good for having slept so long, and also felt nowhere near as stupid as he had felt last night.

Which just proved he was so dumb that he couldn't even remember the lessons he had learned from his previous mistakes.

Eric was sitting bent over at the kitchen table, his head resting on his folded arms, an empty coffee cup beside him. Somebody had put some cut flowers down the neck of his shirt, so he was basically functioning as a vase. Danny smiled to see it.

"I'm glad you're feeling a bit cheerier today."

A man of about fifty, slender and average in height, but with a rather distinctive salt-and-pepper beard, was standing near the fridge, drinking a tall glass of some hideous-looking dark-green concoction. Just as in the attic closet the night before, Danny hadn't been aware of him till he spoke.

"Are you Mr. Stone?"

"Stone is my first name."

"What's your last name?"

"Stone is the only name I need in this house," said Stone. "I see you like what Lana did with the table flowers. Are you in love with her?"

Danny shuddered. "I hope not. I don't think so. She's

not in love with me." And then, because he couldn't help looking pathetic, he added, "Is she?"

"She is definitely not in love with you or anyone, though she has a bit of a crush on her therapist. Danny? That's your name?"

"Yes," said Danny. It was a little late to try and keep himself incognito in *this* house—he cringed to remember sticking out his hand and introducing himself to Lana the evening before.

"Well, Danny, I urge you to be very careful with Eric. He strikes me as being not quite bright enough to know that one doesn't kill the goose that lays the golden eggs."

Eric didn't move. Apparently he really was asleep.

"I haven't laid any eggs yet," said Danny, "but thanks for the advice. That was advice, wasn't it?"

"More of a heads-up. Advice would have been, 'Ditch that loser Fagin, Oliver Twist, and get your rich grandfather to adopt you.'"

"I knew all my grandfathers and grandmothers," said Danny. "I left home because I don't want any of my Family to be my family anymore. Least of all my parents."

"I'm sure you have your reasons, and they're none of my business."

Danny took the hint. He had been on the verge of blabbing even more stuff about how the Family worked.

"Be careful when you go searching for lost objects in people's houses. Some of them get prickly about finding burglars there, and they can afford the very best weapons, whether legal or illegal. Since they hardly ever get to kill people in the normal course of their day, they will naturally have an extra impulsion to fire at you, just to satisfy their curiosity about how it would feel to fire the weapon in anger, so to speak."

"Warning taken," said Danny.

"Well, then, I'm off to work," said Stone. "Remember not to bring anything you take from other people's houses here to my home. Not even for a few minutes while you use the john. If you do, I'll turn you in to the cops myself."

"Got it," said Danny.

"Then by all means, chow down on your breakfast. Or lunch, if that suits you better at this hideous hour of the morning." And with that, Stone was out of the room.

8

Safe Room

⚓

Danny and Eric rode the Metro to Foggy Bottom and then walked to Georgetown. It made no sense that the Metro had no stop in the Georgetown area—how did the servants of all these rich people get to work?

"You think it's an accident there's no stop here?" said Eric. "The rich people made sure there was no cheap, quick way for the slum kids to get here and cause trouble. Why should they care how far their own servants have to walk? They're getting paid for it, right?"

Danny heard the resentment in Eric's voice and he knew he should probably feel the same way toward rich people. But what did he know about rich? The only world he had known before was the North Family compound and the woods and fields and hills. He had watched drowthers during his secret expeditions away from the compound, but there weren't any *real* rich people around Lexington and Buena Vista. Not like the mansions of Georgetown.

"Stop gawking," said Eric.

"Kids gawk," said Danny. "I'm acting like a kid."

"Haven't you ever seen big houses before?"

"Let's see, there was VMI and SVU and some of the buildings at Washington and Lee. I mean, how many classes could you hold in one of these houses? You could put a Wal-Mart in that one."

"No, actually, you couldn't," said Eric.

"Be fun to try," said Danny.

"Why are you so cheerful? Try taking this seriously."

"What's to be serious about right *now*? It's daylight, we're just picking the houses we want to steal from."

"We're not stealing, we're finding stuff lying around."

"In their houses," said Danny. "Come on, I'm new here, let me be a tourist."

A patrol car came along the street and Danny saw how Eric stiffened up.

"I guess we didn't camouflage ourselves well enough," said Eric.

"Maybe he's not going to stop," said Danny.

The cop car stopped. A couple of cops got out.

"Hi," said Danny, when they were still a long way off.

"Try to keep your clothes on this time," said Eric softly.

"You guys know what's with all the flags on this house?" asked Danny.

The cop glanced at the house. "It's the Danish embassy."

"Cool," said Danny.

"We've had a couple of calls—you've been going

up and down the streets, like you were casing the area."

"Casing?" asked Danny.

"He means looking for which ones to rob," said Eric. "Geez louise, what's the crime? Being teenagers without a car?"

"Not a crime yet," said the cop. "Just a misdemeanor."

Danny laughed.

The cop glanced at him and grinned. "Most people are too nervous to laugh at cop jokes."

"So are we getting a warning or are you taking us in?" asked Eric.

"None of the above. I just want to know your business on a day as cold as this."

"He walks me home from my singing lessons," said Danny. "Only today I said, I've never seen the embassies."

"Where do you live?" asked the cop.

Again Danny answered. "A couple of blocks off Wisconsin just past Nebraska."

"And where was your, um, singing lesson?"

"East of the Capitol. Near Lincoln Park."

"And this is supposed to be on the way?"

Eric finally joined in. "He wanted to see Embassy Row. So we got off at Foggy Bottom. His parents have this thing about not wanting to raise a limo kid. So they pay me to get him to and from the lessons so he doesn't get beaten up or kidnapped."

"You're his bodyguard?" asked the cop skeptically.

"I couldn't hold off, like, Al Qaeda, but we don't have any trouble with bullies or pushy beggars."

The other cop finally spoke. "You know what I want?" he asked. "I want to hear the little one sing."

"I'm thirteen," said Danny. "You make me sound like I'm a toddler."

"Sing," said the cop again.

"You got to understand my voice hasn't settled down after changing."

"Doesn't sound changed to me," said the second cop.

"I was a real boy soprano before. I could sing along with 'Un Bel Di' in the original key. So now I'm practically a baritone compared, you know?"

"Still don't hear any singing," said the cop.

So Danny opened his mouth and sang. It was one of the arias that he'd memorized when Baba and Mama used to play a lot of classical music in the house. Not that they ever stopped listening to opera, they just weren't home that much these days. And since Danny was so good with languages, he had no trouble singing along in Italian or German or French, with dead-on pitch. As a little kid he had been killer cute, which was probably one more reason the cousins his own age kind of despised him. But that's why he used the singing-lessons excuse—what *other* lessons could he be taking, without an instrument? Harp or something, maybe. Should have thought of harp.

He gave them "Fin ch'han dal vino" from *Don Giovanni*, and if there were bits he didn't remember, it's not like these cops would be experts, so he sang right through the rough patches. He sang as if he intended to go on forever.

He hadn't sung it in years, and it surprised him how his own, deeper voice sounded. Not very good tone quality, but his pitch was still true.

"You're not very good, kid," said the second cop.

"Hence, the lessons," said Danny. "I was a great boy soprano but you sing a pure tone, like a fife. Now I'm trying to get the vibrato. It's not like I have to sing at the Kennedy Center tomorrow morning."

"Good luck, kid," said the first cop. "Just don't stand in front of any one embassy for too long, and you'll be okay."

"They're not going to start shooting at us or anything, are they?"

"The trigger-happy ones have our own soldiers stationed around them," said the first cop. "Get home safe."

The second cop said, "Don Giovanni has never sounded worse." So there were cops who knew their opera.

"I've never heard him sing it," said Danny.

"Don Giovanni's the name of the . . ."

Danny was grinning at him. "Vocal student humor," said Danny. "Like cop humor, not everybody gets it."

The cops got back in their car and Danny and Eric walked on.

"Was that pure bullshit or did you ever take lessons?" asked Eric.

"Did I *sound* like I've had lessons?" asked Danny.

"You sure as shit sounded like you were singing opera, even if your voice is kind of squawky."

"You pick things up, living with my family."

"Strange family."

"Didn't I mention they weren't normal?" asked Danny. "Okay then, they're not normal."

"I think we'd better not hit any of the embassies," said Eric.

"I'm glad we see eye to eye on that," said Danny. "But what I'm wondering is why we're walking through Embassy Row."

"I didn't know we were," said Eric. "I mean, I've heard of Embassy Row, I just never came here before. Come on, it doesn't go on forever, we'll hit some civilian houses pretty soon."

"At least that explains why they're all so big," said Danny.

Half an hour later they were on 44th Street between Garfield and Hawthorne, looking at the mother of all houses. The mansions across the street would have looked big anywhere else, but compared to this monstrosity they were like dollhouses.

"I think this is the one," said Danny.

"Their mortgage is probably so big they don't have any money to buy stuff," said Eric. "They probably live on shredded wheat and skim milk. And in the winter they heat the house with calisthenics."

"But I'm dying to see what it looks like inside."

"So make a gate or whatever it is and go look."

"Now?" asked Danny. "In broad daylight? On the street?"

"Now's the time when there's probably nobody home," said Eric. "Except the servants. You might have to push them aside to go through the drawers."

"I got to admit, daytime would be easier."

"I'll wait for you over here in these bushes," said Eric.

"Oh, *that* won't look like you're skulking."

"Then *don't* go in."

"Actually," said Danny, "what if I find stuff right now? Why not just take it?"

"Because what if you're caught with the stuff on you?"

"I'll pass it to you through the gate," said Danny "So it won't be on me."

"But I'm not going to go over and stand by the wall. That *would* get us caught."

Danny laughed. "Come on, Eric. Just because *you've* been talking about how I go through walls doesn't mean I actually go through the walls. I mean, I don't open a door in them or anything. I make a gate in *space*. I'll make the gate right here, and when you see my hand stick out with stuff in it, then take the stuff and put it in your pocket."

"What, your hand's just going to appear in mid-air?"

"I don't know," said Danny. "I've never seen it. I've just done it. Sort of."

"I'll stay right here."

"Good," said Danny. "Because if you don't stay here and take what I hand you, I'm not splitting any of it with you."

"You will or I'll make a gate in your ass," said Eric.

"You try that," said Danny, "and let's see how that goes."

"Go on," said Eric. "I'll be here, you go in and take a look around."

So Danny made a gate from right there in the bushes and found himself in the middle of the ultra-posh living room.

It was like no one lived there. Even the big artificial Christmas tree that dominated the room looked institutional, like in a dentist's office. The room was posing for a picture. There were art pieces on the walls and a couple of sculptures and vases, but everything was too big to lug back to the Foggy Bottom Metro station. Though now that they'd walked this far, Danny was pretty sure the Metro station at Wisconsin and Nebraska was a lot closer. Didn't matter—he wasn't touching this stuff.

He stood there and listened for voices or movement. Or alarms. Eric had warned him about motion detectors. He almost wished he could hear someone talking or singing, because then he'd know where they were and he could either avoid them or get out of the house entirely. Silence, though—it could be somebody studying or working or napping, and then they get up and walk in on him and he screams and they scream and . . .

He made his way up the stairs. No creaking. No alarms. Or at least not loud ones. For all he knew bells were clanging in six different police stations, but if the cops showed up, Danny could always leave.

Danny did a quick check of all the rooms. Nobody there to walk in on him. He became more methodical, opening drawers. Lots of jewelry in two of the bedrooms, but it looked cheap to him. Bright colors or funky designs. Plastic. There were a few strands of gold that looked real enough, but they were so light in weight that Danny figured they wouldn't be worth the trip to the fence's store.

As for laptops and computers, Danny wasn't finding any, not on this floor.

He went to the stairs that led another story up. This was mostly storage, and mostly junk. Old clothes, old furniture, things in boxes that hadn't been opened in years. Nothing that would sell.

There was an old safe, a big one that stood on

the floor, but there was nothing in it. Not that Danny could have gotten the lock open if he tried. He just made a little gate and reached inside and felt around.

But the presence of this old floor safe made him think: Maybe there's a more modern safe somewhere else in the house.

Where?

Danny went back down to the living room and out through the gate.

Eric almost screamed.

"Come on, you were expecting me to come back, weren't you?"

"It's just a surprise," said Eric, recovering himself. "Find anything?"

"Cheap jewelry. No laptops. Maybe there's a nice set of knives in the kitchen."

"Big house, no stuff," said Eric. "I knew it."

"I haven't checked the cellar yet. I only came out here because they have an old floor safe in the attic. Heavy thing—I can't believe they'd carry it up the stairs. But I'm thinking, the old safe is in the attic because they have a *new* safe somewhere in the house. I mean, these are the kind of people who own a safe, which means they think their good stuff needs to be in a safe place."

"Good thinking. Only I don't know how to open safes," said Eric. "Remember how we're supposed to find stuff lying around?"

"But where would they *hide* a safe?" asked Danny.

"In the cellar?" asked Eric.

"Maybe, I'll look."

"Behind a painting?"

Danny nodded. "That makes sense. Where else?"

"In case you forgot, this is my first time as a burglar, too."

Danny didn't believe him. He just thought it was Eric's first time going after really valuable stuff. "Back in a minute," said Danny, and he went through the gate again.

There was nothing behind the paintings in the living room. He went down the stairs into the cellar. It was as big as the house in every direction, and here was where the computers were. Two complete offices, with windows opening out onto the back yard. File cabinets in both, but nothing stashed there except papers and knick-knacks. Danny picked up a laptop from the man's desk—unless the woman was so vain she kept a picture of herself on her desk—and then stuffed it into the bag that was obviously designed to hold it.

Instead of going back up to the living room, Danny made a new gate—a small one, just big enough for the laptop in its bag. He pushed it through, knowing it would be hanging in the air right next to the original fullsize gate. Nothing. Eric didn't take it.

I'm an idiot, Danny thought. He had made this new gate connect to the wrong end of the other gate. He had been holding the laptop case in the living room of the house he was burgling. He made the new gate more carefully, and this time Eric had the thing out of his hand almost at once.

At least he assumed it was Eric who took the bag.

So they had one laptop. And, after he went through the woman's office, an iPad, which he passed to Eric through yet another little gate. But no safe.

Where would they put it?

Danny walked around the cellar one more time,

and this time he noticed that in the storage room under the kitchen, the walls had a lot of bracing in one corner. As if there were something really heavy above them. That's it, thought Danny.

He bounded up the cellar stairs and headed into the kitchen. He saw at once that instead of a safe, the bracing was to hold up a really huge oven. Pair of ovens, actually.

There was a half-eaten sandwich on the table. Was someone here after all?

Danny touched the sandwich. The bread was dried out. So it was from earlier in the day. Or yesterday, maybe.

He walked around the main floor and now he realized that the little half-bathroom for guests wasn't big enough to account for all the distance between the living room and the big room with the TV and the fireplace.

Danny couldn't see any kind of entrance. On the main floor, anyway. But what if it was accessed from upstairs?

Back up the stairs again. He scouted around, looking for what was directly over that inaccessible space on the main floor. It was under the man's closet in the master bedroom. Danny knelt down and pulled up the carpeting. It folded right back and, yes, there was a trap door.

Danny opened it.

A horrible smell rose from the hole. He knew the smell. A dead animal. He also knew how to deal with smells. He breathed through his mouth, with his nasal passages closed at the back of his throat.

A light had come on down inside the space when he opened the trap door—it flickered at first but now it was steady. The entry was halfway between a ladder and a stairway. Danny went down it carefully, and found what he was halfway expecting—four bodies lying tied up on the floor. The man was the one who stank—bullet hole through his forehead, and his body was rotting.

But the other three—one white woman, one black woman, and a white pre-teen girl—were not rotting. They weren't conscious either, however, and Danny guessed that they had been here a pretty long time without water—long enough for the husband to start stinking.

If I bring them water and waken them, they'll see me and wonder how I got in. And my fingerprints are all over the house. I touched all the frames of all the paintings on the main floor. I touched doorknobs.

Then again, my prints aren't in the police records anywhere. And on the good side, whoever did this to them probably disabled any security cameras or burglar alarms.

There was a sturdy-looking floor safe in the corner. The door stood wide open. Nothing inside.

We *would* pick the one house in the neighborhood that had already been hit.

Danny made a new gate that he could fit through, straight from the safe room to where Eric was waiting in the bushes.

"All done?" said Eric. "Let's go."

"Give back the laptop and the iPad," said Danny.

"What? You're not getting soft on me, are you?" asked Eric.

"I found the family. The father's dead. The others are unconscious and probably dying. We're not going to go trying to sell a laptop that came from this house."

"Shit no," said Eric. "What have you got me into?"

"Me? Got *you* into it? You are a piece of work." Danny took the proffered bag. "The iPad?"

"I put it in the bag," said Eric.

Danny went back through the gate into the safe room. He took the iPad and laptop out of the case and wiped them down, then set them near the safe. Then he went back up the ladder and picked up the phone. No dial tone. Dead. The lines must have been cut by the first burglars.

Danny left the house for the last time. "Come on," he said to Eric. "We've got to find a phone."

"Phone? Why a phone?"

"To call the cops and tell them about this so they can maybe save the ones who aren't dead yet."

"None of our business!" said Eric angrily. "We were never here. It's that simple."

"But we *were* here," said Danny, walking north toward Nebraska. There were businesses at Nebraska and Massachusetts. Eric followed him. Grabbed him by the arm. "Stop it, man!"

Danny snatched his arm away and then made a gate to Nebraska and Wisconsin, even farther away but near a Metro station.

There were a couple of churches—St. Ann's Catholic and Wisconsin Avenue Baptist. They'd have phones. And if they were closed, so much the better—no need to ask permission or make explanations.

The Baptist church had some kind of meeting going on, but the doors of the Catholic church were locked. Danny gated his way into it, located the parish offices, and gated inside. Nobody there. He picked up the phone and called 911. He gave them the address of the house he had been burglarizing and told them what they'd find inside the safe room accessed from a trap door in the floor of a closet in the master bedroom. "The man's very dead, but I think the others might be alive. Three of them. I'd send ambulances."

"We're dispatching them right now. Where are *you*, young man?"

"I won't be at the house. I'm not coming anywhere near it, never again."

"Who *are* you? Are your parents around? Can I talk to one of them?"

Do I sound like a *child*? thought Danny. "I'm not from around here," he said aloud. "A tourist."

"Please stay on the line—I have someone here who needs to speak to you."

But Danny figured they were just trying to keep him immobilized while a cop car headed for him. So he wiped the phone on his shirttail, then set it on the desk without hanging it up. He went back through the gate into the main meeting room, then through the other gate to Nebraska and Wisconsin. Nobody seemed to notice him arrive, and judging from the lack of disturbance, nobody had seen him disappear a few minutes ago. But people in cars don't notice pedestrians unless they've got nothing else to watch when they're stopped at a light.

Danny quickly found the gate leading back to where he had left Eric, and went through it.

Eric was about a hundred yards away, walking with his shoulders hunched and his hands in his pockets. They could hear the sirens heading toward the murder house. Danny didn't want to run to catch up with Eric, or some passing cop might think he was "fleeing the scene." Danny had read enough mystery novels to know how to behave. So he gated his way to some bushes just ahead of Eric and stepped out to confront him as he passed.

Eric nearly had a heart attack. "Don't do that!" he said angrily.

"Sorry. I called the cops."

"Yes, I hear the sirens. Thanks for doing it while I was still close to the crime scene, moron!"

"There's restaurants and stuff up on Wisconsin, we can eat."

"With what money?" asked Eric. "I seem to remember your getting *nothing* out of that house except stupid, stupid trouble."

"The money from *my* begging that you've got in *your* pocket," said Danny. "We weren't even going to do the job today, remember? And now we're not going to do that house. So we can afford to spend exactly as much on lunch as we were planning to in the first place."

"First rule of being a burglar—you don't call the cops," said Eric.

"Are you a human being or not?" said Danny. "There were two innocent women and an innocent little girl, probably dying, and they'd just spent a couple of days in the same room where the girl's daddy was dead and rotting."

"Exactly—they'll never recover from the experience, their lives will be shitty, they'll wish they had died, so what exactly did you accomplish?"

"If I hadn't called the cops it would have been the same thing as murdering them myself."

"No, it wouldn't," said Eric. "It would be the same thing as never going into the house and therefore not knowing."

"But I *was* inside the house and I *did* know. What's *wrong* with you?"

"What's wrong with *you*!" demanded Eric. "You're nothing but a liability."

"Okay, fine, I get it," said Danny. "Seeya back at the house." And he gated straight to the attic bedroom in Stone's house. He went down the stairs to the bathroom, peed, washed his hands, and then headed down to the kitchen to find something in the fridge.

As he ate the sandwich he had thrown together, it occurred to him that there was a dead man in a safe room who would never eat another sandwich in his life. And there was a little girl who would have a good many years before she could look the world square in the face. Yet it did not make Danny's sandwich taste any worse, or take away any of his pleasure in it.

Am I no better than Eric, then? Able to tune out the suffering of others as if it mattered not at all?

No. I'm enjoying this sandwich because I already did all that I could. And because I was hungry—*I* was. Nobody else feels my hunger, and nobody else is half as interested in feeding me. This is the body I have, and since evolution developed it so that it registers pleasure when it eats, I have nothing to be ashamed of in taking pleasure while others suffer.

At least that girl knew her father loved her when he died. At least she didn't ever have to find out that both her parents would be perfectly willing to kill her if one particular thing happened to be wrong with her.

Yet with that thought—of his parents, of their willingness to put him in Hammernip Hill, of the Family with their strange hatred for their own kind—he found that the sandwich lost its savor for him.

Well, isn't that interesting. Other people's grief salts my food, but my own grief makes it bland. Tasteless. Nauseating, even.

He set down the sandwich.

"Shit," he said aloud. Even in DC, they could reach out and wreck things for him.

9

Orphans

ﻉ

Danny had made up his mind that he was not going to become a burglar, even before Eric got back to Stone's house. For that matter, he was sick of partnering with Eric on anything.

Yes, Eric had shown him the ropes and helped him stay alive and get to DC. But hadn't Danny figured out shoplifting all on his own? There were a few moments of extravagant drama—or was it comedy?—before he got out of Wal-Mart, but he *got* out, didn't he? With the clothes he wanted. It's not like he owed his life to Eric. More like he owed a few meals and rides to him. A debt that could be satisfied with cash—not one that required Danny to let Eric tell him what to do, day after day and job after job.

They had parted company that first day in DC, back on the Mall. If only Danny had been more careful when he gated into the Library of Congress. If only Eric hadn't followed and watched him. Then he'd be completely free of him.

Of course, then Danny wouldn't have found his way

to Stone's house. Or would he? Stone's door was open, but not to everyone. And Stone hadn't been bothered by seeing Danny gate into the attic room. Or if he was, he hadn't shown it, last night or this morning. Stone knew things, and maybe he could help Danny figure stuff out. That is, unless he was tied in with one of the Families. In that case, Danny would simply gate away and hope that *this* time the lesson about not trusting strangers would stick.

Then Eric got back, and instead of coming into the kitchen to try to boss Danny around—or even apologize—he went straight to the TV and switched on the local news.

"Danny, you here?" Eric called loudly. "Get in here, man, you want to see this!"

If Eric hadn't said "man," Danny would have told him to go rub his butt on a splintery board. But somehow "man" made it seem more like they were equals. In fact, "man" was sort of a cool way of saying "please."

Anyway, Danny came into the living room eating an apple—the sandwich was an hour and a half ago— and there on the screen was a reporter outside the house Danny had gated into.

"Mr. Wheelwright had retired from electronic game design and announced his intention to devote the rest of his career to managing his and his wife's charitable foundation, which is funding the development of prosthetic limbs and other devices that wire directly into the brain.

"Again, Abel Wheelwright is dead, murdered in the course of a home invasion. His wife, Eleanor Wheelwright; their daughter, Hannah; and Mrs. Wheelwright's personal assistant, Dana Redd, are being treated for dehydration and various minor injuries. All are listed in fair condition.

"Police are asking for any information about the child who called 911 to report the situation in the Wheelwright house. Without that phone call, it's likely that Wheelwright's widow and daughter and Ms. Redd would have died.

"According to the police, this child is *not* a suspect but is believed to have been inside the house and may have further information that the police need in order to apprehend the perpetrators of this crime."

As police contact information appeared on the screen, the station played Danny's voice on the 911 call. Eric turned around and grinned.

Ced was in the room, too, and set down his book to look at Danny. "That's you, isn't it?"

Danny shrugged. "Who can tell?"

"*You* can, buddy," said Ced.

"It's him," said Eric. "We were there. My boy there's a hero."

"That's not what you said earlier," said Danny.

"What did I know then?" said Eric. "It was cold. I was tired. You saved three people. That's a good thing."

"Maybe there's a reward," said Ced.

"Maybe I'm not going to let them find me," said Danny.

"Why not?" Ced asked.

"'Yes, Officer, I was in the house looking for peanut butter to make a sandwich, while my friend Eric waited outside to receive any sandwiches I might bring out to him. Then we returned to Mr. Stone's house near Lincoln Park, the place where I was molested by Nearly Naked Lana about thirty seconds after I arrived there.'"

"Why would you bring *her* into it?" Ced protested.

"Why wouldn't I?" said Danny. "If anybody reports that I'm the 911 caller, I'll make sure I bring down the whole house."

"This kid is a real biter," said Eric, somewhere between proud and annoyed. "Whatever might make us a buck, he completely rejects and does the opposite."

"And whatever might get us caught with our pants down, Eric wants to do," said Danny.

"Hey, you're the one who took your *own* pants down," said Eric.

Ced was a little upset by that. "*Nobody* took his pants down. Well, a couple of inches but it was a *prank*."

"Lana was not pranking," said Eric. "And besides, I was talking about earlier yesterday, before we got here. When Danny mooned a couple of security guards who were hassling us."

"You *mooned* a *cop*?" asked Ced admiringly.

"He was three feet away," said Eric. "I mean, he spread his cheeks and *starred* him!"

"I'm glad the women and the girl are doing fine," said Danny. "That's *all* I care about." He went back into the kitchen.

Stone was sitting there. "So you made the news," he said.

Danny nodded and went to the fridge.

"Yeah, I've been doing great things since I got here." Danny felt bitter and knew he sounded that way, too.

"Saved some lives, that's not nothing," said Stone.

"And mooned a cop—I sure wish they had a video of that on YouTube. You can imagine how proud I am."

"So you're a kid."

"The cousins moon each other all the time. Especially when they . . ." He almost said "when they're in clant form," but surely there was a limit to his stupidity, and maybe this was it—to avoid saying "clant" in front of a stranger.

"So it was a reflex," said Stone.

"I'm just one big reflex," said Danny. He thought of his response to Lana. The fact that he still thought about that moment and wished he had kissed her. Touched her. And yet was ashamed of feeling that way.

"You're thinking of Lana," said Stone.

Danny almost jumped, he was so startled. Could Stone read his mind? "Who *are* you?" he asked.

"A man who was once thirteen," said Stone. "Oh, come on, I saw you blush."

"I don't blush."

"I saw your face redden and a weird kind of half-smile come to your lips."

Danny covered his face with his hands. "Why don't I just wear a billboard."

"Come on, Danny," said Stone. "You're very good at concealing when you're lying. You're a natural con man, which isn't actually a surprise. But there aren't many males who can hide it when they're thinking of a woman."

"Why isn't it a surprise that I'm a 'natural con man'?" asked Danny. "That's not a talent I'm proud of, if it's true."

"But it kept you alive and got you to DC."

"Eric got me to DC."

"Eric told you what to do. He didn't make you good at it—that's inborn."

"Yeah, I'm a born criminal."

"You're a born gatemage," said Stone.

Danny froze.

"Relax," said Stone. "You think I'm from one of the Families. That I'll tell somebody and they'll kill you. Or that I'll kill you myself."

"It crossed my mind," said Danny.

"How can I put this nicely? I don't give a flying fart about the Families and their treaties and their fears and their rules. When Loki closed the gates it wasn't just the Families that got shut out."

Danny felt his world reeling. What was Stone *talking* about? How much did he know?

"The kitchen is not the place for this discussion," said Stone. "Judging from what I'm smelling from the living room, several people are going to have the munchies before long." Stone arose from the table. "Grab what you want and come to my room."

Danny took a bottle of drinkable yogurt out of the fridge. He looked for a glass, and then decided he'd simply drink the whole liter himself. He followed Stone up the stairs to the room at the front of the house, the one with the best view and the least climbing.

Stone was sitting in a comfortable chair that looked out onto the street. Danny sat in the slightly less padded one beside him.

"You haven't killed me yet," said Danny.

"If I tried, you'd just gate away," said Stone.

"True," said Danny. "You know about gates, but you're not in any of the Families, is that it?"

"That's it," said Stone.

"So who are you?" asked Danny. "Why does somebody living in a townhouse in DC know about the Families and gates and *me*?"

"Come on, you know the Family history—or the 'myths,' as anthropologists call them. Zeus and Eros and Ares and everybody else and his duck siring babies on mortal women, Aphrodite and Athena and even chaste Diana seducing whoever they wanted. And that's just the Greeks. How many stories about the queen of the teeny-weeny fairies drawing off mortal men to some secret kingdom where they hump like bunnies for a while till she gets tired of him and sends him back? What do you think happened to all the babies they made?"

"You?" asked Danny.

"Not me personally. A half-dozen distant ancestors of mine. All those demigods like Herakles—didn't you ever wonder about him? Wandering the Earth, not able to live on Olympus? Actually, there were about three dozen sons of about a dozen Zeuses who took the name of Herakles, which is why there are legends about him in so many places in Italy and the Balkans. There was a while there when being named Herakles and being able to raise a clant or some other little spark of divinity could get you laid even quicker than money."

"How old are you?"

"Forty," said Stone. "Don't get distracted by your own assumptions. You Families all talk as if you were the only wizards in the world. Pure Westilian bloodlines and all that. But there are a lot more of us—*way* more—who aren't part of any Family except whatever parents and siblings we happen to have. We didn't take part in any of your stupid wars, and mostly we stay out of your way. Thor from your family—you're a North, right? Perfect American accent and all that, though from a gatemage that doesn't really prove anything—your Thor has his network of bribed observers, but he's so sure of his own superiority that it never crosses his mind that most of us are not in awe of him and we'll tell him only what we want him to know."

Danny leaned back in his chair. "And you just talk about this, right in the open?"

"I'm far more discreet than *you've* been. Now Eric knows what you can do, and you can bet it won't be long before Ced and Lana do, and anybody else who follows the smell of Westil to this house."

"Smell of Westil?"

"The flowers I grow. Not native to this planet. I specialize in Westilian flowers—different species all year round. Their pollen calls to those who have the scent of it in their blood."

"You're really a Rootherd?"

"More like a Meadowfriend," said Stone. "It's one of the disadvantages of not being in a Family. I'm not quite sure *what* I am, because I'm mostly self-taught. Just the basic principles—love and serve the sources of your strength. If they prosper under your hand, you prosper from the association, too. But who knows what I might have become if I had been guided and taught? My father was a bit of a Puddlekin, my mother a Muckminder. What could they teach me? For all they ever knew, they were born to be Watersire and Claymistress, only they were as untaught as I was."

"Nobody's taught me anything, either."

"I know," said Stone. "How could they? They're sworn to kill your kind whenever you crop up. Not that they wouldn't cheat if they thought they could get a decisive advantage from training a gatemage. The thing is, it doesn't work. It won't work with you, either, sad to say."

"What are you talking about?"

"Gatemages don't last."

"What does *that* mean?"

Stone paused, and it seemed to Danny as if he was choosing which lie to tell. "You're tricksters. You piss people off."

"But we're great at the fast getaway," said Danny. It felt odd, though, to say "we," as if he knew so many other gatemages, as if he were a member of a vast fraternity.

"Danny, you need training."

"Meadowfriends can train gatemages?" asked Danny.

"There are general kinds of training that work for everybody," said Stone. "But no, I'm not the one to train you. I'm just the one to find you."

"That's what bothers me," said Danny, though he had only just realized it. "Out of all the houses in Washington DC, how did I end up in the one house where my disappearing and reappearing didn't send the owner into a tizzy?"

"I cast my net, and mages fall into it," said Stone.

"Well, I wasn't the one who fell," said Danny. "It was Eric who found this place. A friend of his knew about your no-rent policy."

"A friend of his?" asked Stone.

"An acquaintance."

"Think back," said Stone. "Had Eric ever met Ced before?"

Danny thought back. Ced was just there, talking to them. On the street. But no, come to think of it, the first person he talked to was Danny. And what he said was, "Who the hell are you and what do you want?" Which he had said only because Danny walked right up to him and just stood there, close.

Why did I do that?

"You were serious about that pollen? From Westillian plants?"

"It clings to Ced's clothing, because he lives here. Let me guess. You didn't even know why you went up to him. Like that children's game, where the one who's 'it' is searching for something, and the other kids tell him 'warmer' and 'colder' as he gets closer or farther. When you caught a whiff of that pollen, you felt like you were getting *safer*. On familiar ground in a strange city. And the closer you got to him, the safer you felt."

"And that was the pollen?"

"It's worth keeping these plants alive. Especially since I can't get more," said Stone.

"I honestly thought Eric knew him."

"Ced has a way of talking to people as if he's always known them," said Stone.

"So you found me. Your Westilian plants sucked me here with the illusion that I was safe. Why?"

"There's a group of us. Mages, of a sort. Lost Westilians. We call ourselves 'the Orphans' because we aren't part of a Family, and we don't want to be—but we still want some of the benefits. Training, support, protection. We learn a lot from each other. We do research into the origins of magic. We try to understand why it works and why some people can do it and others can't. Everybody does what he does best. Me, I raise these plants, they thrive for me. And so I recruit. I bring in whoever responds to the pollen, I keep them around to see what kind of people they are, and if they seem to be decent folks then I offer them what I offered you. A teacher."

"But not you."

"I'm the recruiter. And I'm also pretty much out in the open here. The pollen that lured you here will draw any Westilians who are searching for you."

"What about Ced and Lana? How did a couple of drowthers end up with you?"

"Ced is not a drowther," said Stone.

"He's a mage?"

"He's a Westilian, an Orphan like me, and there's no way to find out where his ancestry branched off from one of the great houses. But from what he's told me since he got here, his mother was a pretty talented beastmage—she flew with birds, he said, though I suspect he's repeating what she *called* it. She certainly didn't fly herself, in her body—I assume she rode a heartsblood bird and told her son about it. He grew up knowing that such things were possible—he saw how certain birds came to her, how she served them. She died when he was about ten. He tried to develop his own birdmagic, as he called it. But it turned out, to his bitter disappointment, that he's not a beastmage at all."

"What, then?"

"Wind," said Stone. "He can do things with wind. Make little whirlwinds and dust devils and such. But he can also sustain a breeze. Dry the family's laundry on the line—he used that one when they were broke and couldn't afford a dryer. He's also useful to have when you're sailing."

"And he can raise a storm?"

"Oh, no, not yet anyway."

"Not much of a windmage, then," said Danny.

"You have the Family snobbery," said Stone. "But how many truly great mages do *you* know?"

Danny was taken aback, but when he thought about

it, he realized that the total was pretty easy to calcu-
late: Two. Baba and Mama. Nobody else had their
power and their ingenuity to use it in the modern
world. "Two," he said aloud.

"And the rest of your Family? How many are at
about the level of Ced?"

"Some."

"And what level would the others be at without a
speck of training, except the general things that a
Meadowfriend can teach?"

Danny shrugged. "Okay, I'm sorry," he said. Then
his curiosity got the better of him. "What can Lana
do?"

"Absolutely nothing," said Stone. "I tolerate her
here because Ced has taken her on. As his responsibility. The way I tolerate Eric for your sake."

"But I hate Eric."

"Not true," said Stone. "He just scares you, because he's so absolutely selfish."

"I don't want to do what he says."

"Then don't do it. There are several places around
the world where you could live with people who
would mentor you, and where none of the Families
would ever find you."

To Danny, the idea of going to a safe place was in-
finitely appealing. He had not imagined there was any
such thing as a safe place in the whole world.

Which is why the word "sucker" kept flashing in his
mind.

"I don't think so," said Danny.

"Why not?"

"Because I don't trust you enough to put my survival in your hands. How do I know that I won't be
walking into a trap? Death, or a prison, or straight to

one of the Families so they can use me as a pretext to restart the war with *my* Family?"

Stone sighed. "Your caution is admirable. Where was it when you were joining up with Eric? Here I tell you more than anyone else ever has about you and your power, but you can't bring yourself to trust the guy who tells you the truth, you'd rather trust that petty con man who wants to use you as a burglar."

"I owe him," said Danny.

"You already paid him everything you owed," said Stone. "You're square with him."

"I owe him," Danny repeated.

Stone said nothing, just looked at him.

Danny sat there under his gaze a few moments longer. He wanted to explain to Stone about how Eric had mostly been patient with him, had taught him. Yes, Eric was a bossy jerk. But what was between them wasn't just a debt. It was an obligation of the heart. It could not just disappear because he realized now that he didn't like what Eric wanted him to do. But the feeling wasn't logical. He couldn't defend it. He had nothing to say.

Stone sighed. "You can leave my room now."

"Are you mad at me?" asked Danny.

"I think you're a fool, but I'm also glad that at least you're learning some caution."

"I've got to do one job with Eric so he has some money ahead when I leave."

"Leave?" asked Stone. "Where are you going?"

"Like you said. To my new teacher."

Stone sighed again, but now with relief instead of sorrow. "I'll find out who's in a position to take you," he said.

"And I'll try not to burglarize a house with dead or dying people in it."

"Remember what I told you—none of your swag comes here."

"I made the deal, I'll stick to it."

Stone nodded.

"And thanks," said Danny. "For calling me here. For offering me a teacher."

"It's nice to know you're not alone in the world, isn't it?" asked Stone.

But I *am* alone in the world, thought Danny. No other gatemage. Nobody I've known longer than a few days. The name of Stone's group was well chosen. Orphans.

That's what I am, thought Danny. Nice to have a name for it.

10

Inside Man

ى

There was a greater-than-usual police presence in Georgetown, so Eric ruled it out for their "first" real burglary. "We didn't actually take anything," Eric explained, "so the Wheelwright house doesn't count. That was a rescue, anyway, not a burglary." Eric was talking now as if the whole rescue thing had been his idea.

"Calling *any* burglary our 'first' implies that there'll be a second one," said Danny.

Eric gazed at him with icy calm. "You won't be able to stop."

"Who's going to make me?" said Danny. This was sounding more and more like an ordinary argument with one of the cousins.

"Not me," said Eric. "I know I can't make you do anything."

"Then I'll stop," said Danny, "when I say I'll stop."

"Say what you want to," said Eric, "you're going to do it again because you actually like it."

"You don't know anything about me."

"To be inside a stranger's home, while they're there asleep, knowing you didn't trip any alarms because you didn't open any doors, knowing the motion detectors are off in case somebody in the family gets up to go to the john during the night, so you can go wherever you want, take whatever you want. You're like an angel, you're so powerful."

"So you've done this before," said Danny.

"A couple of times," said Eric. "When I was about your age. Nobody had alarms or motion detectors, not in Buena Vista, not in the kind of neighborhood my family lived in. A lot of people slept with their windows wide open. Yeah, I walked around a little. Took a couple of things. Looked at a couple of girls who slept naked on a hot night. Who wouldn't?"

"Me," said Danny.

"What are you going to be when you grow up, a minister?"

"Not a burglar," said Danny.

"Gay, that's what you'll be, if you won't look at a naked girl in her sleep."

"Keep it up," said Danny, "and I'll decide the Wheelwright house was the last."

"Lighten up, Danny," said Eric. "I'm sorry if you think I'm irritating, but I promise you, I'm the normal one."

"It's depressing, but I believe you," said Danny.

They both pretended they were joking.

Eric led Danny to a neighborhood called Spring Valley, out Mass Ave, almost to the Dalecarlia Reservoir. There was a sidewalk running along one side of Sedgwick Street, and they strolled along like any ordinary teenagers, scouting the houses.

"Three dormer windows. Big house," said Eric.

"Kids," said Danny. "Lots of them—bikes and a tricycle. They won't have any money."

"Or they have so much money they can *afford* kids."

They went on like that around the corner onto Tilden. Suddenly the money kicked up a notch—a house with a pool, another with a three-car garage, then one with a boat parked in the driveway.

"Okay, we're home," said Eric.

"All right," said Danny. "Where do you want to be when I hand you the stuff?"

Eric started looking around for a likely place. "Long way from the bus stop," he said.

"So what?" said Danny. "I wasn't talking about you waiting around here—what's the point? Then we have to carry everything a long way, plenty of time to get picked up by suspicious cops, right? So you pick a place near the store where our reluctant fence has his office, and I'll hand it to you there."

Eric looked at Danny with consternation. "You can do that?"

"It's like punching a hole in the air," said Danny. "I'm in the house, I punch a little hole, I reach through it and hand the stuff to you wherever you are."

Eric shook his head. "Sounds too convenient to be true."

"Yeah, well, it has its inconveniences, too," said Danny. "My question is, how much do we want to get?"

"How much what?"

"How much money?" asked Danny. "How many of these houses should I hit? How many laptops, how many Xboxes, how many iPads? How much jewelry?"

"I don't know," said Eric. "A lot. He's going to discount it all like crazy—lucky if we get ten cents on the dollar."

"Lucky if we get anything at all," said Danny. "I still think he'll just take the stuff and give us nothing."

"He wouldn't stay in business very long if word of that gets around."

"And the word would get around how? Are you all that connected to the criminal underbelly of the nation's capital?"

"You talk like the news," said Eric.

"I just think that no matter how much I steal, you're going to need another fence."

"He's the one we know about," said Eric.

"All right, then." And with that, Danny made a gate directly to a small townhouse garden he had taken note of on their visit to the fence. It was only two doors down from the store, and Eric could make a pile of stuff there, hidden by the bushes from anybody walking along the street.

Standing there on the street, it occurred to him that it was kind of rude to leave Eric to make the long trek back alone, so he popped back through the gate to Tilden Street, where Eric was standing right where Danny had left him.

"What did you do?" asked Eric.

"What I told you I would," said Danny. "There's a gate now from here to there. I wish I could bring you through it. Save us the bus ride back."

"When you disappear like that—what if somebody was watching?"

"What would they say they saw? 'A boy just disappeared for a couple of seconds and then he came right back.' The cops'll believe them right away, and they'll stake out the spot all night waiting for me to come back."

"You don't have to get snotty," said Eric. "I just thought you didn't want to be noticed."

"If you'll notice where we are," said Danny, "nobody can see us except from *that* house, and nobody's there right now."

"Tonight they might be."

"And tonight it'll be dark. See any streetlights?"

Eric shrugged. "Your magic trick, you get to decide."

"What about it?" asked Danny. "You want to come through the gate with me and save the trip home?"

"No," said Eric. He shuddered. "I told you, I'm never doing that."

"Mind if I go home that way?" asked Danny.

"Do what you want," said Eric, sounding irritated.

"No, that's fine, I'll take the bus with you."

"Oh, you sweet boy," said Eric sarcastically. "Would you go to all that trouble for little old me?"

Danny would have kept him company, but not if he was going to be a complete jerk. He stepped back through the gate, then walked to the fence's store to get something to eat and drink. A bottle of orange juice and a Payday bar later, he was back on the street, walking home to Stone's house. He was sorely tempted to make a gate into the fence's office and see what he was doing, but decided against it. What if the guy saw him?

Then again, what if Danny didn't bring his whole body through? If he could push his hand through a small gate, why not his face?

He dodged into the garden where Eric would receive the stolen goods tonight. Then he made a small gate that debouched high up on the wall inside the fence's back office. He pressed his face into it, just enough that his eyes were inside the office and he could see.

The fence was at his desk, doing paperwork. Danny scanned the room. No obvious stolen goods here—everything looked like cartons of stuff for the store to sell. Maybe the fence didn't take deliveries here. Or maybe he just stashed stuff into one the cartons to have it hauled out later.

The door from the store opened and the clerk came in. "Thought you'd want to know—one of those kids came in just now and bought a candy bar and a coke."

Orange juice, you moron, thought Danny. Not a soft drink.

The fence reached behind him and picked up an aluminum baseball bat. "I kind of hope they *do* come back," he said. "I haven't smashed anybody up in a good while."

"So you want me to let them in?"

"Buzz me first so I can be ready."

"Why not just buy what they have to sell?" asked the clerk.

"They're cops," said the fence.

"The little one looks twelve."

Thirteen, said Danny silently. Can't you get anything right?

"They get young-looking ones so I'll do something stupid. Come on, you think those kids have ever done any kind of job? Even if they're not cops, they're gonna get on some camera somewhere, or steal something with a radio transmitter or something."

"Then you better not mess them up too bad, Rico," said the clerk.

Rico. So much for his being an Arab.

"I know my business better than you."

"I like my job. How you gonna pay me, you in jail for assault? Or murder?"

"I won't kill them. Much."

"I'll just make them go away, Rico. I won't send them back to you."

"Do what you want, *Mother*," said Rico.

"Somebody's gotta watch out for you, keep you from doing something stupid."

"You're working as a store clerk, moron. What do you know from stupid?"

The clerk turned to go back out the door. Then he stopped and whirled back around so he could look up at the spot on the wall where Danny had his face pushed through the gate.

Danny backed out of the gate the moment he realized he had been seen. The expression on the clerk's face was memorable—horror, like he'd seen a decapitated baby or something. Though, come to think of it, what he'd seen was probably almost as horrible—a human face with working eyes, hanging on the wall without any head or body attached.

Danny sat down and laughed for a moment. He could imagine the clerk trying to explain to Rico the Fence what he had just seen on his office wall. No wonder so many mages couldn't resist playing pranks on drowthers—sending a misty clant to haunt a house, pretending to be a ghost. Making tiny clants out of leaves and petals, to flitter around a garden like fairies. Any mage who could handle their outself at all could make such apparitions at will.

Of course, Danny had no outself and therefore could make no clants. But he could make a gate and stick his face through, and that was sort of similar. He could get a taste of the fun. Considering how many mages played such pranks, it made no sense to Danny that gatemages had a reputation for being especially tricky and deceptive. Unless gatemages could do more stuff than Danny knew about, regular mages were all capable of more and cooler tricks.

He took a bite of his Payday bar and drank off the rest of the orange juice. Then, because he couldn't resist it, he made another tiny gate and pushed the empty orange juice bottle through it. When the clerk got back to the counter, he'd find it perched right in the middle. Then Danny unwrapped the Payday and pushed the wrapper through, as well. Let him freak out a little. Maybe Rico the Fence would think he'd gone crazy and fire him. It'd be the best thing that ever happened to the clerk, to stop working for a creep like Rico.

Danny walked along the street until he'd finished the Payday and swallowed the last of it. Then he began to jog and then run all the way back to Stone's house. Gates were fine, but using his body at full speed still felt good, his legs loping along like an antelope's—or so it felt to him. Probably more like an ostrich.

If I were a beastmage, he thought as he ran, I'd want to have an ostrich or an emu as my heartbound. Two-legged, loping along on legs like stilts, faster than cars can go on these residential streets.

Of course, there weren't any ostriches or emus close by, except in zoos or on farms. He'd have to live in Africa or Australia for those to be convenient heartbeasts.

Maybe my heartbeast is a thirteen-year-old boy, thought Danny. No shortage of *those* around. Maybe I'm somebody else's heartbound, and he's been riding me my whole life and I never knew it.

But that would be manmagic, which was truly evil.

To take possession of the mind and body of another human being? That would be slavery. Not that anybody would mind if one of the Family did such a thing to drowthers. But if you could turn a drowther into a heartbound, you could do it to a Westilian, and that's what made it an unspeakable crime.

Whatever magery such a Westilian had learned, the manmage could make use of it while possessing his body. So if a manmage had a stable of mages that he possessed and controlled, he'd have all their power. The most dangerous of mageries, manmagic was, to turn a Westilian into a slave. It might as well be cannibalism.

Being a gatemage carried a death penalty in all the Families right now, but it hadn't always been that way. There was nothing inherently evil about gatemagic. What if I had been born a manmage? What if I had taken possession of Gyish or Zog and made them do what I wanted? Danny felt a chill, even though his running had worked him into a sweat. Who'd want to be inside one of those nasty old coots, working the levers? But it would be fun to use their arms to beat Lem and Stem the way they used to beat Danny.

What kind of person am I becoming? thought Danny. I guess that once you do one forbidden kind of magic, the worse ones start looking better. They can only kill me once, after all. They might as well snap my neck for a goose as a duck.

Lana was waiting in the living room when Danny got home, sitting on the back of the couch with her feet on the cushions. She looked over at him only long enough to register who he was, then went back to staring at the television. Only it wasn't on.

"What are you watching?" asked Danny.

"The only good program on TV," said Lana.

"It's my favorite, too," said Danny.

Lana looked at him coldly. "If you think I'm going to put out just cause you're being cute, you can forget it."

Danny was appalled. "Is that the *only* thing you think about?"

"It's the only thing *you* think about."

"You don't know what I think about."

"I think I settled that the first time you walked through that door."

Angry now, Danny could say things plainly that he would ordinarily have been too shy to talk about. "Oh, right, you're half-naked, you press yourself against me, breathe in my face, push me down to the floor, what *else* can I think about? Why didn't you try a *conversation*?"

"You would have been thinking about boffing me the whole time," said Lana.

"Maybe I would," said Danny. "Maybe when all you're wearing is a white shirt that I can partly see through, maybe I sit there wondering how hard it would be to undo the buttons. But right now? Dressed like a regular person?"

"Right now you're thinking about how I looked when you first saw me."

"You're such a piece of work," said Danny. "What I *was* thinking when I came in just now was how cool it was that you were looking at a turned-off television and then had something funny to say about it, and I thought I was joining in the joke, and then *you* turned the conversation to 'putting out.' *You're* the one who can only think about one thing, and I don't care how hard a life you've had, you're still the creepiest girl

I've ever known, and I've known some seriously creepy girls."

"Creepy?" she said mockingly. "Oooh, I'm so *creepy.*"

Danny suddenly darted toward her and threw himself on the couch, landing against the back of it and using his weight and momentum to rock it over backward. He had done that more than once with the even-heavier old couch on the back porch of the schoolhouse at home. He could tip it over with just one of his girl cousins sitting on it. If there was more than one, he'd have to coordinate the raid with one of the other boys, but they were always happy to do it. Finally the girls started getting up from the couch whenever they saw him running toward them, and that was fun, too.

Lana, however, was not prepared at all, so she toppled over backward with a scream. Danny was on top of her at once, tickling her mercilessly. She laughed until she cried.

"Stop it, I'm wetting myself! Stop it, you little bastard!"

Danny stopped and knelt up to look down at her. "I'm thirteen years old, Lana," he said. "*That's* what I come up with to do with girls." Then he got up and walked to the kitchen.

Ced was sitting at the table, reading a thick book with tiny print. "Tickled her, eh?"

"She liked it," said Danny. "I could tell." He went to the fridge and decided that after the o.j. and Payday he wasn't hungry after all.

He heard the door swing open and Lana was there, braced against the doorframe.

"You made me wet myself, you stinking little brat!"

"That's just what I expect from a *girl*. All that girls

can think about is pee. 'I need to go to the bathroom.'
'I've got to take a potty break.' 'Who's coming with me
to the little girls' room.' Girls make me want to *uri-
nate*."

She ran to the dishdrain and picked up a table knife.
"I'm gonna kill you, you little prick!"

"With *that* knife?" said Danny. "All you can possibly
do is spread me with mayo or something."

Ced was laughing now, and Lana whirled on him.
"If you were any kind of husband, you'd protect me
instead of laughing!"

"You're the one with the knife," said Ced.

"You know I hate being tickled!" Lana screamed in
his face.

"Well, maybe the kid hates being half-raped," Ced
answered mildly. "So now you're even."

"Now I have to change my pants!" she said.

"Bet *he* did, too," said Ced.

"I did not," said Danny.

"Oh, bad news, Babe," said Ced. "You're losing
your touch."

Lana lunged at Ced with the knife, but he caught her
wrist. It looked to Danny like she hadn't really been
stabbing at him. Like she wanted him to stop her.

Ced dragged her down onto his lap and kissed her.
Or, rather, kissed *at* her, since she kept dodging her
face out of the way. So he kissed her neck.

"Stop slobbering on me!" she shouted.

"I'm going to go up to my room now," said Danny.

Ced picked her up and set her on the table in front
of him, right on top of the book.

"If that's a library book, they're going to make you
pay a fine," said Danny.

By now Lana and Ced were locked in a kiss so deep

that Danny was surprised they weren't gagging on each other's teeth.

"Are you guys vampires?" asked Danny. "Trying to bite each other's necks from the inside?"

They paid no attention to him.

Danny went down the hall toward the stairs. "I'm never getting married!" he said loudly as he left. "It's just too sickening." But actually he was feeling kind of triumphant. He had gotten a little of his pride back, what with tickling her so she lost control of herself. Even steven now, he said silently.

Well, almost even. Because while he was tickling her, he enjoyed touching her body, even through her clothes. She kind of had a point about what boys think about. Apparently it never switched completely off, once he'd started thinking of her that way. He hadn't known that, what with the only girls he knew being his cousins who despised him.

Danny only made it to the top of the first flight of stairs. Stone was waiting in his doorway, brandishing a piece of stationery-size paper. "I've got a name and address for you."

"Already have a name," said Danny, "and I was kind of hoping this was my address."

"A teacher," said Stone. "And a place you can live. None of the Families know about them. And you'll notice that I'm not saying their name out loud. Please do likewise."

Danny walked to him. "I don't know if I want to leave DC," he said. "I like this town."

"Or you don't want to leave Lana?" said Stone. "She's married."

"I know," said Danny. "I got that. But what I said was, 'I like this town.' Why should I go?"

"Suit yourself," said Stone. But he still folded the paper over and pushed it into Danny's pants pocket.

Danny backed away. "Put it in my hand," he said. "Keep your hands out of my pockets."

Stone rolled his eyes and handed it to him. "Not everyone in this house wants to molest you."

Danny unfolded the note and looked at it. "Marion and Leslie? Is either one of them a man?"

To Danny's shock, Stone slapped him across the face—hard. Danny staggered to the side and he couldn't help it that tears came to his eyes.

"You think it's all a joke?" said Stone. "How do you know somebody's outself isn't in this room, listening to what you say? These people are willing to take in and train a gatemage, even though it might bring the wrath of all the Families down on their heads, and you treat it as a *joke*?"

"If they could hear me," said Danny, "they could read your stupid note."

"You think I don't know how to keep their outselves away from me?"

"Then why do you think they're here to listen?"

"Because if you knew anything, you'd know they could be in the next room and still hear you, and I wouldn't know they were there."

"Still didn't give you the right to *slap* me."

"It's somebody else's life on the line, you selfish little pig," said Stone. "Get it through your head that other people matter besides yourself."

"I'm a Westilian," said Danny scornfully. "Nobody matters as much as me." He had meant the words to be ironic, maybe even apologetically so, but they clearly hadn't sounded ironic to Stone.

"You're not a Westilian," said Stone. "Any more

than all those Americans out there are Celts or Germans or Italians or Poles or Russians or wherever their family came from. It's been nearly fourteen centuries since any of your ancestors lived in Westil."

"I know," said Danny. "Look, I'm sorry I said their names. I honestly forgot that I wasn't supposed to say them."

"I just told you not to!" said Stone.

"Like I told Lana, I'm thirteen! I forget things as soon as you tell me. The Aunts always complained about it, but I wasn't the only one, you know."

"Being young and stupid doesn't excuse anything. If you get them killed or even hurt, I'll kill you myself. Get it?"

"I didn't say their address," said Danny. "I didn't say their last name."

Stone reached out and snatched the note out of Danny's hand. "I take it back. I'm not sending you there. I'm not sending you anywhere, except back out on the street. You're too selfish and stupid to be worth helping."

"I'm a gatemage," said Danny, "so I matter to you and your Orphans even if you think I'm stupid."

"Maybe I'd rather we wait another millennium to get a smart one."

"I'm sorry," said Danny. "I'm really, truly sorry. I won't be careless like that again. I'll take it seriously. I take a lot of things seriously, you know. There's a reason I wasn't killed a long time ago."

"It seems to me that the only reason you're not dead is that your Family was too lazy to kill you."

"You have an ugly mean streak in you, Stone," said Danny.

Stone refolded the note and handed it back toward him.

Danny refused to take it.

"Take it," said Stone. "I shouldn't have gotten angry, you just seemed so flippant about it."

"I don't need it," said Danny.

"Don't be defiant, kid. You won't last long here in DC. Word's going to get out about a disappearing kid, and the Families are going to figure out it's a gatemage and come after you."

"I meant that I don't need the note," said Danny. "I already memorized it."

"Oh," said Stone.

"I'm sorry," said Danny. "I keep screwing up without meaning to. I really don't mean to be flippant. Things just come out that way."

Stone nodded. "I forget that that's just how gatemages are. Never taking anything seriously, like it's all a big joke."

"But I do take things seriously."

"Story is that a lot of people already hated Loki before he closed the gates," said Stone. "Most gatemages have a hard time making any permanent friends, at least among the Westilians."

"Yeah, well, the tribe of Slapping Horticulturalists probably doesn't make a lot of friends, either."

"I kind of left a mark on your cheek," said Stone.

"How interesting," said Danny. "A bruise, maybe?"

"Maybe. But it isn't bleeding."

"You got to learn to put your weight behind it," said Danny.

"Flippant. See?"

"So slap me." Danny turned away and trudged up

another half flight and stopped at the bathroom. This was turning out to be a really fine day. He'd probably get shot in one of the houses.

But he didn't. Eric came home, tired and out of sorts from his walk and bus ride. They watched television and had dinner and watched TV again, this time with Ced and Lana, who made fun of all the shows with equal fervor. Finally it was dark, and they walked down toward Rico's store. Danny showed Eric where to stand, and then he went through the gate to Tilden Street.

Nobody was home at the house with the pool, which meant there might be motion detectors. Danny went in anyway, and simply gated his way from room to room so he never walked down the halls. He found a safe and reached through a minigate to pull out what was inside—some serious-looking jewelry and a bunch of cash and bearer bonds, along with birth certificates and other worthless personal papers and pictures. Danny held out what he wanted to keep and put the rest back inside. Then he gated out of the house instead of prowling around looking for fencible electronics.

Back on the street, Danny tucked the bearer bonds and cash into his clothes, then made a new gate into the house on Sedgwick with the three dormers on the roof and all the bikes in the yard. This house was full of sleeping people, except for the mother and father, who were watching a movie in their bedroom.

That was fine with Danny. He located two Xboxes and two Wiis. With each one he found, as soon as he unplugged it from the television, he made a minigate and pushed the item through to Eric. He waited until he could feel Eric tugging on it before he let go. He also pushed through all the game disks he could find. It would do the kids good to live without their brain candy for a while—at least that's what the Aunts always said when they explained why the Family only had one game system, an old Sega, and three games, and even then hardly anyone got permission to play them.

There were three laptops in that same house, two of them in kids' rooms and the other one in a briefcase. They went through minigates, too. In the garage, Danny looked at the Mercedes and the giant SUV and wondered if he could *drive* something that big through a gate. That'd be a wake-up call for Eric, if suddenly a Mercedes started backing through the gate.

But Danny knew they had no way to get cash out of a car—that was a whole different kind of operation, and he didn't want to meet the people who were in the stolen-car business. Besides, it probably wouldn't work—he had no idea how he'd do it. Maybe *he'd* go through the gate, but the car would be too big so when he disappeared it would just keep going. Then again, without his foot on the accelerator, it would probably slow down and stop. Not for the first time, Danny wished anybody had let him learn how to operate a car. Or even the tractor they used for hauling stuff.

Without going back to the street, Danny gated through the other houses he and Eric had decided probably had good stuff in them. One of them was a complete bust—as far as he could tell, the owners had bought way more house than they could afford, so apart from the living and dining rooms, the rest of the house barely had furniture. But the other four houses yielded jewelry, wallets, credit cards, laptops, iPads and Kindles, even a couple of really expensive-looking vases, though for all Danny knew they were Wal-Mart copies.

If that wasn't enough to set Eric up for a while, then too bad. The small, easy pickings from half a dozen houses was all the burglary Danny intended to do. In his life.

Unless he actually *needed* to, for survival. For food. He wasn't going to rule anything out, but he certainly wasn't going to go into burglary as a career. It would be too pathetic, for the first surviving gatemage in who knew how many years to use his power to make a living by stealing stuff from drowthers.

Danny first gated to the place on Tilden Street, just to see if any alarms had gone off or any cops had shown up. Nobody. The street was absolutely quiet. In the morning there'd be a lot of consternation and complaining, but for tonight, everybody was going to get their sleep.

Danny went through the gate to the garden, where Eric was sitting surrounded by a stack of laptops and rows of other electronics. He was shivering a little. The two vases were lying in the grass. "I think those vases are either crap or brilliant," said Eric.

"Or something in between," said Danny. "But I'm betting on crap. Want to break them to keep warm?"

"No," said Eric. "Because hey, here they are, what if they're worth something after all? You didn't do anything stupid like writing IOUs and signing your name, did you?"

"That's an excellent idea," said Danny. He stepped back through the gate, waited for a count of five, and then returned to Eric. Now Eric was standing, and when he saw Danny he visibly sagged with relief. "What kind of moron are you?"

"The fun-loving kind," said Danny. "I'm not an idiot, of course I didn't sign my name to IOUs."

"Good."

"I signed yours."

"Yeah, right. So the way I see it, it'll take us a few trips to get this all into the store."

"I, uh, spied on them a little bit this afternoon," said Danny. "The clerk isn't going to let us in."

"What kind of all-night corner store turns away customers?" said Eric.

"Customers carrying a bunch of laptops aren't the normal clientele."

"So how do we get in there?"

"I'm thinking we start out by me pushing these all through a gate into Rico's office."

"Rico? You're on a first-name basis with him now?"

"That's what the clerk called him."

"When you were spying."

"The clerk saw me. Just my face. He probably thinks he was hallucinating."

"So maybe when we come in he'll run out screaming," said Eric.

"No," said Danny, "I don't think I should make this stuff magically appear. Last thing we want is for Rico to know how we do it."

"So what? He can't catch you."

"But he can catch *you*," said Danny, "and hold you hostage to get me to burgle every house in Washington, and then probably kill you anyway when I'm done."

"Oh," said Eric. "Yeah, you're right, you shouldn't show them stuff popping out of thin air. Though I've got to tell you, there's no way you can know how cool it looks on the other end, when you hand the stuff through to me. Like the night air is giving birth to high-price electronics and jewelry and I'm the doctor there to catch them."

Danny was still focused on the transportation problem. "What if I pop them into an aisle of the store, out of sight from the checkout desk?"

"Then we can show him where they are, and he won't have to know how we got them there," said Eric. "That works."

Danny made a minigate at floor level and slid the laptops through all at once. They were heavy when you stacked them up, but he did it smoothly and the stack didn't tip over. Then he made a series of other gates, sliding everything through in bunches until he imagined they were all lined up in the aisle.

Since they weren't hearing any tumult from the sidewalk in front of the store, there probably hadn't been a customer inside watching the stuff appear. Either that, or the poor sap fainted. Anyway, it was all inside except for the jewelry, which Eric had wrapped up in his shirt, which he was now carrying like a parcel.

"Cold now?" asked Danny.

"Jewelry makes me warm," said Eric.

They walked around to the front of the store and came in the door.

The clerk saw them and got a weird look on his face. "Get lost," he said softly. "You don't want to see him."

"We need the money," said Eric, "and he needs the stuff to sell."

"You don't know him," said the clerk softly. "He thinks you're small-time trash and he's going to send you to the hospital."

Eric set the shirt-wrapped parcel on the counter and opened it.

"Holy shit," said the clerk. He reached under the counter and apparently he pressed a button, because out came Rico from the back room, carrying the aluminum bat.

"I thought I told you little assholes what would happen if you came back," said Rico.

"Maybe you oughta look at the stuff," said clerk. "They're not a joke, Rico."

Rico glared at Danny and Eric, then stepped between them and looked down at the shirt-load of jewelry on the counter. "Fakes," he said.

"How odd that they'd keep their fakes in a safe," said Danny.

"People do that," said Rico. "I'll give you fifty bucks for it."

Eric reached out and started refolding the shirt over the jewelry.

The bat came down lightly across his arms. The blow was only just hard enough to make Eric cry out and snatch his arms back. "A hundred bucks," said Rico. "If you don't like that, then I pay nothing plus two broken heads."

"So what you're saying," said Danny, "is that you don't want to see the rest of the stuff."

"That isn't all?" said the clerk, impressed.

"Shut up, José," said Rico.

"Ah, José," said Danny. "Nice to know your name."

"What else do you have?" asked Rico.

"Nothing, for a fence who offers a hundred bucks for fifty thousand dollars worth of jewelry."

"Maybe five thousand street, not fifty, which means five hundred from me to you," said Rico. "And yeah, okay, I low-balled you a little because I told you little assholes not to come back here and you came anyway."

"We thought you were a serious businessman," said Danny. "But now you've hurt my friend."

"Let's just get out of here," said Eric. He looked like he was about to cry. He was hugging his own arms like a girl who was afraid of getting hit in the chest with a baseball.

"I don't think so," said Rico. "I think your friend is staying here while you bring in the rest of the stuff."

"Oh, it's already in here," said Danny. "We sort of pre-delivered."

"Where?" demanded José. "I didn't see you guys bring anything in here but that stuff."

"At the back of the store," said Danny. "You were kind of napping."

Rico glared at José.

"I was *not*," said José. "I wasn't even reading or watching television, I was sitting here watching the damn door."

"Come on back and see for yourself," said Danny. He led the way down an aisle. When they rounded the corner, there were the laptops and the game consoles. Only now did Danny realize that some of the console cords and cables seemed to be cut—they disappeared in thin air. Apparently in the dark outside, Danny hadn't realized that some of the cords didn't make it all the way through the minigates. He reached down and pulled the offending consoles away from the gate and the cords slid fully into view.

"That's a lot of electronics," said Rico.

"Good laptops," said Danny. "Top of the line."

"Bullshit," said Rico. "They're all used. Most I can pay for any of them is a couple hundred. Maybe twenty-five bucks for each console."

Eric grumbled at that. "You shittin' me, man? You can get a lot more than that."

"Give him a break here," said Danny. "He's got to make his profit and overhead. He's got to pay José's salary. And what if some of it doesn't find a buyer? We don't know what condition these things are in, they might not run at all."

"Smart boy," said Rico.

Eric didn't like it, but Danny held up a hand to silence him. "Come on, George, that's more than we were hoping for from our first haul. He likes our stuff, finds out he can sell it for a good price, he'll start raising our percentage."

"You got that," said Rico.

And Danny was pleased that Eric hadn't blinked when Danny called him George. No reason to give Rico their real names. Danny's didn't matter so much, but Eric could be hunted down if this guy didn't like how the deal worked out.

"Come on into my office and I'll give you the payout," said Rico. "José, bring the parcel from the counter."

"Right, boss," said José, and he walked back down the aisle to the front.

"And lock the door!" Rico called after him. "Can't believe I let you show me this stuff with the door unlocked."

Then he suddenly had Danny slammed up against the display shelves with his shirt up around his ears, and he was frisking him. "Can't have a wire in here," he said. "Can't have you entrapping me into a crime I would never have committed otherwise."

"We got no wires," said Eric. "Get your hands off the kid, you perv."

"It's okay, George," said Danny. "He's got to be sure we're not plants." Then Danny laughed at his own words, conjuring up an image of him and Eric sprouting out of the ground, with Stone sprinkling them from a watering can.

"Something funny?" asked Rico.

"Tickles," said Danny.

"Yeah, well, you're clean enough. You, George, drop trou or I'll feel you up and maybe I'll accidentally hurt your nads for calling me a perv."

Eric dropped his pants and showed that he didn't have a wire concealed either. "First time anybody ever *asked* me to moon them," he said.

"Pull 'em up, smartass," said Rico. "All right, come on into the office."

Danny went through the door first and headed for the desk. Eric was right behind him, but then he heard a cry of pain and a thud and he whirled around to see Eric sprawled on the floor, writhing in agony, and Rico just unwinding from a massive swing of the bat.

"You little assholes, didn't I tell you what would happen if you came back here?" said Rico, softly but harshly. "Didn't I give you fair warning?"

José was in the doorway now, holding Eric's shirt with the jewelry inside. "Ay Dios," he said. "Santa Trinidad."

Danny now had Rico's desk between him and the baseball bat.

"Hold still and take your medicine," said Rico. "Or

I'll just keep smacking your buddy's head till it pops like a melon."

"You don't want no bloodstains on the floor," said José.

"Don't start thinking you know what I want and don't want," said Rico menacingly. Then he lunged forward, swinging the bat as he came. It would have caught Danny at chest level, except that he gated his way back outside.

Man, it was cold out there. He only stayed a couple of seconds before he gated back into the office, but this time right next to Eric. His plan was to get him up and make a run for it, but Eric cried out in pain when Danny tried to pull him.

Rico was off-balance, recovering from his wild swing. He whirled around, looking baffled for a moment as he staggered and leaned on the desk. José, for his part, had a sick look on his face. He, at least, seemed to know what he had just seen—Danny disappearing in one place and reappearing a moment later in another.

"Quick little bastard, aren't you?" said Rico. "Run all you want, I'll just take it out on your friend. He ain't getting up, not without a stretcher. I cracked half his ribs, if I didn't break his back." And now the bat was high over Rico's shoulder as he readied the bat to come down on Danny's head.

What choice did Danny have? He got a firm grip on Eric's wrist and then pulled with all his might to drag him through the gate he had just created. He knew as he did it that it couldn't work—even though Danny was through the gate himself almost instantly, it would take time to drag Eric's body through, and who knew what Rico might do—beat him more, or just grab onto his leg and pull back, stronger.

So Danny reflexively did something he didn't know he could do. He moved the gate. Slid the mouth of it right over Eric's limp body.

It worked. Eric was lying in the garden, still unable to get up—but out of Rico's office.

Only Rico was holding onto Eric's leg. Just the man's heavy arms coming through the gate. Maybe Rico could have come through all the rest of the way, if Danny hadn't let go of Eric. Without that connection with Danny, Rico seemed to be unable to pull his arms back or push them farther through. He was stuck.

Danny didn't dare grab Rico's arms or do anything to him at all—if he touched him, Rico might come the rest of the way through or drag Danny back.

So instead, Danny created a new gate into the office.

There was Rico, looking terrified, with his arms reaching down toward the floor but disappearing just below the elbows. "Let go of me, you little shit!" he shouted when he saw Danny.

"I'm not holding you," said Danny.

José was sitting in the doorway, his back against the frame, looking at Danny wide-eyed. "I did see you on the wall," he said. "I'm not crazy, I saw you."

"You sure did," said Danny. "Where does this asshole keep his money?"

"The store safe is right behind the counter out front."

"No," said Danny. "The *real* money."

"He'll kill me," said José.

"With no arms?" asked Danny.

Rico groaned and wailed. "Let go of me!"

Danny went behind the desk and opened drawers.

Nothing. Then he looked carefully at the jumble of cabinets, shelves, papers, and salable goods against the wall. He started gating his hands into every cabinet and feeling around. Finally he brought his hands out clutching several stacks of bills. Some were stacks of hundreds, some of twenties.

He reached back into the same cabinet and came out with a pistol and a box of bullets. He slapped those down on the desk and said, "Time for you to shut up, Rico."

Rico shut up.

Danny counted out ten hundreds. "Here's what I expected to get for the stuff I brought. A thousand." He counted out twenty more hundreds. "I'm betting this will cover George's medical bills." Then Danny picked up the rest of the money and carried it to José.

"No, man, I don't want none of that."

"Think again," said Danny. "You just saw this asshole get humiliated. You think he's not going to kill you first chance he gets? Take this money, get yourself out of DC, out of this part of the country, out of the United States. You get it? This is unemployment here. Severance pay."

"I got to stay here, I got family to support."

"This isn't enough to take care of them for a while?"

"Eight kids," said José. "It takes that much to get me back into the States. I can't go."

"Tell you what," said Danny. "There's the gun. There's a box of ammo. You want to be safe from him, you get some of those rubber gloves from the janitorial closet, you do what you got to do. I'm not going to kill him, but I don't care if you do."

"No, man, no," said Rico. "Come on, José, I've got

your back, man, I'm not going to hurt you, just put the money back, take that gun, shoot this kid. You save my life, see? I know how to treat my friends."

"We brought him a bunch of jewelry and electronics to sell," said Danny, "and you saw how he treated us."

"We're friends, José!" insisted Rico. "Pull me back into the room, kid. I mean it, you can have all that money, you can take back the stuff, just get me my arms back."

Then Rico's eyes grew wide. "Who's got my hands!" he demanded. "Something's grabbing my hands!" Then he screamed.

Danny had no idea what was happening to Rico's hands. Was Eric doing something? Or was there a dog out there? Or a raccoon? Or was Rico just faking it? Danny needed to get back to Eric in case there was something hurting him outside.

"I'm going now," said Danny. "I'm taking only the fair price for the goods and George's medical bills. I'm leaving the goods. I didn't cheat Rico, I didn't steal from him. When I get out there I'm going to count to ten, then I'll push his arms back into this room. You can take the money here and get out. Or you can shoot his ass. Or both. I recommend both."

José stood up and walked out of the room.

"I guess he doesn't want the money *or* you dead, you lucky bastard," said Danny to Rico.

Then José came back into the room, pulling on a rubber glove.

"No! Oh, no, no, man!" cried Rico.

Danny gated back out to the garden.

Eric had twisted himself into position to gnaw on Rico's right thumb. It was spouting blood, which was pouring out of Eric's mouth. He had a feral look in his eyes, like one of Zog's hawks, hyper-alert but utterly soulless.

"You got to stop that," said Danny. "If I touch you while you're touching him, he gets free. Let go of him. Stop it."

But it was like Eric didn't hear him. He was growling like a dog, like a bear. Then he fell backward and spat out the thumb. And spat again and again, trying to get the blood out of his mouth.

"That was ugly," said Danny. "But fair."

Then he heard a gunshot. It was muffled and far-away, on account of having taken place inside the store a couple of doors down.

Danny didn't touch Rico's arms. Instead, using his newfound skill, he pulled the gate away, drawing it over the arms until no part of them remained visible.

"I made it through the gate," said Eric with a grin.

"Yeah, so I see," said Danny.

"And I feel a lot better."

"You shouldn't have moved. He probably broke your ribs, he might've broken your back."

"I don't think so," said Eric. "I mean, that's how it felt right after he did it, but now I feel kind of better." Eric got to his feet. "In fact, I feel great. Except maybe I hurt my jaw taking off his thumb."

"I can't believe you did that."

"I don't want that asshole ever holding a baseball bat again," said Eric. "You hadn't got rid of his hands, I was taking the other thumb, too."

Danny held out the three thousand dollars. "I think I cheated him, if you're okay. I mean, a thousand of this was for the goods we sold him, but the other two thousand were for your medical expenses."

"You kidding? He owed us at least five. So you

gave him a discount. Let's say his thumb was worth a thousand. He's still a thou ahead."

"I think he's dead," said Danny.

"You killed him?"

"No," said Danny. "I was just an accomplice before the fact. I think José just shot him."

"None of our business," said Eric. "And you saved my ass, man. You're the one who told me he'd do that, and I didn't believe you. I'm the streetwise guy, right? And you're the one who knew."

"You knew, too," said Danny. "You just didn't want to believe it."

"My life as a burglar is over," said Eric.

"Glad to hear it," said Danny. "Now let's take the money and get out of here."

"Um," said Eric.

"What?"

"Maybe after that gunshot we shouldn't be seen walking down this street away from the store."

"Well, I'm not going *toward* the store," said Danny. "Who knows but what José would shoot us, too, if he saw us? If he hasn't already got himself halfway to Union Station."

"Get your head in gear," said Eric. "You just proved you can get me through one of your gate things alive. So let's get back to Stone's house."

"No," said Danny.

"What do you mean? You can do it, it's easy."

"You're not going back there," said Danny. "And neither am I."

"The hell I'm not!"

"You're covered in the blood of a murdered man," said Danny. "You're not tracking any of it into Stone's house. You've got three thousand bucks, you're going to get yourself into a restroom and wash up as best you can and then you're getting out of DC and back on the road."

"My stuff's in Stone's house!"

"So is mine, and it's all worthless, you can replace all you left behind for a hundred bucks," said Danny.

"I'm going back there whether you take me or not," said Eric. "You tell me I'm not the boss of you? Well, you're not the boss of me, either."

Danny sighed. "Okay, fair enough. I'll take you back there, and *then* I'll go. Because I'm not bringing any of this down on Stone's head."

"Fair enough. Once I get my stuff and wash up and all that, I'm going too. I promise."

Danny figured he probably meant it. For the moment. But then he'd decide to stay a few more days. And he'd start bragging about taking a man's thumb in a fight. And since the cops would be looking for whoever bit off Rico's thumb and left it in a garden a couple of doors down, there was a better-than-decent chance it would lead the cops to Stone's door sooner or later.

"Give me your hand," said Danny. "Hold tight so you don't get stuck in between like Rico did."

Eric got a sudden look of fear in his eyes. "You're not going to leave me partway, are you?"

Danny rolled his eyes. "You hold on to *me*, then," he said. "Hug me like your mama so you go through when I do."

"I think I'll walk," said Eric.

"I saved your life," said Danny. "You think I'm going to hurt you now?"

Eric thought about this. "How come you gave me all the money? How do I know you aren't going to kill me and take it back?"

"The money was always for you," said Danny. "Don't you think I could gate my way into any bank vault in the world and get all the money I want?"

Now Eric got angry. "Why didn't you say so! Why did we go through all this burglary shit and this crap with Rico if you could just get nice clean money!"

"Dye packs," said Danny. "Serial numbers on FBI lists. I've seen cop shows. Come on, I did *your* plan and I got you paid and I got you out of there before he could beat you any more than he already did. Come on." Danny held out his arms like he was going to hug a long-lost brother.

Eric stepped into his embrace and wrapped his arms tightly around Danny. "You're the best thing ever happened to me, kid," said Eric.

"I know," said Danny.

Then he gated them back to the place where they had met, behind the shops near the Lexington Wal-Mart. It was just starting to snow.

It took Eric a moment to realize where they were. By then Danny had pulled free.

"You got your three thousand bucks," said Danny. "And you're in your home town. Go home, wash off that blood. Get seen by witnesses. Nobody's going to be looking for the mysterious thumb-biter around here, but if they do, you've got an alibi—you can't possibly have done the thumb-biting because fifteen minutes later you were seen two hundred miles away."

"You lying sack of shit," said Eric. "You tricked me."

"It's what I do," said Danny. "Just remember that

when you're spending three thousand bucks of my trickery."

Eric still looked furious, but he was calming down. "I can't let my family see the money or it's gone."

"How about if you let them see a thousand bucks of the money because you want to help them live a little better for a while."

Eric grinned. "They'd just drink it up."

"What'll *you* do with it?" asked Danny.

"New clothes. A bus ticket. And then I'll eat and drink the rest till I have to start begging again."

Danny admired his self-knowledge. "Then thanks, Eric. For watching out for me for a few days. I learned a lot from you."

"And you're a freakin' Houdini. I didn't learn shit from you."

Danny grinned and waved and then he was gone.

He had gated himself to Parry McCluer High School a couple of miles away on a hill overlooking Buena Vista. He had come to the woods above the school several times in his ventures out of the Family compound and watched all the drowther kids—the teams practicing in the ball field, the kids coming to and going from the buses and cars in the parking lot. The faculty. He knew the place would be empty this time of night. And it was full of computers.

He gated himself inside the foyer, and then into the office. The computers were off. Danny turned one on, waited for it to boot up. Then he googlemapped the address of Marion and Leslie Silverman on Highway 68 near Yellow Springs, Ohio, where it was called Xenia Avenue. He used the satellite mode to zero in on their house. It was a good-sized farm, surrounded by fields, but with housing developments close by to the east.

Danny tried to imagine a ground-level view of what he was seeing. Could he really do this—jump somewhere that he had never been, just from a Google Maps satellite picture? What if he only gated himself inside the computer and everything blew up?

He had made a lot of jumps to places he had never seen before during his jaunts outside the Family compound, but they had only been jumps of a mile or two or five. And he had made them without thinking, without even knowing he was doing it; it was all just part of running to him, running really fast and wanting to get places, see things. He didn't even know what he wanted to see. That's how he first got to Parry McCluer High School, skipping clear over Buena Vista itself. But come to think of it, he probably *saw* the hillside where he ended up before he ever jumped.

Well, if I can't get there in one gate, I can get there in a few dozen. Or a few hundred. It's not as if I have to *pay* for these gates.

He closed his eyes, picturing the tree-lined driveway leading from Xenia Avenue up to the house. Thinking of the address. Thinking of the names.

Then he made a gate, and he was there. In the driveway in the middle of the night. Snow everywhere that hadn't been shoveled, but the sky was clear. Danny walked to the street. Brookside Drive should meet the other side of Xenia just a rod or two north of the Silvermans' driveway, and there it was.

Danny walked back to the gate he had just made and returned through it to the office at Parry McCluer. He zeroed out the browser history and then cleared out all the cookies and all the temp files. Then he uninstalled the browser itself. It took a while, but he figured he had done all he could to make it so nobody could find out that the last thing the browser had shown was a certain address in Ohio.

Then he was back through the gate to the Silvermans' driveway. He wasn't going to wake them up in the middle of the night. He made his way to the barn, which was heated by the bodies of a couple of dozen cows, and curled up in a corner to sleep.

11

Servant of Spacetime

و𝒾و

Marion and Leslie Silverman were old enough that all of their own kids were grown and gone. The day Danny arrived there, Leslie—Mrs. Silverman—proudly showed him the pictures of five little families on the top of the upright piano. Danny was inept enough to ask, "Are any of them Orphans?"

Leslie raised her eyebrows. "Don't you think that if any of them were, they'd all be?"

In a moment, Danny realized how it had sounded to her. "I meant, are they mages . . . like you."

"I have no idea what you're talking about," said Leslie, looking truly puzzled.

"Have we taken in the wrong stray?" asked Marion from the kitchen, where he was making pies.

"He thinks one of us is dead," said Leslie. "Or both of us."

"No," said Danny. "I just thought . . . Stone told me . . ."

"Now he thinks that he can talk to rocks," she

called out to her husband. "What do you think, Marion, is he a keeper? Or a discard?"

Danny was completely baffled. They had brought him into the house the moment Leslie found him in the barn—before dawn, because apparently the cows got testy if they weren't milked every day at the same time, and it was a very early time. He had assumed they knew exactly what and who he was. But no, apparently they took *all* strays into the house.

"Look, call Stone," said Danny. "He sent me here."

"Now I'm supposed to talk to rocks," said Leslie. "Marion, what did you put in those omelets? Am I going to start hallucinating, too?"

"Only if you forgot to take your meds, darlin'!" Marion called back. "Now hush, please, I can't have any emotion going on when I make the crusts or they won't be flaky and delicious."

"I'm yelling to be heard, not because I'm angry."

"Yelling's yelling," called Marion. "We're scaring the dough."

"So he makes the pies, and you milk the cows?" asked Danny, changing the subject since it was apparent they were bent on pretending not to know anything about magery or why Danny had come here. Unless they weren't pretending, in which case this was some elaborate hoax Stone had pulled. At least Danny could give Stone credit for sending him to such a hospitable couple.

"We each do what we like most," said Leslie, "or if it's a job that has to be done and we both hate it, then whoever hates it least. Or we trade off. I'm milking because I'm an early riser, and he's pies because pies don't like me so the crust never behaves."

"I thought maybe because you both have names that could be either male or female, you got all mixed up on men's work and women's work," said Danny. He smiled and started to laugh, thinking he was being kind of funny and clever.

Apparently not.

"Sorry," he said.

"Don't know what for," said Leslie.

"Should I leave now?" asked Danny.

"Heavens no," said Leslie. "We've hardly started to get to know you."

"I just seem to be saying everything wrong," said Danny.

"Not at all," said Leslie. "Where did you get such an idea?"

"I didn't just happen to come here, I had your address. Your names. I didn't just make it up. I'm not a vagrant."

"I'm so relieved," said Leslie. "To know you came here on purpose—well, that eases my mind no end."

Was there irony in what she said? Danny couldn't be sure. He couldn't read these people the way he could read the Aunts. It was more like trying to understand what Mama and Baba were getting at when they talked over his head. He understood all the words, he just had no clue what was going on. The Aunts said what they meant. Or at least they meant what they said.

No, they didn't, Danny realized. He simply had known them longer and had practice figuring out what they meant.

So he sat and thought for a moment. "You're just careful, aren't you?" said Danny. "Because you don't know if I'm a trap."

"I know what a trap looks like, darlin'," said Leslie. "At least, the kind we use for mice that get confused and think they're welcome inside the house. If you're a trap, I wonder what we'd use for bait, and where we'd put it."

"How about I put myself in a trap so you know I'm not one?" said Danny.

He gated from the chair he was sitting in to one across the room.

Leslie turned and looked at him in his new location, shaking her head. "Well, you've certainly proven that you trust *me*."

"If I were a spy from any of the Families, would I do that?"

"If you had a brain in your head, would you do that?" she retorted.

"Well, I certainly proved that you know what mages are, because you didn't start screaming and carrying on when I gated across the room."

"I can't scream and carry on," said Leslie. "Marion is making pies."

"Didn't you get a message from Stone about me?" asked Danny.

There was no more pretense she didn't know who Stone was. "Apparently you got here faster than the internet can send mail."

"I don't think Stone knew I was going right that moment. I left in kind of a hurry, on account of I was involved in something stupid and illegal, and I didn't check in with Stone."

"Stupid and illegal," said Leslie. "So you act as your own character reference, apparently."

"I'm an excellent burglar," said Danny, "but not a very good negotiator with insane criminal persons who just broke my stupid greedy friend's ribs with a base-ball bat."

"Am I going to have to warn my neighbors to lock their windows and doors at night while you're here?"

"Are you serious?" asked Danny. "They can't keep me out if I want to get in. I'm not here as a burglar. I'm here as a student."

"I'd suggest you learn farming at an agricultural college somewhere, darlin', on account of we're not really serious farmers. It's kind of a hobby."

Danny sighed. "Have you got a television?" At least he could amuse himself, if they did.

"No, I'm sorry, we got rid of the old black-and-white years ago."

"They've got color now," said Danny. "And flat screens. And cable."

"Aren't you sweet to point that out," said Leslie. "We had cable for a while, but it came down to this: I thought there was nothing worth watching unless we had cable, but Marion said he wasn't paying for television since God meant it to come free out of the air and not out of a hose and paid for at fifty bucks a month."

Danny couldn't help laughing at that, and his laughter made Leslie smile.

"Sure we have television," said Leslie. "But is that really the best thing you can think of to do with your free time?"

"We didn't get to watch a lot of it back on the Family compound."

"Which reminds me," said Leslie. "You learn any useful farming skills?"

"Why would I?" asked Danny. "I had no affinity for plants or animals. All I had were my two hands, and the Aunts thought it was dangerous to let me loose near living plants. I think they thought I'd kill whatever I touched."

"How are you doing on that?" asked Leslie.

"On what?"

"On *not* killing whatever you touch," she said. There was a bit of an edge to the question. She was not asking about plants.

Danny regarded her steadily. Why would she ask such a question about killing, if she *hadn't* been in contact with Stone? He could only assume that Stone knew something about what happened in Rico's office, because Eric would have told him. And Stone would have passed the story on to the Silvermans.

"I didn't kill anybody," said Danny. "Even though he tried to kill me and my friend. I figured I could always get away, so why bother? But there was a man who worked for the guy who was trying to kill us, and *he* was in serious danger. So I made a gun available to him, but I also got him plenty of money to get out of the country, if that's what he wanted. The choice was his."

"What about cannibalism?" asked Leslie. "You much for human meat? Like it *en soufflé* or on kabob? Or is it just the little parts you hanker for now and then? Served body temperature, tartare?"

"*Eric* bit off Rico's thumb. I didn't know he was going to do it, and he was just spitting it out when I got back to him. For what it's worth, he was aiming to take the other one, but I didn't let him."

"Taking candy from a baby, eh?" asked Marion. He was standing in the kitchen door. "Sounds like you got in *way* over your head. But Stone says Eric backs up your story." He had a cellphone to his ear.

"You were letting Stone listen to what I was saying?"

"You left a bloody path behind you in DC. We had to decide whether we thought you were worth teaching," said Leslie. "I'm still not sure. Though at least I'm pretty sure we aren't going to kill you."

"Kill me?" asked Danny. He jumped to his feet. "*That's* what you were deciding? While you fed me and treated me so nice?"

"Somebody who can jump through a gate at the first sign of danger," said Marion, "you think we're going to let you *know* we're thinking along those lines? Look, gatemages have always been a problem. You can't discipline them, you can't—well, if they become civilized it's cause they plumb felt like it. Even the ones that don't do any serious damage to fellow Westilians are pretty much a living horror to the mortals they decide to play pranks on. Kidnapping people by dragging them through gates. Pretending to be one person by voice and manner, while really you're another. You Lokis and Hermeses and Mercuries, you cut such a caper."

"The only people I played pranks on were my cousins."

"But they were the only people you knew who weren't bigger than you, and that was before you even knew you *were* a gatemage, am I right?" said Marion. "Let's get something straight here. We may be Westilian by blood and training, but we're not part of any of these Families and we live amongst drowthers all the time, and we like them. In fact, we think we're mostly drowther blood ourselves, and we won't have you here if it's going to cause grief for our friends."

Danny sat back down. "What can I say? If I *were* that kind of nasty trickster, I would assure you that

I would never *ever* do any such thing to the local drowthers. I'm *not* that kind of nasty trickster, but what can I tell you except the exact same thing?"

"Well, at least he's logical," said Marion.

"You say that like it's a good thing," said Leslie.

"Tell you what," said Marion. "What if *I* teach him, but if we decide to get rid of him, *you* make a pie and we get him to eat it?"

"Too dangerous," said Leslie. "The dogs might get into it and die first."

Danny kind of wanted to laugh at the way they were talking, but it was too life-and-death for him to really think they were funny. "I ran away from home because they were fixing to put me in Hammernip Hill. I'm not going to stay here if you're also deciding every day whether I'm to be allowed to live."

"Hammernip?" asked Marion.

"*Hamar-gnipe*," said Leslie. "'The peak of a crag.' Throwing people off *hamar-gnipen* used to be a prime way of sacrificing them to the gods." She turned to Danny. "I went to college, Marion didn't. So I educate him when I can."

"And I spit in her soup," said Marion brightly.

"Our Hammernip isn't much of a crag," said Danny. "More like a hillock. A down. A barrow." He looked at Marion. "I haven't gone to college yet. I just read."

"Darlin'," said Leslie, "everybody on Earth stays alive day to day solely because everyone they meet decides, every single day, not to kill them. For instance, you could gate your way into my chest and pull my heart out right now. Or squeeze it hard and make it stop."

The thought made Danny almost gag. "That's just sick," he said. Yet at the same time, he couldn't stop himself from thinking: Cool. Why didn't *I* think of that?

"Gatemages have done it before," said Leslie.

"We're taking you on as a student," said Marion. "Let that be enough for now."

"Not so fast," said Danny. "You act like you're doing me this big favor and it's okay for you to test me before you'll 'take me on'—but you're not gatemages. You've never known a gatemage in your life. There's no manual on how to do gatemagery or how to train a gatemage. What in the world are you going to teach me?"

"There are certain basics that you don't know," said Marion.

"So tell me."

"Not till the pies are done." Marion went back to the kitchen.

"Isn't he simply maddening?" asked Leslie. "But he's a Cobblefriend, and he's been able to sense the presence of large deposits of both oil and coal in various places, using his credentials as a geologist—he actually did go to college, all the way to a Ph.D.—and the royalties from the wells and mines allow me to maintain my farming habit. I dropped out of college to marry him and put him through school. And in case you're wondering, I'm a beastmage, most specifically a Claw-sister, though it hardly seems the right term to use when my heartbeasts are all cows. Still, it's better than 'Udderbuddy.'"

"You're a Cowsister?" asked Danny. "No wonder you have to do the milking."

"They never kick me, if that's what you mean. We get along very well. Sometimes I wish I had an affinity with a different kind of beast. I'd love to experience leaping like a gazelle, or pouncing like a lion, or soaring like a hawk."

"My Uncle Zog is a hawk sometimes. When he isn't a vulture."

"How metaphorically apt," said Leslie. "I once knew Zog, if he's the same one. The way you Families recycle names, it's hard to be sure we're talking about the same man."

"There's only one Zog," said Danny, "and he's an angry, vicious piece of work."

"And yet I don't recall him leaving someone behind with a bloody stump of a thumb and a bullet in their brain."

"That's because he eats his kills," said Danny.

Leslie laughed. "Oh, you're funny."

"I wouldn't put it past him," said Danny.

"Well, when he's riding his heartbound, of course he experiences eating whatever the heartbound eats. I can tell you that I know the sweet pleasure of chewing cud, for instance. Yet grass, half-digested or fresh, has *never* passed *these* lips."

Danny felt a little relieved, but also disappointed. "I thought the longer you rode your heartbound, the more like them you became."

"In temperament, perhaps, not in diet. I'm very calm, though I'm also skittish and prone to stampede."

"What are the basics you can teach me? Because I could never do any of the things they taught the other kids to do."

"And what was that, exactly?"

"Finding your outself. Making clants. Love and serve the source of your strength. That sort of thing."

"And why do you think you weren't doing those things?"

"Because nothing ever happened."

"And mightn't that have been the fault of your teachers?"

"Maybe," said Danny. "But what would a gatemage 'love and serve'? Doors and windows? And if you don't *have* an outself, you can't very well do anything with it."

"Everyone has an outself, Danny. Even the most commonplace drowther, whether he knows how to set it loose or rein it in."

"I don't," said Danny stubbornly.

"Well, then, we have a long way to take you, since you do have one. But let's start by telling you something that *is* known about gatemages. You could not make a gate without an outself. Gates are your clants, you see. Each of them is built around a small portion of your outself, and it opens and closes—or disappears completely—under your complete control. Call in your outself, and the gate doesn't just close, it dies. It's gone."

"So when Loki closed the gates, he was just calling in his outself?"

"That would close only the gates that *he* had made. He closed *all* the gates, even those made by long-dead mages."

"But if a gatemage dies, how can his gates continue, if they're clants?"

"What happens to any other mage if someone kills his body while his outself is controlling a clant or riding the heartbound beast?"

"The clant begins to fade," said Danny, thinking back to lessons he'd been taught. "And it keeps going through the motions it was last assigned by the dying mage. They told us that was how legends of ghosts began—people seeing a fading clant from a dead mage."

"And if you die while riding your heartbound?" asked Leslie.

"Then we have a beast that can talk, or at least understand human speech. Which is where the idea of talking animals and werewolves comes from. But the outself gradually fades and gets lost in the mind of the heartbound."

And Danny made the extrapolation to his own magery. "So every gate I've made remains after I die, for a while at least."

"Only the ones you haven't already closed and gathered in."

Danny didn't like confessing a weakness, but how would he learn if he didn't? "I don't even know what that means."

Leslie regarded him steadily for a long moment. "You mean you don't know how to close your own gates?"

"How would I know anything at all?"

"They're all still there? How many?"

Danny reviewed his mental map of his gates. "I'm not sure how to count them. What about the ones that I made twice, once in each direction?"

"I think those are two gates," said Leslie. "They just go the same places."

"I don't know," said Danny. "They *feel* like one gate to me, only doubly strong."

Leslie nodded, frowning in thought. "Perhaps that's how gatemages create gates that are strong enough to persist centuries after they die—they knit two or more gates together. I really can't say," said Leslie. "You realize that without a serious gatemage in nearly fourteen centuries, we don't know much, and what we do know is mostly guesswork or logical deduction."

Meanwhile, Danny had been enumerating each group of gates. The largest batch was all the nonce gates he had made inside the Family compound before he knew that he was making gates at all. "I might have over-looked some, but I think I've got about two hundred and fifty gates."

"Mercy me," said Leslie. "All at the same time?"

"Well, I can only go through one at a time. And some of them are just little stutters, getting me through a wall or up a tree. You've got to remember I didn't know I was making them. I didn't know I was going through them. I just thought I was a good runner and climber."

"You do understand that this is extraordinary. Great mages can often maintain up to a dozen separate clants, or ride two heartbeasts at once, sometimes three. But each division of the outself diminishes what remains. You should have run out of outself after the first dozen gates or so. In ancient times, the great gatemages used to treasure their gates, take pride in them, yet always hold a bit of outself in reserve, so they could get out of emergencies."

Danny heard the implication loud and clear: He was doing something even the "great mages" couldn't do.

"Of course, I don't know how much of your outself each gate requires," said Leslie. "Maybe all gatemages can maintain as many as you seem to have, and pre-tended to have only a few. They can't be that hard to control. After all, the gates don't *do* anything, they just sit there, yes?"

"Unless I move them."

"You can move them?"

"Either end. I can slide the gate over somebody and sort of make them go through it."

"So you can move people through your gates against their will?"

"Do you want me to show you?"

"I want you to promise you will never move me like that."

"Even if you're lying helpless in front of an oncoming train or semitruck and I can gate you out of the way?"

"I will try to avoid getting in the way of large oncoming vehicles," said Leslie, "so it won't come up."

Danny was already learning—but perhaps a little more than they had meant to tell him. And they were learning from him, too. Leslie meant him to know that he *had* an outself, that his gates were his clants. But she had had no idea that either end of a gate could be moved or that a single gatemage could maintain so many at once. This seemed to Danny to be useful information.

"Since I could never find my outself, I didn't pay much attention when they were teaching the other kids about calling it in. I know there was some kind of danger that the outself could get lost. Or that it could drag too much of your inself with it, and so you could lose track of where your body is. But I don't see how any of it applies to gates. I always know where they are, and where I am. I don't *feel* like there's any part of me *in* them. How can I call them?"

"How can I explain it? When I'm riding my heartbound, I just . . . gather it in, when I want to return to myself."

"I don't know what that would even mean."

"At least now you know that each gate *is* a part of your outself."

"That's like saying that gravity makes things fall. Naming it doesn't mean you understand it or can affect it in any way."

"You know how it feels when you send *out* your outself."

"I know how it feels when I make a gate," said Danny. "You're telling me it's a sending of my outself, but it still feels like . . . making a gate."

They sat and looked at each other.

"This isn't working," said Danny. "Everybody *but* me knows what you mean by 'gathering in your outself.' And you have no idea what it feels like to make a gate. Why are you so sure they're the same thing?"

"I'm not sure."

This was discouraging. There was going to be too much of the blind leading the blind in this "education" he was launching into.

Yet it was also exhilarating to be discussing magery with someone who didn't regard him with pity or dread or contempt. To be spoken to as an equal, or at least as someone worthy of respect. Just the fact that these two, like Stone, took him seriously as a mage— maybe a great mage—changed his estimation of himself. Things like mooning the security guy at the library didn't feel so funny and clever anymore. Danny realized now that they were the actions of a defiant child, someone who feels small and weak and therefore has to show contempt for power—if he thinks he can get away with it.

I have this rare and frightening power, he thought, and all I could think of to do with it was bare my butt and say nanner-nanner, because I knew they couldn't punish me.

But how much of the behavior of Lokis and Mercuries in the legends and Family histories came out of precisely that same childish sense of being inferior and yet capable of escaping punishment?

So he wanted to keep this adult conversation with Leslie going. "I'm trying to think," he said, "what it is that I love and serve to gain the power to make gates. *If* gatemagery really works according to the same principles as all the other magics."

"No one knows," said Leslie. "Some say that gatemages don't love or serve anything, which is why they're so dangerous and irresponsible and childish."

That stung a little, but since Danny had just been thinking the same thing, he couldn't really take offense.

"But in recent years, in discussions among the Orphans, a theory *has* come up."

"I'd love to hear it, because as far as I know, I tried with all my heart to love and serve trees, potato plants, mice, dogs, and rock, to no effect. They didn't notice I was there, except the plants, and they withered."

"It takes time."

"It takes time to get really good at it," said Danny. "But for those with a real affinity, it takes no time at all for some *spark* to show up. Like me—whatever it is I have an affinity for, I never knew I was 'loving and serving' it. I just had the power to make gates, and then it was a reflex. Automatic. I didn't even know I was gating."

"So do you want to know the theory?" asked Leslie.

"All ears," said Danny.

"Spacetime," said Leslie.

"So I'm, like, the servant of physics?"

"That's science, not magery," said Leslie with only a little contempt. "Physics is *measuring* it; you *change* it."

"Okay, so I love and serve spacetime. I can't say it makes *no* sense, because how does it make sense to love and serve stone or lightning or water? But spacetime? That's kind of . . . *everything*. How can I love and serve *everything*?"

"It's the bed in which everything else exists, but it's not, in itself, anything."

"Now, see, that has to be offensive. To spacetime, you know? Which is why you can't make gates." Danny grinned.

"Danny, being flippant and making jokes isn't going to help you."

Danny felt abashed, but then his defiant streak made him think of a contrary argument. "How do you know it *isn't* going to help me?" asked Danny. "How do you know jokes aren't how spacetime is loved and served? I mean, spacetime is the causal universe, right? The set of relationships between everything that exists in space, which implies dimension, and in time, which implies causality." Danny was rather proud of being able to toss out these terms, though he was pretty sure he barely understood them.

"You must be a whiz of a student," said Leslie. "A real show-off in class. But I do understand you. Besides, I married a class show-off."

"You know the saying 'Shit happens'?" asked Danny.

"I saw *Forrest Gump*," said Leslie.

"I have no idea what that is," said Danny.

"Things happen, bad things, good things, seemingly at random. Yes, I get it."

"That's spacetime, right?" said Danny. "I mean, this is *your* theory, right?"

"It's *a* theory. It is certainly not mine."

"As far as I can see, spacetime *is* a prankster. Weird stuff just happens. Insane coincidences that mislead people into making false assumptions about how the universe works. You pray for somebody and they phone you. You keep bumping into the same stranger as if you were somehow meant to be together. Only there's no meaning to it. It just happens. Spacetime is pranking us."

"So you're saying that by making flippant jokes, you're loving and serving spacetime?"

"I'm saying that when I pranked people, I made shit happen," said Danny, "and maybe that's why spacetime gave me the power to make gates."

"Well, it makes a perverse kind of sense," said Leslie. "The tradition is that Loki and the other gatemages have all been tricksters and con men. It's one of the signs."

"Getting people to believe things that aren't true, so we can cause them to do things they would never do in a rational universe."

Leslie nodded. "So your brattiness is the source of your power?"

"Hey, I'm not the one who said that gatemages love and serve spacetime."

"I'm intrigued. I think this bears looking into. Makes the theory stronger. So how about this one: Gatemages are also extremely good with languages. How would that tie in?"

Danny shrugged, though he was thrilled that she was asking *him* to come up with a guess. "Language is figuring out what other people mean by the noises they make, and then learning how to make the noises that will get them to do what you want. Right? Language gives us the illusion that we're talking about reality, but in fact we can say false statements as easily as true ones, and get people to act on them as if we had changed reality." Danny was liking this idea. "In fact, isn't language just a system for coming up with false temporary realities? Isn't it just our way of creating realities for each other?"

"That is a deeply perverse way of saying it, but I suppose it could explain the affinity."

Marion was back in the doorway. "This boy is bullshitting you, Leslie. He's making stuff up as he goes along."

"Maybe that's just what gatemages do," she said with a shrug.

"How do you know it isn't true?" asked Danny. "I come out of Wal-Mart wearing shoplifted clothes, and who do I run into but a kid who can get me to the very city where some magic pollen leads me to Stone who leads me to you, so I can get some training. How is that even believable, except that spacetime is grimly determined to make *me* a more effective prankster?"

"Why would spacetime care?" asked Marion.

"Why does stone care about getting shaped into . . . stone stuff? By stonemages? Why does water want to flow the way that watermages tell it to flow? These are inanimate objects that come to life under the ministrations of a mage that loves and serves them."

"Maybe," said Leslie, "spacetime hates the way that all its pranks have been so severely limited by the closing of the gates in 632 A.D."

"That's it," said Danny. "And it's been getting more and more frustrated because the Families have been killing gatemages all these years—and so spacetime has squeezed *me* out and somehow set things up so I *didn't* get killed. Maybe spacetime brought me into being so I could make a Great Gate and get some real power back into the magery of the world."

"A mission in life," said Leslie. "Just don't count on spacetime being reliable. As soon as you count on it, it'll prank you."

Danny got the implication—that if they trust *him* they might get that same result.

"Maybe spacetime wants the Great Gates restored, but it isn't just the Families' killing of gatemages that has kept us Gate-free for fourteen centuries," said Marion.

"Far from it," said Leslie, nodding.

"Killing all the gatemages isn't enough?" asked Danny.

"The Families only kill the gatemages they know about," said Marion. "We outsiders, we Orphans, we've had six gatemages that *we* knew about and the Families never found."

"Well, why aren't we going to Westil, then?"

"The Gate Thief," said Marion.

"Gatemages don't last long," added Leslie.

Stone had said the same thing. "Why not? Who's the Gate Thief?" asked Danny.

"As soon as somebody gets strong enough to attempt a Great Gate to Westil, the Gate Thief comes in and steals their gates," said Marion.

"Steals them. How?"

"If we knew how, maybe we could prevent it," said Marion. "The gatemage lives through it, he just can't make gates anymore. It's as if his whole outself was stolen from him."

"Who can do that?" asked Danny.

"The Gate Thief," said Marion.

"But who's the Gate Thief?"

"The person who steals the gates," said Marion. "It's very circular."

"I'd rather believe it's all a prank by spacetime," said Leslie. "For one thing, the Gate Thief has been at work for centuries. Nobody lives that long. So why not figure spacetime causes all the gatemages to lose their outself?"

"Spacetime loves the gates," said Marion. "If it didn't, it wouldn't have allowed them in the first place."

"Then the Gate Thief is the enemy of spacetime," said Danny.

"Exactly!" said Marion.

"That's why we're hoping," added Leslie, "that spacetime—or fate, or raw random chance, or whatever—will create a Gatefather with the power to withstand the Gate Thief."

They looked at Danny in silence.

"The pie crusts are almost certainly done," said Marion, "if they aren't burnt." He went back into the kitchen.

"You hope I'm the one who can stand up to the Gate Thief," said Danny.

"*You* hope you are, too," said Leslie. "Because if you can't stand up to him, then you won't be a gatemage anymore. Not after your whole outself is ripped away from you."

"What if the Gate Thief is a gatemage who loves and serves spacetime . . . by playing tricks on spacetime itself?"

"Tickling the tickler," said Leslie.

"If I never try to make a Great Gate, will the Gate Thief leave me alone?"

"We don't know who it is, if it's a person at all, and

either way, we can't ask," said Leslie. "As far as we know, the Gate Thief doesn't steal any gates at all until somebody bridges the gap between Westil and Mittle gard."

"So I'll never make a Great Gate."

"Then you're an even bigger waste of time than I thought," said Leslie. "We're not training you so you can burglarize houses or steal state secrets or whatever course of action you decide to devote your life to. Nor even to get the healing power that comes from passing through a gate. You're worth helping precisely and solely so that you can open a Great Gate so that mages can pass between the worlds and build up reverberations of their power."

"And you want it to be a student of yours so that maybe you can control this new access to power, break down the Families, and rule both worlds."

Leslie nodded. "Now you understand."

Danny laughed. The heroes were unmasked. "You Orphans are no better than the Families."

"But we *are*," said Leslie. "Because we want the Great Gates open to everyone. Even drowthers, so they can wake up the potential affinities inside them."

"How egalitarian," said Danny.

"What an elitist thing to say," said Leslie.

But Danny couldn't help it—he despised the self-delusions of the Orphans as much as he despised those of the Families.

"I'm thirteen," said Danny mockingly. "This is all over my head."

"You're a gatemage," said Leslie. "You understand everything that anybody says."

Did he? Was that why he was such a good student? "It's not that easy."

"Serve spacetime," said Leslie, "and let's work on learning how to close your own gates."

"But *you* don't even know how to do it," said Danny. "How can you teach *me*?"

"I'll keep describing to you how it feels to gather in your outself, and you keep trying to produce that feeling so you can see if a gate closes. Maybe someday, between us, or through dumb luck or getting older, you'll hit on it."

Danny thought about this. "It doesn't sound like a complete waste of time."

"How low our expectations have become," said Leslie.

"So," said Danny. "It's a deal. Let's get started."

"I think we just did," said Leslie. "And my brain is tired. I think you bruised it with your idea that pranking serves the whimsical nature of spacetime."

"So when is our first real practice session?"

"Tomorrow after breakfast," said Leslie. "No, I take that back. Tomorrow morning at milking time."

"Why so early?"

"Because I'm going to teach you to milk cows."

"I can't tell a cow from a camera."

Leslie smiled. "A cow with autofocus, you just point it at the scene and yank its tail."

"You think I need vocational training? That if you get me to milk cows I can become a beastmage whose heartbeast is a grazing animal?"

"I want you working hard and concentrating on something besides your gatemaking."

"How will *that* help?"

"It might not," said Leslie. "But it's worth a try. Danny, I think we have some good ideas here. But the only way to know if they're workable is to try to make them fail. If we fail to fail, then maybe we're on the right track."

"Why don't we try something else first?" asked Danny. "Why don't you show me some of the gates those earlier gatemages made? Then maybe I can learn how to close *their* gates, the way Loki did."

"I can't," said Leslie. "Loki closed all the old ones, and the Gate Thief takes all the new ones. There are no gates left. Right now, yours are the only gates in the world."

"So why doesn't he step in and stop me now? Why wait?" asked Danny.

"I'll put that question on the agenda when I meet with him next week," said Leslie.

That was how Danny's education in the rudiments of magery began all over again. But he had some hope this time. Before, when the Aunts and Uncles were trying to teach him, everyone felt that he could do no magery at all. Now, the Silvermans and Danny knew that he could do some pretty good magery, so maybe they could get better results.

They spent weeks and months at it. By the next summer, Danny had reached the conclusion that it would be easier to squirt snot out of his elbow than to figure out how to gather home the outself fragments that maintained each of the gates he made. But apart from farm chores, did he have anything better or more important to do than to try to get control of his gatemagery?

Life on a small dairy farm beat burglary. Living and working with the Silvermans was way better than hanging out with Eric and Ced and Lana. And maybe someday he'd have a breakthrough and get the hang of it all at once.

If spacetime wants me to close gates, it'll happen, one way or another. And if it doesn't, then I never will learn it no matter how much I study.

Meanwhile, Danny reminded himself, he was safely out of the reach of the North family and all the other Families that would regard him as a threat that needed killing or start a war over who got to use any Great Gate they could get him to make. So even if he never learned to do everything the Orphans wanted him to do, his life was still better in Yellow Springs than it had ever been in Virginia.

12

The Queen's Hero

ᶂ

Wad knew every path and passage of Nassassa Castle, for he had explored them all.

He knew the public spaces from climbing high in the beams and rafters, or burrowing into thatch. No one ever looked up to see him looking down, or if they did look up, his face was hidden in smoke or they were partially blinded by the dazzle of candles.

He knew the corridors that everyone walked, and the corridors that only the servants used, and the passages that allowed the soldiers to get to the arrow-ports and spyholes and oilspouts and secret sallyports that protected the castle.

He knew the abandoned rooms whose doors were heavily locked and into which no servant came; he knew the private rooms whose doors were hidden behind tapestries and furniture, or under rugs, or *as* furniture, and he knew who came and went. For it was in such private rooms that the secret government of Iceway met and tried to influence the decisions of the king, and it was in such private rooms that King

Prayard met with Anonoei, his concubine, to conceive the sons that the whole kingdom hoped would inherit from him someday.

He knew the spaces that were not rooms at all, but rather architectural accidents, which had no passages that led to them, except in the attics, and only when sections of old roof were torn up to be replaced by new tiles or thatch. Then the workmen saw such places; but the others, in the foundations of the castle, in the airshafts that provided ventilation to deep places, in the spaces between rooms where stones had not come out even during construction and gaps had been left behind, no one but Wad ever saw those, for there was no way to reach them, unless you were a Pathbrother or Gatefather.

For Wad understood now that he was indeed what Hull had said he was on his first evening here, in the shade garden on the hill behind the kitchens. He had not known it until she said it, but then he realized that what he had thought of as "finding the door" was really making a gate.

He reached into himself, into the maelstrom of dream and memory and habit and reflex of his mind, and found out how to make gates exactly where he wanted them, and move them when that was necessary, and call them back into himself when they had served their purpose, so he never dissipated his outself by maintaining too many gates at once.

He kept only a dozen or so permanent gates, and otherwise used feet and hands to get from place to place. All his gates were in hidden places where no one could ever see him go or come. Instead, people who bothered to look at him would see him climbing, swinging, groping, balancing his way up walls and tapestries, out along beams and girders, and into narrow ducts and passages. Thus he earned a reputation as a squirrel, seen only as he slipped out of sight; a rodent skittering through the castle.

Since people thought this of him, it was natural that if anything was stolen he would be suspected of it. Suspicion led to questions, and Wad hated questions. He didn't like to talk to people. Talking led to argument, and he was tired of argument. He didn't remember why he was so tired of it, for it was lost in his distant past, his time before the tree, which was still chaotic and unfathomable to him. He only knew that he had wearied of talking long ago, and then had simply acted. Had done *something* that made him both satisfied and ashamed, so he could hardly face anybody's gaze without looking away, and yet always knew that he had done right.

He had stolen something, he knew that. Stolen many things. But he was done with stealing now, as far as he knew. So one of the things he watched for was to make a constant inventory of everything that anyone brought into the castle. Then he would track it, remembering whose it was, where it was kept, whom it had been given to, and where *they* now kept it, and so on, in an intricate web of exchange.

If something was missing, he usually knew it before the owner, for he checked the inventory frequently during the night, making small nonce gates that let him probe the insides of trunks, drawers, cabinets, boxes, bowls, and under beds and behind tapestries and inside nooks and crannies.

Then, when he was questioned—usually by Hull—about whether he knew where some item or another had been left, he had an answer. "It's in Rudder's chart chest," he said once, and two days later the man once named Rudder was hanged over the sea wall, and a new man was elevated to his place and given his name.

Another time he knew that a particular wanted item was exactly where it was always kept, and the accuser was lying. This he said to Hull, and the kitchen girl who had lied got a beating and then was sent back to her home in disgrace.

Over time, instead of suspecting Wad of stealing things, most people stopped stealing or lying about where things were, because they knew that he always knew. Some feared him because of this, and now and then there was an effort to have him expelled from the castle, but when it came to the King, he said, "And then I'd have to replace Hull as baker and night cook, and I won't do it. Besides, I've found that most people who complain about Wad are the very ones he has caught stealing or lying about someone else stealing." Then the King would look at them with innocent amusement and watch them retreat in confusion.

But King Prayard had his own worries about Wad, and one day he began speaking aloud in a private room where he was waiting for Anonoei to come to him. "I have let you live here, my boy, because your discretion is perfect. You tell nothing you see. You also notice that I ask nothing of you, for you are not my spy."

Wad said nothing, but trembled a little on the beam where he was lying.

"I'm sure that you have watched me with Anonoei many times, but you have grown careless and I found bits of straw on the floor and saw your foot when I looked up. Anonoei is a very shy and modest woman, and if she saw you she would be embarrassed and hurt. Please try to be more careful."

Wad still said nothing, for how could he tell the King how many times Anonoei, lying on her back with Prayard about his business atop her, had looked right into Wad's eyes and winked the eye that Prayard could not see? Instead, he found a different vantage point to watch from in this room, when he felt the need to know what King Prayard and his mistress were discussing together.

Hull still thought of herself as Wad's protector, and in truth she was. But Wad also knew he had the protection of the King, and Prayard's reminder that he had never asked Wad to spy for him was, as far as Wad could see, a clear warning that the King would one day use him in precisely that way.

Indeed, Prayard did not have to ask, for along with his inventories, Wad kept a vivid memory of all the conversations he heard between the King's enemies and friends. Wad had overheard so much duplicity that he kept a complicated mental sorting frame of all the people in the castle.

There were the King's friends who were truly loyal to him, the friends who were playing their own games, and the friends who were secretly serving the Queen and her servants from Gray. Then there were the Queen's friends who were truly loyal to Bexoi's older brother, the Jarl of Gray; her friends who were actually in the pay of Prayard to spy on her; her friends who were in Prayard's pay but fed him false information; and the Queen's friends who were loyal to her nephew Frostinch, the Jarling or heir of the Jarl of

Gray, who came and went from the castle at will and had his own plans and designs that often contradicted the intentions of his father.

The Queen had no friends who were loyal to her. She confided in no one, said little, complained never. She was married to a man—Prayard—who treated her with elaborate courtesy and made a ceremony of coming to her bed once a month, but spilled his seed on her belly and put nothing inside her that might make a baby. Yet she said nothing of this humiliation, though Wad had seen her more than once, after he left her, as she tried to collect her husband's seed and put it inside herself.

Wad wanted to tell her, O Bexoi, even if this worked, do you really think he would believe you if you claimed to have got his child in such a way? If he thought a child by you would be useful, he would be trying to conceive one; since he does not, he would condemn you in privy council for your supposed adultery, and then would have you returned to your father's house in public shame. Where would your child be then, O Bexoi?

He wanted to say that, but never did, because he and the Queen were not on speaking terms. She was not on speaking terms, really, with anyone, and so she intrigued Wad more than any other person in the castle, for he did not know what she wanted, what she hoped for, what she feared, what she planned, what she felt or thought about anyone or anything—not in words, anyway. He only saw what she actually did.

How could a person remain so perfectly hidden from Wad, when he watched so closely and often?

A strange thing happened, though, as he watched

her over the three years he lived in Nassassa. He fell in love with her.

He did not give his feelings that name at first. He would only admit to himself a certain curiosity in her doings, and then a bit of an obsession. He thought of his watching of the Queen as a bad and dangerous habit, and tried to avoid doing it; but within a day or two he'd find himself studying her again from one of his dozen vantage points in her suite of chambers.

He finally had to admit that he loved her when Frostinch's chief agent in the castle, Luvix, who was officially there as her huntsman and master of horse, despaired of getting a chance to arrange her death by hunting accident, since she never hunted. Wad heard him arrange with his lover of the moment, Sleethair, Bexoi's chief lady-in-waiting, to be seen vomiting drunkenly in a public corridor at precisely the moment when Luvix would be entering Bexoi's room to force a quick-acting poison down her throat.

Wad, learning of the plot, did not even *decide* to break his longstanding do-nothing policy. He simply gated his hand into Luvix's sleeve where he had the vial of poison concealed, and took it.

But Wad also had an imagination, and he thought of what might happen when Luvix showed up in Bexoi's chamber, woke her to force the poison into her, and then found that it was missing. Would he allow her to live, knowing that he had laid forcible hands upon her? He would not.

So on that night, after Sleethair lovingly left her mistress to fall asleep inside her safely locked bedchamber, Wad dropped down from the ceiling. As he had expected, Bexoi made no sound, though he had certainly surprised her. Bexoi's self-discipline was perfect, which was one of the things he loved about her, since he strove for a similar perfection. Because Wad knew that Luvix had a man stationed at the door, listening for any sound within that might cause him to abort his plan, he put his finger to his lips and then beckoned to her to get out of her bed.

To his great relief, she made no argument and attempted no discussion. Instead, she nodded, then rose and slipped a warm robe around her shoulders, for the air in the castle was frigid on that autumn night— yet not cold enough that anyone had been authorized to lay fires yet.

When she was out of bed, Wad began to arrange pillows to form a human-like shape under the bedcovers. To his surprise, she laid a hand on his shoulder to stop him. She returned the pillows to their proper place, and then, to his shock, she began to form the flame of her candle, the dust of the walls, and the straw on the floor into a clant.

And not just an ordinary clant, but rather a perfect image of herself, though perhaps a little younger and more perfectly beautiful than Bexoi herself. Wad wondered if this was deliberate, or if she simply thought of herself that way and did not realize how her years in Nassassa had aged her and torn the bright happiness from her face.

The clant was naked, and as it slid back under the covers, Wad marveled at how smoothly and gracefully it moved. He had not seen such expert handling of a self-seeming clant since . . . since . . .

He could not remember that time, it was so far back, but he knew that there had once been a time when many mages had the power to self-clant so perfectly that it fooled almost everyone except Wad himself, though in those days he had borne another name and served other purposes. When was it? Who was I then? He could not remember, for when he tried to think back that far, all he could see was the wood of a tree all around him, the grain of the wood permeating his own flesh in rivers of life that sustained him in his ageless, mind-empty state.

Why was I there? What was I hiding from? What had I done before I entered the tree? Why would I choose such a living death and then rest there in a dream? How long was I asleep?

No answers came to mind. But he had drawn tantalizingly near to a real memory of the time before the tree, and it distracted him momentarily. Bexoi had to come stand directly in front of him to remind him that he had a specific errand here. She reached out and touched his chest, and he came to himself again, and nodded.

She has shown me that she is a truly powerful mage, and a mage of fire and light, rather than the pathetic Feathergirl that everyone else believes her to be. So I will not conceal myself from her, either. Instead of opening the trap door and leading her down into a tunnel from which she can see nothing, I will take her into the wall and show her all as it unfolds.

Wad reached out his hand to her and she took it. He led her to his permanent gate in her chamber, which was in the same wall against which her bed stood. He pointed to the stone in which he had placed it, and pointed to the exact point on the face of the stone where the gate opened. There was a curious indentation in the stone at that spot, which was why he had chosen it.

He pushed his finger into the gate and her eyes widened. Then he pulled his finger back, took her hand, and pushed *her* finger into the gate. He had deliberately doubled the gate into a sturdy one through which anyone could pass—if they knew where it was. Now she knew. Whether he was there with her or not, she could find this passage in times of future danger, and go through it to safety.

He nudged her forward, and she followed her finger into the gate. As her body neared the stone, the gate embraced her, flowing around her body as Wad had designed it to do. She went through it without his holding her hand at all, proving to her that it was available to her even when she was alone. Then Wad followed her.

The space between the walls was an inadvertent space left by the architect; the other wall supported a military stairway up to an oilspout. So this empty space had a very high ceiling near the outside wall, which descended till it met the floor about three feet before reaching the opposite wall of her chamber.

In the darkness, she had kindled a silent flame without fuel, as only a Firemaster or Lightrider could do. It hung in the air instead of being attached to her finger, so she was a Lightrider indeed, the strongest kind of firemage. Again, Wad was touched by the thought that he had not seen such power since . . . since . . .

He led her to a spot just inside the canopy of the bed, and created a nonce gate for her. When she pressed her face to the stone, she would be able to see from a spot on a bedpost just under the canopy, where she would have a full view of all that happened on her bed. Wad made another such viewport for himself.

Then they waited, still in perfect silence.

The door opened. Luvix came in. He saw the clant lying in the bed, and closed the door behind himself and locked it.

The clant sat up and said nothing. Wad did not know if this was because Bexoi was making the clant do what she would have done, or if she was simply not capable of making the clant speak well enough to be convincing. He could hardly expect *that* level of perfection in her clanting—in these days when no one could augment their power by passing through Great Gates to Mittlegard, such skill would be almost impossible to achieve.

And he realized: All the great self-clanting and fire-making I've been comparing her to was before the closing of the Great Gates. I have memories from four-teen centuries ago. That's how long I was in the tree.

Luvix reached into his sleeve. There was nothing there.

Wad pressed the vial of poison into Bexoi's hand. She did not look to see what it was. Perhaps she guessed. At any rate, she did not take her eyes from the viewport.

Luvix realized that he had to kill her anyway—Wad could see the fearful realization come to his face. Poison could have been concealed and denied. But a bloody wound or a broken neck could not be covered up. It would be recognized as murder. It would be investigated. If Luvix succeeded in hiding his role in her death—not a perfect certainty, and he would probably have to kill his lover Sleethair to be safe—then the murder of the younger sister of the Jarl of Gray would be blamed on Iceway and the war would start up again. And if Luvix were caught, it would probably trigger an attempt by Frostinch to depose his father and take his place as Jarl of Gray. Either way, chaos and misery, blood and death.

Luvix took out, not the knife he openly carried, but a dagger concealed in his boot.

"Please," said the clant of Bexoi. The voice was husky, half-whispered, but completely believable. Wad was giddy with admiration for her. If gatemages could create a clant, he thought, I'd want mine to be as good as this.

"I'm sorry, Lady Bexoi," he whispered in reply. Then he gripped the top of her head and pushed the needle-like blade into her eye, then churned it around the fulcrum of the hole in the bone through which the optic nerve would pass, if it had been a living woman.

The clant must be so solid that it felt real to Luvix's fingers; and solid inside, so the blade would encounter just the right kind of interference and resistance from bone and brain and the back of the skull. If Wad had not loved the Queen before, he would love her now for the sheer magnificence and perfection of her creation.

When Luvix drew out the blade, a spurt of blood followed it, and brain and eye matter seemed to cling to it. It was so real that Wad reached out and touched the woman beside him, to be sure that *she* was the real one, and was not disappearing as the woman in the bed was killed.

Luvix wiped the blade on the bedsheet, and a stain appeared. Then he reinserted the dagger into his boot, walked to the door, unlocked it, and left, closing it behind him. Wad noticed that as soon as his back was turned, the illusion of a stain on the bedsheet disappeared. There had been no blood or brains on the dagger, and therefore none on the sheet, and now that

Luvix was not watching, Bexoi no longer needed to maintain it.

No doubt he is going to a place where Sleethair can see him. Then she will return here and discover the body, screaming and bringing everyone to see.

"We have a few moments," said Wad quietly. "Will they find the bed empty? Or you alive in it?"

The Queen withdrew her face from the viewport and turned to look at him. "I have shown you what no other has seen," she said.

"And I, you," said Wad.

"You are a Gatefather," she said.

"And you are a Lightrider," he said.

"I have concealed it from everyone, all my life. No one knows in all the world but you."

"Hull knows something of what I am," said Wad.

"And you let her live?"

"She would not betray me."

"Will *you* betray *me*?" she asked him pointedly.

"If you doubt me," he said, "give me back that vial of poison and I will drink it now."

A smile came to her lips. "On my doubt alone, you'd choose to die?"

"Not until I saw you safely through the gate and back in your room," said Wad. "I would not want you to languish here, if I'm not as strong as I think, and the gate dies with me."

"I will have to talk more with you," she said. "I'm not sure what to do with a confidant—I've never had one before."

"Talk to him," said Wad, "and he will talk to you."

"Oh, my," she said. "The two most silent people in the castle, and here we are chattering like biddies in the henyard."

"What will they find?" asked Wad again. "A dead clant? Or a living queen?"

"I think the living queen," said Bexoi. "Let Luvix wonder what happened to his lovely murder. Let him try to guess. Let him, in fact, try again—now that I know a place where I can go. The gate will be there?"

"Always open to you. And I'll leave your viewport here as well, so you can control the clant."

"I don't really need that," she said.

"You can see through the clant's eyes?"

"I'm very good at it."

Wad looked back through the viewport. The body of the clant was still intact, still naked and beautiful, still empty-eyed and stained with the blood that had spilled out onto the cheek. "What a perfect creation," he said. "And how clever of you to pretend that your weak affinity for birds was all you had."

He felt her brush past him as she moved back toward the gate. "How do I find it from this side?" she asked.

"I left it shimmering," said Wad. "Since no one can see it from this side except someone who has already passed through it."

She doused her light. Sure enough, the shimmer was there, a single spot in the stone. She touched it with her finger, pushed through it. She turned her face to smile at him just before she disappeared.

He stayed to watch. The clant simply vanished. Then Bexoi turned her back to him as she let the robe fall from her.

Naked, she turned back around, shaking her head. No doubt she realized that Wad had already seen her naked self-clant, and that if he chose to observe her nudity, he could choose vantage points anywhere in her chamber. She could never hide from him, so there was no reason for her to try.

And now that he knew he loved her, he deliberately chose not to look at her naked body. Instead he watched the door.

It opened. Sleethair came back in, accompanied by a lone soldier in the uniform of Gray—no doubt the same conspirator who had stood watch at the door. Luvix would not have involved more than these two, besides himself.

They looked at the bed. At Bexoi sitting there, exactly where Luvix had said he left the murdered clant. Both her eyes were open and undamaged.

"I thought you had gone for the night," said Bexoi. "And what is he doing inside the door without my invitation? Put yourself under arrest, man. You will be sent back to Gray as soon as I tell my husband of this breach of propriety. Consider yourself lucky that I do not have you flogged."

The soldier ducked out at once.

"I'm— I'm sorry to bother— bother you," said Sleethair.

"Well, now that you're here, stay the night," said Bexoi. "I had a strange dream and it has left me wakeful and restless. Here, beside me—spend the night with me."

"But your majesty, I . . ."

Wad waited to see what excuse she would come up with, for of course she was desperate to get to Luvix and tell him that he had not killed the queen after all. Or to accuse him of lying to her. Or simply to get out of Nassassa.

Sleethair got into the bed beside the queen.

"Usually you smell like Luvix," Bexoi said coldly. "But tonight you smell like vomit. Are you ill?"

"Yes," said Sleethair—almost eagerly. Wad knew she was thinking: This is my excuse to get out of the room!

"Well, I'm glad you emptied out whatever was bothering you. If you need to puke again, you can do it over that side of the bed onto the floor and then clean it up yourself in the morning. I will not be left alone tonight."

And that was that. Wad stifled his laughter. Let Luvix spend a miserable night wondering what has gone wrong, why there was no outcry when Sleethair "discovered" the body. Let Sleethair spend a sleepless night beside the woman she conspired to murder. With any luck, Luvix will go ahead and kill the hapless soldier without finding out that Bexoi is alive—and then Sleethair will wonder if he would have killed her, too, as soon as her usefulness was over.

I saved her life, thought Wad, by taking the poison and then coming here to give her warning. But she might well have saved her own life without any help from me, even if it meant causing the traitor to burst into flame as soon as he drew the knife, or make the poison burn up and evaporate completely when he opened the vial.

Bexoi still had the vial, come to think of it.

Wad gated back to the kitchen then, and took his place among the nest of sleeping boys behind the stoves.

The next morning the castle was abuzz with the tragic news that Sleethair, Queen Bexoi's chief lady-in-waiting, had died in the night. Those who had seen her vomiting attested that she was quite ill, but that they had thought her much recovered. Meanwhile, Luvix was seen looking haggard and haunted, and when he departed that afternoon to return to Gray, everyone chalked it up to his grief for his mistress's death—for *that* secret had not been well kept at all.

Wad came to the queen three nights later, after things had quieted down. As soon as her new lady-in-waiting closed the door, Wad came down the wall from the ceiling. Again, he said nothing.

Bexoi beckoned to him, and he came. She was almost exactly his height, for she was a tallish woman, and Wad was still boyish, like a gangling adolescent not yet come to his full manly size. She put her hands on both sides of his face and kissed him firmly yet sweetly. It was not the kiss of a queen to her royal subject, or even the kiss of a rescued woman for the hero who saved her. It was the kiss of a lover, and Wad recognized it as such, though he knew not how.

"I accepted my brother's plan for me," she whispered in Wad's ear, "because Prayard is one of the mightiest mages alive, and I wanted his children. But he refuses to give me any. You are a greater mage than he is, my little savior; your seed has more value to me. I want it. I want your baby."

"The King will know it isn't his," whispered Wad.

"I will tell him I scooped his seed inside myself after he left. I've tried it, and it doesn't work, but he'll at least pretend to believe it. He'll hardly dare accuse me of adultery, because that would mean confessing that he hasn't given me his seed, which violates the treaty."

Wad nodded. Her thinking had been more subtle than his own.

She let fall her robe and began undressing him.

"I'm older than you think," said Wad.

"Good. I was afraid you were too boyish to do the job," she whispered.

"I'm older than anyone else alive," said Wad. "I don't know if my seed is still alive."

"If it isn't, then we'll at least take pleasure in the experiment," said Bexoi. "You are the first person in my life that I have trusted. We will make babies together, and we will talk about everything, and no one will suspect for a moment that the wall-climbing Squirrel, the kitchen boy called Wad of Dough, is the father of Queen Bexoi's magnificent, kingdom-inheriting son."

"Or sons," said Wad.

"And daughters," said Bexoi. "But if Prayard stops visiting me, then we'll have to stop too, alas."

"Eluik and Enopp will try to kill any child we have," said Wad. "If Anonoei doesn't try it herself."

She laughed lightly and softly. "The moment I'm pregnant with this baby," she whispered, "I will have her sent away, and the boys too, for dear Prayard won't be able to contradict me. My child will be heir, and the people will rejoice, and if Anonoei remained here they would be outraged. The moment I have a child, her two boys become bastards and potential rebels. No, they won't be close enough to our babies to lay a hand on them."

"You've thought of everything," whispered Wad, who by now was in the bed beside her, discovering that his hands knew exactly what to do with a naked woman, even though he had no clear memory of ever being with a woman before.

"I always knew you watched me," said Bexoi. "Now I'm glad I never told the king to have you killed."

"It's always an option, if you get tired of me," Wad
pointed out.

"Father me a baby, and I'll never get tired of you,"
She kissed him into silence.

13

Veevee

అ

At fifteen, Danny was getting more and more frustrated with the solitude of his life with the Silvermans. It was the same problem he had had at the Family compound when he was younger. He could get a good education by reading whatever he could find on the internet and studying books from the library, so it's not that he was behind his grade level in school. In fact, he was doing college-level work in most subjects, and when Marion and Leslie periodically quizzed him about what he was learning, they always ended up nodding and saying, Carry on. What Danny missed was associating with people his age. With friends.

Now that some time had passed, he could look back on his association with Eric and realize that the reason he let Eric boss him around was that even though Eric didn't seem to particularly like him, or see him as anything but someone to use, he was the closest thing Danny had ever had to a friend. And now, though he didn't have to deal with cousins who despised him, he still felt like the only prisoner in a minimum-security facility.

He still ran, the way he had run when he lived in the Family compound. Now, though, it wasn't a secret, he wasn't escaping—he had permission. He was running openly on the roads around Yellow Springs. He would run up and down Xenia Avenue, or cut through the fields and run on East Enon Road—or County Road 18A, depending on where you were. That was the worst and best place to run, because it passed Yellow Springs High School.

Sometimes, when he ran in the daytime during the school year, he would turn left on the Dayton–Yellow Springs Road, which ran along the north side of the high school. He would see high school kids running on the track—not the track team, usually, but just kids in P.E. class, and he would wonder what it might feel like to have a dozen or two dozen kids running along the same road with him. At such times he would pretend that there was someone with him who would say, "Was that as fast as you can go, slowpoke?" or "I saw the way you jumped over that big puddle, good job." And sometimes he would deliberately splash in puddles as if he were trying to soak an imaginary friend—a prank (of course a prank, wasn't he a gatemage?). Or he'd set himself a goal as if a friend had challenged him.

But there was no friend.

He knew better than to wish for a competition, however, because he knew that if he ever started to care who *won*, then he would always win. While he hadn't made the great breakthroughs as a gatemage that he had hoped for, he had learned to refine and control the techniques he already knew. So he could make a series of tiny gates, by reflex rather than by concentration, that would hurry him along in fine increments, so that to any observer he would seem to be faster than the other runners, but no magic would be visible. If he cared about winning, it would become tempting, if the race was close, to give himself just a little bit of a magical boost. And that would be cheating. What honor would there be in seeming to defeat someone who was actually faster than he was? Yet how could he bear to be bested? So he would never race. If he encountered another runner out on the street, the moment they seemed to be competing with him he would stop and contemplate the scenery for a while, until they were far enough away that competition was impossible.

Just because he *had* the power of a gatemage, or at least some of it, Danny didn't think it was necessarily right for him to use it. Gating Eric out of Rico's office was necessary, he did not regret that, for it healed Eric and it kept him from getting beaten to death. Using his gatemagery to immobilize Rico was also the right thing to do, he was sure, because it was the only power he had to stop the man from doing more of his murders. But using gates to defeat a high school athlete? To break into people's homes or spy on them?

He was not ashamed of all the spying he had done as a kid, because he hadn't known he was a gatemage then, and he was trying to survive in a compound full of mages who had no qualms about using *their* powers against him or anybody else. He had to know whatever he could learn. But now? He never created a gate that would let him see into Marion's and Leslie's room or spy on them when they were talking with each other or with interesting strangers. They would tell him what they wanted to tell him. He was not going to spy on them.

But if they asked him to spy on someone else, he would do it in a second, because he would trust their judgment that it was useful and necessary to do so. It hadn't come up, but in his lonely hours he had played through many a scenario in which they really needed one of his skills to save them from some dire circumstance, and he came through for them.

Such were the fantasies that filled his mind as he ran, as he did his chores. He would see the girls emerging from school buses or getting out of their cars in the morning as he ran past Yellow Springs High, and wonder what it would be like to talk with one of them. "You left your homework on your desk at home? Let me get it for you—here it is."

But then he had darker thoughts, ones he was ashamed of. If he wanted a career as a peeping tom, he could do it from his own bedroom and no one would ever know. He couldn't let himself indulge such fantasies, let alone act them out. Drowthers shouldn't sacrifice their privacy just because he happened to have a little power that gave him access to anything, anywhere. And he knew that if he really cared for a girl, he could never do such a thing to her; and if he didn't really care for her, then—as he learned with Lana—he didn't want to think that kind of thought about her.

So many moral dilemmas he wrestled with—wishing that they might actually come up in the real world. Wouldn't it be nice to actually know a girl who wasn't his cousin? But it would be so hard to be a real friend to someone his own age without letting them know what he was and what he could do. And that would be the end of the friendship, he was sure. Not because they would reject him, but because he would stop being Danny Silverman—he was using their last name now—and instead be That Kid Who Can Jump Through Gates In Space.

Danny was lost in thought, as usual, when he came loping down Xenia Avenue and saw a middle-aged woman materialize in the driveway in front of his house. In fact, she appeared in exactly the spot where *he* had first appeared the night he came to the Silvermans for the first time.

She had come through a gate. More to the point, she had come through *his* gate.

He hadn't been touching her or leading her. She had to have found it on her own. Which meant she was a gatemage herself.

Danny glanced around to make sure no one was watching him, and gated to a spot right behind her. He was so flustered that he failed to allow for the fact that he was still running, so he barreled right into her and knocked her down in the driveway.

"Sorry," he said, getting up. "You seemed to come out of nowhere."

"So did you," she said.

"I was just running along Xenia and there you were."

She sat up and looked back the way he indicated. "You're the gatemage," she said. "You just made a gate from there to here."

So she *was* a Westilian. And therefore dangerous. "And I'm about to make a gate and stuff you through it," said Danny, "unless you tell me who you are and why you came through my gate."

"If you want a gate to be private," she said, "then hide it or close it."

Danny said nothing.

She looked puzzled. Then her face brightened. "You don't know how, is that it? You can make them, but you can't hide them or close them?"

His dread was giving way to curiosity. She obviously knew more about gatemagery than Stone or the Silvermans. "I didn't know you *could* hide a gate from a Finder."

"You can if you're powerful enough. But I'm more than a Finder. I think I'm a Keyfriend! Of course, I didn't *know* that until I saw one of your gates for the first time in Washington DC. You have no idea how important that was for me."

So maybe she didn't know as much as he had hoped. "What are you doing here?"

"Sitting on the gravel of the driveway with my nylons torn to ribbons and my palms and knees skinned and bleeding."

"Sorry," said Danny.

"No you're not," said the woman. "You were testing to see how much I knew about you and whether I meant to kill you."

"Still wondering," said Danny.

She beamed. "Here's what I know. I jumped through a half-dozen of your gates in the DC area, as soon as I saw the first one and realized what it was. You can imagine, it's frustrating being a gatemage at a low enough level that I can't actually make gates myself— because with all the Pathbrothers and Gatefathers murdered whenever they're found, and all the old gates gone, when would I ever even *see* a gate? I had no idea what a gate would even look like, despite all my research over the past thirty years. And there I am in a taxi, riding along Wisconsin Avenue, and there's this shimmering off to the right. It's not something I'm seeing, just a heightened awareness of a certain place. Only the place I'm sensing is *inside* a church! I'm sensing it through the walls! Naturally, I stopped the cab. Paid him and then hurried over and knew the horrible frustration that even though I could get inside the church, I could not get inside the room where the shimmering was!"

"I take it you eventually did?"

"In a backward way," she answered. "I found that when I stood in a certain position, I could tell there were two gates. One was the exit point of a gate that took someone into the church, and the other was the entrance point of a gate leading away. I couldn't very well ask a priest to let me into his office, because then he'd see me use the gate—if it was actually a gate and if I was actually a Keyfriend or Lockfriend."

"I see the problem," said Danny.

"Of course, he would probably interpret it as some kind of heavenly visitation. Those Semitics are so eager to believe that their gods are still talking to them— fourteen centuries after the gates were closed!"

"Semitics? I thought that meant Jews and Arabs."

"The people who follow the Semitic gods. Jews, Christians, Muslims. The non-Westilians."

In his entire life, Danny had never heard that there were any gate-traveling gods besides the Westilians. "I always thought their God was . . ." But he couldn't think of exactly what he had thought their God was, because he couldn't remember ever particularly thinking about it at all.

"Really God?" she prompted, amused.

"A myth. Like Santa Claus."

"You mean . . . like Zeus? And Thor? And Shiva? And Hermes? And Pan?"

"I guess I thought that we were the only real ones," said Danny, and then he laughed at his own naiveté.

"That's what all the gods think," she said, nodding. "Anyway, I'm outside the church on Wisconsin, and now I realize that I can tell where the one gate came from and the other gate led! It took a lot of walking to get to a starting place that didn't require me to break into somebody's house—all the gates. You are a naughty burglar boy, aren't you!"

Danny was about to snap at her, but she held up a hand. "Do you think *I'd* stay out of people's houses, if I could make gates?"

He wanted to protest that it was Eric's idea, but she was going on with her story.

"I didn't mind wearing out a pair of shoes—it was worth it. Because until that day I had no idea whether I was really a gatemage or not! And now I know that I'm a pretty good one! I can open all your gates and I know where they lead before I step through them, and I can even see glimpses of what's going on where they come out. And then it turns out I can actually *go* through them! Only one way—the direction you went in—but I'm a gatemage, dammit!"

"So you aren't here to kill me," said Danny.

"Kill you! I want to worship you!"

"Please don't," said Danny.

"I want to follow you everywhere."

"It seems like you already have."

"You just *made* that gate, didn't you? You saw me standing here and you just stopped and made the gate and came through it."

"I didn't *stop* and make the gate, I just made it and then realized I was running too fast and couldn't stop, which is why I knocked you down, and I'm sorry."

"All right then, make it up to me."

"How?" said Danny.

"Make a gate—just a little one—so I can go through it and get that amazing rejuvenation! It will heal me, won't it? My research suggests that gatemages weren't *also* healers, it's just that going through a gate heals whatever's wrong with your body at the moment. Certainly I feel *wonderful* after gating around after you all day!"

Danny didn't make the gate. If she was actually an assassin—something he could not rule out merely because she said she wasn't—he wanted her to have every disadvantage he could arrange. "Doesn't stop you from getting older."

"I've always wondered. Does going through a gate regenerate lost body parts? I mean, if I lost an ear, then went through a gate, would the ear grow back?"

"I have no idea," said Danny. "But I think not, because a man once lost his thumb when he was halfway through a gate, and when his arm went back through the gate, the thumb was still missing. Though come to think that may not prove anything because he was dead before his hand came back through."

"Well, we need to conduct experiments then, don't we! We need to find out how this thing works!"

Danny didn't like the way she was assuming they were partners now. "I don't think so."

"Oh, we definitely need to know the exact rules of gating. How can we control the process if we haven't codified the consequences of various gatemaking actions?"

"The part I'm disagreeing with is the words 'we' and 'us,'" said Danny. "I don't even know who your half of 'we' *is.*"

She blinked. "Oh my. I haven't introduced myself." She thrust out her hand. "I'm Victoria Von Roth, but you *have* to call me Veevee." Then, in mid-handshake, she threw her other arm around him and gave him a huge hug. "I love you, strange gatemaking boy! You are the most important person in the world to me!"

"I hope you won't take this wrong, Veevee," said Danny—and it felt weird to call an adult by a nickname without a title in front—"but I don't love you. In fact, you terrify me."

"That's just silly, I couldn't hurt a fly."

"You could tell certain people where I am," said Danny, "and *they* would certainly kill me."

"But *anybody* can find where you are. Just follow your gates! I admit there were a few interesting side-trips—why in the world did you go to that office in that high school . . . Parry McCluer?"

"You're the only living soul I've ever met who can follow my gates." Then he added, mostly to himself, "Unless the Greek girl can."

"There's a Greek gatemage?"

"Probably a Finder. Maybe someone more like you. I don't know."

"Won't you tell me your name, O handsome young Gatefather?"

"We're not sure I'm a Gatefather. Maybe I'm a Pathbrother—they can make gates, too."

"Name! Name! What do I call you? Sweaty Careless Running Boy?"

"So then you go back through the gates until you find the people who are searching for me in order to kill me, and because you know my name you'll confirm to *them* that you know me, and so they'll make you take them to me."

"I would never do that!"

"And I would be sure of this because . . . ?"

"Because I can't go through your gates backward. So I can't track back to where you came from."

"Says you," said Danny.

"My, but you're careful," said Veevee.

"That's why I'm still alive," said Danny.

She patted his arm. "No, you're still alive because of dumb luck. You are *so* careless, despite trying to be careful. You've already told me, first, that you're from one of the Great Houses; second, you aren't one of the Greeks; third, you're afraid of someone killing you. You speak English with an American accent. So you're a North, and if I wanted to sell you out I could let them know where you are without even knowing your name."

Now Danny saw the craftiness and amusement in her eyes.

"We gatemages," she said, "we're not stupid and we know how to pretend to be dumber than we are. Am I right?"

"Sadly, yes," said Danny. "I'm Danny Silverman."

"You're actually using the Silverman name? Do you want *them* killed, too?"

"Why, are you planning on killing me after all?" And then, realizing that her answer might be delivered with a bullet or poison or a knife, he gated three steps back and to the left.

"Relax," said Veevee. "I was just pointing out that if you use their name, you put them at greater risk of discovery."

"Not as great as if I called myself Danny North."

"Danny, I have to say it again: I've never been so

happy to find out that another person existed since my mother first put her titty in my mouth."

That was such an unpleasant, disrespectful way to speak about one's own mother that Danny wanted to end the conversation. Why was he still talking to her anyway? He should have gated into the house as soon as she appeared, warned the Silvermans, and let them deal with her.

Part of that program was still available. "Maybe we better go inside and have you meet the Silvermans."

For the first time, her enthusiasm failed her completely. "Oh, the Silvermans already know me, and I them."

"And you don't like them?" If she didn't like the Silvermans, that was a huge black mark against her.

"Like them? I almost married Marion. I would have, if that *cow* hadn't come between us!"

"These are my foster parents you're talking about," said Danny coldly.

"Oh, keep your shirt on, Danny," she said. "Leslie *is* a cow. That's her heartbeast. Lighten up."

"That's not how you meant it."

"You don't *know* that," she said, with a coy look.

"Don't call Leslie a cow ever again." Danny turned his back on her and walked toward the house.

"Aren't you going to invite me in?" asked Veevee.

Danny did not answer her at all. Let her come to the porch and knock on the door herself, if she wants in. If Leslie and Marion already know her, they probably already hate her. Let the three of them work it out.

"My knees and palms hurt!" Veevee called from behind him. "Make me a little gate!"

Danny made a gate directly in front of her. Then he turned and beckoned to her like a traffic cop—one hand pointing to her, the other beckoning for her to move forward.

It wasn't necessary—she saw the gate. She smiled and stepped into it—and found herself across Xenia Avenue, facing away from the house. She spun around, confused at first, then furious when she saw Danny, but Danny just turned and continued into the house. Supposedly she could see where his gates led, and gatemages were known to be pranksters. Why hadn't she looked before she stepped?

He stepped into the house and called out, "We have a visitor!"

"Don't shout in the house!" shouted Leslie from upstairs.

"A gatemage followed me home," called Danny, and then, perhaps a little louder: "Victoria Von Roth."

Leslie practically flew to the top of the stairs and then seemed to ski down them, she moved so quickly. "That miserable bitch really *is* a gatemage? And she's *here*? Oh, of course she's here. Wherever she's not wanted."

Leslie seemed more than annoyed—flustered, really, and vaguely embarrassed. It suddenly seemed likely that at least part of Veevee's story was true—they had been rivals for Marion's affections.

"Relax," said Danny. "Marion chose *you,* didn't he?"

"What did she tell you? That the only reason he married me instead of her was because everybody thought *she* was drekka, and I was a real mage, even if I was only a Cowsister?"

"I don't think she's here to try to persuade Marion

he made the wrong choice," said Danny. "I think she's just excited to finally have proof she's a Keyfriend."

"Oh, a Keyfriend no less! Naturally she'd claim to be the very highest kind of gatemage that can't actually make gates."

"I think it's true. She found my gates and went through them without my help or even my knowledge."

"That's bad news. You should have felt her using them."

"You never told me that. I can sense when people use gates I made?"

"Obviously not," said Leslie. "Go find Marion and tell him he'd better get in here."

"No," said Danny. "I think I need to be here when Veevee gets to the door."

"What do you think I'm going to do, moo at her?"

"I think you and Marion should be together when you see her for the first time in all these years."

"Oh, suddenly little Danny North is a peacemaker. I don't remember what kind of magery that is!"

"It's the I-don't-want-any-bloodshed kind," said Danny.

"Gate to the barn and drag him back here, then," said Leslie.

"You said not to gate around the farm—"

"This is an emergency, you boneheaded bratling." She was peering through a slight gap in the curtains. "Oh, she looks just the way I expected. Always tarting herself up like she was a senator's wife. I'd say 'duchess' except she forgot her coronet."

So the bitchiness ran both ways. It was easy enough to understand why. They both believed—Veevee with spite, Leslie with dread—that Marion had only chosen Leslie because their children were likelier to be mages.

Danny gated out to the barn, where Marion was inscribing a headstone. Now that he was retired from geology, he did stonework just because he loved to work with rock. He charged more than the local stonecutters so that they wouldn't think he was trying to put them out of business, though it took him fifteen minutes to do an intricate carving that they would spend three days to do. And as a Cobblefriend, he could help the stone find a smooth, sealed finish that would not erode for centuries. He also had a bit of a flair so that even with headstones, there was a sense of dash about them. Some people thought it was undignified and in bad taste; they had plenty of other stonecutters to choose from. And there were always people who thought Marion's stones expressed the character of the loved one they had lost.

This one had the silhouette of a mountain at the top of the stone, with the figure of a mountain climber very small against both the front and back surfaces. It would be the gravemarker for a young husband and father who had died on a mountain while trying to save a fellow climber who had fallen and broken a leg. The young man's parents were outraged that his widow was putting a representation of the thing that killed him on the headstone; but the widow was the customer, and *she* said that he was never happier than when he was climbing. "He had a love for the stone itself. He said he sometimes felt as if, when he climbed, his fingers caressed the rock and the rock caressed him back. He died as a hero on the mountain, and that's what I want our children to see when they visit his grave."

Marion had told this story over supper just last

night, and then added, "I have no doubt the young man had an affinity for stone."

"So he was Westilian?"

"I doubt it."

"You know I don't believe all that nonsense of Westilians originating here on Earth," said Leslie.

"Believe what you want, my dear," said Marion, "but Westilians and Mittlegardians interbreed quite readily, and there's no reason to think there isn't latent magery in the population of Earth."

"I think that the male Westilian habit of seducing drowthers is a sufficient explanation of affinities cropping up in general population from time to time. There's hardly a soul on Earth who doesn't have *some* Westilian blood by now."

So here was Marion, carving the headstone for a fellow stonemage, or so he supposed. It was part of the camaraderie of the mages, stone for stone, fire for fire, heartbeast for heartbeast. They felt a kinship, those who shared an affinity, regardless of Family barriers.

And Veevee, thought Danny, is the only person in the world, except perhaps the Greek girl, with whom I might find such kinship. It was clear that Marion had shaped the headstone with great respect—he had taken hours giving intricate detail to the stone. Danny, on the other hand, had knocked her down in the driveway, injuring her, and even when he healed her, he had sent her across the street.

"Marion," said Danny.

Marion looked up from his work. "Did you *gate* in here?"

"Leslie asked me to. Victoria Von Roth is here."

"Here!" Marion looked annoyed. "What for?"

"She found my gates and followed me through them. She's a Keyfriend."

Marion absorbed the information with a blink.

"I think Leslie needs some reassurance. Veevee's almost at the door by now. May I gate you back so you can face her together?"

"Don't imagine that you know *anything* about what passed between me and Veevee and me and Leslie all those years ago," said Marion.

"I only know what's likely to pass between Leslie and Veevee in about fifteen seconds," said Danny.

Marion reached out a hand. Danny helped him to his feet and then gated him into the parlor. Veevee was knocking and Leslie was about to open the door.

"Let Danny open it," said Marion. He strode to his wife, drew her back into the parlor, and stood there with his arm around her waist. This must be how Christians stood when they faced the lions in the Roman arena, thought Danny.

He opened the door. "Veevee!" he said with exaggerated warmth. "How lovely of you to drop by!"

"You're something of a devil, Danny," she said with mild reproach, "but I still adore you. Or at least I adore your gates." She turned at once to the Silvermans and inclined her head. "What a pleasant surprise," said Veevee, "that this young man's gates should lead me to your door. I can't imagine a better place for him to seek shelter and training than in this house."

Danny was almost disappointed that Veevee was behaving so graciously. But it did amuse him that Veevee's tone made it impossible for Leslie to show any of the feelings that he knew were seething just under the surface. Marion held out his hand and Veevee shook it firmly. "I'm glad to see that both of you look so well," she said.

Leslie had no choice but to offer her hand as well, and Veevee smiled at her. Warmly, to all appearances, because Leslie made some effort to shape her face into a genuine smile.

"And how are all the happy little cows?" asked Veevee, her warmth undiminished.

Danny almost whooped aloud with laughter—it was hard to remain silent. Veevee really *was* a bitch, but she certainly had style.

Leslie glared. "The herd is quite contented, thank you. There's always room in the barn for more, if you need a place to stay."

No, Leslie, please, Danny said silently. Don't try to match wits with Veevee. You sound petulant where she is cool.

"I have no plans," said Veevee, "so I may take you up on that, depending on the freshness of the hay." She turned to Marion. "Imagine this, Marion! I *am* a gate-mage after all. Not so advanced as your dear wife, of course. But I think I may be singularly useful in the training of your young ward. Gatemagery has been my study for thirty years, as part of my—what was the term, Leslie, dear?—my 'elaborate sham,' wasn't it? And since it turns out, to everyone's surprise, not least my own, that I really *am* a gatemage, perhaps I might have some information that Danny might find useful."

She turned to Danny. "You wouldn't mind if I told you some of what I've learned?"

"I hope you'll tell me all of it," said Danny. "But only if you refrain from discussing cows while on this property."

"Fortunately, the closest I ever come to dairy nowadays is low-fat yogurt and cottage cheese," said Veevee. "And I never eat beef—after knowing Leslie for so long, it would be like dining on a friend."

"We eat beef whenever we like," said Leslie. "Cattle are a prey animal and expect some of their number to die from time to time. Like you, we do our slaughtering with tenderness."

"I have an excellent idea," said Marion. "If Danny wishes to learn from you, he can make a gate from here to wherever you live. He can go to you for a few hours a day, and then return here for meals. Unless you've learned to cook in the intervening years."

And there it was. Marion had declared himself. He was completely on Leslie's side, and Veevee was not welcome here. Danny was rather relieved. He could learn from Veevee, but he wouldn't have to deal with all this history.

14

Public Gate

❦

Veevee wouldn't even let Danny gate her back to her car in DC. "I'll call the rental company and tell them where to pick it up. I'll say I had a family emergency—and I did, didn't I!" Instead, he gated her home to Naples, Florida, where she lived in a penthouse condominium overlooking the Gulf of Mexico. As soon as they arrived, she went to the kitchen to take inventory of the refrigerator and call out for a grocery delivery.

"This is going to be so fun," said Veevee.

Danny wasn't sure. Her enthusiasm still bothered him. So far, all he really knew was that she could travel through his gates. But what did that amount to? He already knew how to create gates. He didn't need her to confirm that it worked.

And yet he *was* excited. He wasn't the only gate-mage in the world, and Veevee had spent her life studying a magery she only hoped she had.

She went into the bedroom and came out in a modest scarlet one-piece swimsuit which flattered her without pretending that she was any younger than she was. "First things first," she said. "I want a gate that takes me down to a spot near the beach, and then another gate that brings me back up here."

"Is that why I'm here?" asked Danny. "To save you waiting for elevators?"

"Why, does it cost you anything?"

"Well, supposedly each gate costs me part of my outself."

"Are you running out?"

"I don't know."

"Then do it, Danny. We have to have something to work with, don't we? We can't work on the gate back to the Silvermans' cowshed every time, can we? And what if you do learn to close or take back your gates? Do you want it to be *that* one?"

She always had an argument like that. She always would. Compelling reasons for him to do *exactly* what she wanted—now. If he didn't put his foot down now, would he ever?

Probably not. But it would be worth it, if she could actually help him get control of this thing.

So they leaned over the Gulfside balcony of her condo and chose a spot mostly sheltered by palms near the condominium tower next door. She could come and go from there without being observed. So he created a gate to the spot and she gleefully went through it. When she appeared down in the sand, she waved merrily to him and then held out her arms like a two-year-old wanting to be picked up.

Danny decided to make it a challenge for himself. Instead of going through the gate himself and then making another to bring them both back up, he decided to try to make the second gate from right there on the balcony. After all, it's not as if he touched anything or connected to the gates when he made them. So why would it matter if the starting point was far away, and the endpoint was right next to him?

But as he started to form the gate down near Veevee, on impulse he made the beginning of it be the exact point where the first gate exited, and the endpoint the exact beginning of the original gate. Wasn't that what Leslie had asked about? What would happen if he made gates with the exact same start and end points, only going opposite directions? He'd never tried to make two gates exactly overlap before. But it wasn't hard—he could clearly see the exact points where the gate was anchored at both ends.

Down below, Veevee's hands clapped to the side of her face like a mime portraying stunned surprise. She reached out a finger to the endpoint of the gate and then she was beside him on the balcony. "You little devil, you didn't tell me you could do that!"

"Do what?" he asked.

"Oh, don't pretend with me."

"I know I made the beginning and endpoint coincide with the first gate, just in reverse," said Danny, "but wasn't that the obvious thing to do?"

"But that's all? Because to me it looked as if the gate went from being a tiny tube to being the interstate. Well, not quite, but very big, and going both ways at once. It's not as if you merely doubled it. It must be ten times bigger."

"Well ain't that cool," said Danny, impressed. Partly with himself, but mostly with the discovery about how gates worked.

"Now it's my turn," said Veevee.

"Your turn to do what?" asked Danny. "Do you think you can make a gate?"

"The more I study what you do, the better my chances, don't you think? But no, what I mean is that Keyfriends are sometimes Lockfriends, too."

"And that would mean . . . ?"

"If I can figure out how to close and lock one of your gates, maybe *you* can see what *I'm* doing and learn the skill from me!"

"Since you're the only one who can use my gates," said Danny, "and any locking I did wouldn't keep out a Keyfriend, what's the point?"

"To learn! Isn't it fun just to *learn*? Come on, you aren't one of those kids who hates school, are you?"

Danny shrugged. "It's worth it for you to know how to close them."

"Especially that one you just made. Because I think you've hit on how to make a gate public."

"And that's a bad thing?"

"A public gate is one that anyone can use—a Finder, of course, but also any drowther who happens to run into it."

"Oh," said Danny. "So you mean a drowther could walk into that spot and just pop through the gate and be on your balcony."

"Honestly, that might be a pretty good way to get a date," said Veevee.

"Or a burglar," said Danny.

"Oh, I don't need a burglar." Then Veevee laughed. "Oh, have some fun with this!"

"So we need to lock the gate—if it's public—so that people won't accidentally use it."

"Imagine if I had somebody over for lunch and

they walked out on the balcony and then suddenly—
poof! They think they somehow fell off this tower
and lived!"

"Okay," said Danny. "Close the gate. Lock it. Whatever you do."

"If I can do it. Opening your gates was easy
enough—I came, I saw, I poked it with my finger."

"Kind of like what you did to Marion and Leslie,"
said Danny, for no better reason than he thought of it.

Veevee whooped with laughter. "That's exactly what
I did! Oh, Danny, you have such a *dirty* mind for a
child."

Dirty? Danny had no idea what she was talking
about.

"All right, let me fiddle around for a little while
trying to close the gate, and you do it too."

"Do what?"

"Close it!"

"Do you think I haven't tried? I'm like a little kid
trying to wish really hard. I make my hands into fists,
I close my mouth and squinch my eyes shut and then
I puff out my cheeks and think, 'I wish I wish I wish.' "

Veevee didn't laugh this time. "I know," she said.
"That's what I spent more of my life doing. Couldn't
raise a clant, couldn't find my outself. But I made
a lot of wisecracks and played tricks on people and
learned foreign languages easily, so I thought, I must
be a gatemage! Then I did just what you described, or
the mental equivalent. Wished really hard that I could
make a gate."

"So you know that isn't the most likely way to succeed," said Danny.

"We give up, then? And hope nobody ever walks
into the gate on my balcony?"

"I'll move this end of it, if you want," said Danny.

"See, that's the strange thing. Nobody ever talks about moving gates. They just talk about closing them or gathering them in." Then she started to laugh. "Yes, Danny. Move the gate. By all means. Move it straight into the middle of your own body."

Danny closed his eyes and thought for a moment. "Not to put a damper on your idea or anything, but that would only send me through the gate. That's how I force other people through, anyway—I move the gate to them. Almost like I use one end of it to eat them."

"Now, that's an interesting thought. Which end do you bring to them?"

"The mouth end, of course. The entrance."

"What if you moved the exit to them?"

"I don't know," said Danny. "Want me to try it on *you*?"

Apparently she didn't. "What if you moved the exit right to the entrance?"

"Then I wouldn't be closing the gate, I'd be making it useless," said Danny.

"Well, that would be something, anyway, wouldn't it?"

"Now that I think about it, there's all kinds of weird things I could do," said Danny. "What if somebody was falling off a cliff, and I make a gate under him and the exit is over him. So he falls into the lower gate, comes out of the upper one, and falls down and keeps going back up, like a yo-yo!"

She almost fell on the floor laughing about that one.

"Of course it would have to be a public gate," said Danny. "If that's what we've actually got here. Something that anyone could fall into, and not just a Finder."

"Think that would make the news?" said Veevee. "'Man jumps off building in suicide attempt, keeps changing mind.'"

Danny laughed, too. She had the same sense of humor he had. Or close to it, anyway.

"Of course, you'd probably just make a gate with the exit back up on top of the building or whatever, and then move the mouth of it over him to catch him and drag him up," said Veevee. "That's what a good person would do, anyway."

Danny caught something she said, though he had used the term himself only moments before. When she said it, though, it triggered a chain of thought in his mind. "The *mouth* of the gate," he said.

"Just a figure of speech," said Veevee.

"Not in English, it's not," said Danny. "People don't talk about gates having mouths. I mean, to them a gate is just a gate—you step through it and you're in the same place, plus a step. There's no mouth, there's no entrance and exit. So why did you call it a mouth?"

"Well, the kind of gate *you* make isn't really a gate, like in a picket fence. In some ways it's like a tunnel. Tunnels have mouths."

"And maybe that's all there is to it," said Danny. "But when you said it just then, it made me think of something I read. Something very old."

"You're right," she said. "It *is* called a mouth in some of the legends and histories I've found. That's what gates are called in several of the Persian inscriptions, and there's one tantalizing Hittite passage—I've been reading so many of them for so many years—you'd be surprised how much there is about gates in the ancient writings, if you know how to read them. Which, as a gatemage, I do."

"So let me tell you a runic inscription I read in the Library of Congress."

"I've already been there," said Veevee. "Many times. Which one do you mean?"

Danny started to recite it. "'Here Tiu dashed the ships of Carthage against the rocks, because they would not pay tribute to the valkyrie.'"

"Ships of Carthage?" she said. "I've never read *this*."

"I'm not surprised," said Danny. "It was an untranslated copy embedded in a Danish book about something else."

Veevee listened closely as he repeated his English translation. Then she walked to where her laptop sat on the kitchen table, right by the napkin holder, the salt and pepper shakers, and a butter dish. She turned it on and brought up her word processor and then said, "Tell it again."

She typed as he dictated. When it was all recorded, and he affirmed that she had it exactly right, though there were a few unfamiliar words whose meaning he had guessed at, she printed out two copies and they sat there looking at them.

"I think this is practically a manual," said Veevee.

"It didn't make any sense to me, but I was still new at making gates and my mind was on other stuff," said Danny. "And at the time I hadn't figured out how to move the mouth of a gate over somebody to force them through it. But see, when you *call* it a mouth then you're eating them, right? Or your gate is, or whatever. So when it says that the 'dark gate of Bel carried off the hearts of brave men to eat at his feasting table,' we're talking about Bel moving the mouth of that dark gate over people and passing them through, right?"

"I don't know," said Veevee. "It's the thing about

hearts that makes me wonder. 'The Carthaginians had eaten the old gate,' right? So that means a gate eating a gate—do you think that's possible?"

"I don't know," said Danny. "Should I try it?"

"No, let's just sit here and theorize until we die," said Veevee.

Danny made a gate right there on the table. It was short—a foot long. He moved the mouth of it over the butter dish and it popped over to the exit, near the napkins. "There's the gate," said Danny. Then he took the mouth of the gate to the exit and moved it back and forth over it. "Nothing," said Danny.

"You were moving the mouth of the gate over its own tail, right?" said Veevee. "Only it isn't a tunnel and it isn't a snake, so you can't tie it in a knot."

Once again Danny felt a little thrill at the thought that somebody else could actually *see,* or at least sense, what he was doing. "Yes," he said.

"So a gate can't eat itself. Why not make another gate and try to use the mouth of it to eat the first gate."

So Danny tried it.

The first gate—the whole thing, both ends of it— went through the new gate and popped out the other end.

"Wow," said Danny.

"Wowee zowee," said Veevee. "You ate a gate."

"No, I *moved* a gate."

"Why not call it eating? Anybody who was using the first gate regularly wouldn't know where it was anymore. To them, that gate got eaten!"

"I'd already shrunk that first gate down to nothing, trying to get it to eat itself," said Danny. He turned toward where he had made the public gate on the terrace. Even though he couldn't actually see the terrace itself—there was a wall in the way—he could still sense the location of the gate. So could Veevee, though perhaps not as clearly, since it wasn't hers.

He created a new gate with its mouth inches from the public gate down to the beach. The exit of the new gate was right there in the kitchen with them. Then he moved the mouth of the new gate over the entrance to the public gate.

That entrance popped into the kitchen.

Meanwhile, though, Danny pushed the mouth of the new gate over the public gate's other end, too, on the beach below—and now both ends of the public gate were there in the kitchen.

Veevee laughed and slid a chair into the public gate. It reappeared a few inches away—as if it had suddenly hit a patch of oil and slid incredibly swiftly and silently across the floor.

Danny was in awe. "So a gate that was six stories high—I mean the entrances were six stories apart—I ate both ends, and now they're only a few inches apart."

"Why are they apart at all?" asked Veevee. "You passed both ends of the gate through the same mouth and out the same exit. Shouldn't they have ended up in the exact same spot?"

"I don't know the rules yet," said Danny.

"This is so *weird*," said Veevee. She shuddered and then laughed again. "It's creeping me out! I've only known about gates for a day and suddenly I'm finding out they do the coolest things!"

"But we still don't really understand that inscription," said Danny. "The bit about the jaws of Bel seizing Loki's heart, but instead Loki's heart holds the jaws, and then when he finds the gate of Bel he moves it—I'm trying to picture what he was doing."

"The heart of Loki—is it his outself?"

"How can it be, if the sun has a heart, too? Do stars have outselves?"

Having asked the question, Danny immediately tried to answer it. He closed his eyes and thought back to the book and the inscription—the actual runes and the Fistalk words he had read them as. Enough time had passed that his mental picture of it wasn't perfect. And he had to check to make sure that he hadn't blown his translation. Was it really the Fistalk word for *heart* every time?

Maybe. Danny just couldn't be sure if he was really seeing the signs for the syllables for *heart* when it referred to the sun, or something else. It certainly seemed like something else, now that he examined it. He didn't recognize it, whatever it was, though for all he knew it was a trick of memory. An eidetic memory didn't mean you really took a photograph. It was subject to all the ordinary flaws of memory—including the tendency to insert into the picture exactly what you want or expect to see.

"Maybe we're onto something and maybe we're not," said Danny. "We set out trying to close gates, and we ended up capturing them and moving both ends. Is that 'eating a gate'? The thing is, it was my own gate I 'ate,' so I already knew where both ends were. And all I did was bring them into the same room as me. I didn't *eat* them."

"Yes you did," insisted Veevee.

"Okay, maybe that's all that's meant by 'eating' a gate. But there still has to be a way to close a gate—or what would being a Lockfriend even mean?"

"But we know what the last Loki did, don't you see? He *took* all the gates in the world—just the way you took that public gate—and he ate them. Moved them. They aren't where they used to be—but that doesn't mean they aren't *somewhere*."

Danny saw it, too. "But what good would it be to find them? They're out of place. They've been moved. They don't lead whence or whither they did before." Then he grinned, because in all the world, only another gatemage would delight in using the old words as much as he did.

"Are we looking for those stolen gates?" asked Veevee. "What's our project here, to restore all the gates that Loki stole? I don't think so!"

"Loki stole gates," said Danny. "But what about this Gate Thief who tears the outselves out of gatemages? Just strips them so they can never make another gate."

Veevee read aloud from the sheet with Danny's translation of the four runic inscriptions. "The jaws of Bel seized his heart to carry it away."

"Is that the Gate Thief?" asked Danny. "The ancient god of the Carthaginians? Gatemages can break their outselves into fragments, leaving bits here and there as gates—but we *must* hold the rest of them inside us somehow. Maybe Bel can find the unspent hoard of the gatemage's outself and swallow it up in a gate. Maybe he just moves it out of the gatemage's reach, as if he had spent his whole outself on gates and then forgotten where they were."

"Do you think it might be vengeance?" asked Veevee. "Maybe this inscription—maybe we're still living in that story. Maybe Bel has taken thousands of years to get even."

"Or maybe it wasn't Loki who closed all the gates back in 632 A.D.," said Danny. "It's not as if anybody saw him do it. It's not like he left a note. What if Bel recovered from what that earlier Loki had done to him, and then came back and ate all the Westilian gates as retaliation—and then found the newer Loki and stripped him or even killed him. Maybe we've been blaming him all these years, and it wasn't his fault, he was the *victim*."

"Wouldn't that be ironic," said Veevee. "Yet it *would* make a perverse kind of sense."

"Especially if we think of spacetime as a trickster," said Danny. "Loki gets blamed for his own demise, and so the Westilians deprive themselves of the only kind of mage that could fight Bel."

"Oh, that bastard spacetime," said Veevee. "You gotta love his sense of irony."

"And ever since then, Bel—or the fiftieth-generation mage *called* Bel—watches the Westilians and eats the whole outself of any gatemage who tries to make a Great Gate."

"You think he's *still* getting vengeance thirteen hundred years later?"

"Like the Families don't hold grudges at least that long?" said Danny.

"Yes, why shouldn't Bel be as mentally unstable as those inbred Families," said Veevee.

"I'm the result of one of the most ridiculously inbred marriages ever," said Danny.

"Sorry, I really didn't mean to insult you," said Veevee.

"I'm not insulted," said Danny. "I was proving your point."

She jumped up and gave him a hug and kissed his cheek resoundingly. "If you were any smarter or funnier or cuter I'd eat you alive." Then she giggled. "Oh, this whole thing has given completely new meanings to sayings with 'eat' in them. 'Eat your heart out.' 'Eat *this*.' 'Eat me.'"

Danny joined in. "'Have your cake and eat it, too'?"

"Have your *soul* and eat it, too, you mean."

"You eat everything on your plate or you won't get dessert," said Danny.

Veevee shook her head. "I think I already did all the funny ones."

"Maybe," said Danny, a little embarrassed.

Veevee laughed and gave him a tiny light punch on the arm. "Eat like a king!"

"I could eat a horse!" said Danny triumphantly.

"You really could, couldn't you," said Veevee in delight.

"We still haven't made any progress toward closing and locking gates," said Danny.

"I think we've made a lot of progress for only our *first session*, please remember," said Veevee. "And now here in my kitchen I've got this public gate that goes nowhere and I still can't get down to the beach."

"The nice thing is, the public gate is still mine—I moved it using another gate, but I can just as easily put it back where I found it."

"Except not starting from the balcony," Veevee reminded him.

"Where, then?" asked Danny.

"My bedroom," she said. "Look, right here—inside my underwear drawer."

"What?" said Danny, following her into the bedroom.

"It's not like I have to *walk* into the gate. I just find it with some body part and push my way through, right? So put it inside my dresser, so I can open the drawer, put my hand in, and have access to the gate. But nobody else can ever stumble into it accidentally."

"Right," said Danny. "And when you come back to your room, you end up inside your drawer and your dresser explodes around you."

Veevee giggled. "Oops," she said. "I forgot it went two ways."

"Let's not put it in your shower," said Danny. "You don't want to accidentally step through it and end up wet and starkers on the beach."

"You prankster, you were tempted to do it, weren't you!"

"I can't fool somebody who can see the gates," said Danny.

"Oh, well. It would have been a funny prank. It still might be, someday. To play on someone who *isn't me*."

Danny put the entrance to the gate right up against her linen closet shelves. Nobody was going to press their body into that space, and when she came back to the room, she'd simply appear in front of it, facing away. Veevee tried it out, both ways, several times. "Very convenient," she said.

"Just remember to check your shower before you get in," said Danny.

"I know how you think," said Veevee. "You just told me to check the shower because you want to distract me so it doesn't occur to me that you really placed a public gate just above my toilet seat."

"Never crossed my mind," said Danny. "But I wish it had."

The grocery delivery arrived. Danny helped her put things away. Then she made him a couple of sandwiches—one cucumber and watercress on white bread, and one peanut butter and honey on whole wheat. They were really good. Why couldn't any of the Aunts have been like Veevee?

He returned home through the gate to the Silvermans' with half the peanut-butter-and-honey sandwich still in his hand. Leslie eyed it suspiciously.

"That's what she's feeding you?" she asked.

"I had to steal it," said Danny. "She won't let me eat or drink or use the bathroom or anything."

"Ha ha," said Leslie. Then, more seriously, "Do you think she'll help you?"

"We're making progress," said Danny.

"Just keep safe. That's all I care about," said Leslie.

Danny realized that she was telling him the truth. It touched him, to think she actually cared about him—enough to let him go study with the woman she probably hated worst in the whole world.

Danny gave her a hug and kissed her cheek.

"You still have the stink of her deodorant on you," said Leslie. But she hugged him back.

15

The Queen's Squirrel

ᴥ

It was in the kitchen that Wad first heard the rumors that Anonoei was plotting to kill Queen Bexoi. It began with Hull quite out of temper, though she wouldn't tell anyone why. But she was storming and stomping around the kitchen, ready to snap at anyone who asked the most innocent question, and as for those who made mistakes, they were doomed. Hull was generally not a violent person, but brooms were laid against backs and an iron pot was thrown and dented against a stone wall.

Wad knew that it was time for him to intervene, for though the pot was badly aimed, it had been thrown hard and if it had struck the head of poor Gunnel, he'd have been dead or a halfwit, which Wad knew would consume poor Hull with grief.

"Pardon me," said Wad softly.

"Speak up, you Wad of half-risen dough!" shouted Hull.

Wad spoke even more softly. "I think we have a fungus infestation in the shade garden."

"Do you think I'm an idiot?" demanded Hull. "Do you think I don't know you're trying to get me out of the kitchen to calm me down?"

"The undersides of the basil leaves are white with it, like an upside-down snowfall," Wad persisted, even more softly.

"Then pull them out and burn them, you fool! Don't bother me with it."

"You told me your grandfather once found a way to kill fungus," said Wad.

"You scheming little squirrel," said Hull. "As if you actually knew what was for my own good." She stalked out of the kitchen and headed for the shade garden.

Wad loped after her, passed her, and had the door to the garden unlocked and open for her when she arrived. Hull came in and slammed the door shut behind her. "Well?" she said.

Wad just looked at her.

"I know you can talk, Wad. Don't play dumb with me."

Wad smiled slightly.

"I wasn't really aiming at Gunnel's head!" Hull said.

"What if you missed and hit him?" asked Wad softly.

"Then I'd feel worse than I do right now, which is hard to believe."

Wad's silence was another question.

"They tried to put poison in the Queen's tea," said Hull. "They thought because I'm fat and getting old that I wouldn't see the movement behind my back. But I saw, and I turned and told him to drink the tea himself or I'd pour it down his throat. So he picked it up with trembling fingers and threw it on the floor."

She laughed. "It was a tin cup and it didn't break, and a minute later I had that cup up to his lips and him pressed against the wall and he started to cry and begged me not to make him drink, that it wasn't his idea, that he was only trying to serve the King."

"How would it serve the King to kill his wife when she's pregnant with his first legitimate heir?"

"They don't want a legitimate heir!" said Hull.

"Who is 'they'?" asked Wad.

"And what will you do about it if I say?" she retorted.

"I don't know," said Wad. "Who?"

"I don't know either," Hull confessed. "'They'll kill my family if I say,' he says to me, and what can I do then? I'm too merciful, that's what I am. But if the Queen dropped dead of poison, who would they blame? Me, who was carrying the tray myself! Who else? I could protest all I wanted, but there was two they intended to kill with that poison—the Queen and me. Not that anyone would care about me. I barely care about myself. But I'd never forgive them forcing me to die with a traitor's and assassin's shame on me, when I don't deserve either name!"

Wad stepped right up to her and put his arms around her. She noticed that he was a little taller than he had been when he first came to Nassassa nearly two years ago. But still not as tall as he ought to be, after all this time. "Using my grandfather's name to force me out of my own kitchen," she murmured. "Shame on you."

"I didn't say his name," whispered Wad. "Because I don't know it."

"You invoked his memory and made me stop ranting and throwing things, and I *wanted* to rant and throw things!"

Wad shook his head against her shoulder.

"I did so! I may not have wanted the *consequences* of ranting and throwing, but I certainly wanted things in that kitchen to hit other things, and hard!"

"Then next time throw at me," said Wad. "I won't mind."

"Oh, and what would you do, gate out of the way? Show everyone what you are? *If* you still are?"

"I wouldn't gate away," said Wad. "I'd let you hit me. Then you'd stop."

"Why? Because you think I love you?"

Against her shoulder, Wad nodded.

"Presumptuous little squirrel. Nobody loves squirrels! They're too clever, you can't stop them from stealing!"

"I don't steal," murmured Wad.

"I don't know who tried to kill the Queen," said Hull. "Whoever it was had that weak-kneed coward's family in their power and any man who has children, he's no longer free, they can control him, and that's the truth. And no, I won't tell you who the weak-kneed coward was, either!"

"Are you afraid I'll kill him?"

"I'm afraid that someone will find out that you know, and kill you for it."

"And I'm afraid that someone will kill *you* for it, because by now they certainly know that *you* know."

Hull pushed him away a little. "They wouldn't dare," she said.

"If they dare to try to kill the Queen . . ."

"Who would put blood in the King's bread!" said Hull.

"Tell me," said Wad. For in truth it surprised Wad

that there could be any conspiracy that he didn't already know about.

"I don't know," said Hull, "but I do know this: Whoever it is wants the Queen dead so that her baby will never be born, so that Anonoei's little halfway bastard boys can take the place of the rightful heir who died unborn."

"And why would they do that?"

"Because the Queen is from Gray," said Hull. "Don't pretend you don't know the politics of this house, I know you go a-spying whenever I don't have you at a job, and sometimes even when I do."

"Then why don't you want to see Anonoei's Icewegian sons inherit?"

"I'm old enough to know how things work in this world," said Hull. "If both those boys are heirs, then they'll fight between each other and we'll have a civil war. Or one of them will kill the other, and then we'll have a fratricide on the throne—always a proud day for a kingdom. Old Oviak made war on Gray and lost it, and he swore to the bargain that brought peace. Queen Bexoi and that baby in her belly are the price of it, and no Icewegian with honor can go back on the word of the old King, even if he *is* dead."

"So it's not because you love the Queen," said Wad.

"I don't even know her. When I bring her breakfast—with my own hands, mind you, because Her Fancyship demanded it—she hardly looks at me and never says a word, not even thanks."

"Why do you think she demanded that *you* bring her breakfast?"

Hull thought for a moment. "Well, I'm glad to know that I'm trusted even by those I don't much like."

"You saved her life today."

"I can't throw myself on her protection, though, can I?"

"Try the King's protection," said Wad.

"How do I know he isn't part of the conspiracy?"

Wad did not believe the King would do such a thing, but he couldn't be sure of it.

"So now you've calmed me down and I won't kill any of the idiots who work in the kitchen. I won't tell on the conspirators and that should satisfy them, too."

"Should it?"

"I'm busy." She turned for the door, then stopped. "*Was* there any fungus?"

Wad shook his head.

"The King doesn't want this baby," said Hull, "because everyone knows the Queen is a drekka, or nearly so. She can call finches! How useful! Her children will have no greatness in them. But that's the promise old King Oviak made to Bexoi's brother, and King Prayard is bound by it, and by his own marriage oath! I hate it that I don't trust him, but how can I trust anyone? Except you, Wad. You're the only faithful man or boy in Nassassa." And with that she went back to the house.

Faithful man or boy? Wad laughed bitterly inside himself. Faithful to my Queen, and to the boy or girl, half mine, growing inside her womb. Faithful to you, Hull. But to none else, especially if they threaten any of my beloveds.

Behind this fierce loyalty, though, there was another Wad, an older one, who knew secrets he wouldn't tell this tree-born reborn squirrel. And that Wad was laughing—at the word *beloved*. There is no love, said that ancient Wad. There is only hunger and possession. You huddle like a starving man over his food, you fool, saying, "Touch not what is mine, I'll kill you if you touch it."

Well, I will, Wad told that ancient self. See if I don't.

Just another killer, no different from any other, said the cynical worm that dwelt in his ancient heart. *You* love, and so your greed is noble and your hate is righteous. *You* desire, and so you plan to kill whoever wants to take away from you the things you have no right to have because they belong to someone else. You are the lover-by-stealth, the thief of the King's throne, for you want to put your cuckoo's egg upon it, denying the King's own sons. Do you speak of nobility? Those who would kill the Queen would only avenge *your* crime—your treason and betrayal of a man, Prayard, who has done you only kindness.

Wad sank down upon the ground in the shade garden. Why did I come to this place? he asked himself. I needed no one till I came here, and now I love three, and they will make a killer out of me in the effort to protect them.

While Wad was bitterly condemning himself, Hull went into the kitchen, where no one dared to look up from their work, and stalked off to her own room, to meditate upon the kind of foolish old woman who takes out her anger on the innocent. That was what was on her mind when she stepped into the darkness of her room, holding no candle because she knew the place by heart. She only heard one breath, one step, and then the dagger was in the top of her spine, just under the neck. *Whick whack,* back and forth, and she felt no pain as she dropped to the floor until her head struck stone. Even then, she was only dazed. She felt her brain fading because of lack of air. Breathe, she told herself. Breathe. But her body obeyed nothing.

The door closed behind her. Alone in the dark, her brain starved from lack of air, and without pain or even fear, Hull died.

It was Wad who found her, an hour later, when the kitchen servants came to him and begged him to make sure she was all right. "She hasn't told us that we're done. We dare not leave the kitchen till we have her leave." Everyone knew that Wad could approach her no matter how angry she was.

He found her door locked, but that was no barrier to Wad. He gated inside, found her body, and wept. Where was I when they did this? I knew they would try to kill her, but did I watch over her? No, I pitied and condemned myself as a killer, as being no better than any other. But who did I kill today? No one. If I had killed the right man, Hull would be alive.

Yet he could not unthink all that he had thought. The very fact that he longed to add to the blood already on his hands from handling and weeping over that good woman only sickened him and grieved him more. Kill kill kill, that's all we do, despite our powers. For magery didn't change the fact that ultimately the only way to stop a man was to threaten to kill him, if he was weak or fearful, or to kill him outright, if he was strong and brave and dangerous. Murder is the only power that we know. Am I better than they are? Hull was better than any of us, because she never killed, because she kept on trusting even when she had the proof that she was dealing with assassins. And she is dead. Does that mean that only the murderers can live? What world is that to live in?

Hull, why did you take me in, if not to be your protector? And since you have no son, who but me is your avenger?

But would you, even now, want vengeance for your death? Or simply peace?

Wad laid her back down on the floor, his tears still on her face. He gave no alarm. Let someone else discover her and raise the cry of murder. Wad had work to do.

He gated to a place he knew by a brook in a narrow canyon many miles from Nassassa. There he washed himself in the cold snowmelt mountain water of early summer. Hull's blood was sent back into the world through that stream, to be part of the sea again one day. As for his clothing, he burned it, lest the blood be seen and anyone accuse *him* of the murder of the well-loved night cook.

Naked as the hour he came out of the tree two summers ago, he gated back into the castle and closed the gates that he had made to Hull's room and to the brook where he washed. Then he made a viewport into Anonoei's room.

She was supposed to be preparing to leave Nassassa. At the Queen's request—and the demand of the agents of Gray who surrounded her—King Prayard had commanded that Anonoei and her two sons be sent away. A ship was going to take her to a place of exile, where she would be guarded so that neither she nor her sons could endanger Queen Bexoi's child when it was born. The ship was supposed to leave the next day, but Wad saw no sign of preparation for a move. Oh, there were three open trunks in her antechamber, but there was nothing in them, not even a pile of clothes waiting to be sorted.

She knows, thought Wad. Whether she is part of the plot or not, someone told her that she need not pack, because she would not leave. She knows they mean to kill my Bexoi and my baby, and she is content.

But angry as he was, and grieving, and wracked with guilt for not having protected Hull, he still did not reach through a gate into her heart and squeeze it into stillness, or pull it out and throw it in the King's face. Instead, he made sure that her two sons, six-year-old Eluik and four-year-old Enopp, were in her chambers, too.

Wad knew a place that dated from the ancient days, two thousand years before, when the first portion of Nassassa Castle was built. As the stonemages hollowed out the crag to make the chambers, halls, and corridors of the inmost keep of Nassassa, they created three tunnels down which they poured the rock they fluidized. These tunnels opened out three hundred feet above the deep volcanic lake that formed a part of the perimeter of the castle. From there the slag had fallen and been lost in the lake. Then the tunnels were filled with seamless stone. But at the mouth of each tunnel, a shallow cave remained, where the last hot slag had poured away when all the stone behind it had begun to harden. They all sloped sharply upward, the floor more steeply than the roof, so there was scarcely any level ground inside.

Wad could do no work with stone, but still he could make each cave into a prison cell. He simply made a gate across the mouth of each cave, a gate so wide that you could not get around it. If you fell from the cave, you were caught in the gate, which took you to the narrow back of the cave. If you were careless, you could then roll right down again to the gate at the cave's mouth, and fall again, and be caught again and returned to the back of the cave—over and over, until you finally caught yourself and held on to the stone and clung there.

It was a terrible prison, a cruel torment, but Wad kept telling himself, It is not death. No one can call me murderer.

Then Wad formed a gate just behind Anonoei and passed the mouth of it over her, carrying her into the steepest of the caves. He heard her scream as she tumbled down to the cave's mouth, and back to the top, and down and out of the mouth again. It was a delicious sound to Wad, in his rage and hate.

He took Eluik and Enopp the same way, each in turn. They, too, screamed—and Wad wondered if their mother could hear them. Let them all do their screaming, thought Wad. Hull was not allowed to scream; they scream for her.

Then he went back to Anonoei's room, passed gates around the open trunks, and bore them each to a cave. There he fastened them in place, using a technique he had not known that he knew, though it came with the ease of old habit the moment he desired it. Each lay longwise along the side of one of the prison caves, with a gate at the bottom end that led only the tiniest fraction of a fingerwidth higher up the slope. So the trunks were constantly falling, yet never perceptibly moved at all.

The prisoners caught themselves on their trunks, then climbed in and lay down or sat inside them, weeping and crying out, but safe from the terror of the yawning cave mouth. That torture was over—but the memory of it would never end.

They would know that some powerful mage had

done this to them—but what kind of mage, and who? Perhaps the children had no idea of their mother's plotting, but they would learn of it eventually, and recognize that whatever mage had done this could not be resisted. When eventually he released them from the cave—after Bexoi's and Wad's firstborn child was openly proclaimed the heir of Prayard—they would think twice before they plotted again, for they would know what could be done to them, and how powerless they were to resist.

Each day, Wad would gather up the scraps from the King's table—a duty he had often performed—and instead of carrying them to the pigs or to the compost bin, he would divide them into three bags and push them through a tiny gate into the trunk in each cave, along with a pitcherful of water, which would pour down into the bottom end of the trunk, where they must drink it from their scooping hands, or lap it up like dogs, before it leaked away. His prisoners would quickly learn to be glad of the water and the scraps, would press the sack into the bottom of the trunk to soak, and then wring out the last drops of water from it.

He took pleasure in all the cruelty of the way that he would provide for them, make animals of them, even though he knew that the children, at least, could not be blamed for anything. They must learn fear! he told himself. Only fear will keep them from threatening my child when they grow older.

Meanwhile, another part of him, that ancient soul, roiled within him, as if it were a thousand souls, and all of them angry and afraid of him, all of them crying out that he had no right to such power as he had, if this was how he used it; and crying out, Is this all you can do? Make prisoners of the innocent, because you have someone else you would protect? Are we not all your prisoners here, and have you no compassion for our imprisonment, either?

And Wad wondered how his ancient soul had become so shredded, that it thought itself to be a multitude.

His work done, his prisoners' first meal and drink provided for, Wad came naked to the Queen in her nightbed. He wrapped his arms around her as, only that morning, he had wrapped his arms around beloved Hull, and whispered to her that she was safe. No one would kill her or the baby, not when they did not know where Anonoei was, or the sons King Prayard had begotten on her. Who would be the heir then? Not knowing, they would not dare to harm the Queen.

"What have you done?" said Bexoi.

Wad told her of how Hull had saved her life, and then been murdered for it. And then he told her every detail of how he had abducted Anonoei and her sons and how he would provide for them.

"Good," said Bexoi. "But wouldn't it be simpler to remove the gate at the mouth of each cave and let them fall to their deaths?"

"What if they slid into the water and came out alive?" asked Wad.

"Then gate them down to the bottom of the lake," said Bexoi.

Wad did not know whether to be happy or horrified that his beloved was as cruel as he. He laughed.

But he did not kill Anonoei or her sons, and he did not tell Bexoi that he would not kill them. He owed her no obedience.

We are gods, thought Wad. All the great mages are. And gods make no apologies or explanations.

Be silent, he said to the many voices deep inside himself, as they cried out against his arrogance. If you had any power, he said to them, then you would stop me. But you are weak and I am strong. Be still.

16

Warden

ب

How long can you behave monstrously before you become a monster? The first rage that Wad had felt toward Anonoei and her sons had long since passed. Hull was still dead, Eluik and Enopp still posed a threat to Wad's and Bexoi's baby, but the grief and fear had faded with time, as they always do. Humans, even great mages, get used to anything.

Yet the tedious work of pushing food into their hellish cells continued, day after day. Ashamed of what he was doing to children, Wad soon changed their fare from slops to bread and cheese, which he gated out of the locked pantry every day. It was driving the new Hull—a man this time, who had once been her apprentice Hatch before he got the night cook job and the night cook name—mad with frustration that his count was always off by three loaves and a fair-sized cheese.

Wad also sent his prisoners clean jars filled with water, which they returned to him empty, and open bowls for their bodily wastes, which they returned to him foul. He cleaned them himself, with his own hands, as penance for the terrible thing that he had done and continued to do.

Meanwhile, Bexoi's belly grew, and when King Prayard's frenzy over the loss of his lover and their sons faded—as all such feelings fade—he began to notice that the woman who was his lawful wife was with child.

But was it *his* child? Wad watched, of course, as Bexoi explained to him how she had pushed his seed into herself again and again.

"That doesn't work," Prayard repeated.

"It only had to work once," said Bexoi. "And think of it—this baby is of the hardiest seed of his father, the most determined, the most ambitious. The luckiest."

"You say 'he,'" said Prayard. "Will this baby be a son?"

"It might be," said Bexoi. "But if it's a girl, we can try again. Now that you know I'm not barren after all."

"I never thought you were barren," said Prayard.

"But you made sure everyone else thought so."

"And you never told anyone that I was preventing it," he said.

"Because I didn't want to start a war," she said. "I wanted to start a baby."

At last the day came for the baby to be born. Wad, of course, was not officially present, though he watched closely. There was a while when the baby's head seemed to be stuck, unable to press forward to emerge. So Wad made a little gate, and the baby seemed to shoot forward into the midwives' hands. "It was like magic," said one of them to the other. "Did you see?"

"Born to be a great mage, then, do you think?" asked the other.

What Wad cared about was Bexoi. Once the baby

had passed through the narrow gap in her bones, she was bleeding profusely and the healer attending her was unable to do anything. "At times like this," the healer said, "we can be consoled that at least she left her child behind her when she died."

Wad just shook his head at such a thought. He made a gate that swallowed Bexoi whole and then returned her to a spot a tiny fraction of a fingerwidth away. Nobody noticed the movement, or thought it only a momentary twitch; at least no one remarked on it. And suddenly she was not bleeding. Suddenly she was happy and tired and perfectly healthy in every way.

"Thank you," she whispered.

The healer assumed that Bexoi was speaking to her, and said, "But I did nothing, your majesty."

"I know," she murmured kindly. "You did your best, and I am well, and that's enough. Give me my son."

"His name will be Oviak, of course," said the healer, "after his father's father."

"Naming is not your business," said Bexoi softly. "And I will not give my son the name of a man who lost a war. His name will be Oath, for by his birth a covenant was kept alive."

But hearing this, Wad thought: By his conception the sham of marriage between Prayard and Bexoi was utterly broken by me. So that will never be his name in my heart. I will call him Trick, for that is how he came into this world, and what his life will always be— a trick that Bexoi and I played on everyone.

After Oath had lived for seven days, he was presented to King Prayard, who declared him to be his son and heir. That very night he came to Bexoi, saying that he only meant to talk to her, for she was still recovering from childbirth. But she laughed and said, "I am well and whole and hungry for my husband," and for the first time he acted as a husband should, and left his seed inside her.

Within the week, Prayard moved the Queen into his own chamber, to be protected by his most trusted men. The message was clear to all: Bexoi, not the lost Anonoei, was the woman who was sacred now to Iceway. She was the mother of the heir, and whoever raised a hand against her was the enemy of all.

Bexoi herself responded by cutting off the ambassadors and representatives and agents of Gray. They still lived in Nassassa and saw her every day—but only in a public room, with King Prayard's own ministers in attendance. There was never a word in private with the Queen, and they soon realized that this was not because she was being held prisoner, but because she wanted nothing to do with them. "I will not be used against my husband and my lord," she said to them in one such public meeting. "When I was childless, and had no friends, my brother the Jarl and my nephew the Jarling and all of you conspired to use me as a pretext for war or as a means of humiliating Iceway. Now I am truly Queen, and my only care is that Gray and Iceway stay at peace, as equal allies against the enemies of both. I will not be used for any other purpose."

Word of the Queen's change of loyalty was taken back to Gray, and while the Jarling Frostinch raged and railed about his aunt's "treason," her brother the Jarl wept with joy. "She has set the example for us all. A girl without magery or beauty, with no weapon but her heart, has tamed the savage seamage. In their son will peace come to us all."

Frostinch quickly saw that he must hold his tongue and pretend in every way to submit to his father's will. But he saw his father's acceptance of Bexoi's treason as a fatal weakness in the old man. As once he had plotted for his aunt's death, to provoke the war he wanted, so now he began to look for ways to help his father's reign reach a peaceful, happy, and swift conclusion. Then they would see how much peace the birth of Oath had brought between the kingdoms of Gray and Iceway.

In Iceway, the reclusive Bexoi began to venture out, not with nurses bringing the baby along behind her, but carrying Oath herself, and showing quite openly that she herself was giving suck to the baby. This astonished the people, but it reminded the old ones that this was once the way that all Icewegian heirs were nurtured in their youth. "What milk but royal milk should the royal baby drink?" they said. And she herself said, "I am not ashamed to show the breast from which Oath suckles, for this breast is Iceway's breast, and it is now and always will be from the people that he draws his food and drink."

And still no one guessed that she had any but the feeble beastmagery of small seed-gathering birds, or that Oath, with his tiny waggling arms, was really the son of two great mages—both of them far more powerful and skilled than the seamage Prayard who thought he was the father.

To Wad, these changes were all to the good. He understood well enough that with Bexoi in the King's chamber every night, their trysts would be few—but now and then she used a gate he had made for her and joined him in one of the many secret rooms he knew of in Nassassa. For months they only talked; Wad asked for no intimacy with her body, and she offered none.

And then, during one such encounter, when the boy that she called Oath and Wad called Trick was ten months old, she took him to her body passionately. When he was spent, lying beside her on the pile of their clothing on the floor, she told him she was pregnant again.

"So soon?" said Wad. "I thought that when you nursed a baby—"

"Who knows what happened when you healed me there on Oath's birthbed? My body was made ready for Prayard's seed. I waited until I was pregnant with his body before I slept with you again. This new baby will truly be his. That is a kind of faithfulness to my husband, isn't it?"

Wad heard those words and smiled, but his smile was a lie. The Queen had long wanted Prayard's son. By having Wad's, she had finally won the attention, then the affection of her husband, and now had his baby in her womb. What did that mean for the future of little Prince Oath?

Now, when he fed his prisoners, Wad began to see that they had not been the only threats to Trick's inheritance—or, indeed, to his survival. Bexoi was a strong woman, he knew. She would do whatever she thought was necessary to achieve her ends. She had confided in Wad more than once that her nephew Frostinch was the greatest danger to Iceway, and that sooner or later it would come to war between them.

But Wad had finally come to see that she meant this in the fullest sense—that Frostinch would be Jarl of Gray, and that Bexoi would be, one way or another, the ruler of Iceway when that war came. Wad had given her a baby who was named the heir; Prayard had given her the position of the mother of the heir. Now another baby was coming, so Oath was no longer so essential to her plans.

Wad had seen enough now of the machinations of the court to know that Bexoi would never be content until she ruled as regent for a beloved baby king. The question was: Which baby would it be? Bexoi would have to choose between them.

Wad had only one pawn in this game.

Or three, if you added in the two elder sons of King Prayard, who brought with them a rival regent, Anonoei. This woman of Iceway had once had many friends and perhaps still had them, if she were to emerge from her hiding place.

Now Wad understood why he had been so reluctant to kill his prisoners when Bexoi insisted. He had known from the start that he could not trust Bexoi any more than Prayard could. He simply hadn't known that he knew it.

Wad, as their warden, began to give the prisoners food from the King's own table, pilfered gatewise from the tables and sent to Anonoei and Eluik and Enopp in fine bowls and basins. For Anonoei there was wine as well as water, and, for the boys, sweets as well as bread and cheese and meat.

He did not expect them to learn to love the jailer that they never saw. In part he gave this better food to them, and washed up the pans of their shit and piss, as penance for his crime of keeping innocent children as solitary prisoners in a terrifying place. But there was something else that he only now and then allowed himself to know—they were the answer to a question: Who will stand against Queen Bexoi, should there come a time when it were better if she fell? It was a question only he was asking, and so for now he kept the answer to himself.

17

Birthday Present

ملم

In the middle of the summer of 2010, Leslie and Marion sat Danny down in the living room with so much ceremony that Danny thought they were going to announce that they were fed up with his commuting from Yellow Springs to Naples and he was going to have to move out. Which he definitely did not want to do, since he delighted in Veevee, but only in small doses, while Leslie and Marion were the closest things to parents he had ever known.

"As you know," said Marion, "your sixteenth birthday is approaching."

"It's July thirtieth," said Danny. "My birthday is September fourteenth. It's approaching in the sense that Christmas is approaching."

"Some preparation is needed," said Leslie.

"Preparation for what?" asked Danny.

"Your driver's license," said Marion.

"We have to enroll you in driver's education right now," said Leslie.

"Because we've decided that your birthday present will be a car," said Marion.

"You're a very responsible young man," said Leslie. "You work hard at everything you do. You're careful and skillful. We think you'll be an excellent driver."

"I think my word was 'adequate,'" corrected Marion.

"It won't be a *new* car," said Leslie. "Insurance is expensive for sixteen-year-old young men."

"Again, my word would be 'boys,'" said Marion.

Danny was touched. He could imagine such a scene playing out in any normal drowther home. It made him feel like . . . an American. An Ohioan. A human being.

"You are so wonderful," said Danny. "I wish I had grown up in your house."

"You still are growing up," said Marion. "And in our house."

"Mostly," said Leslie.

"But the thing I can't figure out is . . . why would I want a car?"

They looked at him, nonplussed.

"I even go grocery shopping by gate," said Danny.

"We didn't appreciate the shopping cart in the kitchen," said Marion.

"Now, it was just the once," said Leslie. "And he took it back himself."

"I always pay for everything," said Danny. "I haven't stolen anything since I've lived here with you."

"What about in Florida?" asked Leslie. "I suppose the rules are different there."

"I made gates for Veevee to her favorite stores and malls, yes," said Danny, "but always to a spot outside, so she still has to pay. More to the point, *I* always pay.

Even to go into the movies. I want to live by drowther rules. I'm doing it better than a lot of drowthers."

"By drowther rules," said Marion, "you need a car."

Danny put his hands in shrugging position. "Why? I already have better transportation than the President."

"In a word," said Marion, "dating."

"You can't very well gate a girl to the movies, Danny," said Leslie, "and very few of them will be impressed if they always have to walk."

"Or maybe you expect the girl to drive," said Marion. "They are not impressed by this."

"I think you're overlooking the biggest point here," said Danny. "I don't need a *car* so I can date. I need a *girl.*"

Marion and Leslie looked at each other, and Marion coughed. "Uh, Danny, in, uh, drowther culture, in *this* country, anyway, teenagers of opposite sex are generally expected to find each other without adult interference."

"And you know where they do that?" asked Danny. "At high school."

Again Marion and Leslie looked at each other, then back at Danny. "Are you saying you want to go to high school?" asked Marion.

"You've already taken the PSAT and the SAT and the ACT," said Leslie. "Your self-education has been superb, and your scores prove it. You'll be able to get into any college in the world."

"You two are wonderful teachers," said Danny.

Marion gave a hoot of laughter. "Danny, the most we've ever done is brought you a textbook now and then."

"And listen at the dinner table when you go on

about Mongolian history or the uses of differential calculus or the principles of calculating vertical load versus horizontal flexion or whatever it was in bridge building," said Leslie.

"And how many parents would do that?" said Danny. "I don't want to go to high school for the classes, I want to go to high school because that's where they keep the girls. And the *friends*. You two and Veevee are my only friends in the world, and no offense here, but you're all old enough to be my parents."

"It's not safe for you to spend a lot of time with drowthers," said Marion. "You could do or say something—"

Leslie interrupted. "They could ask something you couldn't answer—"

"If any of the Families was alerted to what you are . . . ," said Marion.

"I have to be able to function in drowther society," said Danny. "Drowthers go to high school. They talk about music and movies. I don't know what movies and music they talk about, except what I see discussed online. It's not the same."

"You don't *like* any of that music," said Leslie. "You always switch away from hippity-hop or whatever it's called."

"Hippy-hop," corrected Marion.

"Hip-hop," said Danny, rolling his eyes.

"Aha!" said Leslie. "See? You *already* know about that kind of thing."

"If you have friends, they might come over," said Marion. "Unannounced. You'd have to stop using any of your gates around the farm."

"I only have a few gates here," said Danny. "You wouldn't let me."

"The parents of the girls you date would want to meet *your* parents," said Leslie. "All you have is us. How do you explain that?"

"Uncle Marion and Aunt Leslie," said Danny. "And wouldn't it be hilarious in a kind of terrifying way if some girl ever did have to face my real parents. Even supposing they didn't kill me and whomever I brought with me on sight, they'd despise her for being a drowther, and she'd despise them as uneducated country bumpkins."

"So you see why high school just wouldn't work," said Leslie.

"He doesn't look persuaded," said Marion.

"I'm not proposing that I go to high school here," said Danny.

Again, Marion and Leslie traded looks. "But why not?" asked Leslie. "The high school is just through the fields and up the road."

Danny laughed.

Leslie took umbrage. "I don't see what's funny about what I said."

Marion undertook the explanation. "We just told him all the reasons why going to high school while living here wouldn't work out, and then you seemed hurt that he wasn't planning to go to high school here."

"There is no contradiction in what I said," Leslie retorted.

"It's okay," said Danny. "It has nothing to do with you. The kids at Yellow Springs High have seen me running past. I've been noticed and mentioned—I've seen them pointing and telling each other about me. Wondering why I'm not in school, I'm betting. Speculating on the reason. I can only guess what they say. The point is that I'm already kind of legendary at Yellow Springs High. There is zero chance I'd have a normal high school career there. It'll be bad enough that I'm coming in as a junior. A 'new kid.'"

"How do you know what they're saying?" said Leslie.

"Why are you arguing for him to go to high school here," asked Marion, "after telling him why you didn't think he should go?"

"I'm arguing for him not going away to some other place for high school," said Leslie, "because even though he's skinny as a rail, I can't imagine him getting any decent food in Florida."

"I don't want to go to high school in Florida, either," said Danny. "And I know what kids must be saying about me because I've been reading about high school kids and how they talk and think."

"'Young adult novels,'" said Leslie. It was her turn to roll her eyes. "When you've already read the classics."

"It's research, *Mom*," said Danny, deliberately using a term she didn't like him to use, or at least said she didn't. "Isn't it kind of pathetic that the only way I can learn about the life of a drowther teenager is by reading *Bruiser* and *Friend Is Not a Verb* and *Holes*?"

"I notice that you keep reading about teenagers with magical powers," said Marion.

"Not always," said Danny, "but if I ever go to high school I'll *be* the kid with magical powers, won't I? So that's part of my research—how they cope."

"By hiding who they are and becoming social misfits and pariahs," said Leslie. "Is that what you plan to do?"

"Of course he plans to hide what he is," said Marion. "Or word will get out and the Families will find him and they'll zap him with lightning or have the earth swallow him up and crush him before he can gate away."

"You've been reading my novels," Danny said to Leslie. "You really *are* my mom."

"Your mother is a great mage," said Leslie. "I don't deserve to receive the respect you owe to her."

"'Mom' isn't a term of respect," said Danny.

"You say that and I don't even know what you *mean*," said Leslie. "Our kids always called me Mom and they respected me!"

"What he means," said Marion, "is that it's a term of affection."

"Love," said Danny. "It's a term for the woman in my life who loves *me* enough to read the novels I'm reading just so she can try to figure out what they're teaching me."

There was a silence in the room until Leslie asked, in a somewhat smaller voice, "Do you call *her* Mom?"

Danny laughed. "Veevee? *Mom?* Oh, right. She's a *colleague,* Leslie. We *work* together."

"I notice that when I brought her up, you stopped calling me Mom," said Leslie.

"Don't make him explain," said Marion. "You and I can have *that* fight later. This is his birthday we're talking about, and I think what he's saying is that he wants to go to high school, but he doesn't want to do it here *or* in Florida."

"That's it," said Danny. "I want to go to Parry Mc-Cluer High School."

"I've never heard of perimacluing," said Leslie. "How do you perimaclue and why do they devote a whole high school to it?"

"It's the name of the school," said Marion. "But it's

nowhere near Yellow Springs or I would have heard of it."

"It's in Buena Vista, Virginia," said Danny. "And yes, it's within twenty miles or so of the North Family compound. But the family never goes there—if they even come close, they go to Lexington. They have no business ever in Buena Vista."

"It's a needless risk," said Marion.

"If they're still looking for me—" Danny began.

"They are," said Marion.

"You've heard something?" asked Leslie sharply, suddenly worried.

"No, of course not, I'd have told you both," said Marion. "What would *we* hear? Who would we hear it from? But they're looking for you, Danny, count on it."

"But they won't be looking in a town so close to home," said Danny. "Not after nearly three years. One town is as safe or dangerous as any other. We don't know where their spies are. But Thor, the one in charge of the spies, said that he doesn't want me dead."

"Which might just mean that he doesn't want you wary," said Marion. "But you're right. After all this time, they can't be expecting you to locate near them— nor to do something as bizarre as go to high school."

"What's so special about this Perry McDonald High School?" asked Leslie.

"Parry McCluer," said Danny, "and there's nothing special about the place except that when I was a kid and I first started gating out of the Family compound— though I didn't know I was gating then—I used to go up to the woods above the high school and watch them. Like I watch the kids here, only I wasn't just glancing as I ran by, I could sit there for a long time and kind of study them. They were all older than me then, I was just a kid, but I kept thinking, If only I could be one of them. Getting on their buses or into their cars. Girls getting into guys' cars, whole groups of them piling into one car and driving off yelling out the windows. Stuff like that."

"Girls getting into boys' *cars,*" Marion pointed out helpfully.

"What were they yelling?" asked Leslie suspiciously. "I don't like teenagers who yell out of car windows."

"That's not the point," said Marion. "He wants to *be* one of the teenagers yelling out of car windows. He wants to find out why they yell what they yell."

Danny nodded.

"How could you possibly go to high school there?" asked Leslie. "I hope you know we're not moving. And the school authorities will have *drastic* questions about a boy who shows up with no parents, no birth certificate, no school records, no records of immunization—"

"I've kind of already planned that out," said Danny. "I haven't talked to anybody about it yet, because, well, I wanted to talk to you first. And this wasn't the day because I hadn't worked up the courage yet, only you brought up cars and dating and, you know."

"What's your plan?" asked Marion.

"Veevee has a lot of money, apparently," said Danny.

"We have a lot of money, too," said Leslie. "Just because we keep farming doesn't mean—"

"Veevee has enough money that she could rent a small house in Buena Vista. Within walking distance of the high school. It's way up a steep road and it isn't the city's best neighborhood, but it's the right place for me to live. Veevee will pretend to be my aunt, and when I need her to she'll dress in an appropriate costume and meet with any parents who visit. But I'll make gates between her condo in Florida and the rental house so she can really keep living at home."

Leslie held her tongue—but so painfully that it was obvious she had quite a bit to say about Veevee's involvement in the plan.

"I haven't asked Veevee any of this, but you know she loves to playact and there's no chance she'd turn me down. I'll also make gates between there and here, so I can come home on weekends and holidays and stuff." Danny could see that calling their house 'home' smoothed some of Leslie's ruffled feathers. "I'll even make a public gate between here and there, if you want to be able to drop in and check up on me."

"No public gates here," said Marion. "Not until you learn how to lock them."

"Yes," said Danny, "it would have been better if Veevee had been a Lockfriend instead of a Keyfriend. But then I probably would never have found her, or vice versa, and I'm learning a lot from her—mostly from all the research she's done over the years, but also because she can see what I'm doing and give me feedback and ideas. That's just a fact of life—something that nobody in the world right now except for her could have done. So she has to be part of my life. But Mom, Dad, you are the people I love like parents. This is the place where I was happy for the first time in my life. I'm not trying to get away from you. I'm just trying to learn how to live in the drowther world. I'm trying to find out how to be a normal human being. And I can't learn that here."

Danny had seen that Marion picked up on his calling him "dad" and that it meant perhaps more to him than "mom" had meant to Leslie. But Danny wasn't saying those things as a trick, even though he knew that, as a trick, they would absolutely work. He said them because they were true.

"Mama" and "Baba" had been titles of awe and fear more than love. Occasionally as a child he had referred to them that way as a claim to special status for himself, when he was young enough that his drekka status had not yet become clear. But "mom" and "dad" were words that had remained as empty placeholders in his mind and heart until he came to Yellow Springs and the Silvermans.

Danny had often wondered if Stone's choice of Leslie and Marion as his guardians and trainers didn't have more to do with the fact that they were such great parents than with any particular skill they would have at training him—though they had schooled him as much as possible in the disciplines of magery. What he learned from them was a lot more about being a decent human being and taking responsibility for his actions and treating people who were weaker than himself with decent respect. And not playing tricks on people just because he thought of them.

"What about a birth certificate?" asked Marion.

"I was thinking I'd go back to DC and ask Stone. He'll know how to get one made. Maybe find somebody who was born on the same day as me, but died young. Or maybe just buy a flat-out forgery. Or maybe I gate into some county's records office and fill out the forms myself and insert them into the records. We'll make it work."

"So you're back to criminal activities," said Leslie.

"Come on," said Danny. "I have to have a birth certificate. An identity. There's no safe *and* legal way for me to get one."

"She knows that," said Marion. "And we both know that to get on in the drowther world you're going to have to have all that identification sooner or later. It sounds to me like you've thought this all through. Like you're exactly the careful, responsible, intelligent young man we thought was ready for a car. Only instead you're ready for something much bigger."

"He'll still need a car, even in Buena Vista," said Leslie.

"No, I won't," said Danny. "I'm going to show up there poor, not prosperous. No car. Walking to school. Of course I'll gate to the grocery store since the nearest decent one is *miles* away. But I don't want to come in there in a showy way, with money and a car and nice clothes. I want to be unobtrusive. Somebody that most people will pretty much ignore. It's fine if they think I'm weird—just not *legendary* weird. I think I'll make a better grade of friends and maybe get to know a better kind of girl than the ones who are impressed with guys for their cars and clothes and money."

"You do remember that those young adult novels are *fiction*," said Leslie.

"But if they didn't get the details of the kids' lives right, the kids wouldn't read them," said Danny. "*I* was reading them as an anthropologist."

"You were reading them as a romantic young teen-age boy," said Leslie. "And you bought into the endings where the poor-but-decent lonely boy ends up with the nicest, smartest girl."

"That too," said Danny with a grin.

"It's a true story," said Marion. "Don't you think, Leslie?"

Again the look between them, but this time it was

saying an entirely different set of things that were really none of Danny's business.

IT WAS GOOD to see Stone again. The house hadn't changed, though Ced and Lana were long since divorced and gone—Ced to study windmagery with an old Galebreath in Oregon, and Lana to a business school where, as Stone said, she had a fair shot at learning how to be something that didn't involve prostitution. "Though she'll probably become a secretary, seduce the boss, break up his family, and then make his life a living hell till he divorces her," said Stone. "But if he can't keep his fly zipped, he's the natural prey of angry damaged women who are careless about underwear."

And then, seeing Danny's rueful look, Stone said, "She was just practicing on you. Thirteen-year-olds are too easy to be sporting."

"I still dream about her," said Danny ruefully.

"And you probably always will," said Stone with a sigh.

Danny explained what he wanted.

"And you actually expect Victoria to be able to bring this off?" asked Stone.

"Why?" asked Danny. "You know her?"

Stone rolled his eyes. "You've been working with her for—how long?—and she's never mentioned me?"

"No. Not really. I don't think so."

"I'm her husband, Danny," said Stone. "My name is Von Roth. Peter Von Roth. She was Victoria Bland until she married me."

"*Bland*?" asked Danny.

"Really. Her parents' name. I think she's spent her whole life denying that name. Maybe she only married me because my last name was so Germanic and strong. *Von Roth!*" He gave it a strongly German pronunciation. "Sounds like the anger of the gods, yes?"

"But . . . she talks about her alimony."

"She doesn't get alimony," said Stone—or Peter, apparently. "We're still married. But her father is still one of the top mucky-mucks in the Department of Agriculture—he's really a first-rate Sapkin—and her mother inherited *her* father's land in northern Virginia, and sold off some nice chunks of it as they were building up Tysons Corner into a shopping mecca, so her family is awash in dough. Her 'alimony' is checks from mommy and daddy."

Danny had to laugh. "She really *is* a trickster. I never had a clue."

"Well, I can tell you, our lives would have been very different if there had been any way to know that she was a gatemage instead of a drekka. She always *said* she was, but how could anyone believe her? She was so showy and dramatic, we all believed it was part of a pose."

"But you married her."

"I always talked with her as if she were a gatemage. I joined her fantasy, as I supposed. And come on, Danny, until you came along it *was* a fantasy. She had no more idea she was a gatemage than anyone else. We'd been married no more than a year when she realized that I didn't really believe that she was a gatemage. That I was sort of humoring her. I didn't mean to let on—I had always talked as if it were true, and I made no slip—but you know how gatemages are. You can read meanings in human speech or facial expressions that no else can see. Part of the language gift, maybe. Sometimes it makes me wonder if gatemagery isn't right next door to manmagery. Anyway, she realized that I was only playing along, and it really hurt her, and she began spending less and less time at home, until I realized she was ... gone. I'm telling you more than I should. But if you're going to pin your whole plan on her being reliable ..."

Danny nodded. "I appreciate your concern. But remember, we gatemages are tricksters and con men, too. She'll bring off the only thing I really need her for—getting me enrolled in high school, setting me up in a cheap rented house with an allowance for necessities, and then popping in when I need to show off my flamboyant aunt."

Stone smiled. "Oh, you gatemages aren't the only tricksters."

"Really?" asked Danny.

"Here you were, a genuine gatemage. And there I was, the man who still loves that infuriating woman. I thought, Maybe she really is a gatemage. I could never have gotten her to come *here* to see the gates you made—she now pretends to be allergic to the pollen of the plants I grow—but one day when she was visiting with her parents in Fairfax, I talked to her on the phone and reminisced a little about the restaurant Dona Flor, which used to be our favorite place to eat— they had risolli with a habanero sauce that could take the top of your head off—and she was as predictable as the tides. She drove off out Wisconsin where I knew you had some gates and ..."

"And she was a gatemage after all."

"The real thing. It's not as if I ever said she wasn't!" said Stone, as defensively as if Veevee were in the room.

"And she'd have killed me if she'd known I planned it. 'Trying to trap me into revealing that I couldn't see a gate that you *knew* was there, is that it?' "

His imitation of Veevee was dead on, and Danny laughed.

"But I wasn't testing her, I was giving her an opportunity. I wanted it to be true—I always did. I knew it was an affinity that couldn't be tested as long as there were no gates in the world, unless she was a Pathsister or Gatemother herself, which was hardly likely. *You* are hardly likely, Danny. But I never said she *couldn't* be a gatemage."

"You were agnostic."

"Agnostic but hopeful," said Stone. "Or maybe . . . wistful."

"And your wist came true," said Danny with a grin. "Though I'll bet Leslie wasn't thrilled when Veevee showed up."

"I get the feeling that . . . well, to put it unkindly," said Danny, "you were second choice."

"She hadn't met me when she had her fling with Marion," said Stone. "And Marion flat out refused to accept her claim of gatemagery. He's a stonemage, for heaven's sake, *and* a geologist. He's not going to willingly live inside someone else's dream. And how could Veevee ever love or live with a man who didn't at least try to believe? If only she didn't have such a keen eye for pretense herself," said Stone. "I'd still be happy to have her with me. But the final break was when she tested me. 'Come to Florida,' she said. 'If you love me, get out of this miserable town and come to Naples.'

"But I couldn't leave my work here." Stone sighed. "America and a lot of the rest of the world come to

DC. This is the place where my pollen can gather in the Orphan mages. The Families know about me, of course, but they don't care—to them Orphans are no better or more interesting than drowthers. I've found nearly a hundred mages since I've lived here. How many would I have found in Naples, Florida? At best, a handful of old coots who are way too old to train."

"You still love her."

"Everybody still loves her," said Stone. "Even the people who hate her—that's why she makes them so angry. I bet Marion still thinks of her."

"The way I think of Lana?"

"Well, no," said Stone. "Veevee's not that kind of woman, if you know what I mean. More like . . . Marion still wishes he *could* have lived inside her dream. And now that it turns out it wasn't just a dream, she really *is* a gatemage, you can imagine how that must make him wonder and regret—even though he loves Leslie like crazy. Might-have-beens are a bitch."

To Danny it was as if Stone had just unlocked everybody's diary and he felt like a sneak for knowing so much about Marion's and Leslie's and Veevee's past. And yet it was a relief to know.

"I'm glad you told me all this," said Danny.

"I always kind of thought you knew. That somebody would have explained. But now that I'm saying this, it's such a ridiculous idea. Which of them would ever see the need to explain any of this to you? Not one of them is proud of their behavior. Well, Veevee is, but she's not an explainer."

"She and I are doing our best to explain gatemagery."

"Oh, come on," said Stone. "She and you are trying

to *invent* gatemagery. The best her research and yours can do is give you clues and hints and point you in interesting directions."

"We've made some progress," said Danny.

"Know how to make a Great Gate yet?" asked Stone.

"Not a clue," said Danny.

"Keep it that way," said Stone. "I don't want the Gate Thief to strip you and make a drekka out of you."

"At least then I'd be safe from the Families," said Danny.

"Don't count on it," said Stone. "They'd assume it was a gatemage's trickery and kill you anyway, just to be sure."

"Yeah," said Danny ruefully. "They would."

"I'm not going to put you in touch with counterfeiters and crooks who sell fake i.d.s," said Stone. "In the end, those things can always be tracked down and then where would you be? But I've helped other fugitives from Families get more-or-less legitimate identities, and a gatemage like you should be able to get one that's a lot realer than usual, without having to bribe half as many people."

After Stone explained the system and identified a likely county that hadn't fully computerized their old records, it took only an hour for Danny to learn the ins and outs of record keeping in West Jefferson, North Carolina, which Stone had chosen as his new birthplace. Inserting his birth into the records wasn't hard, so that when he and Veevee showed up asking for a duplicate, while Veevee shed a tear for her dear dead sister and brother-in-law, Danny's fictitious parents, they got a copy of the birth certificate with no trouble.

Stone looked at the birth certificate and made a face. "Why didn't you use 'Silverman' as your last name?"

"In Ashe County, North Carolina? That's not going to be a believable name."

"But 'Danny Stone'? I'm flattered, but—"

"It's the one I thought of while I was in the records room," said Danny. "Since it's not really your name, I didn't think you'd mind. And since I didn't use 'Von Roth,' I figured Marion and Leslie would be fine with any other name I chose that *would* be believable in Ashe County."

The Social Security number was a little trickier. There was a lot more information coded into the number than most people suspected. But Stone had a Westilian friend in the system who could pluck out whatever unused numbers met the paradigms—Social Security numbers of children who had died without ever having anything added to their records in the system. Attaching Danny's pertinent information to one of the numbers took very little time.

Then there was the matter of recording false childhood immunization records, but that was another job that a gatemage could do after hours in the office of a pediatrician who had been in the trade in the same town for a long time.

As for Danny's actual immunizations, Stone insisted that he owed it to the other children to actually get the shots and vaccinations.

"I can always go through a gate and heal myself whenever I start to feel sick."

"I thought you were educated, Danny," said Stone. "Don't you know you can be contagious for days before any symptoms show up?"

The fact is Danny didn't want anyone poking him with needles. It had never happened to him and he was pretty sure he wouldn't like it.

"Danny," said Stone, "it's just a matter of distraction. Wiggle your toes while they're giving you the shots. Concentrate on that, and the needles themselves won't bother you."

As usual, Stone was right. But toe-wiggling did nothing for the sore arms. And Stone wouldn't let him go through a gate until he was sure the immunizations had had time to work. "If you 'heal' your body by gate before the injections have a chance to stimulate the immune system, then the shots will have been for nothing. *Think*, Danny. Don't be such an adolescent."

I'm going to high school, Danny wanted to say. But he knew that Stone was right. He could not afford to be self-indulgent the way other teenagers could. He might be planning to live among drowthers, but he was not a drowther, and he could not afford to forget it.

When he was ready, Danny made a public gate between the attic room where he had slept at Stone's house and a spot against a wall in Veevee's condo. He doubted they'd discover it by accident, so at some point, when he judged it might be a good idea, he'd tell them about it.

Veevee was marvelous as his aunt who was moving to Buena Vista to explore opening up a small clothing factory. "For certain boutique clients in New York and L.A.," she explained, "who *must* be able to tell their customers that the clothing is made in America by seamstresses who are paid a fair wage with full benefits. Though it will take time to assemble the funding, you understand. And since this will be my most *stable* address, poor Danny and I agreed that this is where he should live." The principal seemed happy to know that there might actually be a new employer in town; and in the meantime, Veevee's story would have no impact on Danny's desired image as a not-rich kid who lived pretty much alone in a semi-crummy house. If anyone asked about his aunt's plans to start a clothing factory, he'd simply roll his eyes as if there was little truth in it, or she was crazy, or whatever teenagers assumed.

Danny intended to be a good student, but not speak up much in class; to dress decently but not too well; to be a little wild, but not dangerously so; to be funny but never the class clown. He might try out for the school play. He knew that boys were always at a premium, and he figured that a con man like him would be a decent actor. He knew he could memorize the lines. There'd be girls in the cast.

He had it all planned out.

18

The Father of Trick

꙳

The boy called Oath had walked at nine months of age, having never spent much time upon his knees, as King Prayard often pointed out. He was talking in clear sentences at fourteen months. It was far too soon to look for signs of any affinity, but this was Iceway, and so every time the boy even glanced at water it was taken for a token of things to come. The King had carried him upon his shoulders, taken him to councils, shown him off before ambassadors, flaunted him especially before the representatives of Gray.

But then, as Bexoi's belly began to grow with yet another child, a strange thing happened. The King became solicitous of Bexoi and spent more time with her. He wasn't often seeking out Prince Oath. And though the tot was only sixteen months of age, he felt the change; he felt it as a loss. "Where is Papa?" he would ask. And his nurses would answer, "He's the King, and he must do his work."

But in truth King Prayard was not working, he was rubbing salves into the tight-stretched skin of Bexoi's belly, hearing her say, "*This* is the child you put inside me on purpose, *this* is the child that will be the product of your love, and not your contempt."

"Don't taunt me with my old mistakes," King Prayard murmured.

"I'm celebrating our newfound love," said Bexoi. "Politics are finally gone. This will not be a political child."

"I hope that she's a girl," he said, "and that she looks like you."

"So you can marry her off to some foreign king, and we'll never see her again?"

"But a boy will be a rival to Oath," said Prayard.

"A boy will be a protection for the kingdom," said Bexoi. "This boy that is so ripe that in two months he'll burst forth into the world, he will step behind Prince Oath in every way, ready at a moment's notice to take his place, if something dreadful were to happen to his brother."

"You fear your nephew Frostinch, don't you?" asked King Prayard.

"Your heir will have so many enemies. Two sons will serve the kingdom better than one. Look what happened to the children of your concubine."

"You know I never think of her," said Prayard, "and yet you grieve me by mentioning her again and again."

"I think of how she disappeared so tragically, and her sons—you can never have too many sons."

Wad heard all of this. He heard, and knew that Bexoi knew he heard. These were subtle threats against the boy that she called Oath and he called Trick. Yet what could he do? He was Wad the kitchen boy, Wad the Squirrel, Wad the silent roamer and runner of errands; now that Hull was gone he had become less than nothing, barely tolerated in the kitchen, and not endured at all anywhere else. If he was found in the stables they thrust him out as if his presence would poison the horses; if he was found in the armory, he was treated as if he would dull the blades of all the swords.

How could such a one be granted even a moment in the presence of the Prince?

But Wad the Gatefather, Wad the Man in the Tree, Wad the lover of a queen and warden of three royal prisoners, the Wad that no one knew of but Bexoi herself—how could he be prevented?

So while she lay there, manipulating the King's affections, Wad was listening, yes, with half an ear, opening the tiniest of gates between his ear and her chamber so he heard without having to see what passed between Prayard and her, he also kept a tryst of another sort.

He gated little Trick to a garret room that Wad had set up as a child's playroom—not overpopulated with bright-colored toys, as fools think children want their world to be, but thick with dust and ancient furniture and trunks and weapons and other forgotten detritus of bygone kings and queens and stewards and princes, where there are nooks and dens and lofty places and deep but tiny dungeons to explore. Here he and Trick would play at hide and seek, or Wad would let the toddler dress him up in dusty old clothes, or they would play with toy soldiers and carts and carriages.

"I will always call you Trick," Wad told the boy, "because it's a trick on everybody when we play together. You can't tell anyone or I'll be sent away. You must pretend that you don't see me when you're with your nurses or your mother or the King. Pretend that I'm invisible. Because I am."

And then he winked out of existence in one spot, and then winked back a few feet off, and Trick clapped his hands and laughed and shrieked.

Meanwhile, back in his nursery, a lifesize wooden baby doll pretended to be young Oath, the well-tended Prince, asleep in his high-sided bed, the one that kept him safe—but also quite invisible to his lazy nurses, who dozed or gossiped or did needlework while supposedly he slept. When, even after an hour's nap, he seemed fitful and tired as if he hadn't slept at all, they took it as a sign that he missed his father the King, never realizing that the father he was missing was the much-despised kitchen boy whose presence in Nassassa no one understood.

Sometimes, though, Trick fell asleep while he was with Wad in their secret garret playroom. Then his father would sit and look at him, and whisper to him silently: Your mother is a monster of ambition; your father a monster of cruelty for her sake. She plots against you. She plots your death. But I will keep you safe. She will know that she dares not harm you, for the consequence would be too dire.

Deep inside himself, Wad felt the answering echoes of hundreds of other minds. Usually they were a sea of turmoil, and for long years he had not understood what they were, thinking them to be a part of himself. Now, however, he knew this much: They had memories that could not be his own. They had wills that would not choose what he had chosen, and when he acted in a way that distressed them, any of them, they'd protest, a sort of indigestion in his mind. How he came to have such madnesses within his mind he could not guess, but he must live with them, he knew. They were powerless to harm him.

When it came to Trick, however, they were of one mind and heart with him. He is your son, they echoed, when he said, He is my son. You must protect him now because that's what a father does. You must die for him, kill for him. Whoever puts the boy in danger, even if it is his very mother, is your enemy. If you can't control the woman, she must die.

19

Rope Climb

On Danny's first day of school, he ran. He had no books to carry, and though it was going to be a hot day, the morning wasn't too warm for a good run. Dressed in tee-shirt, jeans, and running shoes, with a pen in his pocket and a spiral notebook in his minimal backpack, Danny locked the front door behind him and started loping along the street.

He wasn't running particularly fast; he simply saw no reason to walk when running would do. Nor did he have any need to slow down just because the last stretch of road that wound up the hill to the school was so steep. Danny had been running up and down steeper hills than that, with much less even ground and a lot more obstacles, since he was little. To him, it was an easy jaunt. He wasn't even out of breath when he reached the office to get his class assignments.

"Coming in as a junior, Mr. Stone," said Principal Massey, "we thought you might appreciate a little help getting acquainted with the school."

That explained the presence of a bored-looking girl without a hair out of place.

"That's cool," said Danny. "Thank you."

"Here's your class schedule," said Massey. "Laurette will help you find your classes."

"Thanks, Laurette," said Danny. He gave her a big smile that was designed solely for Massey's consumption. Danny had read enough young adult novels to know that Laurette was probably popular and bound to look down on him.

She flashed him a quick cheesy smile—also for Massey's consumption.

"I'm glad you came early," said Massey. "That'll give the two of you time to get familiar with the layout of the school."

They left the office together. "Why are you all sweaty?" asked Laurette as soon as Massey couldn't hear.

"Because you're so amazing," said Danny.

"Ew," said Laurette.

"Because I ran to school."

"What are you, some kind of jock?" she asked.

"I don't have a car," he said.

"Well, I guess you won't need to know about parking passes."

Danny laughed.

"What's funny?" she asked.

"What's your story?" asked Danny in reply. "Why did you get stuck with showing the new kid around?"

"Because I mouthed off to my English teacher so I've got to do service hours."

"This is the first day of school," Danny pointed out.

"I have three weeks of service hours left over from last year."

"You must have some mouth."

"This is the hallway," said Laurette. "That's a class-room. Can you count?"

"Usually," said Danny.

"Then you can probably figure out the room numbers. They're mostly in order. Any questions?"

"Will you be my best friend?" asked Danny.

She barked a laugh. "If you're going to run to school, invest in a better deodorant."

"For a girl who doesn't care if anybody likes her, you sure go to a lot of effort to show off cleavage," said Danny.

She reached up and spread the lapels of her blouse about an inch farther. "Got your eyeful?" she asked.

"No. I'll be studying your cleavage all year."

"You've got a filthy mouth, Danny Stone," she said.

"I'm betting that the average total will turn out to be two."

She walked away from him.

So far so good, thought Danny. Either she likes me now, or she hates me. That means either her friends will hate me and her enemies will like me, or vice versa. No way does this girl not have friends and enemies.

Danny had first period English. He made it a point to answer no questions the teacher asked, even though he was interested in some of the things she said and he had a strong temptation to blow the teacher away with all the cool stuff he knew about the language. Instead, he said nothing at all, barely looked at her, and adopted the slightly sullen attitude he saw some of the boys wearing. He knew he could always be smart later, if that turned out to be a better strategy. But once you admitted to being smart, there was no going back. At least that was his hypothesis as a high school anthropologist.

Calculus was going to be easy and dull—a repeat of stuff Danny had mastered the first year he was living with the Silvermans. AP history was going to be funny, because everything the teacher said was either misleadingly incomplete or flat-out wrong, but it didn't matter because the students weren't listening anyway.

Lunch was what mattered. Where would he sit at lunch.

He got his tray and carried it over to the table where Laurette was sitting. She had three girlfriends with her. One was chubby but dressed like she thought she was thin, complete with bulgy bare midriff. Another was doing Goth, and the third had medium bad acne and a sour-looking expression that made the Goth look cheerful. Compared to them, Laurette looked like a cheerleader.

"Look," said Laurette when he sat down. "We're not friends."

"Oh, I know," said Danny. He looked at the Goth. "I just had to know why you aren't wearing any of your piercings."

"None of your business," said the Goth.

"Just tell me and I'll go away," said Danny.

"Go away now," said the Goth.

"He thinks he's cute," said Laurette. "He talked about my cleavage."

"Ew," said Chubby and Goth.

"Everybody talks about your cleavage," said Sour.

"Not to *me*," said Laurette. "It's, like, rude."

"I'm betting," said Danny to Goth, "that either there's an anti-piercing policy here that everybody ignores except you, or your parents won't let you wear them to school, or you walked too close to a really powerful magnet, or your piercings get infected a lot so you have to give them a rest." It was an easy enough deduction—two of the pierced spots were red and inflamed.

Goth pointedly looked away from him.

"Thanks," said Danny. He started to pick up his lunch tray.

"She didn't say anything," said Laurette.

"Yeah, but I give up easy," said Danny.

As he walked away, he made a gate directly in front of Goth and passed the mouth of it over her. It only moved her a quarter of an inch forward. Her friends didn't really notice it except as some kind of twitch, but *she* felt it.

"Hey!" she said loudly.

Danny stopped and turned around.

"Did you shove me, smelly running boy?"

"Oh, so Laurette *did* talk about me," said Danny. He set the tray back down on their table.

Goth's piercings were all healed. As in completely gone. As if never pierced at all. None of the girls noticed it. Danny started eating.

The girls got up and left. As they went, he made a gate right in front of Sour, jumping her forward two inches and up a half inch, and curing her acne. Nobody noticed the immediate improvement in her complexion, however, because the jump made her trip and drop her tray. Danny didn't even watch, though he heard her eloquent fecal-centered discourse, along with Goth's and Laurette's laughter as they helped her pick up the mess.

On a whim, Danny made the gate public in both directions. Anyone who walked through that exact spot in the lunchroom would become healthy—and, quite probably, trip and drop something.

After a few minutes, a couple of guys—one of them really tall, the other overweight with way too many piercings and his hair half shaved off—sat down, Too Tall beside him, Half-Hair across from him. "You actually hit on Laurette?"

"She say I did?" asked Danny.

"She said *you* said you were going to be watching her breasts all year."

"Doesn't everybody?" asked Danny.

"She practically sticks them in your face," said Half-Hair.

"Not *his*," said Danny, pointing to Too Tall. "She's not tall enough."

"Did you really run to school?" asked Too Tall.

"Yeah."

"Why?"

"It was there," said Danny.

"Where you from?" asked Half-Hair.

"Ohio," said Danny.

"Your aunt really going to start a clothing factory in town?"

Danny rolled his eyes.

"What's the rest of your schedule?" asked Too Tall.

"Gym after lunch," said Danny.

"You really in AP History?" asked Half-Hair.

Danny nodded.

"I got gym next period, too," said Too Tall.

"Am I going to have a wonderful time in physical education this year?" asked Danny.

"Depends on whether you suck up to Coach Bleeder," said Too Tall.

"I take it you don't."

"There's too many guys already kissing his butt," said Too Tall. "Can't wedge my face in."

"I bet you don't even try," said Danny.

"If you run," said Half-Hair, "he'll want you for the track team and you can be his best friend."

"I don't compete," said Danny.

They studied him for a few moments, as he made a stack of potato chips and then pushed the entire stack endwise into his mouth, crushing the chips in the process.

Half-Hair made a smaller stack and tried to eat it the same way. He ended up with potato chip fragments all over his shirt. Danny reached over, picked one off, and ate it. Initiation over. They finished eating their lunch with him and he knew he had a place with them the next day. Danny knew these guys were not generally regarded as cool. Not a problem. He would make them cool through their association with him.

So far Danny was having a great time at high school. Too Tall turned out to be named Hal Sargent. He was apparently Coach Lieder's favorite target of abuse. As in, "Everybody hit the floor and do twenty so I can see what I'm working with this year. Hal, the floor is the wall-to-wall wooden thing that you couldn't hit if you dropped a shot put. Lay your face on it and then peel it off twenty times."

Hal seemed resigned to the ridicule.

Danny passed a gate over Coach Lieder just as he was turning around. The gate lifted him an inch above the floor. He lost his balance and fell heavily on his butt.

Everybody stopped doing pushups.

"Keep going, you morons, haven't you ever seen anybody fall down before?" said Lieder.

Danny did his pushups quickly.

"New Kid," said Lieder.

Danny started a second set of twenty.

"New Kid," Lieder demanded. "You call those push-ups?"

"Yes sir," said Danny. He started clapping his hands at the top of each pushup.

"You a show-off, New Kid?"

"Sometimes, sir," said Danny. He pitched his voice exactly right—completely respectful, and yet dryly sarcastic. A couple of kids laughed. Danny finished his second twenty and stood up.

"I saw you running to school this morning, New Kid," said Lieder.

Danny didn't say anything.

"I didn't tell you to stop doing pushups."

"You said to do twenty," said Danny. "I did forty."

"Everybody outside," said Coach Lieder. "Daniel Stone, the show-off new kid, is going to lead you all in running the hill, down and then back up again."

Everybody groaned.

"Keep it up and you'll do it twice," said Lieder.

Danny jogged lazily down the hill, not leading anybody. He walked back up with Hal and a couple of others who weren't in running shape.

"I thought I said to run," said Lieder when Danny reached the top.

"I was told I needed to get a better deodorant before I ran the hill again," said Danny.

"Are you getting smart with me?" asked Lieder.

"Simple truth, sir," said Danny.

"I said for you to show them how to run it."

Danny said nothing.

"Run it alone," said Lieder.

"I run for pleasure, sir," said Danny.

"So give *me* the pleasure of watching you run," said Lieder. He pulled out a stopwatch.

Have I goaded him enough? Danny asked himself. Do I really need this enemy?

Yeah, he answered himself. Everybody hates him. I definitely want him on my case.

Danny took off down the hill. He loped lazily all the way to the stop sign at the bottom, turned around and ran back up at exactly the same speed.

"That the best you can do?" asked Lieder.

"I ran the hill," said Danny.

"You were running faster this morning."

"This morning I was eager to get to school," said Danny.

"I was timing you," said Lieder.

"I know."

"So why didn't you run your fastest?" asked Lieder.

"Because I run for pleasure," said Danny. "And that's how fast it pleased me to run."

"You and I aren't going to get along this year, New Kid," said Coach Lieder.

"I can't see why not," said Danny. "I'm a nice guy." There were some stifled laughs.

"You're an insubordinate jerk," said Coach Lieder.

"Well, yeah," said Danny.

The laughs weren't very well stifled this time.

"Run this hill five times," said Coach Lieder.

"No sir," said Danny.

"What?"

"It's too hot," said Danny. "It's still summer. You can't make a kid run this hill five times in hot weather right after eating lunch." The words "hospital" and "lawsuit" went unsaid.

Coach Lieder stood there regarding Danny in stony silence. "Everybody get back into the gym." He turned to lead the way.

Danny started running the hill, this time as fast as he could go, both ways. It didn't take long.

When he got to the top of the hill again, Lieder's face was red. The other kids were still gathered around. "What do you think you're doing?" he demanded.

"Heading into the gym, sir, like you said."

"You ran the hill," said Lieder.

"Yes sir," said Danny.

"After you told me you wouldn't."

"I only said you couldn't make a kid do it five times in hot weather right after eating lunch."

"But then you did it."

"It was my pleasure," said Danny.

"You knew I wanted to time you," said Coach Lieder. "You started when my back was turned."

"I don't like being timed," said Danny.

"I'm going to be timing you all semester."

"Takes all the pleasure out of running," said Danny.

"Timing each part of your run is how you get better."

"I don't want to get better," said Danny. "It's *already* fun."

Then Coach Lieder played his trump card. "Parry McCluer High School needs you on the track team."

"No it doesn't," said Danny.

It obviously bothered Lieder that Danny was not flattered to be offered a place on the team. "How much of this do you think I'm going to take from you?"

"Track is voluntary, sir," said Danny. "And I don't race."

"You don't *race*?" asked Lieder.

"I like running *with* people. When you race, one of you is supposed to leave the other behind. What's the point of running *with* somebody, if you end up by yourself?"

Lieder was going to have a stroke. "To win!" he said.

"To win what?" asked Danny.

"The. Race."

"I don't race." Danny started walking back to the gym.

"Run that again and let me time you this time!" demanded Lieder.

Danny just kept walking. "I've already run it twice. It's going to be ninety-five today. I'm going inside."

After gym he had biology and then drama. In biology he sat there silently, judging how current the teacher's information was. In drama, he made a huge splash just by being male in a class with eleven girls and only two other guys.

By the end of the first day, Danny was legendary in exactly the way he wanted. Everybody knew his name. He had defied a teacher. He had shown that he could really, really run. Yet he didn't care about winning. And Sin—Cynthia Arnelle, the Goth who was allergic to her piercings—was convinced that he had done something magical to heal her. "He even erased the holes," she was telling people.

"They just grew over," Laurette told them adamantly. "*He* didn't heal anything."

Danny was leaving school right then, jogging past. "Hey, you!" Sin shouted. Danny jogged over to her. "You erased my piercings, you asshole."

Danny looked her over closely. "You have piercings?" he asked.

"Not *now*," she said. "Thanks to you."

"When did I do this?" asked Danny, showing a puzzled expression.

"When you got up from the table at lunch. You jostled me, and now my piercings have completely healed over."

Danny looked from Sin to Laurette and the other girls. "Wow," he said. "For a girl named Sin, she's doing pretty well with faith-healing."

Sour Girl's complexion was now clear, and if she smiled she'd probably be pretty. Danny reached out to stroke her cheek. She slapped his hand away, assuming, no doubt, that he was mocking her. She didn't like to be touched on a cheek covered with zits.

But now that Danny had almost touched her, Laurette and Sin were staring at Pat's smooth skin, probably for the first time, since as friends they had trained themselves not to notice her complexion.

Now my work here is done, Danny said silently. He jogged off down the hill.

This was going to be a great year.

IN THE FIRST two weeks of school, Danny never ran fast except when Lieder wasn't timing him. It was a running joke and got him called to the principal's office.

"He can time me whenever he wants," said Danny. "He times me a lot."

"But you never run fast when he's timing you," said Principal Massey.

"I don't like being timed."

"That's like saying you don't like being graded."

"I don't," said Danny. "Takes all the fun out of it."

"But your teachers tell me you're doing excellent work, and *they* all grade you."

"So far I was interested in all the assignments."

"Listen, Danny Stone, I know you were home-schooled, but you need to understand that in public school, you fulfill your assignments, you obey your teachers."

"I fulfill my assignments, sir. I obey my teachers."

"Listen, Danny, I'm telling you: Obey Coach Lieder. Let him time you at your best!"

"I can't help it if he drops the watch," said Danny. "Or falls down. I run my fastest a lot, but the only runs he ever manages to time happen to be the slower ones."

"You have an attitude," said Principal Massey.

"How can I *not* have an attitude?" said Danny. "Everybody *always* has an attitude, even if it's only apathy."

"See? It's smart remarks like that . . ."

"How is that a smart remark? It's just . . . true."

"Get out of here," sighed Principal Massey.

Thursday of the second week, a few girls discovered the healing properties of the Tripping Place in the lunch-room and word of it quickly spread, even among those who regarded it as an urban legend. Those who tested it were freaked out when it worked, but more and more girls were arranging to pass through the spot.

As far as Danny could tell, though, only one person connected him with the Tripping Place. "You did this," said Pat, touching her cheek.

"Did what?" asked Danny.

"I had the worst acne in the school," said Pat. "Now it's gone."

"So you grew out of it. What does that have to do with me?"

"You did it," she said. "The Tripping Place in the lunchroom—I was the first person to trip there. You did it, and it healed me."

"Just like that?" asked Danny. "Wow, I must be, like, really magic."

"You show up at Parry McCluer and strange things start happening."

"So I'm in control of, like, the spacetime continuum."

"Why did you decide to cure my acne and heal over Sin's piercings?" demanded Pat.

"You and Sin seem to think I care about you way more than I actually do."

"Then why do you keep sitting down at the same table as us during lunch? And bringing those dweebs Hal and Wheeler with you? Are you trying to destroy our reputation?"

"Just studying Laurette's cleavage," said Danny. "She's still averaging two, but I keep hoping for changes."

Pat called him a name and walked away. But she couldn't fool Danny. He had seen the smile playing around the corners of her mouth. She liked her new face. She liked *him*. And pretty soon she'd work up the courage to admit it to Laurette and Sin and Xena.

Danny enjoyed doing things for people. Especially for his friends.

Unfortunately, Danny also enjoyed toying with people who weren't his friends. Especially jerks who were begging to get pranked.

But Danny didn't want to be the typical gatemage, playing nasty tricks on people and laughing at them without compassion. If there was anything he had learned from the Silvermans, it was that you should use your magery to make the world a better place. And he already learned for himself that you don't walk away from somebody else's need, not if there's something you can do about it. Even Coach Lieder didn't deserve to be abused; whenever he left Danny and Hal alone, Danny left *him* alone.

One night, when Danny was having dinner with Veevee at her favorite little Italian spot in Naples, he asked her, "If this whole theory about gatemages serving spacetime is true, then if I *don't* play vicious pranks on people, does that make my power to influence spacetime weaken or go away?"

"I have no idea," said Veevee.

"Okay," said Danny. "Just wondering."

"Danny, you're a natural smart aleck. You can't help it. It just doesn't stop. And the worst thing is, when you want to, you get away with it. *That's* how you prank spacetime itself—you don't ever have to suffer the consequences of your pranks."

Danny didn't really set out to prove her wrong about consequences. It just happened.

On Danny's sixteenth birthday, he went to school as usual. It was a Tuesday. Over the P.A. system in the morning, Danny's birthday was read out by somebody from student government. It was cool how many people commented on his birthday as they passed him in the hall between classes. And at lunch, Laurette and Sin and their friends got him outside at lunch to sing him a deliberately off-key version of "Happy Birthday" that replaced the word "to" with another word that started with *F*.

"Is that, like, my present?" asked Danny.

"Somebody had to say it to you," said Sin, "or it wouldn't really be your birthday." She had gotten two new piercings on one ear, and one of them was already infected. A slow learner, Danny figured. Not his job.

"Well, thanks," said Danny.

Coach Lieder had also noticed the announcement. "Sixteen years old, right, Stone?"

"Yes sir," said Danny.

"Well, I have a present for you." He pointed to the thick rope dangling from the ceiling near one wall of the gym, with a bunch of mats under it. It hadn't been hanging there yesterday.

"We're having a hanging," said Danny. "Cool."

"Climb it," said Lieder.

"I don't know how to climb a rope," said Danny.

"Your other teachers tell me you're a quick learner."

"But, see, *they* make an effort to teach me," said Danny.

"Put your hands on the rope and pull yourself up," said Lieder. "Then grip the rope with your legs so you don't slide down, while you reach up to raise yourself to the next level. There, I've taught you. You have a new skill. It's my present to you, Birthday Boy."

It took three tries, but Danny made it to the top without using a single gate. His legs and hands were raw. And getting down without rope burns was nearly impossible. But Danny made it a point not to show any reaction to the pain—though he also refrained from using a gate to heal himself. He wanted the other kids to see that even though his skin was red and raw, he showed no sign of minding the pain.

It clearly rattled Lieder that Danny made it up the rope and didn't complain about the discomfort. So he started in on his favorite victim. Hal was tall, but he was skinny. There wasn't an ounce of muscle on his body. His arms looked like Amish buggy whips. His leg muscles looked like he went home to a concentration camp every night.

Hal couldn't lift himself up by his arms. Period. Not even a chin-up. Certainly not the first upward surge of a rope climb. And even when a couple of guys lifted him up off the ground as a "boost," he just slid down, yelling in pain the whole time.

"Get him up the rope," Lieder ordered Danny.

"What do you want me to do?" asked Danny. "Push him up?"

"I want to see him at the top of the rope," said Lieder.

"Sorry, dude," said Hal to Danny.

"Not your fault," said Danny. Of course, Danny *could* get Hal to the top of the rope whenever he wanted. But it might be a little too spectacular. As in, make-the-newspapers.

Danny remembered what he used to do for himself, before he even knew he was a gatemage. Short little gates that he didn't even realize *were* gates.

Danny had vowed never to use gates to help himself win a contest. But to help a friend silence a tormentor? That was different.

Danny tried to figure out how to do it so it wasn't obvious, even if someone was watching. Maybe a spiral set of gates, so you couldn't see as easily that Hal's hand movements had nothing much to do with his rise up the rope.

Lieder was busy yelling at some other poor sap, and everybody was watching him. Danny grabbed onto the rope and then set it—and himself—to spinning. While he spun, he made a series of gates rising up the rope.

He figured that if Hal was twisting on the rope while he climbed, it wouldn't be so obvious that what was happening was unnatural.

Then, as the rope started unwinding, Danny made another bunch of little gates spiraling back down from the ceiling.

Danny beckoned to Hal, who really was in pain from rope burns on his thighs and hands. "Try it again," he said softly. "Keep your hands moving so it looks like you're really doing it."

"What are you talking about?" asked Hal.

"Just grab onto the bottom of the rope and start spinning clockwise. You'll see."

Nobody was watching at the moment, which was a good thing. Because it didn't work at all the way Danny expected. Hal grabbed on, started spinning, and *shot* upward in a spiral. Only he didn't stop at the top. He just disappeared.

About half a minute later, though, he reappeared spiraling down the rope. He fell on his butt and then flipped over and crawled along the mats to get away from the rope. All his rope burns were gone.

"What happened?" Hal demanded hoarsely.

"I don't know," said Danny. "What do you *think* happened?"

"I start spinning, and suddenly it's like I'm a mile up, looking out over the whole Maury River Valley, I mean I can see the cars going into and out of the Mc-Donald's drive-through in Lexington, I'm up so high. And I feel great. But I'm still spinning, see, and then all of a sudden I start to fall, only whatever it is catches me and sucks me down, still spinning. To here. I think I'm going to puke. Motion sickness. Fear of heights. You're a dangerous friend to have, man. What is it, some kind of drug? Cause if that was a hallucination, it seemed pretty damn real."

Danny had made gates that all led to points on the rope. None of them could have taken Hal past the ceiling. Danny hadn't made anything like the gate Hal was describing.

Hal reached for the bottom of the rope and handed it to Danny. "You try," he said. "Show me how to do it right, if that was wrong."

Danny grabbed on and started spinning.

He really did spiral upward. But it didn't stop at the roof. Just as Hal said, the gate took Danny to a spot about a mile over the school—and held him there.

Before the gate began to let him slip downward, another kid from gym class joined him in the middle of the air at the south end of Buena Vista. "This is freakin' awesome," he shouted. "How'd you get it to do this? You some kind of freakin' magician or something? I want to learn how to do this trick!"

Danny spun down. All the guys in the class were lined up to "ride the rope."

Coach Lieder was sitting down, watching his students grab onto the rope and flat-out disappear. He looked at Danny with hatred and fear. "They're riding it like at a carnival," said Lieder. "You did this."

Danny had no answer. This was the worst thing imaginable. Word would get out. It would attract media attention. Especially once somebody set up a telephoto lens outside to see the kids hanging in midair before they spun back down. And Danny had no idea how to shut it down.

"Where are you really from?" asked Coach Lieder. "What damn planet, New Kid?"

"I don't know how this works," said Danny

truthfully. "Hal must have done it." Please, please, let Hal get all the credit in the media. Not that the story wouldn't still bring all the Families to Parry McCluer. And that would be the end of Danny's high school career.

A couple of weeks and it would be over. All because Danny *had* to use gates to impress his friends. No, oh no, it was to *help* his friends. *Except* Danny knew better. He really was a show-off. He had been so careful not to use gatemagery to cheat at athletics, and here he was using it to cheat and win at high school life. What had he been *thinking*? He had fallen into the same trap as the typical nerd hero in young adult novels, who gets himself in serious trouble by trying too hard to make a good impression on the other kids.

I learned nothing, thought Danny. And now I'm going to lose it all. I have to get away from here. Preferably now.

He might have gated away on the spot, gone home to Yellow Springs, and confessed all to the Silvermans, except that one of the guys at the rope shouted, "Hey! What's going on?"

Danny looked. The kid was spinning and spinning on the end of the rope, but nothing was happening.

The kids who had already gone up the rope kept coming down, so it was obvious that the gates were still working. Except the bottom one.

Danny looked at the gates. Or rather, *felt* the gates with that inner sense that had nothing to do with his eyes. They had been changed. They looked like his old gates. Only this was the first moment that he actually registered the fact that his old gates and the gates he made now were different. When had they changed? And why had *this* gate changed back?

As he watched, other gates in the spiraling sequence also changed. It was as if they were getting pinched. Closed. Someone or something was closing his gates *right now.*

Has the Gate Thief found me?

The last kid was back down the rope, and now the downward gates pinched off, one by one, until all the gates were locked.

All my old gates looked just like this. They must have been locked when I created them, so I was the only one who could go through them. But when Veevee found them, she unlocked them. She's a Keyfriend, that's what she does. Only once I saw what my gates looked like *open,* I started creating them that way. I imitated what she did with my gates without even realizing it.

Had Veevee figured out how to lock gates as well as open them? Was she checking up on him and saving him from his own mess? If so, he would *not* be angry. The kids could say what they wanted, Coach Lieder could tell all to the media, and nobody would believe them as long as the spiral gates no longer worked. Unless a camera saw it happening and showed it on the news, it never happened at all, and the only story that would reach the papers was if Lieder was stupid enough to insist on the story until he got fired or committed.

Veevee had probably saved Danny's butt. She had to be just outside the gym somewhere—her range wasn't anywhere near as long as Danny's, she could only affect gates that were within a few blocks of her unless she actually saw them get made.

Danny was glad to see that the disappointed boys were pestering Hal about the fact that the gates no longer worked. It would give him a moment to slip out and apologize to Veevee for his stupidity and promise that he would never, never do it again, and as long as she was closing gates, could she please do something about the Tripping Place in the lunch room?

Danny stepped through the outside door and scanned for Veevee. Not there. She must be around the other side of the building.

So he ran in search of her, rounding the first corner in only a few steps. Rounding the second corner.

It wasn't Veevee.

It was the Greek girl.

A Family had found him. Even without the story hitting the papers. There had to be a whole bunch of the most powerful Greek mages poised to zap him with whatever powers they had. Filled with immediate terror, Danny did the only thing he could do. He gated away.

20

Locks

⚓

Danny was glad that he had never gated from his little house in Buena Vista up to the school or back again, even in the rain, because otherwise the Greek girl would be able to go from there to Veevee's house in Florida or the Silvermans' in Ohio or Stone's house in DC. Yet she had found and followed him from somewhere, and she would no doubt follow him now.

His first jump had been by reflex, to the place up in the woods above the school where as a child he used to sit and watch the high schoolers. From there, he gated to a rest stop on the road to DC where he and Eric had waited for three hours before they could find a ride, though they did get a couple of lunches and a lot of nearly finished bags of snack food. Danny had made no gate there.

He thought he might have a moment of safety in which to think about what had just happened and what he had just learned. But he had only been at the rest stop for about a minute when the Greek girl was right there beside him.

"Please wait!" she said.

If she said any more, he didn't know what. He created a gate to the spot in front of the Library of Congress where Eric had confronted him and where he had mooned the security guards. Now that he understood the difference between locked and unlocked gates, he could see that these were locked. What did he know about the Greek girl? She knew how to lock gates. Could she unlock them?

Danny passed through his own gate into the restroom alcove inside the library. He felt through all the gates in the library—all locked. If Lockfriends could unlock gates as well as lock them, then she would be inside the library in no time.

But she didn't come.

Was it that easy to lose her?

Did it even matter? Now that she had found Parry McCluer High, he could not remain there. Not that he hadn't already ruined everything himself, with his stupid spiral gate that took people a mile higher than he ever meant to, and which was public even though he didn't do any of the things that he thought making a public gate required.

No time to think about that, to regret the high school years he wouldn't have after all. All that mattered was staying alive, period.

And that would require that he learn how to take conscious control of the locking and unlocking of his gates.

The gates he had made ever since meeting Veevee were open; all the gates before that were locked. Why had he changed? *How* had he changed? Did Veevee's mere presence suddenly reshape the gates he made? Or did she deliberately change them, opening all his gates without his realizing it?

No. Veevee wasn't changing them—he'd know it if she were, just as he knew when the Greek girl closed the spiral gates at the climbing rope in the gym. They were already open for her when he made them.

Danny made a gate between the bathroom alcove and a spot right in the middle of the catalog room. It was a gate he never meant to use. He just had to see how gates came out of him now.

It was unlocked. If the Greek girl were inside the library, she could find it and use it.

But what was it about the way he shaped it that left it open, when before he had made all his gates prelocked? What changed when Veevee came on the scene?

It wasn't just that she unlocked his gates when she used them. He hadn't even noticed the difference. Maybe it was the way Veevee changed his *attitude* toward gatemaking. Her exuberance. Her enthusiasm. She made gatemagery fun.

And before it had always been something fraught with peril. Escaping from the Family compound, knowing he'd be killed if he were caught. On the run with Eric, getting into the library, doing burglaries—those gates were about survival. Or crime. But once Veevee came on the scene, and he realized he was making the gates as much for her as for himself, it became a pleasure. But how did his mood change the way he shaped the gates? And how could he control his mood for gate-shaping purposes?

He made gate after gate to various points around the library, trying to refine his mood. The trouble was, it *couldn't* be the mood he was in, because at this exact moment he was terrified, and yet none of the gates was locked.

To judge from my gates, he thought, I'm having all kinds of fun.

He remembered the pinching feeling that he experienced when the Greek girl was closing the gates. *That* was what he needed to duplicate, not his emotional state.

He tried to feel the pinch as he made his gates, but nothing happened.

There were now thirty gates leading from the alcove all over the library. Fortunately, none were public, though all were unlocked.

Stop making gates, you idiot, Danny told himself. Start trying to lock the ones you have. If a Lockfriend can do it, then a Gatefather like Danny should be able to do it in his sleep.

When Danny had started gatemaking, he wasn't even aware it was happening. He wasn't even conscious of the fact that he knew the location of every one of them, mouth and tail. Once he realized that he was a gatemage, however, and started making new ones, he had become aware of his map of all his gates. It had been there all along; he'd been sensing them all along. Likewise, before Veevee came, he hadn't been aware of whether gates were locked or unlocked, because he had nothing to compare them to, and *he* could go through any gate he made without unlocking it. After she came, he had noticed the difference unconsciously; it changed his gatemaking, though he still didn't realize it until now. So there were things he knew that he didn't know that he knew. Somewhere inside himself, he knew how to lock a gate.

He calmed himself and thought through his entire map of gates scattered from Virginia to Ohio to DC to Florida. Not a very large swath of the world, he realized. He wasn't exactly ready for the jet set. But regardless of distance, he was aware of every one of them. He could *move* any of them, as well.

Move them! Of course. If he moved all the gates so they no longer began or ended where they used to, then the Greek girl couldn't use them to follow him.

He reached out to the gates outside the library, one of which had just conveyed him inside, and pulled the mouth ends in.

In where? He hadn't really thought of *where*. Just . . . in.

But when he went to look for the gates he had just gathered, they were nowhere to be found.

And he gasped and leaned against the wall. He had just eaten his own gates. The thing that felt like "gathering in" was actually the long wished-for command to erase a gate. He had pulled them back into his— what, his inner satchel of potential gates? His outself.

What I thought of as "in" must be what it feels like for other types of mages to pull in their outself, stranding whatever clant they had made, or leaving their heartbeast to itself. And it had been as natural as breathing, just as the Silvermans had told him. Just as Uncle Poot had said.

If he had only known how to do this before the Greek girl came to visit the North compound, he could have left no trace of gatery for her to find.

But that would have required understanding that was beyond him. He could gather in his gates *now*.

This was no time for tidying up. He had to learn how to lock . . .

All the gates he had just made there in the library were locked.

While his attention was distracted, the Greek girl must have locked them. Of course she could sense where they were through the library walls. If she had followed him from the rest area to the mooning spot outside, then been blocked by the locked gate he originally made there, she could still reach in and lock his gates.

Now, though, he had a better idea of what was going on. Gathering in his gates was closely akin to simply moving them. Locking and unlocking were not different in kind from making.

It turned out to be so easy he almost cried with relief. He reached out to one of the gates the Greek girl had just locked, and did a faint almost-making at the mouth, only . . . wider. There was no muscle involved. There were also no words. It was more like conversing with someone by mental gesture. But the result was that the gate was no longer locked.

I have opened a gate, he realized.

When he tried to close it, nothing happened.

He could do what Veevee did, but not what the Greek girl did. He was half there.

The gate he had just opened closed again. The Greek girl was still at work. He felt once more the pinching off sensation. Only this time, having learned how to sense the opening of a gate, he realized that the closing was not at the mouth, it was at the tail.

The difference was a subtle one, since there was no distance between the mouth and the tail. From the outside there was, of course, but from inside a gate the mouth and tail actually occupied the same space at the same time. They were geometrically adjacent—there was no space between the inside of the mouth and the inside of the tail, no matter how far apart they were.

So until this moment he had not realized that in the making of all his earliest gates, he had inadvertently pinched off all the tails as he made them; but after meeting Veevee, he knew she would be coming after him and so, as automatically as holding a door for one of the Aunts or Mama, he had left the tail open behind him.

He unlocked one of the gates, then locked it again himself.

He unlocked all the gates that began inside the library. Then he locked them all. Now that he understood it, it was easy.

All these years of working to try to master this art, but with nobody to teach me or explain it to me . . . it's not their fault, or mine either. They had no words to explain it. Maybe even now, if Danny described how locking and unlocking felt to him, Veevee and the Greek girl would look at him as if he were a madman and tell him that it felt *nothing* like that to them.

He sensed something being attempted with one of the locked gates, but he couldn't tell what. It had to be the Greek girl, but what was she doing?

She was trying to see if she could open a locked gate.

He felt another thrill of fear. I just learned how to lock gates by watching her lock them. Have I now taught her how to *un*lock them, by letting her watch *me*?

He calmed his fear: Terror is not conducive to clear thinking, since it moves decision-making from the conscious mind to the limbic reflexes. What matters is not that she's trying to learn to open locked gates.

What matters is that she was actively trying to help *me* learn how to lock them.

What else could her locking of all the new gates in the library have been? She couldn't *use* them. She must have understood that he was trying to learn how to lock them, and so she locked them all just to show him. To help him.

Was it possible that she hadn't followed him in order to point him out to assassins?

He made a viewport. He had learned to do this by making gates to push his face through, as he had first done in Rico's office. In the effort to keep his face from being visible, however, he had kept shrinking the gate until the mouth of it was a pinprick in size, and the tail was at the lens of his eye. Now he understood that each such viewport was really a half-made gate, which was locked at both ends, so that only he could see through it.

He looked through the viewport at the mooning spot.

There she was, looking angry and frustrated and, yes, a little scared.

Then she noticed the viewport—not with her eyes, of course, but with her gatesense. She turned, reached out a finger, touched it. The effect was not to block his vision, but rather to include her whole body in it. To let him sense what she sensed.

It was profound and disturbing. It was no longer a visual connection. It was as if he had, not the use of her body, but a glimpse of her selfsense. How her body felt inside itself.

He could also feel her gatesense—how his gates looked to her. Could she feel his? Was he laying himself just as bare to her, his inner map of all the gates that he had ever made? And could she sense that he was sensing her this way? Was that what she intended?

He let the feeling of her selfsense wash over him, through him. He shuddered with a kind of terrifying ecstasy. Would it be this way with anyone who knew where a viewport was, and touched it?

With this kind of intimate contact with her gate-sense and selfsense, could he also learn what she was thinking? What she intended?

No. There was no language in this, and it was not, strictly speaking, her mind that he was involved with here. The inself and outself were something quite different from the mind, though they responded to the mind's instructions. It was as if the inself were the skeleton of the puppet that the mind controlled, while the outself was the strings that hung down to animate other puppets.

Could he use this connection to control her?

No. Danny stopped himself without even making the attempt. Even if it were possible, which he doubted, it would be manmagic to do it. A mage did not take control of another mage, even his worst enemy, even if it was in self-defense.

He pulled back the viewport from her finger so that he could see her visually again.

As soon as he did, he saw her double over, then drop down to a seated position on the grass and cover her face with her hands. She was crying. Sobbing, great heaves of her shoulders. What had he done to her?

He widened the viewport and pushed his face through it. "Did I hurt you?" he asked.

She shook her head.

"Why are you crying?"

She took her hands from her face, but also turned her face away.

Of course he could move the tail of the viewport wherever he wanted; but if she wanted him not to see her face, he would respect her wish.

"You were teaching me how to lock and unlock gates, weren't you," said Danny.

She nodded.

"Why?" said Danny. "Where's the rest of your Family?"

"They don't know where I am," said the Greek girl.

"Are you going to tell them?"

"I can't go back," she said. Her English was perfect, though it had a British tinge.

"Why not? They knew you were a gatemage."

"They thought I was just a Finder. That justified letting me live, despite the treaties and laws, because I couldn't actually *do* anything with gates. I never dared to show them I could move through your gates. *I* didn't even know I could until I finally came across an open one. But then . . . I had to go. Don't you see? I've been hungry for this my whole life. I felt so much hope when I first found you three Christmases ago, there in the North fortress. But all your gates were locked, and I couldn't open them. I could lock them more tightly— but what good was that, with you as the only other person in the world who could find them!"

She looked right at him, wiping tears off her cheeks as she did. "Then I found the open gate you made for your Keyfriend, there in Florida. Yes, I was in her flat, and no, she never saw me. If she had, don't you think she would have followed? I couldn't have blocked her. Anything I can lock, she can open."

"And anything she opens, you can lock."

Danny made the viewport into a complete gate and passed through it to sit beside her on the grass. "Are you saying that you're in as much danger now as I am?"

"I'm a real gatemage, am I not?" she said. "Not just a Finder, but someone who can change the gates. Who could lock down any but a Great Gate, who can tell where gates lead as well as where they start. They were with me walking through the mall in Naples, Florida, shopping—my parents, an uncle, the cousin they think I should marry—and I saw the open gate in a corridor leading down to the mall restrooms. I went right up to it and stepped through. I didn't care that it would cut me off from my own Family. I didn't even care where it led. I just knew that at last, after all these years, I had found a gate that I could use. And I locked it behind me."

"So you brought no one," said Danny.

"I came to meet *you*. But then I realized that you didn't leave all your gates open because you wanted to, you didn't even realize you were doing it. And when I got to the high school and saw that you were trying to twist a Great Gate—"

"I was?" asked Danny.

"Didn't they teach you anything?" asked the Greek girl.

"'Twist a Great Gate,'" he echoed. Then he began quoting the runes. "'Here Loki twisted a new gate to heaven.' I thought 'twist' was just the Fistalk term for making a gate. But it was about making a gate that spirals, making it while the gatemage is spinning."

"What do you think whirling dervishes were imitating?" asked the Greek girl. "They had seen a gatemage spinning while he made a gate to heaven. The Tower of Babel—Nimrod was one of the earliest gatemages to reach Mesopotamia, a mighty hunter who built a tower from which he suspended a rope, so he could wind himself up and then create a gate while spinning a long, long time. Doesn't your Family have these stories?"

"Nothing about gatemages," said Danny. "You can understand why."

"Of course they didn't tell you. Even in my family, they gave me access to the records of the gatemages only because they wanted me to be able to recognize whatever gates I might see. Not that it helped—there were no gates in all of Europe and Africa and Asia! Your Last Loki was thorough. All the gates in the world were gone. Until we drove into the North fortress and I saw gates everywhere. It took me a while to realize that's what I was sensing, and to realize that the ones located behind buildings and inside trees were as plain to me as the ones out in the open."

"So when you walked up to the wall where I was hiding . . ."

"I just wanted to see you. The only other gatemage I'd known of in my life. I could see the gates burning inside you—"

"What?"

"Your hearthoard," she said. "Gatemages don't have the normal outself, because it's already fragmented, ready to be made into gates. In your case, it's divided into bits so fine they almost seem like dust to me. That's what I was looking at. A million possible gates, all contained in a single vivid point inside your body."

"I've never felt that."

"What *did* you feel then, when you reached into me just a moment ago?" she said.

"No," Danny said. "It was you who reached out to *me*."

"I had to persuade you somehow that you could trust me. So I touched you to lay myself bare to you. Not in body, but my hearthoard. You could have stripped it away from me and added it to your own hearthoard. Sometimes lesser gatemages do that, so that a Pathbrother or Gatefather can have enough in his hearthoard to make a Great Gate. The lesser mage is left with nothing, but if the Great Gate is made, then it is deemed to be a worthy sacrifice."

"I don't know anything," said Danny. "Nobody I knew could teach me."

"I had books," said the Greek girl. "Nobody in *my* Family actually knows anything, either."

"Thank you for trusting me," said Danny. "I had no idea what was happening between us, when you reached into my viewport and I felt you."

"You understood enough to trust me and come out and join me here."

"I'm still afraid that it's all a lie," said Danny. "That some Grassbrother will make the lawn here swallow me up or something."

She took his hand. "Whatever happens to you will happen to me, I promise it. I will do whatever I can to protect you, when the time comes to make a Great Gate."

"I don't want to use up your . . . heart . . ."

"Hearthoard. Heart magazine, heart arsenal . . ."

"I don't want to take it away from you."

She laughed. "Don't you understand? I have never heard of a gatemage with a hearthoard like yours."

"You said it was only dust."

"No, no," she said. "The hearthoard is the same *size* in everyone. The potential gates expand to fill the size, or shrink to fit within it. Mine has only a few coarse granules. According to the books—well, *book*, the only one that discussed the hearthoard—the most powerful Gatefathers have so many gates inside that they are like grains of sand. But yours . . . yours are—"

"Dust," said Danny.

"That's what I saw when you were hiding there in the wall. A gatemage with so much power . . ."

Danny sat there digesting this.

"And then you were twisting a Great Gate there in the school, all by yourself."

"I had no idea what I was doing. I thought I was making a series of tiny gates to help my friend get to the top of a climbing rope in gym class."

She looked puzzled for a moment.

"Physical education."

"No, no, I understood you very quickly. I *am* a gatemage, you know, even if only a lesser one."

"Without you, I don't know if I would ever have learned locking and unlocking. Or even eating gates."

"You didn't eat any gates," she said, laughing a little.

"The gates that were out here—I took them back."

"Yes, you gathered in your own gates, but that's not *eating* them. Eating is when you take someone else's. It's a bit of their outself, so you're connected to them, then. That's eating. You can't eat your *own* gates."

"I don't know anything," said Danny. "Sixteen years old and I'm like a baby."

"Because they gave me five books to read," said the Greek girl. "Only five that talk about gatemages, out of our whole library—but it was five more books than anyone gave you."

She was still holding his hand.

"Do I know your name?" said Danny.

"Yllka," she said. "That's my public name. But the secret name my mother and father gave me, when they realized I must be some kind of gatemage, was Hermia."

Danny understood at once the classical reference to Hermes—the generic name for Greek Family gatemages. "So they thought you would be a gatemage like me? Despite the law?"

"Why do you think they brought me the books to read? I had all the signs—good with languages, a bratty trickster, no outself, no clant-raising ability, no affinities at all, yet very smart. I might have been drekka, but my parents hoped for more."

Danny shook his head. "All these years, everyone pretending that they hate the thought of having a gatemage, promising to kill the first one to show up—"

"My Family have been trying for years to persuade the others—not yours, of course—that the drowthers have become so powerful that the weak mageries that are within our reach are not enough to protect us. Where is the stonemage who can take apart an atomic bomb without touching it? Where is the Tempester who can blow a missile off its course? Where is the Sandfather or Claymaster who can swallow up a tank? And as for stopping a bullet or bending its course—there is no magery to deal with that. Not unless we can pass through a Great Gate once again and make ourselves strong. Instead of fighting each other, we must be preparing to protect ourselves against the drowthers."

"It sounds almost noble," said Danny.

"It isn't," said Hermia. "They miss being gods. They know that nobody will worship any of us in our present condition, let alone pay us tribute or obey us or regard us as anything but psychics or magicians—charlatans, yes?"

"And you thought I was making a Great Gate?"

"For your Orphan friends. That's who my Family fears most in this world—the Orphans. They've tried, you know. Gatemages have been born to them before this."

"They told me," said Danny. "The Gate Thief gets them. Which is why I would *not* have made a Great Gate today if I'd had the slightest clue that that was what I was doing."

"Well, it was pretty feeble, anyway," said Hermia. "It only went up a mile. You don't actually think there are any planets that close to the surface of the Earth, do you?" She smiled.

Danny laughed a little, but a new question came to mind. "How would I create a Great Gate anyway? I don't know where Westil is."

She shrugged. "We've never had to," said Hermia. "Make a gate that's large enough, and twist it so it shoots out beyond your conscious control, and . . . it ends up on Westil. Then twist it all the way back, and you have created a Great Gate. Public, powerful. Not only healing but enhancing. Strong men and women made stronger—like Herakles and Goliath. We couldn't make such drowthers into mages, but we could take them through the Great Gate—"

"Take them to Olympus," murmured Danny.

"And then bring them back many times stronger than they were."

"I should make one just for Hal," said Danny, thinking aloud.

"But that's why you need me there," said Hermia "To lock the other end of it the moment it reaches Westil. Otherwise, who knows what kind of person or beast would come down from Westil?"

Danny remembered something he had read in Leslie's King James Bible. "'And the great dragon was cast out,'" Danny recited from memory. "'That old serpent, called the Devil, and Satan, which deceiveth the whole world: he was cast out into the earth, and his angels were cast out with him.'"

"Is that the Bible?" asked Hermia.

"It just seemed appropriate," said Danny.

"Only that's not referring to Westilians," said Hermia.

"Who else, then? And why not us?"

"There were plenty of wars on Westil over the millennia that the Great Gates were open. But nobody in their right mind would cast their enemies out of Westil and send them to Mittlegard through a Great Gate. That would be like healing all their wounds and replacing their spears with artillery and their chariots with jet fighters. You lock them *out* of the Great Gates that you control and go back and forth yourself."

"So if I had opened a Great Gate before I knew how to lock it . . ."

"Great Gates are made up of hundreds of small gates woven together," said Hermia. "Like rope. But all the gates lead to Westil. You make them here but then as you twist them you're almost throwing the ends of them out into the universe, like casting a rope up to someone waiting on a cliff. There's no way you can do that while thinking of whether the gates are locked or not. So it doesn't really matter if you know how to lock them, as long as you have someone with you who does."

"And you're offering your services," said Danny.

"It's not really an offer," said Hermia. "It's more like . . . a desperate plea. I have no safe place in the world now. When you make the Great Gate, I need you to take me through it. Where in Mittlegard can I hide from the Family of Zeus?"

"I've done okay hiding from the Family of Odin."

"Zeus isn't one-eyed," said Hermia with a grin. "And I'm not a true Hermes who can always stay one step ahead of him. When I'm caught, there's no escape for me, unless *you've* made gates for me."

"So we're allies," said Danny.

"You don't need me as much as I need you," said Hermia. "But I really can help you. Please don't shut me out of your gates, Danny North."

21

Great Gate

֎

They gathered at the high school gym, because the rope was already there. It was night, and the building was dark, but for this work they needed no more light than the green of the glowing EXIT signs over the crash doors.

It made Danny sad to come back here, for he knew there would be no returning here to this school. Nobody but Hal Sargent actually knew that Danny had anything to do with the weird behavior of the rope; Danny might have gotten away with it and stayed in school, especially now that he knew how to lock a gate or return it to his own satchel.

But tonight Danny was going to try to make a Great Gate. Since he had already proven that he had the power to start one, there was little doubt that he would succeed. After all, solitary Orphan gatemages had made Great Gates before. No, the likeliest outcome was the same one the other gatemages had had: The making of a Great Gate, and then the loss of the mage's entire outself to the Gate Thief.

If that happened—when that happened—there was no way Danny could continue in Buena Vista. Without gates to connect him to Veevee and the Silvermans, Danny would be entirely alone. Without the power of a gatemage to go anywhere at any time, he would be at the mercy of clowns like Lieder and Massey; he would have nothing to offer his friends. He would truly be what his Family so long had thought him: drekka. He would have to make his way in the drowther world, but it only made sense to do it close to home, in Yellow Springs. He would simply have to live with being the Weird Running Kid, make straight *A*'s, keep his head down, and get to college.

They had already worked it out in the meeting he assembled in the Silvermans' living room. Veevee, Stone, the Silvermans, and Hermia—once Stone was convinced that she was on the level, and persuaded the others—they had charted the possibilities.

"If the Gate Thief strips you," said Marion, "we will go to the North Family, tell them all that you did, and that you have lost your outself. Maybe they'll let you alone, then, knowing that you're no longer a mage of any kind."

"Not likely," said Danny.

"But your only chance," said Stone, "if you no longer have the ability to gate away from anyone trying to kill you. Hermia and Veevee will be just as vulnerable—without your gates, they'll have nowhere to go and no way to get there."

"I don't see why we have to do this at all," said Leslie. "Why not just let Danny live his life? The power he has right now can open Mittlegard to the Orphans. If Hermia is right and he has a vast store of gates inside him, why not link all the major cities of the world with big public gates and let the drowthers move every-where freely?"

"The Families would still hunt him down and kill him," said Marion sadly. "And then his gates would slowly fade, like the ghosts left behind when clants are stranded."

"I hate it," said Leslie. "Why not wait, at least? Why does it have to be now?"

"Every day that we wait is a day in which one of the Family spies might spot him or Hermia."

"If the Gate Thief is just going to take him—"

"Mom," said Danny—which silenced Leslie immedi-ately, though it filled her eyes with tears. "All the other gatemages who tried a Great Gate were alone. No other gatemage with them. I have Hermia and Veevee. There's a chance they can keep the gate locked against the Gate Thief."

"Or something," said Hermia. "Since we don't know what the Gate Thief actually does."

Veevee shook her head. "I agree with Leslie. I think that this girl and I will make no difference at all—we'll just have a clearer view of how Danny gets stripped."

"Even that will move our knowledge forward," said Stone. "We can write it down, we can spread it among the Orphans. Maybe we'll learn something that will let us do better on the next attempt."

"This is all moot," said Danny. "I'm doing it. I'm doing it tonight. Either there'll be a Great Gate or there won't. Not only that, you'll all be there."

"Getting bossy, isn't he?" said Veevee.

"Because *if* I make a Great Gate, it might last for a few seconds. I want all of you to go through it as quickly as you can. Get to Westil and then, if you can, come back *instantly.*"

"What's the point of that?" asked Leslie. "What if we get stranded there? We won't know *anyone*, they'll probably kill us the moment they notice we're there. The Gate Thief might be the ruler of the whole world there, for all we know."

"But we'll be the first mages to pass through a Great Gate in fourteen centuries," said Stone. "We'll be more powerful than anybody."

"What does that mean to me?" asked Leslie. "I'll be the world's most powerful cow?"

"She's got a point," said Veevee. "Maybe she shouldn't go."

"But Marion has to, and Leslie won't stay behind alone if he goes," said Stone.

"That's right," said Leslie.

"And Marion's a Cobblefriend," Stone went on. "After passing through the gate, he'll be the strongest stonemage in the world."

"We don't know that," said Marion. "I'll be much stronger in the things that I can already do. But none of the literature suggests that a Great Gate can turn a Cobblefriend into a Stonefather. The Great Gates make a difference in degree, not in kind."

"We'll try it," said Danny. "If you think we should, Stone, I'll go get Ced and bring him along. He's a windmage, and you say he's got a lot of ability. Maybe a Galebreath. If we bring him through the Great Gate, then whichever side he ends up on, he can protect the others. None of the Families will have a windmage to match him, once he's gone through a Great Gate, and the same will likely be true in Westil, if he gets stuck there."

"You can ask him," said Marion. "Nobody should go if they don't want to run the risk of being stuck in

Westil. Think of everything that's happened in Mittlegard since 632 A.D. All of modern technology, for one thing. Immunization against plagues. Medicine. If they don't have gates, they can't heal people easily. Flush toilets. The Copernican model of the solar system. Microscopes. Telescopes. There's no reason to think they have any of that stuff."

"Or they might have better stuff," said Danny. "For all we know, the Gate Thief isn't a person at all. What if it's a machine that sucks the power right out of any mage? We don't know anything."

"And it's time we did," said Marion. "Leslie's and my kids are grown. If we're stranded there, we'll miss them, but they don't *need* us."

"Why are we having this conversation?" said Hermia. "The gates will probably be sucked out of Danny before anybody can go anywhere."

"Greeks are so cheerful," said Veevee.

"For what it's worth," said Hermia, "we're not really Greek. We were never Greek. We're Pelasgians. We were the gods of the Illyrians, the Albanians, the Danae. When the Dorians and Ionians came, we wiped out their Families and they worshiped us. But we're *not* Greek."

"Thanks for the history lesson," said Leslie.

"I think it's fascinating," said Danny.

"Oh my, Danny's in love," said Veevee. "Danny and Hermia, sitting in a tree—"

"Give it a rest, Veevee," said Stone. "Everybody's a little crazy tonight. But Hermia's right. The most likely outcome is that the Gate Thief will swallow all of Danny's gates before anybody makes it to Westil, let alone back again. And there we'll all be in Buena Vista, Virginia, which isn't exactly a metropolis, without any gates to get us home. Somebody's going to have to rent us a car so we can drive to the airport in Roanoke and get the hell away from there. *With* Danny, whatever kind of shape he's in."

"I'll do it," said Veevee. "Danny can make me a nice gate between the airport and this rope in the gym—"

"Why do we have to do it there?" asked Leslie. "Surely there are other ropes hanging from gymnasium ceilings that aren't a stone's throw from the North fortress."

"That's the one that worked today," said Hermia. "Danny proved he can make a Great Gate, and he did it there."

"If we can make a Great Gate," said Danny, "then maybe we can break down this system of miserable, hate-filled, paranoid, inbred Families."

"And replace them with miserable, lonely Orphans," said Marion. "Sorry to be cynical, but I'm not optimistic about our ability to do any better. Whoever has the power will become the gods of legend—capricious, cruel, tyrannical."

"And yet you're going to go through the gate?" asked Veevee.

"It's going to be made, isn't it?" asked Marion. "If it's going to happen, I want it to be us that go through it first. Maybe we can make it less awful for the world than it might otherwise be."

"I think we're done here," said Danny. "I've got some gates to make. From here to Parry McCluer High School, so when the time is right you can all just step through. From there to the Roanoke airport so Veevee can rent a car. It'll take her about an hour to get it up I-81 to B.V. Meanwhile I'll go get Ced, if he'll come. Stone, maybe you should come with me."

"And me," said Hermia. "I'm staying with you." She turned to Veevee. "And no more jokes about being in love. You and I are both *nothing* without him, and you know it."

"I do," said Veevee, chastened before her fierceness.

"If you're lying to us," said Stone to Hermia, "and you're setting him up to get killed, I swear I'll kill you with my bare hands."

"I'm glad you're so loyal," said Hermia without batting an eye. "But I am no liar and no spy."

"Good, that's settled then," said Danny. "Since I'm the idiot who set this all in motion by playing around with the rope-climb in a high school gym, I apologize right now for everything that goes wrong with this. With any luck, I'm the only one who gets zapped in the outself, and everything else goes on like normal for the rest of you. But if terrible things happen, please remember that I meant well, and that I did my best. That's what I promise you. I'll do my best to try to fight off the Gate Thief and get this thing done right. It's up to you to make the most of it, if you can."

Leslie burst into tears. Danny walked over and put his arm around her shoulder.

"Oh, don't bother with her," said Veevee. "Comforting her is Marion's job. We have work to do. Move it, Gate Boy."

Everyone laughed, even Leslie. Danny stood up and made a public gate from the Silverman living room to a space near the bleachers in the Parry McCluer gym. Then he took Hermia's hand and stepped through it. Veevee took Stone by the hand and followed them.

CED CAME WITHOUT argument—he knew the chance of a lifetime when he saw it, even with the risk of getting stranded on Westil. Veevee rented a big SUV and made it to the high school without getting lost. Danny pulled in all the little gates that had propelled so many students a mile up into the air, so the area was clear.

"All right, Hermia," said Danny. "Close all the public gates I just made. I don't want any students to stumble their way to Yellow Springs or Roanoke tomorrow."

"Don't worry," said Ced. "The Gate Thief will probably eat them all before morning."

Nobody laughed.

"Sorry," said Ced. "Thought I'd brighten the mood."

"Oh, you did," said Stone. "Now everybody hopes you'll make it to Westil and stay there." That did get a few chuckles.

Danny looked at Hermia and Veevee. "Are you ready?"

"We'll be vigilant," said Hermia. "And if there's anything we can do to help you, we'll do it."

"The main thing is to tell everybody the moment the Great Gate is complete, so they can go through it. Tell them where to enter. Make it so this isn't wasted, if it's possible at all."

"I think I should go with them," said Veevee.

"Absolutely not," said Stone. "You need to be with Danny, not distracted by zipping through a gate."

"What if the Gate Thief locks the Great Gate and I'm the only one who can open it?"

"Open it from this side," said Hermia. "Our job is to stay with Danny."

Veevee sighed. "I know," she said.

"She just doesn't want to lose her loving husband," said Stone cheerfully.

"Leslie gets to go with Marion," Veevee pointed out.

"Nobody goes with anybody until I make the gate," said Danny. "Which is now."

He walked to the rope, gripped it with his hands, then raised his legs up so his feet rested on the big knot at the bottom. "Wind me up, ladies," he said.

Hermia and Veevee began to spin him.

"Slowly, I don't want to be dizzy before I even start," said Danny.

They slowed down.

They turned him and turned him until the thick rope began doubling and Danny was rising noticeably higher above the floor.

"Enough," said Danny. "Now everybody be quiet. Only talk to me if it's something urgent that you think I don't see. It takes concentration to spin out so many gates at once."

They had already decided, from Hermia's reading, that the average Great Gate was really ten or twelve gates intertwined and twisted together, all of them spanning the whole distance. Some Great Gates had fewer, some more, and the more there were, the longer the Great Gate would last after the death of the mage that made them. But they figured average was good enough for today.

"Let go," said Danny. "But carefully, so I stay centered." Then he closed his eyes. Vision would only distract him.

Veevee and Hermia looked at each other. "On three," said Veevee. "As in 'one, two, let go.' All right?"

Hermia nodded.

"One," said Veevee. "Two. Now."

Danny began to spin.

He immediately started to form gates until he had twelve, all of them with their mouths close together at the height of the knot in the rope, facing the west wall of the gym. The tails ended at the ceiling, but that was only temporary, as he carried the mouths with him in his accelerating spin.

Hermia and Veevee were watching for the moment of maximum acceleration, when the rope was at its full length, before it started winding up again in the other direction. But Danny didn't wait for their signal. He knew from what Hermia had read in the books that Great Gates had usually been made by Gatefathers who were simply turning around and around on their feet, like children playing at making themselves dizzy. This would certainly be fast enough.

He took the tails of the twelve gates and threw them upward into space, with no destination in mind except a vague idea of "there," wherever there was. "There" meaning Westil. Meaning the natural home of the mages. Meaning the place where the Gate Thief was waiting for him.

It took less than an instant. "There," he thought, and the tails of the gates arrived. Just like that.

"It's open," said Hermia. "This way."

Danny had no time to notice whether anyone was going through the gate or not. For the Gate Thief was there, just like that.

"Oh God," said Veevee.

The Gate Thief had him, just the way Bel had Loki in the runic inscription: "The jaws of Bel seized his heart to carry it away." But that had been followed by "Loki held tight to his own heart and followed the jaws of the beast."

Danny understood now exactly what the inscription meant. He could feel his entire outself, all the gates he could ever make, moving away from him. He could simply let them go, or he could concentrate on them, try to keep control of them.

But no, fighting the Gate Thief wasn't the way. "Loki tricked Bel into thinking he was captive, but he was not captive. His heart held the jaws; the jaws did not hold his heart."

Danny stopped resisting, though he maintained his concentration, his awareness of all the gates as the Thief dragged them away. He also felt it as the Gate Thief began to slurp up all the gates that Danny had ever made in his life, sucking them in like noodles from a bowl of soup.

Then suddenly his gates, his outself *arrived*. Inside another person, so it was no machine—but there was a powerful impression of a thousand other outselves as well. The Gate Thief had all the outselves he had stolen kept in one place, and Danny was among them. Yet he also sensed that he was stronger than any of them. No, he was stronger than all of them. His mass of potential gates was greater than the entire satchel-ful of outselves combined.

Which of them belonged to the Gate Thief himself? Easy to find: the largest. And in that moment Danny became aware of the entire map of the Thief's active gates.

What mattered, though, was the satchel, the repository where the Thief kept his unused outself and the outselves of all the mages he had ever stripped and all the gates that he had stolen. Danny knew that he was more powerful than all of them combined, but he also knew that the Gate Thief knew things that Danny did not. He wants me to fight him. If I try to pull my own gates back, that's the moment when the jaws snap shut and cut the gates from me, like breaking a fully stretched-out rubber band.

Instead, Danny held his gates right where they were, inside the Gate Thief's stash. Then he created all his gates at once, his entire outself as one vast mouth, with the tail of it in Danny's own heart, his inself. Mouth to tail, a million gates, uncountable gates. He widened the mouth and engulfed the Gate Thief's entire satchel within it, just as he had swallowed Eric when he dragged him out of Rico's office.

His gates were back, just like that. And along with them had come all the stolen gates in the Gate Thief's satchel. And all the Thief's own gates that had not yet been made, his unused outself.

He could feel the Gate Thief pulling back on his own outself—doing exactly the thing that would allow Danny to cut it off entirely, to swallow it and leave the Gate Thief bereft.

Because he still had the Gate Thief's map of gates inside his mind, Danny knew that he was leaving them behind, not stripping the Thief entirely. But Danny had no idea how to suck them in the way the Thief had sucked in Danny's, and he didn't want to take the time to try, for fear it would give the Thief time to recover.

Instead, leaving behind the few gates the Thief had deployed in Westil, Danny broke the connection between all these outselves and the Thief himself.

The Gate Thief was gone. His map of gates was gone. But Danny had most of the Thief's gates and all the stolen ones.

Alone with the outselves of a thousand mages, Danny suddenly became aware that they were screaming. And loudest of all, the huge and powerful outself of the Gate Thief. They weren't *doing* anything, but they were filled with fear and hatred and hope and hunger all at once, and they were screaming in his mind, and all that he could do was scream back at them until he dropped from the rope onto the floor of the gym, screaming and gasping and screaming again. He could not hear his own mind, no matter how loud he screamed. I am Danny, he was trying to say. I am Danny, this is *my* heart, not yours. It belongs to me.

It had never occurred to him, because he had not foreseen this outcome, that to take other mages' outselves into his heart would be the equivalent of a heartbound beast allowing the outself of a mage to ride him. And if Danny was not strong enough, not skilled enough, they would control him like a clant.

And Danny had no skill with this at all.

22

Justice

ᥫᶩ

Queen Bexoi seemed happy to see Wad when he appeared in the nursery. He had been watching her for more than two weeks, and she was never alone. He knew it was no coincidence, no accident. Whenever Prayard left her, she made sure someone else was with her—usually a court official, but when necessary, one of the nurses tending her child. Wad had seen her do exactly the same thing when avoiding the agents of Gray, only it had been even more difficult, of course, to avoid Wad, since he would know whenever she was alone and could get into any room. So when Queen Bexoi suddenly had not so much as a moment of privacy—she who had once had hours to herself every day, and who *could* have solitude with a wave of her hand—Wad knew exactly what was going on.

Today, though, she had finally slipped. The nurse who was supposed to be in the nursery when Bexoi arrived had stumbled on the stairs and was now in the kitchen, having her wound bathed and bandaged by the day cook, Mast. So when Bexoi left her ladies-in-waiting at the door and came inside the nursery, she had no company but the baby, Oath. And, in a moment, Wad. They were alone together at last, unseen by anyone except the baby and whoever might be watching at the open viewport he had created in Anonoei's old room.

Yet Bexoi didn't bat an eye when he appeared. She smiled warmly, resting her folded arms across her huge belly, which was one month from delivery, and said, "Oh, Wad, I've missed you so much, my only friend, please, sit down."

He did not sit. He was here to make sure she knew that she could not harm Prince Oath with impunity. He had no time to waste. "I realize that things are over between us, Bexoi," he said, "and I am not angry."

"Over?" she said. "Friendship does not *end*."

"But I will never be in your bed again, and I'm content," said Wad calmly—as deceptive as she was, and better at it.

"I have a husband, now, of course," said Bexoi. "My lonely vigil is over. You have been such a blessing in my life, do you think I could ever forget your kindness? You have my friendship and loyalty forever."

Wad wondered how many times she had rehearsed the speech, knowing that for any normal man it would be infuriating, would stir him to violence or ranting or grief. Was that what she wanted from him? Wad did not care—he was not here to follow her plans, but to bend her to his own.

"I came," said Wad, "to ask you whether Prayard's baby is doing well."

Bexoi smiled beatifically, opening her arms to stroke the sides of her own belly with affection. But Wad saw her also become more tense, more alert. "Why do you ask? Have you heard that I am unwell? That the baby is in danger of any kind?"

"How could a baby inside your womb be in danger?" asked Wad. "Who would dare to reach inside your body and pinch off the cord until the baby died? What kind of monster would do such a thing, even if there was a man who could?"

There. The threat was made.

She grew solemn. "I have a friend who makes sure that babies pass out of my body in their proper time, healthy and undamaged. He tends my body as well, so I suffer no ill effects. That friend is the most precious person in my life."

Oh, yes, my love, he answered silently, do remember how childbirth nearly killed you—would have killed you, without my help. Think of that before you raise a hand against my son. "Not more precious than Prayard," said Wad. "Not more precious than the baby you carry. Not more precious than the baby Oath whose birth has made you Queen and wife in fact as well as name."

"Who can measure one love against another?"

"That is my question," said Wad. "I have in my possession, you see, a woman who was once the King's beloved, who gave him sons that once he loved. These last two weeks, as you avoided me, I found it harder and harder to get food for them unnoticed."

"How unfortunate," said Bexoi, with real sympathy in her voice, if not her eyes.

"It occurred to me that perhaps it is time, now that you occupy your proper place as Queen, for me to bring forth the prisoners who have spent a year and a half in my care. These were children the King once loved with all his heart. Think how happy you would make him, to produce them for him in his own bedroom, and their once-beloved mother, too. How he would thank you for having kept them alive all these months."

Bexoi continued to smile, but her eyes were hard. "I thought they must have passed from the land of the living many months ago. I know I asked you from the start to send them plunging to the bottom of the lake."

"What kind of warden would I be if I allowed such a misfortune to befall them? It's true that they could fall at any time, right out of their prison cell, but who knows where the gate that catches them might lead? Right now it leads to the top of the same cave. But it could lead here to the nursery. Or to the King's chamber."

"Why are you threatening me like this?" asked Bexoi softly. "When my husband's love is so new and fragile? You threaten my unborn baby, you threaten to return my husband's old lover and his bastard sons. Why would my friend betray me like this?"

"Why did you shun me?" asked Wad. "Why did you cut me off without a word? What am I to think, except that you are plotting something?"

"I couldn't face you," said Bexoi. Now her performance changed. Instead of happiness to see him, instead of utter innocence, she was now a helpless little girl, asking him for help, for understanding. "I thought you would be angry. I was afraid."

"You thought I'd take the hint and go away," said Wad.

"You helped me when I was in need," she said. "I was showing you I was in need no more."

"Telling would have been better than showing."

"Asking would have been better than showing up uninvited," she answered.

"You know I can't approach you openly. The kitchen boy? The castle monkey? The one that was named 'Wad of Dough' by the only one who loved him?"

"I loved you," said Bexoi. "I love you still."

Wad ignored her. He knew this game. "How quickly would they act to swat me away, to throw me out of Nassassa? Or imprison me, if they thought I meant to speak with you alone?"

"If you know your place so well," said Bexoi, "perhaps you ought to have stayed there."

Her words stung him. "On the night when Luvix meant to poison you or stab you to death, should I have stayed in my place?"

"That night your place was with me."

"And when Oath was conceived, should I have been in my place?"

"Your place was in bed with me, because I bade you come."

"But now my place is back where I was before, as if you owed me nothing."

"You slept with the Queen of Iceway, sister of the Jarl of Gray," said Bexoi. "You have had your reward. There is no other. My need for you has passed."

There it was, stated nakedly, without pretense. "Then all is clear between us," he said.

"No it isn't," she said. "You have threatened my unborn baby."

"You know I'd never harm a child," said Wad.

"You have kept two children prisoners in a cave, for a year and a half," she said contemptuously.

"You charge me with a crime that I committed for your sake?"

"For *my* sake you would have murdered them. I don't know for whose sake it is that you have kept them alive for all this time."

"I didn't need to share your bed, Bexoi. I know that's your husband's place. I could have continued to be your protector and ally, if you had only asked me."

"Then I regret that I did not. I ask you now."

"Too late," said Wad.

"Alas," said Bexoi.

Wad expected her to attack him. So he was taken by surprise when she flicked a hand and the high-sided bed where Prince Oath slept erupted in flames.

Wad did not hesitate. He gated to the crib, his arms already outstretched to seize the child between his hands.

But the baby was not there. Instead, there was a mannequin, the doll that Wad himself had used to hide Trick's absences. And as he hesitated in the realization, Queen Bexoi engulfed the wooden doll in unnatural flame that created bitter smoke. The doll had been painted with something, and the smoke from its burning dulled his mind.

It was a clever enough plan, to make him think that he was saving his son, to use his own trick against him, and to place him for a long moment in the agony of fire and the stupidity of the drug.

How else could you murder a gatemage, except to entice him into the midst of poisoned smoke and hold him there until he lacked the wit to gate away?

The poison was not quick enough, the pain of the flames not sharp enough, his confusion not long-lasting enough. He gated out of the castle entirely, to a spot atop a hill overlooking Nassassa from across the fjord. He was healed in that moment by the gate itself, so his mind was clear.

He had no more than a moment to wonder where the baby was, and how she had removed him from the crib without his noticing. Only a moment to realize that she must have arranged for the nurse to "stumble" and be absent, that Bexoi had used that decoy to distract him and, with luck, assassinate him. He had not discovered an opportunity to be alone with Bexoi, he had fallen headlong into the trap she laid for him. He had never been in control of anything; whatever the risk to her or to her second child, she wanted him dead before the child was born.

He could not think about this now, because from his vantage point he saw at once that a dozen men were being lowered over the castle walls on ropes, heading for each of a dozen caves that overlooked the lake below. In three of them, he knew, they would find Anonoei and her two sons. They had pikes. Their plan could not be clearer. And Wad remembered that he had told the Queen what the prison he had made consisted of, but had never told her that the three of them were separated, or which of the caves contained them.

Wad knew how to save Anonoei and her children, but he had no intention of bringing them back to King Prayard. That would only put their lives in danger, for the King was now besotted with Bexoi, who carried his child. If he had taken Wad's advice and watched at the viewport in Anonoei's old room, then he would know that Oath was not his child, that Bexoi had been faithless to him, that she knew who had captured Anonoei and her children, and that Queen Bexoi was a firemage. If he had not watched, he would not know. But either way, there was little hope for Wad's three prisoners if he brought them to a place inside Nassassa. Bexoi would kill them if the King did not.

So instead, Wad cast his inner gaze to a place high in the mountains, where once he had found clothing left by a young girl's hands. But where were the girl and her family, who had picnicked by the tree where Wad had dwelt in silent dreaming for so many centuries? He knew that poor as they were, the family would take in the children and their mother. And the prisoners, for their part, would be so grateful to be free that they would accept whatever meager fare was offered them.

Later, Wad would come to Anonoei and her sons and tell them a useful story about who imprisoned them and how they were set free. Later, he would bring them to the people who still mistrusted Bexoi and believed the kingdom would be better served if Anonoei's children were King Prayard's heirs.

Once, fresh-hatched from the tree, Wad had shadowed the girl and her family along a mountain road. Wad had seen where they arrived. And now he was there, looking down a slope at the lonely house in shaggy fields nearly ready for the poor harvest of the short growing season in the mountains.

He took the gate at the mouth of the cave where the dangling soldier braced his feet upon the sill, poised to jab with the pike into Eluik's body, and pushed the gatemouth up the sloping floor to swallow the child inside. At that very moment he had already moved the tail of the gate to a spot in the dry grass just up the hill from the house of Roop and Levet, and their brave and kind-hearted daughter Eko, who once had succored him.

Wad paused only long enough to see that Eluik was there and alive, then returned his attention to the face of the cliff. Another soldier now was poised at the mouth of the cave that held Anonoei, readying his pike to probe the woman who lay trapped and helpless before him.

At that most inconvenient moment, Wad felt a familiar stirring that he did not understand. It was a burning somewhere deep inside him, in the well from which five hundred voices cried to him. He did not know what the burning meant, or why the voices cried out when the burning came, or who they even were, but he knew that every time he had felt this burning during all his years inside the tree, the only way to still the hunger was to eat.

Not food, but the thing that burned.

Now, though, he was not in the tree. Now he was a woken man, a Gatefather who understood his own magery. So what he had experienced during his long tree-sleep as a burning and an eating, as unconscious as that of a babe inside the womb, he now understood quite differently.

It was the presence of another gatemage that had stirred him up. Or rather, it was the creation of a Great Gate that was not his own which caused him to burn inside. The new Great Gate led from a world that Wad had once known well, but now could not remember. He only knew that if that Gate were left in place, it would destroy everything that mattered in the world.

So Wad reached out, by instinct now, after so many years of habitual response, and ate it. He felt the outself of the other mage, the maker of the gate, react with surprise and try to pull away. He knew that he had felt the selfsame thing at least two dozen times while he had lived inside the tree. But this time he understood that it was a person, and that what he ate was that other person's heart, his outself, the part of him that made his gates. Wad swallowed that heart, and with it dragged inside himself the whole array of gates the other mage had made, sucked them in like noodles that dangled outside the mouth, only to be slurped inside. And in a moment he had them, all the gates.

There were so many. This one had so many gates, and yet they had not begun to exhaust his hearthoard. Wad had never seen a Gatefather with so much potential. But, as usual, the gatemage was naive and did not understand what was happening with him. He had not learned enough to know how to resist Wad's strength and skill and wiliness.

But just as Wad was about to sever the connection between the gatemage and all the gates he would ever make, a strange thing happened. Out of the heart Wad held already in the jaws of his inner mouth, the other gatemage stretched open a mouth much larger than Wad's own, and snapped it over him, over his entire hearthoard, over all the other mages' hearthoards that Wad held inside him. The stranger snapped, he bit, the connection was severed. And Wad was helpless to resist.

If the other mage had not been so naive, he would have sucked in all of Wad's existing gates as well, but he did not. The gates that Wad had made remained. But he had no hearthoard now, nothing with which to form another gate.

In that moment, Wad went from being the greatest

Gatefather that the world of Westil ever knew to being one so frail he had no store of gates inside him, and only a handful of existing gates that he could manipulate.

The soldier stabbed into the cave with his pike, and Wad could not do anything at first. It would take a tiny bit of his outself even to move her gate the way that he had moved Eluik's, and he had no shred of outself left to do even this.

So he sucked Anonoei's gate into himself, to give himself some kind of hearthoard, however small.

Her bleeding body tumbled from the cave mouth toward the lake.

Now Wad had enough reserve that he could move the mouth of Eluik's gate to a place just under the falling woman. It swallowed her; she disappeared in mid-air; but he felt her emerge in the snow near Eko's house, fully healed by the passage through the gate.

He found the cave where Enopp had been held. The soldier there was drawing back his pike from the cave, and on the end of it Enopp hung, gripping it with both his hands, though it pierced him through the belly. If it had been his heart, no doubt it would have been too late to save him, but quickly Wad took back Enopp's gate, gaining even more power and quickness. Then he swung the mouth of Eluik's gate to swallow him. He disappeared.

But because Enopp still gripped the pike, it came along with him, leaving the soldier standing there, balanced between cave sill and taut rope, with empty hands.

Enopp emerged between his mother and his brother in the mountain grass. He was not healed by the gate because the spear still pierced his body and he still held on to it.

Pull out the pike, Wad shouted in his mind. But Anonoei and Eluik just stood there, shivering and terrified. Two years of prison had made them helpless, broken, unresourceful. They could do nothing.

Wad moved the mouth of the gate across the gorge until it swallowed Wad himself. He too emerged on the mountain slope. He pulled the pike from the writhing boy, then dragged the mouth of the gate from Nassassa to this place and passed it once more over the boy, depositing him only inches from where he started, but with no wound in his belly.

Wad stood revealed now before Anonoei.

"You," she said. "The kitchen monkey. Wad."

He turned to her. "Get your sons down the hill and beg these gentle souls for help! Are you a fool? Walk!"

But they could not walk. They could barely stand.

Wad gathered in more of the gates that he still had to work with, a tiny fraction of the outself he was born with, and made a gate to take them down to a spot just outside the door of the humble shack. "Open up!" he shouted.

No one came.

The house was empty.

Wad gated them inside the hovel. It would be warmer there than outside. It was all that he could do right now.

Because he had a greater concern, now they were safe. What had Anonei and her boys ever been to him, except his enemies and then his prisoners and finally his terrible burden of responsibility? For them as human beings he cared nothing, because he knew them not at all.

All he could think of now was: Where is Trick? He was not in the burning crib when I reached for him. Where did she put him?

Wad used the gate at hand, reversed it, and took himself back to the hill overlooking the fjord and Nassassa's steepest wall. Then he closed the gate entirely, and gathered up all the other gates, the ones that once had been his passageways to freedom in Nassassa, the gates that once had led him to the Queen. Now he wished that he had been like the mage who swallowed up his hearthoard, leaving hundreds of gates everywhere. If he had not been so tidy, he would have them now. Instead his entire hearthoard was no more than that of a common Pathbrother.

How could I not have understood that I was the Gate Thief all along? What did I think those voices inside me were, that seething mass of rage and loss and fading memory? I did not think. I did not remember a time when they were not there. But there must have been such a time, because I stole them all. Somewhere among them was Hull's grandfather. So many others. Why was I doing this? Why was it so important that no gates be made in this world, or leading from another world to here?

Wad realized now that his old self, the self that still remembered things, must have hidden inside the tree so he would live for centuries, stealing gates and gatemages' hearts. Why had he become the enemy of all gatemagery? Why couldn't he remember? Had his memories seeped into the tree, lost to him forever? Or did they remain somewhere inside him, waiting to be found?

He gathered in his gates and then used these feeble resources to search Nassassa for his son.

He found Trick's body smothered under the gown of the last nurse who had been on duty. When Wad had been distracted, watching her replacement stumble and go to the kitchen to get her injury attended to, the woman had suffocated the child and carried the body out beneath her clothing. Trick was already dead before Wad went to the nursery to see the Queen.

Wad had supposed that he and Trick were safe until the new baby was born. The Queen had counted on him to believe that, and so she acted in advance, carefully manipulating Wad's attention. Only her failure to kill Wad himself had prevented all from going as she planned. This was the day, the hour she had chosen for all her rivals to die. And she had hidden it from him.

Wad gated the dead toddler out from the nurse's gown and brought the body to his own arms. The gate had no power to heal the child now. He was already cold.

Wad did not kill the nurse. She had only obeyed her Queen. Let the woman be tormented by the memory of the struggling boy, and by the fear of what would happen when the Queen demanded she produce the corpse. When she could not do it, Bexoi would assume that the nurse had given it to someone else. Bexoi would assume the baby was alive, that she had not had the heart to kill it, just as Wad had not killed Anonoei and Eluik and Enopp.

If that had only been the truth, if Wad had found his son alive, he would have spared the nurse who refused to kill him. Even in his weakened state, he would have gated her away to safety. Now, with no corpse to prove her obedience, he would let her suffer the consequence of being thought innocent of murder by the one who ordered her to do it.

For a moment he thought of a terrible justice: putting the body of his son back into Bexoi's womb, to share the space with his half-brother, only a month away from birth. If Bexoi lived through the insertion—and Wad had lost none of his deftness, so she might—the body would decay and rot inside her, and soon wreak vengeance on his monstrous mother and his usurping wombmate.

But Wad had no murder in him now. Grief and fear had overpowered his rage. A Gatefather in another world had proven he was stronger than Wad. Someday that mage would come here to this world, and Wad would have no power to resist him. Now was not the time for meaningless murders. Let Bexoi have her kingdom, if she could keep it, if Anonoei could not find a way to take it from her. Wad had other work to do. Other enemies to deal with.

He sat upon the hill, a Gatefather who was now but a shadow of himself, and wept. For all his crimes he wept, for all who had died before he could save them, for the mages he had stripped of power even more utterly than he had been stripped today. I held their outselves in my hearthoard for a thousand years, some of them, or more. I made myself the thief of hearts, and now I am repaid.

And yet I must stand watch against some enemy whose name I do not know, some danger that I can't identify, some world-ending dread that now will find me nearly empty.

I was the god who was supposed to protect this world. Was it my nemesis who took away my heart today? Or merely some innocent gatemage who happened to be stronger than I ever was, and unknowingly laid the world bare to the real enemy, whatever that might be?

Wad gated himself away from Nassassa to the mountains. He found Eko working in another field beside another house—a larger one. The family had become more prosperous. They had abandoned their old house in the high and meager fields.

Eko knew him when she saw him, and her face brightened. "Tree man," she said.

"Thank you," he said, "for what you did for me."

She knelt before him. "O Man of the Tree," she said, "how can I serve you now?"

"In your old house higher up the mountain, there is a woman and her sons. They are helpless and no one else knows where they are. If the King or Queen should find them, they'll be killed. But they have friends who soon will seek them. Keep them alive until I can find and bring their friends."

"I will," she said, and closed her eyes. Then she opened them, reached out and touched Wad, then drew back her hand as if she had burned herself.

"If there is any blessing in me," Wad replied, "then it is yours."

She arose and ran up the path that led to the abandoned hovel.

Wad gated himself to the tree in the Forest of Mages, where he had lived so long. He gathered in the last of all his gates and pressed himself against the tree. "Take me back," he murmured. "I have failed at everything."

But the tree did not obey. Perhaps without his power it did not know him. Perhaps his time for dwelling in a tree had passed. But Wad remained there, clinging to the rough bark, because he had no other place to go.

"Trick," he whispered. "My son, my son, if only I had died and you had lived. O Trick my son."

23

Gatefather

ॐ

He heard them calling to him, as if from far away. Leslie, weeping over him, saying over and over, Danny, come back, Danny, we need you, please come back. Marion, his voice stern: Daniel North, you have work to do. Get your chores done before you play. Do you think a farm runs itself? Stone, speaking softly, We have to know what happened, Danny. You have to report to us. This is all wasted if we don't understand. Danny, come back to me.

Veevee and Hermia didn't speak to him. Instead he felt them, felt a pinching and a caressing inside himself, probes that moved through him, not in his body, not even in his mind, but in that place where his gates all stayed.

Only gradually did he realize what they were doing. All the screaming outselves that had been drowning out his own thoughts, threatening to swallow him up in their agonized, frustrated wishes and demands, one by one they were closing, closing, closing, as Hermia worked to shut them all. Meanwhile Veevee was touching the ones that Hermia had not yet reached, as if to assure them that they were being heard, they did not have to scream, they would be heard if they only spoke one at a time, each in turn, not all at once like this, patience, patience.

Only one voice inside him was not touched or closed or changed. It was the outself of the Gate Thief, and he was not screaming. Not shouting, not doing anything.

Pulled out of his stupor and terror and solitude by the voices of his friends, freed from more and more of the burden of all the stolen gates by Hermia and Veevee, it was to the outself of the Gate Thief that Danny turned.

Who are you? Danny asked, not in words, but as a kind of exploration. Why did you try to steal my heart? What did you want? What did you fear?

Bel Bel Bel Bel, came the answer. Only it wasn't an answer. It was simply a kind of watchfulness, a continuous probe. Let Bel not come into the world again, he will eat us all this time, he will ride the drowthers, all of them, ride them through the gates to Westil, he will devour us all. Close the gates, all the gates, keep the worlds apart. Is that a gate? Is there a gate? Gate? Gate?

Gradually Danny came to understand that the Gate Thief's outself was simply continuing to do the task that had been set for it, waking and sleeping, for centuries. Watch for a Great Gate, for any gate, wake me when a gate appears, all gates must be stopped, must be eaten, must be owned. No gates anywhere, or the enemy will make it through.

It was still the war with Bel. Carthage was long since

broken, plowed and salted, but still the Gate Thief watched out for the dangerous and implacable foe.

Gate Thief? Danny knew him now. It was Loki. It had always been Loki, the Last Loki, the one who closed the gates between the worlds. Somehow he was still alive, still watching, and until Danny ate his outself, he had still been laboring to keep the worlds apart.

Why? Danny asked, again and again. But Loki's outself did not hear him. Instead it continued its vigil, intensely watching, scanning.

Lying where he was, still hearing the other captive outselves, still feeling Hermia and Veevee inside him, still hearing the voices of Leslie, Marion, and Stone, Danny made a gate, a single gate, going only an inch or two.

Immediately Loki's outself outshouted everything. Gate gate gate gate gate! And Danny felt what Loki's outself made him feel: Must consume the gate, must eat all the gates this mage will ever make. Danny was *hungry.* And yet it was his own gate that he would have to eat, if he was to satisfy Loki's need.

The Gate Thief had carried this hunger around inside himself for more than thirteen centuries.

"He made a gate," said Hermia aloud.

"A locked one," said Veevee. "Very small."

"Was it Danny who made it?" Hermia asked. "Or has the Gate Thief taken him over from the inside?"

Danny opened his mouth and tried to speak.

Leslie cried out, "He's trying to talk! Hush!"

"You're the only one being loud, my love," said Marion.

Danny searched for his own voice, the one the outside world could hear. "It's me."

He opened his eyes. "Still in the gym?" he asked.

"We didn't know if we could move you," said Vee-vee.

"And Ced didn't make it back through the gate," said Marion.

"He didn't want to come," said Leslie.

"But we came back," said Marion. "We touched the earth of Westil and then we came right back. While you fought, we made the passage." The awe in his voice was almost palpable.

"So move us some mountains, tough guy," said Danny, his voice feebler than he expected. "What about Stone?"

"I didn't go," said Stone. "I stayed with Veevee. What would I do with more power? Grow giant tomatoes and get my picture in the paper?"

"Florist shop?" asked Danny. "How long?"

"Half an hour, maybe," said Veevee.

"Who's crying?" asked Danny.

"Leslie, of course," said Veevee.

"And Hermia," said Stone.

"Oh, really?" asked Veevee. "I thought she was still busy locking gates."

"I am," said Hermia. "I'm not crying. Shut up."

"We thought we lost you," said Veevee. "So many gates, so many outselves. We couldn't imagine how you could contain them. Keep them from taking you over. Especially with the Gate Thief's outself in you—so thick with power, so . . . but the dust of your outself overwhelmed him. You're really something, Danny."

"My gates?" asked Danny.

"All inside you," said Hermia.

"The Great Gate?"

"Especially that one."

"Make it again," said Danny.

"Not yet," said Veevee. "You don't know what would happen."

"What about Ced?"

"He *chose* to stay," said Marion. "He could have made it back. You can open another Great Gate in a day, a week. Let him do what he wants to do there. In a month you can go to him. Give him a chance to do what he can do as the most powerful windmage in Westil."

"If he *is* the most powerful," said Stone.

"If you try to make the Great Gate again," said Hermia, "you don't know what the Gate Thief will do. He's not dead. If you open up a way for him to come through, he might know a way to take it all back again—his own outself, the captives, and you as well. He's still dangerous."

Danny nodded. His head hurt. "My head hurts."

"You hit the floor kind of hard," said Veevee. "I'm thinking we need to pass you through a gate. You might have a concussion."

"He might have fractured his skull," said Leslie.

"Can you put yourself through a gate?" asked Hermia.

Danny took the little gate that he had made and passed the mouth of it over his own head, then down his entire body.

He felt fine now. He sat up. Stood up.

"You beat him," said Hermia, grinning. Then she threw her arms around him. "You beat the Gate Thief."

"It's Loki," said Danny. "The Gate Thief is Loki. The very one."

"After thirteen hundred years?" asked Stone, incredulous.

Hermia let go of him, stepped back. "I guess he really wanted to keep the worlds apart," she said.

"Well, Ced is there now," said Stone. "And Marion and Leslie went through to Westil and back again."

"Powerful cows," said Danny to Leslie.

She strode to him and hugged him tightly.

"What now?" Danny asked them all.

"We get the rental car away from here," said Veevee. "Which means I have a drive ahead of me."

"You've put enough miles on the car for them to believe you actually used it," said Danny. "I'll gate you back. The rest of you—Yellow Springs?"

"They certainly don't want to stay in the miserable shack you're living in here," said Veevee.

"Let's get out of here," said Danny. And added, to Marion, "Now that we know how to do it, we can rig our own rope in the barn."

They came to the crash doors, pushed them open.

A huge bird dropped on top of Danny and knocked him to the ground, started pecking at him savagely. Danny instantly gated about ten feet away and, completely uninjured now, jumped to his feet.

Thor was there, about two rods off, and Baba and Mama were with him. Thor was yelling at the bird. "Stop it, Zog! Stop!" The bird was beating with its great wings, moving angrily toward Danny.

Then the bird was calm.

"I can't believe Uncle Zog would give up," said Danny.

"He didn't," said Leslie. "I took the bird away from him."

"You can do that?" asked Danny.

"Nobody can do that," said Thor.

"I've been to Westil," said Leslie. "I still can't ride a beast that isn't bound to me, but I can break anyone's connection with their heartbound. Do you understand me?"

The ground trembled under them.

"Gyish!" cried Baba. "Don't!"

Now Danny saw Gyish standing near the Family's truck. Gyish was paying no attention to Baba. A crevice opened in the ground at Danny's feet.

Danny simply gated to one side.

A new crevice opened.

"Oh, for pete's sake," said Marion.

A gash opened in the earth under Gyish and the old man dropped down into it. So did the truck.

Mama screamed.

"Marion, what have you done!" cried Leslie.

"Don't worry," said Danny. "I gated the old man away and sent him home to the compound as soon as he fell in."

"You didn't have to," said Marion. "I wasn't going to kill him."

Leslie strode toward Baba and Mama and Thor. "Yes, he made a Great Gate. Yes, the Gate Thief tried to take him. But Danny is the greatest Gatefather who ever lived. Get it? He fought the Gate Thief and he won!"

"Oh, Danny!" cried Mama. "It's what we hoped for you!"

"This is why we kept you alive," said Baba. "So you could make a Great Gate for us."

"How kind of you," said Danny.

"Now let us through," said Baba. "Let us go through the gate."

"It doesn't exist right now," said Hermia.

"But you can make it again," said Mama. The greed in her eyes was more than a little scary.

"If I decide to," said Danny. "But one thing is certain, Mama, Baba, Thor. No one from the North Family will ever use it."

If he had stabbed a knife into his father's heart, he could not have looked more stunned. "You're my son!" Baba cried. "We made you for this!"

"How many gatemages before me did the Families murder?" said Danny. "Thank you for not killing me. Thank you for not murdering your own son. What a sacrifice. I have better parents now. If you come anywhere near us, I'll gate you to the Moon. Do you understand me?"

Thor was about to say something, but before he could get any words out, Danny gated them all back to the Family compound.

"So how do you really feel?" asked Stone.

"Give me credit here," said Danny. "I didn't kill them."

"Should I bring the truck back up to the surface?" asked Marion. "It isn't damaged much."

"Crush it," said Danny. "They can buy another, and think of me whenever they use it."

"Can we visit my Family next?" asked Hermia.

"All in good time," said Stone. "What you just did was probably a mistake. It's their worst fears realized—it gives them all the more incentive to kill you. You'll be able to remake the Great Gate and send only your friends—their enemies—through it. It'll be the destruction of their Family."

"I suppose you're right," said Danny.

"We can work it out," said Marion. "Negotiate. No

more killing of gatemages. They turn gatemages over to us as soon as they're identified. And when we make a Great Gate again, each Family can send one member through and right back again. If we promise to share equally, maybe we can keep a war from breaking out."

"And gates for everybody," said Stone. "Leading from Family to Family. Public gates that can't be closed, so everybody can check on everybody else without buying an airplane ticket."

Danny laughed.

"What's funny?" said Veevee. "I wet myself a little when he opened up that crack in the ground."

"I just—we had no plan for this," said Danny. "For complete, total success."

"It isn't total," said Hermia. "The Gate Thief—Loki—he's still there, and he knows a lot more than any of us. The Families can't be trusted even if they make the most solemn promises. We're safer than we were, but only barely."

"You really are a pessimist, aren't you?" said Stone.

"Danny won," said Hermia. "But only by taking Loki by surprise. Now it's time for us all to knuckle down and *study* this. So when Danny faces him again, he'll have a better idea of what he's doing. Did Loki have anything left, Danny, or did you take it all?"

"He has six gates left," said Danny. "Or at least that's all I sensed before I cut him off."

"Maybe enough to make a Great Gate of his own," said Hermia, "and if passing through a Great Gate increases a Gatefather's outself, he might be able to come here and get us."

"Maybe," said Danny. "But if you could hear the hunger of his outself—he's all about eating Great Gates, not making them."

"We need to bring together everything we know. I've had access to five Family books on gatemagery. Veevee's been studying what's available in the public record her whole life. Danny's actually faced the enemy. I think we can put it all together and try to make sense of it."

"Not tonight," said Leslie. She was stroking the head of the bird that Zog had tried to use to kill Danny.

"I don't know if I faced the enemy," said Danny. "I mean, yes, it was the Gate Thief. But he was terrified of something. Of Bel, whoever that is. The god of Carthage, but . . . we need to find out more about that. Before we start undoing Loki's work, we need to understand it. How do we know we aren't going to unleash on the world the very disaster he tried so hard to prevent?"

"Another day," said Leslie. "It's late, we're tired. Danny, are you coming home with us?"

"Or me?" said Veevee. "I don't care which, but Leslie's right. We all need to sleep."

"It's Hermia who needs a place to stay," said Danny. "You want to go annoy Veevee in her condo? Or get much better cooking with Marion and Leslie?"

Hermia looked from Veevee to the Silvermans and back.

"Or my house," said Stone. "I take in refugees from the Families."

"Stick with your fellow gatemage," said Veevee. "Danny, would you be a dear and restore the gates between Yellow Springs and Naples and DC before you go to bed?"

"Yes," said Danny. "And don't forget the gates from all of you to my place here in B.V."

"No," said Leslie. "You're not *staying* here!"

"Ridiculous," said Veevee. "After what happened?"

"Do you really think the Norths will leave you alone?" asked Stone.

"Please let's not argue," said Danny. "I'm trying to make a life for myself here. And tomorrow's a school day."

Inside himself, however, Danny could feel the pull of a thousand different wills, some weak, some strong. And deeper and stronger than any of them, the out-self of the Gate Thief, the ancient Loki. He had felt it surge with exultation when he thrust his own parents back to their home, dismissing them like a lord with a despised underling. He had liked his power far too much.

He needed to get back to school. And no more gates there, no more showing off. He needed roots in the drowther world. Because being a god was too seductive and too dangerous. How many people might he hurt, if he didn't keep this under control? He thought of his friends at school. Who would protect them from the gods, if not Danny? He thought of would-be tyrants like Lieder and weaklings like Massey. Just because Lieder misused his power, and Massey didn't protect anybody with his, didn't mean that in their weakness they didn't need to be treated with fairness and respect. I could dismiss *them,* too, because they have offended me. But there are rules of decency. Or if there aren't, then there should be.

For there was always the possibility that Loki was really a good man after all. That his reason for closing all the gates was real and compelling. That he wasn't just protecting Westil and the Westilians—that maybe he was trying to save the drowthers, too.

I was born with more power inside myself than I ever dreamed. But along with it there came no more sense than any other idiotic kid. Somewhere along in here I need to grow up into a man I can stand to live with. A man who doesn't just survive, but deserves to.

AFTERWORD

I began this book as I have begun so many others—with a map. It was 1977. I doodled it and then began naming the places in it. I connected it with an idea I had been nursing along for more than a year, about a magic system in which you gain power over a type of creature or an element or force of nature by serving its interest, helping it become whatever it most wants to become. So as I worked on the map, I decided to take it seriously.

I traced the coastlines and rivers on a clean sheet of unlined paper (it was first doodled on a lined notebook sheet), then xeroxed it a couple of dozen times on the copier at the office of *The Ensign* magazine, where I was working as an assistant editor at the time. Then I drew in the borders of countries, showing the changes across time. When I named them, I let the names also change with the centuries.

When I was done, it felt to me as if I had a whole history there, with a sense of ancientness and power in it. The kind of feeling I always get from poring over historical atlases. (I once created a type-in program for the PC junior's BASIC language, showing the results of every presidential election in U.S. history as colors on a map. It was another way of containing the sweep of history in a two-dimensional space. The book it was supposed to appear in died with the PCjr, and the program can't run under any existing version of BASIC. So you'll have to take my word that it was great.)

With the maps complete, it was time to try out the magic system. The result was the dark story "Sandmagic." Though the story was rejected with a rude letter by the quondam editor of *Fantastic* magazine, I refused to give up. It was published in an anthology of Andy Offutt's and then picked up for a best-fantasy-of-the-year anthology. That was all the validation that I needed.

The trouble was, I cared too much about the Mithermages world. I thought of it as my best world ever, and my best magic system. I wanted to tell only stories that were worthy of it. And besides, in those days fantasy didn't often sell as well as science fiction. I had a family to support. I stuck with the spaceships and held on to Mithermages for some later date, when I had found a story that could bring out all its possibilities.

Little did I know that I already had part of the story. Jay A. Parry, my closest friend at *The Ensign* (or anywhere, at that time), and I were working on a story idea together, about an orphan or bastard kid who lived in a medieval castle, prowling and spying as he crawled through beams and rafters, secret passageways, roof thatch, gullies, drains, and tunnels. He would know everything that was going on in the castle, yet everyone would ignore or despise him. Jay named him "Wad."

Years later, we even tried to create a collaborative novel that we could sell together. Jay wrote an opening that was very good, but I somehow couldn't carry on with it. Now I realize that it was the magic system we were working with at the time that blocked me—it wasn't strong enough. Yet I couldn't think of a better one.

Skip forward a few decades. I had already published the Mithermages maps in a small collection entitled *Cardography*. (The maps don't appear in this book because they aren't needed yet; they'll show up in the next volume.) Still I had not written a story set in that world since "Sandmagic." Yet the maps and the magic wouldn't leave me alone. I was brooding about it one day when it dawned on me that if Wad lived in the world of Mithermages, *his* might be the story worth writing.

I asked Jay for permission to take Wad and put him in this world of mine. Jay graciously gave his consent, and so I have preserved the name Jay thought of for this lost and lonely boy. I knew at once the place where he would live in the novel—Iceway, a northern kingdom that thrived by trading and raiding on the sea.

For a time the Mithermages project was under the tutelage of editor Betsy Mitchell at Del Rey, with whom I had worked so happily on the book I thought of as the best in my career so far, *Magic Street*. She helped and advised me greatly in developing Mithermages, and it was at this time that I decided that I would stretch the story between our present-day natural world and the magical one, rather the way I had done with *Magic Street* and its immediate predecessor, the contemporary/medieval fantasy romance *Enchantment*.

At once the magic system erupted: It would explain everything. Elves and fairies, ancient mythical gods of every Indo-European culture, ghosts and poltergeists, werewolves and trolls and golems, seven-league boots and mountains that move, talking trees and invisible people—all would be contained within it.

As I was fitting the magic of Mithermages into our world, past and present, I was invited by Gardner Dozois to submit a story to an anthology called *Wizards*. I came up with a new story set entirely in the Mithermages world, at an unspecified but early time period. I called it "Stonefather," and I knew as soon as I finished it that it was one of the best stories I'd ever written. I later brought it out in collaboration with Subterranean Press as a slim stand-alone book with a gorgeous cover by Tom Kidd. I had tangible proof that the Mithermages world was still alive and could give rise to strong stories.

But it was slow going, building up the story of Wad and the simultaneous tale of Danny, the boy born into our world as a gatemage in a Westilian Family. The problem was that the magic system was too thick. There was so much to explain. For years I was stuck in one place: an opening I wrote in which a much younger Danny struggles just to figure out what was going on in his magical family.

By the time I solved the problem, the project had moved to my primary publisher, Tor, and I was working once again with longtime editor and friend Beth Meacham. I realized (finally!) that my whole approach was faulty. Instead of having Danny know almost nothing, and have the reader learn each point as Danny learned it, I started the book afresh with Danny as a twelve-year-old knowing as much as anyone in his family about the way magic worked and how the Westilians fit into the universe.

I was really following my own advice—I tell students in my writing classes that suspense comes, not from knowing almost nothing, but from knowing almost everything and caring very much about the small part still unknown. I had expected to spend quite a bit of time in the North Family compound, developing Danny's relationships with the Aunts and Uncles, the Cousins, and his parents and siblings, but I quickly found the place too cramped and depressing—as Danny did. I had painted him into a corner; he could not thrive there. I had to get him out.

From the moment he left the Family compound and started shoplifting at the Lexington Wal-Mart, the book hummed along right to the end. The scene that I had originally envisioned as the beginning of the novel—a gate that would allow Danny and other kids to shoot right to the top of a climbing rope in a high school gym in Buena Vista, Virginia—now became the climactic scene. Meanwhile, Wad's story, which had stayed stubbornly vague for years, suddenly took on clarity as I wrote the story "The Man in the Tree," always intended as a chapter of this book, and then created the character of Queen Bexoi as Wad's ally, lover, and nemesis.

Only one ingredient was missing, and it came by purest chance. Years ago, Victoria Von Roth, a wonderful actress whom I directed in *Posing As People* in a production in Los Angeles, almost demanded that I name a character in one of my books after her. Since then she had reminded me from time to time, and it happened that one of those reminders came at exactly the moment when I had Danny in Yellow Springs, Ohio, and had no idea how to push him forward on his journey of discovery. "Use my name in this book," Veevee suggested, so I did. I thought of the real Victoria's exuberant personality and genuine kindness, and the character who bears her name in this novel came forth. I ran the chapters past Victoria for her approval; if she hadn't liked the character, I would simply have changed the name. But she did approve, and the name stayed.

Beth Meacham was reading the chapters as they came out of my computer, the first time I have ever let an editor read my chapters at the same time as my wife, Kristine, read them, instead of waiting till after. Beth was helpful at every stage, either with suggestions or needed encouragement; Kristine was also my reliable first reader, helping me walk the narrow line between the earthiness I wanted and some level of decorum that the general readership might enjoy.

Other primary readers—Erin and Phillip Absher and Kathryn H. Kidd—got the chapters in their rawest form as well. They all contributed greatly as I moved the story forward.

With the ironclad deadline for publication looming during the summer of 2010, more than thirty-three years after I first drew the maps of the world I now call Westil (after one of the more important nations in its history), I was compelled to finish the novel despite all other distractions, including teaching two weeklong writing workshops. I wrote a chapter nearly every day as Kristine and I flew to Poland for the launch of the translation of *Ender in Exile*. Chapters were written in jets on the way to and from Poland, in Warsaw, and in Czeszin, where I took part in a sci-fi and fantasy convention that combined the annual EuroCon with the national conventions of Poland, Czechland, and

Slovakia. I met or reacquainted myself with many wonderful people, and came home with all but four of the chapters done.

On the first of September I finished the last chapter, and put the book into the hands of the wonderful staff at Tor, who went the extra mile in making up for my late completion to bring the book out on time. My thanks to all.

Above all, though, I must thank my family—Kristine, of course, and our youngest, Zina—for their patience during the stress it always causes when I have a book under construction. Erin Absher helped many times to make our lives possible during episodes of travel, while my assistant (and the managing editor of my magazine, *Orson Scott Card's InterGalactic Medicine Show* at www.oscigms.com), Kathleen Bellamy, and our webwright and IT manager, Scott Allen, kept the world running smoothly around us.

Explore the stars in this all-new sequel
to Card's *New York Times* bestselling
Shadow of the Giant

ORSON SCOTT CARD

SHADOWS IN FLIGHT

★"Card's latest installment in his Shadow subseries…
does a superlative job of dramatically portraying the
maturing process of child into adult."

—Publishers Weekly

starred review on *Shadow of the Giant*

"A fitting and satisfying continuation to the Ender
series…Card…seems to indicate that he will at some point
return to follow Bean's family and the other Battle School
Children as they expand throughout the galaxy."

—SF Site.com

on *Shadow of the Giant*

At the end of *Shadow of the Giant*, Julian Delphiki—
or Bean—flees to the stars with three of his children.
All share the engineered genes that gave Bean both
hyper-intelligence and a short and cruel physical life.
And now the Delphikis are about to make a discovery that
will let them save themselves, and perhaps all of humanity
in the days to come.

In hardcover January 2012

tor-forge.com